"It's the demon's doing, Palat snarled.

"The demon knows we're down here."

In the next instant, a frightening figure surged from beneath the water. Formed of the rats' bones, the creature stood eight feet tall, built square and broad-chested as an ape. It stood on bowed legs that were whitely visible through the murky water. Instead of two arms, the bone creature possessed four, all longer than the legs. When it closed its hands, horns formed of ribs and rats' teeth stuck out of the creature's fists, rendering them into morningstars for all intents and purposes. The horns looked sharp-edged, constructed for slashing as well as stabbing. Small bones, some of them jagged pieces of bone, formed the demon's face the creature wore.

"That's a bone golem," Taramis said. "Your weapons won't do it much harm."

The bone golem's mouth, created by splintered bones so tightly interwoven they gave the semblance of mobility, grinned, then opened as the creature spoke in a harsh howl that sounded like a midnight wind tearing through a graveyard. "Come to your deaths, fools."

DIABLO®

THE BLACK ROAD

Mel Odom

ISBN: 978-1-9456831-2-1

First Pocket Books printing April 2002
First Blizzard Entertainment printing March 2018

10 9 8 7 6 5 4 3 2 1

Cover art by Bill Petras

Printed in China

THE BLACK ROAD

Oпe

Darrick Lang pulled at the oar and scanned the night-shrouded cliffs overlooking the Dyre River, hoping he remained out of sight of the pirates they hunted. Of course, he would only know they'd been discovered after the initial attack, and the pirates weren't known for their generosity toward Westmarch navy sailors. Especially ones who were hunting them pursuant to the King of Westmarch's standing orders. The possibility of getting caught wasn't a pleasant thought.

The longboat sculled against the gentle current, but the prow cut so clean that the water didn't slap against the low hull. Sentries posted up on the surrounding cliffs would raise the alarm if the longboat were seen or heard, and there would be absolute hell to pay for it. If that happened, Darrick was certain none of them would make it back to *Lonesome Star* waiting out in the Gulf of Westmarch. Captain Tollifer, the vessel's master, was one of the sharpest naval commanders in all of Westmarch under the king's command, and he'd have no problem shipping out if Darrick and his band didn't return before dawn.

Bending his back and leaning forward, Darrick eased the oar from the water and spoke in a soft voice. "Easy, boys. Steady on, and we'll make a go of this. We'll be in and out before those damned pirates know we've come and gone."

"If our luck holds," Mat Hu-Ring whispered beside Darrick.

"I'll take luck," Darrick replied. "Never had anything against it, and it seems you've always had plenty to spare."

"You've never been one to go a-courtin' luck," Mat said.

"Never," Darrick agreed, feeling a little cocky in spite of the danger they were facing. "But I don't find myself forgetting friends who have it."

"Is that why you brought me along on this little venture of yours?"

"Aye," Darrick replied. "And as I got it toted, I saved your life the last time. I'm figuring you owe me one there."

Mat grinned in the darkness, and the white of his teeth split his dark face. Like Darrick, he wore lampblack to shadow his features and make him more a part of the night. But where Darrick had reddish hair and bronze skin, Mat had black hair and was nut brown.

"Oh, but you're up and bound to be pushin' luck this night, aren't you, my friend?" Mat asked.

"The fog is holding." Darrick nodded at the billowing silver-gray gusts that stayed low over the river. The wind and the water worked together tonight, and the fog rolled out to the sea. With the fog in the way, the distance seemed even farther. "Mayhap we can rely on the weather more than we have to rely on your luck."

"An' if ye keep runnin' yer mouths the way ye are," old Maldrin snarled in his gruff voice, "mayhap them guards what ain't sleepin' up there will hear ye and let go with some of them ambushes these damned pirates has got set up. Ye know people talkin' carries easier over the water than on land."

"Aye," Darrick agreed. "An' I know the sound don't carry up to them cliffs from here. They're a good forty feet above us, they are."

"Stupid Hillsfar outlander," Maldrin growled. "Ye're still wet behind the ears and runnin' at the nose for carryin' out this here kind of work. If'n ye ask me, ol' Cap'n Tollifer ain't quite plump off the bob these days."

"An' there you have it then, Ship's Mate Maldrin," Darrick said. "No one bloody asked you."

A couple of the other men aboard the longboat laughed at the old mate's expense. Although Maldrin had a reputation as a fierce sailor and warrior, the younger men on the crew considered him somewhat of a mother hen and a worrywart.

The first mate was a short man but possessed shoulders almost an ax handle's length across. He kept his gray-streaked beard cropped close. A horseshoe-shaped bald spot left him smooth on top but with plenty of hair on the sides and in back that he tied in a queue. Moisture from the river and the fog glistened on the tarred breeches and soaked the dark shirt.

Darrick and the other men in the longboat were clad in similar fashion. All of them had wrapped their blades in spare bits of sailcloth to keep the moonshine and water from them. The Dyre River was fresh water, not the corrosive salt of the Gulf of Westmarch, but a sailor's practices in the King's Royal Navy were hard to put aside.

"Insolent pup," Maldrin muttered.

"Ah, and you love me for it even as you decry it, Maldrin," Darrick said. "If you think you're miserable company now, just think about how you'd have been if I'd up and bloody left you on board *Lonesome Star.* I'm telling you, man, I don't see you up for a night of hand-wringing. Truly I don't. And this is the thanks I get for sparing you that."

"This isn't going to be as easy as ye seem to want to believe," Maldrin said.

"And what's to worry about, Maldrin? A few pirates?" Darrick shipped his oar, watchful that the longboat crew still moved together, then eased it back into the water and drew again. The longboat surged through the river water, making good time. They'd spotted the small campfire of the first sentry a quarter-mile back. The port they were looking for wasn't much farther ahead.

"These aren't just any pirates," Maldrin replied.

"No," Darrick said, "I have to agree with you. These here pirates, now these are the ones that Cap'n Tollifer sent us to fetch up some trouble with. After orders like them, I won't have you thinking I'd just settle for any pirates."

"Nor me," Mat put in. "I've proven myself right choosy when it comes to fighting the likes of pirates."

A few of the other men agreed, and they shared a slight laugh.

No one, Darrick noted, mentioned anything of the boy the pirates had kidnapped. Since the boy's body hadn't been recovered at the site of the earlier attack, everyone believed he was being held for ransom. Despite the need to let off steam before their insertion into the pirates' stronghold, thinking of the boy was sobering.

Maldrin only shook his head and turned his attention to his own oar. "Ach, an' ye're a proper pain in the arse, Darrick Lang. Before all that's of the Light and holy, I'd swear to that. But if'n there's a man aboard Cap'n Tollifer's ship what can pull this off, I figure it's gotta be you."

"I'd doff my hat to you, Maldrin," Darrick said, touched. "If I were wearing one, that is."

"Just keep wearin' the head it would fit on if ye were," Maldrin growled.

"Indeed," Darrick said. "I intend to." He took a fresh grip on his oar. "Pull, then, boys, while the river is steady and the fog stays with us." As he gazed up at the mountains, he knew that some savage part of him relished thoughts of the coming battle.

The pirates wouldn't give the boy back for free. And Captain Tollifer, on behalf of Westmarch's king, was demanding a blood price as well.

"Damned fog," Raithen said, then swore with heartfelt emotion.

The pirate captain's vehemence drew Buyard Cholik from his reverie. The old priest blinked past the fatigue that held him in thrall and glanced at the burly man who stood limned in the torchlight coming from the suite of rooms inside the building. "What is the matter, Captain Raithen?"

Raithen stood like a mountain at the stone balcony railing of the building that overlooked the alabaster and columned ruins of the small port city where they'd been encamped for months. He pulled at the goatee covering his massive chin and absently touched the cruel scar on the right corner of his mouth that gave him a cold leer.

"The fog. Makes it damned hard to see the river." The pale moonlight glinted against the black chainmail Raithen wore over a dark green shirt. The ship's captain was always sartorially perfect, even this early in the morning. Or this late at night, Cholik amended, for he didn't know which was the case for the pirate chieftain. Raithen's black breeches were tucked with neat precision into his rolled-top boots. "And I still think maybe we didn't get away so clean from the last bit of business we did."

"The fog also makes navigating the river risky," Cholik said.

"Maybe to you, but for a man used to the wiles and ways of the sea," Raithen said, "that river down there would offer smooth sailing." He pulled at his beard as he looked down at the sea again, then nodded. "If it was me, I'd make a run at us tonight."

"You're a superstitious man," Cholik said, and couldn't help putting some disdain in his words. He wrapped his arms around himself. Unlike Raithen, Cholik was thin to the point of emaciation. The night's unexpected chill predicting the onset of the coming winter months had caught him off-guard and ill prepared. He no longer had the captain's young years to tide him over, either. The wind, now that he noticed it, cut through his black and scarlet robes.

Raithen glanced back at Cholik, his expression souring as if he were prepared to take offense at the assessment.

"Don't bother to argue," Cholik ordered. "I've seen the tendency in you. I don't hold it against you, trust me. But I choose to believe in things that offer me stronger solace than superstition."

A scowl twisted Raithen's face. His own dislike and distrust concerning what Cholik's acolytes did in the lower regions of the town they'd found buried beneath the abandoned port city were well known. The site was far to the north of Westmarch, well out of the king's easy reach. As desolate as the place was, Cholik would have thought the pirate captain would be pleased about the location. But the priest had forgotten the civilized amenities the pirates had available to them at the various ports that didn't know who they were—or didn't care because their gold and silver spent just as quickly as anyone else's. Still, the drinking and debauchery the pirates were accustomed to were impossible where they now camped.

"None of your guards has sounded an alarm," Cholik went on. "And I assume all have checked in."

"They've checked in," Raithen agreed. "But I'm certain that I spotted another ship's sails riding our tailwind when we sailed up into the river this afternoon."

"You should have investigated further."

"I did." Raithen scowled. "I did, and I didn't find anything."

"There. You see? There's nothing to worry about."

Raithen shot Cholik a knowing glance. "Worrying about things is part of what you pay me all that gold for."

"Worrying me, however, isn't."

Despite his grim mood, a small smile twisted Raithen's lips. "For a priest of Zakarum Church, which professes a way of gentleness, you've got an unkind way about your words."

"Only when the effect is deserved."

Folding his arms across his massive chest, Raithen leaned back against the balcony and chuckled. "You do intrigue me, Cholik. When we became acquainted all those months ago and you told me what you wanted to do, I thought you were a madman."

"A legend of a city buried beneath another city isn't madness," Cholik said. However, the things he'd had to do to secure the sacred and almost forgotten texts of Dumal Lunnash, a Vizjerei wizard who had witnessed the death of Jere Harash thousands of years ago, had almost driven him there.

Thousands of years ago, Jere Harash had been a young Vizjerei acolyte who had discovered the power to command the spirits of the dead. The young boy had claimed the insight was given to him through a dream. There was no doubting the new abilities Jere Harash mustered, and his power became a thing of legend. The boy perfected the process whereby the wizards drained the energy of the dead, making anyone who used it more powerful than anything that had gone on before. As a result of this new knowledge, the Vizjerei—one of the three primary clans in the world thousands of years ago—had become known as the Spirit Clans.

Dumal Lunnash had been a historian and one of the men to have survived Jere Harash's last attempt to master the spirit world completely. Upon the young man's attaining the trance state necessary to transfer the energy to the spells he wove, a spirit had taken control of his body and gone on a killing rampage. Later, the Vizjerei had learned that the spirits they called on and unwittingly unleashed into the world were demons from the Burning Hells.

As a chronicler of the times and the auguries of the Vizjerei, Dumal Lunnash had largely been overlooked, but his texts had led Cholik through a macabre and twisted trail that had ended in the desolation of the forgotten city on the Dyre River.

"No," Raithen said. "Legends like that are everywhere. I've even followed a few of them myself, but I've never seen one come true."

"Then I'm surprised that you came at all," Cholik said. This was a conversation they'd been avoiding for months, and he was surprised to find it coming out now. But only in a way. From the signs they'd been finding the last week, while Raithen had been away plundering and pillaging, or whatever it was that Raithen's pirates did while they were away, Cholik had known they were close to discovering the dead city's most important secret.

"It was your gold," Raithen admitted. "That was what turned the trick for me. Now, since I've returned again, I've seen the progress your people are making."

A bitter sweetness filled Cholik. Although he was glad to be vindicated in the pirate captain's eyes, the priest also knew that Raithen had already started thinking about the possibility of treasure. Perhaps in his uninformed zeal, he or his men might even damage what Cholik and his acolytes were there to get.

"When do you think you'll find what you're looking for?" Raithen asked.

"Soon," Cholik replied.

The big pirate shrugged. "It might help me to have some idea. If we were followed today . . ."

"If you were followed today," Cholik snapped, "then it would be all your fault."

Raithen gave Cholik a wolfish grin. "Would it, then?"

"You are wanted by the Westmarch Navy," Cholik said, "for crimes against the king. You'll be hanged if they find you, swung from the gallows in Diamond Quarter."

"Like a common thief?" Raithen arched an eyebrow. "Aye, maybe I'll be swinging at the end of a gallows like a loose sail at the end of a yardarm, but don't you think the king would have a special punishment meted out to a priest of the Zakarum Church who had betrayed his confidence and had been telling the pirates what ships carry the king's gold through the Gulf of Westmarch and through the Great Ocean?"

Raithen's remarks stung Cholik. The Archangel Yaerius had coaxed a young ascetic named Akarat into founding a religion devoted to the Light. And for a time, Zakarum Church had been exactly that, but it had changed over the years and through the wars. Few mortals, only those within the inner circles of the Zakarum Church, knew that the church had been subverted by demons and now followed a dark, mostly hidden evil through their inquisitions. The Zakarum Church was also tied into Westmarch and Tristram, the power behind the power of the kings. By revealing the treasure ships' passage, Cholik had also enabled the pirates to steal from the Zakarum Church. The priests of the church were even more vengeful than the king.

Turning from the bigger man, Cholik paced on the balcony in an effort to warm himself against the night's chill.

I knew it would come to this at some point, he told himself. *This was to be expected.* He let out a long, deliberate breath, letting Raithen think for a time that he'd gotten the better of him. Over his years as a priest, Cholik had found that men often made even more egregious mistakes when they'd been praised for their intelligence or their power.

Cholik knew what real power was. It was the reason he'd come there to Tauruk's Port to find long-buried Ransim, which had died during the Sin War that had lasted centuries as Chaos had quietly but violently warred with the Light. That war had been long ago and played out in the east, before Westmarch had become civilized or powerful. Many cities and towns had been buried during those times. Most of them, though, had been shorn of their valuables. But Ransim had been hidden from the bulk of the Sin War. Even though the general populace knew nothing of the Sin War except that battles were fought—though not because the demons and the Light warred—they'd known nothing of Ransim. The port city had been an enigma, something that shouldn't have existed. But some of the eastern mages had chosen that place to work and hide in, and they'd left secrets behind. Dumal Lunnash's texts had been the only source Cholik had found regarding Ransim's whereabouts, and even that book had led only to an arduous task of gathering information about the location that was hidden in carefully constructed lies and half-truths.

"What do you want to know, captain?" Cholik asked.

"What you're seeking here," Raithen replied with no hesitation.

"If it's gold and jewels, you mean?" Cholik asked.

"When I think of treasure," Raithen said, "those are the things that I spend most of my time thinking about and wishing for."

Amazed at how small-minded the man was, Cholik shook his head. Wealth was only a small thing to hope for, but power—power was the true reward the priest lusted for.

"What?" Raithen argued. "You're too good to hope for

gold and jewels? For a man who betrays his king's coffers, you have some strange ideas."

"Material power is a very transitory thing," Cholik said. "It is of finite measure. Often gone before you know it."

"I've still got some put back for a rainy day."

Cholik gazed up at the star-filled heavens. "Mankind is a futile embarrassment to the heavens, Captain Raithen. An imperfect vessel imperfectly made. We play at being omnipotent, knowing the potential perhaps lies within us yet will always be denied to us."

"We're not talking about gold and jewels that you're looking for, are we?" Raithen almost sounded betrayed.

"There may be some of that," Cholik said. "But that is not what drew me here." He turned and gazed back at the pirate captain. "I followed the scent of power here, Captain Raithen. And I betrayed the King of Westmarch and the Zakarum Church to do it so that I could secure your ship for my own uses."

"Power?" Raithen shook his head in disbelief. "Give me a few feet of razor-sharp steel, and I'll show you power."

Angry, Cholik gestured at the pirate captain. The priest saw waves of slight, shimmering force leap from his extended hand and streak for Raithen. The waves wrapped around the big man's throat like steel bands and shut his breath off. In the next instant, Cholik caused the big man to be pulled from his feet. No priest could wield such a power, and it was time to let the pirate captain know he was no priest. Not anymore. Not ever again.

"Shore!" one of the longboat crew crowed from the prow. He kept his voice pitched low so that it didn't carry far.

"Ship oars, boys," Darrick ordered, lifting his own from the river water. Pulse beating quicker, thumping at his temples now, he stood and gazed at the stretch of mountain before them.

The oars came up at once, then the sailors placed them in the center of the longboat.

"Stern," Darrick called as he peered at the glowing

circles of light that came from lanterns or fires only a short distance ahead.

"Sir," Fallan responded from the longboat's stern. Now that the oars no longer rowed, the longboat didn't cut through the river water. Instead, the boat seemed to come up from the water and settle with harsh awkwardness on the current.

"Take us to shore," Darrick ordered, "and let's have a look at what's what with these damned pirates what's taking the king's gold. Put us off to port in a comfortable spot, if you will."

"Aye, sir." Fallan used the steering oar and angled the longboat toward the left riverbank.

The current pushed the craft backward in the water, but Darrick knew they'd lose only a few yards. What mattered most was finding a safe place to tie up so they could complete the mission Captain Tollifer had assigned them.

"Here," Maldrin called out, pointing toward the left bank. Despite his age, the old first mate had some of the best eyes aboard *Lonesome Star*. He also saw better at night.

Darrick peered through the fog and made out the craggy riverbank. It looked bitten off, just a stubby shelf of rock sticking out from the cliffs that had been cleaved through the Hawk's Beak Mountains as if by a gigantic ax.

"Now, there's an inhospitable berth if ever I've seen one," Darrick commented.

"Not if you're a mountain goat," Mat said.

"A bloody mountain goat wouldn't like that climb none," Darrick said, measuring the steep ascent that would be left to them.

Maldrin squinted up at the cliffs. "If we're goin' this way, we're in for some climbin'."

"Sir," Fallan called from the stern, "what do you want me to do?"

"Put in to shore there, Fallan," Darrick said. "We'll take our chances with this bit of providence." He smiled. "As hard as the way here is, you know the pirates won't be expecting it none. I'll take that, and add it to the chunk of luck we're having here this night."

With expert skill, Fallan guided the longboat to shore.

"Tomas," Darrick said, "we'll be having that anchor now, quick as you will."

The sailor muscled the stone anchor up from the middle of the longboat, steadied it on the side, then heaved it toward shore. The immense weight fell short of the shore but slapped down into shallow water. Taking up the slack, he dragged the anchor along the river bottom.

"She's stone below," Tomas whispered as the rope jerked in his hands. "Not mud."

"Then let's hope that you catch onto something stout," Darrick replied. He fidgeted in the longboat, anxious to be about the dangerous business they had ahead of them. The sooner into it, the sooner out of it and back aboard *Lonesome Star*.

"We're about out of riverbank," Maldrin commented as they drifted a few yards farther downriver.

"Could be we'll start the night off with a nice swim, then," Mat replied.

"A man will catch his death of cold in that water," Maldrin grumped.

"Mayhap the pirates will do for you before you wind up abed in your dotage," Mat said. "I'm sure they're not going to give up their prize when we come calling."

Darrick felt a sour twist in his stomach. The "prize" the pirates held was the biggest reason Captain Tollifer had sent Darrick and the other sailors upriver instead of bringing *Lonesome Star* up.

As a general rule, the pirates who had been preying on the king's ships out of Westmarch had left no one alive. This time, they had left a silk merchant from Lut Gholein clinging to a broken spar large enough to serve as a raft. He'd been instructed to tell the king that one of the royal nephews had been taken captive. A ransom demand, Darrick knew, was sure to follow.

It would be the first contact the pirates had initiated

with Westmarch. After all these months of successful raids against the king's merchanters, still no one knew how they got their information about the gold shipments. However, they had left only the Lut Gholein man alive, suggesting that they hadn't wanted anyone from Westmarch to escape who might identify them.

The anchor scraped across the stone riverbed, taking away the margin for success by steady inches. The water and the sound of the current muted the noise. Then the anchor stopped and the rope jerked taut in Tomas's hands. Catching the rope in his callused palms, the sailor squeezed tight.

The longboat stopped but continued to bob on the river current.

Darrick glanced at the riverbank a little more than six feet away. "Well, we'll make do with what we have, boys." He glanced at Tomas. "How deep is the water?"

Tomas checked the knots tied in the rope as the longboat strained at the anchor. "She's drawing eight and a half feet."

Darrick eyed the shore. "The river must drop considerably from the edges of the cliffs."

"It's a good thing we're not in armor," Mat said. "Though I wish I had a good shirt of chainmail to tide me through the coming fracas."

"You'd sink like a lightning-blasted toad if you did," Darrick replied. "And it may not come to fighting. Mayhap we'll nip aboard the pirate ship and rescue the youngster without rousing a ruckus."

"Aye," Maldrin muttered, "an' if ye did, it would be one of the few times I've seen ye do that."

Darrick grinned in spite of the worry that nibbled at the dark corners of his mind. "Why, Maldrin, I almost sense a challenge in your words."

"Make what ye will of it," the first mate growled. "I offer advice in the best of interests, but I see that it's seldom taken in the same spirit in which it was give. Fer all ye know, they're in league with dead men and suchlike here."

The first mate's words had a sobering effect on Darrick, reminding him that though he viewed the night's activities as an adventure, it wasn't a complete lark. Some pirate captains wielded magic.

"We're here tracking pirates," Mat said. "Just pirates. Mortal men whose flesh cuts and bleeds."

"Aye," Darrick said, ignoring the dry spot at the back of his throat that Maldrin's words had summoned. "Just men."

But still, the crew had faced a ship of dead men only months ago while on patrol. The fighting then had been brutal and frightening, and it had cost lives of shipmates before the undead sailors and their ship had been sent to the bottom of the sea.

The young commander glanced at Tomas. "We're locked in?"

Tomas nodded, tugging on the anchor rope. "Aye. As near as I can tell."

Darrick grinned. "I'd like to have a boat to come back to, Tomas. And Captain Tollifer can be right persnickety about crew losing his equipment. When we get to shore, make the longboat fast again, if you please."

"Aye. It will be done."

Grabbing his cutlass from among the weapons wrapped in the bottom of the longboat, Darrick stood with care, making sure he balanced the craft out. He took a final glance up at the tops of the cliffs. The last sentry point they'd identified lay a hundred yards back. The campfire still burned through the layers of fog overhead. He glanced ahead at the lights glowing in the distance, the clangor of ships' rigging slapping masts reaching his ears.

"Looks like there's naught to be done for it, boys," Darrick said. "We've got a cold swim ahead of us." He noticed that Mat already had his sword in hand and that Maldrin had his own war hammer.

"After you," Mat said, waving an open hand toward the river.

Without another word, Darrick slipped over the side of the boat and into the river. The cold water closed over him at once, taking his breath away, and he swam against the current toward the riverbank.

Two

Twisting and squirming, hands flailing through the bands of invisible force that held him captive, Raithen fought against Cholik's spell. Surprise and fear marked Raithen's face, and Cholik knew the man realized he wasn't facing the weak old priest he thought he'd been talking to with such disregard. The big pirate opened his mouth and struggled to speak. No words came out. At a gesture, Cholik caused Raithen to float out over the balcony's edge and the hundred-foot drop that lay beyond. Only broken rock and the tumbled remains of the buildings that had made up Tauruk's Port lay below.

The pirate captain ceased his struggles as fear dawned on his purpling face.

"Power has brought me to Tauruk's Port," Cholik grated, maintaining the magic grip, feeling the obscene pleasure that came from using such a spell, "and to Ransim buried beneath. Power such as you've never wielded. And none of that power will do you any good. You do not know how to wield it. The vessel for this power must be consecrated, and I mean to be that vessel. It's something that you'll never be able to be." The priest opened his hand.

Choking and gasping, Raithen floated back in and dropped to the stone-tiled floor of the balcony overlooking the river and the abandoned city. He lay back, gasping for air and holding his bruised throat with his left hand. His right hand sought the hilt of the heavy sword at his side.

"If you pull that sword," Cholik stated, "then I'll promote your ship's commander. Perhaps even your first mate. Or I could even reanimate your corpse, though I doubt your crew would be happy about the matter. But, frankly, I wouldn't care what they thought."

Raithen's hand halted. He stared up at the priest. "You need me," he croaked.

"Yes," Cholik agreed. "That's why I've let you live so long while we have worked together. It wasn't pleasant or done out of a weak-willed sense of fair play." He stepped closer to the bigger man sitting with his back against the railing.

Purple bruising already showed in a wide swath around Raithen's neck.

"You're a tool, Captain Raithen," Cholik said. "Nothing more."

The big man glared up at him but said nothing. Swallowing was obviously a hard and painful effort.

"But you are an important tool in what I am doing." Cholik gestured again.

Seeing the priest's fluttering hand inscribing the mystic symbols, Raithen flinched. Then his eyes widened in surprise.

Cholik knew it was because the man hadn't expected to be relieved of his pain. The priest knew healing spells, but the ones that caused injury came more readily to him these days. "Please get up, Captain Raithen. If you have led someone here and the fog has obscured their presence, I want you to handle it."

Showing restraint and caution, Raithen climbed to his feet.

"Do we understand each other?" As Cholik gazed into the other man's eyes, he knew he'd made an enemy for life. It was a pity. He'd planned for the pirate captain to live longer than that.

Aribar Raithen was called Captain Scarlet Waters by most of the Westmarch Navy. Very few people had survived his capture of a ship, and most ended up at the bottom of the Great Sea or, especially of late, in the Gulf of Westmarch.

"Aye," Raithen growled, but the sound wasn't so menacing with all the hoarseness in it. "I'll get right on it."

"Good." Cholik stood and looked out to the broken and gutted buildings that remained of Tauruk's Port. He pretended not to notice as Raithen left, nor did he indicate that he heard the big pirate captain's slight foot drag that told him Raithen had considered stabbing him in the back.

Metal whispered coolly against leather. But this time, Cholik knew, the blade was being returned to the sheath.

Cholik remained at the balcony and locked his knees so he wouldn't tremble from the cold or from the exhaustion he suffered from spell use. If he'd had to expend any more energy, he thought he'd have passed out and been totally at Raithen's mercy.

By the Light, where has the time gone? Where has my strength gone? Gazing up at the stars burning bright against the sable night, Cholik felt old and weak. His hands were palsied now. Most of the time he maintained control of them, but on occasion he could not. When one of those uncontrollable periods arrived, he kept his hands out of sight in the folds of his robes and stayed away from others. The times always passed, but they were getting longer and longer.

In Westmarch, it wouldn't be many more years before one of the younger priests noted his growing infirmity and brought it to the senior priest's attention. When that happened, Cholik knew he'd be shipped out from the church and placed in a hospice to help with the old and the diseased, all of them dying deaths by inches and him helping only to ease them into the grave while easing into a bed of his own. Even the thought of ending his days like that was too much.

Tauruk's Port, with Ransim buried beneath, the information gleaned from the sacred texts—those things Cholik viewed as his personal salvation. The dark forces he'd allied himself with the past few years willing, it would be.

He turned his gaze from the stars to the fogbound river. The white, cottony masses roiled across the broken land forming the coastal area. Farther north, barbarian tribes would have been a problem to their discovery, but here in the deadlands far north of Westmarch and Tristram, they were safe.

At least, Cholik mused, they were safe if Raithen's latest excursion to take a shipload of the king's gold fresh out of Westmarch had not brought someone back. He peered down at the layers of fog, but he could see only the tall masts of the pirate ships standing out against the highest wisps of silver-gray fog.

Lanterns aboard those ships created pale yellow and orange nimbi and looked like fireflies in the distance. Men's raucous voices, the voices of pirates and not the trained acolytes Cholik had handpicked over the years, called out to one another in casual disdain. They talked of women and spending the gold they'd fought for that day, unaware of the power that lay buried under the city.

Only Raithen was becoming more curious about what they sought. The other pirates were satisfied with the gold they continued to get.

Cholik cursed his palsied hands and the cold wind that swept over the Hawk's Beak Mountains to the east. If only he were young, if only he'd found the sacred Vizjerei text sooner . . .

"Master."

Startled from his musings but recovering in short order, Cholik turned. He tucked his shaking hands out of sight inside his robes. "What is it, Nullat?"

"Forgive me for interrupting your solitude, Master Cholik." Nullat bowed. He was in his early twenties, dark-haired and dark-eyed. Dirt and dust stained his robes, and scratches adorned his smooth face and one arm from an accident during the excavation only a few days ago that had claimed the lives of two other acolytes.

Cholik nodded. "You know better than to interrupt unless it was something important."

"Yes. Brother Altharin asked me to come get you."

Inside his withered chest, Cholik's heart beat faster. Still, he maintained the control he had over himself and his emotions. All of the acolytes he'd bent to his own ends feared him, and feared his power, but they remained hungry for the gifts they believed he would bestow. He intended to keep it that way. He kept silent, refusing to ask the question that Nullat had left hanging in the air.

"Altharin believes we have reached the final gate," Nullat said.

"And has Altharin halted his work?" Cholik asked.

"Of course, master. Everything has gone as you have ordered. The seals were not broken." Nullat's face creased with worry.

"Is something wrong?"

Hesitation held Nullat mute for a moment. The pirates' voices and the clangor of ships' lines and rigging against yardarms and masts continued unabated from below.

"Altharin thinks he has heard voices on the other side of the gate," Nullat said. His eyes broke from Cholik's.

"Voices?" Cholik repeated, feeling more excited. The sudden rush of adrenaline caused his hands to shake more. "What kind of voices?"

"Evil voices."

Cholik stared at the young acolyte. "Did you expect any other kind?"

"I don't know, master."

"The Black Road is not a way found by those faint of heart." In fact, Cholik had inferred from the sacred Vizjerei texts that the tiles themselves had been shaped from the bones of men and women who had been raised in a village free of evil and strife. They'd never known need or want until the population had grown large enough to serve the demons' needs. "What do these voices say?"

Nullat shook his head. "I cannot say, master. I do not understand them."

"Does Altharin?"

"If he does, master, he did not tell me. He commanded only that I come get you."

"And what does the final gate look like?" Cholik asked.

"As you told us it would, master. Immense and fearful." Nullat's eyes widened. "I've never seen anything like it."

Nor has anyone else in hundreds of years, Cholik thought. "Get a fresh torch, Nullat. We'll go have a look at what Brother Altharin has discovered." *And pray that the sacred texts were right. Otherwise, the evil that we release from behind that gate will kill us all.*

Pressed into the side of the mist-covered cliff, holding himself on his boot toes and the fingers of one hand, Darrick Lang reached for the next handhold. He was conscious of the rope tied around his waist and loins. He'd tacked the rope to a ship's spike he'd driven into the cliffside five feet below, leaving a trail of them behind him for the others to use. If he slipped and everything worked right, the rope would keep him from plunging to his death or into the river sixty feet below. If it worked wrong, he might yank the two men anchoring him to the side of the cliff down after him. The fog was so thick below that he could no longer see the longboat.

I should have brought Caron along, Darrick thought as he curled his fingers around the rocky outcrop that looked safe enough to hold his weight. Caron was only a boy, though, and not one to bring into a hostile situation. Aboard *Lonesome Star,* Caron was ruling king of the rigging. Even when he wasn't assigned aloft, the boy was often found there. Caron had a natural penchant for high places.

Resting for just a moment, feeling the trembling muscles in his back and neck, Darrick breathed out and inhaled the wet, musty smell of rock and hard-packed earth. It smelled, he couldn't help thinking, like a newly opened grave. His clothing was wet from the immersion in the river, and he was cold, but his body still found enough heat to break out in perspiration. It surprised him.

"You aren't planning on camping out up there, are you?" Mat called up. He sounded good-natured about it, but someone who knew him well could have detected the small tension in his voice.

"It's the view, you know," Darrick called down. And it amused him that they acted as if they were there for a lark instead of serious business. But it had always been that way between them.

They were twenty-three years old, Darrick being seven months the elder, and they'd spent most of those years as friends growing up in Hillsfar. They'd lived among the hill people, loaded freight in the river port, and learned to kill when barbarian tribes had come down from the north hoping to loot and pillage. When they'd turned fifteen, they'd journeyed to Westmarch and pledged loyalty in the king's navy. Darrick had gone to escape his father, but Mat had left behind a good family and prospects at the family mill. If Darrick had not left, Mat might not ever have left, and some days Darrick felt guilty about that. Dispatches from home always made Mat talk of the family he missed.

Focusing himself again, Darrick stared out across the broken land at the harbor less than two hundred yards away. Another pirate sentry was encamped on the cliff along the way. The man had built a small, yellow-tongued fire that couldn't be seen from the river.

Beyond, three tall-masted cogs, round-bodied ships built for river travel as well as coastal waters rather than the deep sea, lay at anchor in a dish-shaped natural harbor fronting the ruins of a city. Captain Tollifer's maps had listed the city as Tauruk's Port, but not much was known about it except that it had been deserted years ago.

Lanterns and torches moved along the ships, but a few also roved through the city, carried by pirates, Darrick felt certain. Though why they should be so industrious this early in the morning was beyond him. The swirling fog laced with condensation made seeing across the distance hard, but Darrick could make out that much.

The longboat held fifteen men, including Darrick. He figured that they were outnumbered at least eight to one by the pirates. Staying for a prolonged engagement was out of the question, but perhaps spiriting the king's nephew away and costing the pirates a few ships were possible. Darrick had volunteered for such work before, and he'd come through it alive.

So far, bucko, Darrick told himself with grim realization.

Although he was afraid, part of him was excited at the challenge. He clung to the wall, lifted a boot, and shoved himself upward again. The top of the cliff ledge was less than ten feet away. From there, it looked as if he could gain safe ground and walk toward the city ruins and the hidden port. His fingers and toes ached from the climb, but he put the discomfort out of his mind and kept moving.

When he reached the clifftop, he had to restrain a cry of triumph. He turned and looked back down at Mat, curling his hand into a fist.

Even at the distance, Darrick saw the look of horror that filled Mat's face. "Look out!"

Whipping his head back up, some inner sense warning him of the movement, Darrick caught a glimpse of moonlight-silvered steel sweeping toward him. He pulled his head down and released his hold on the cliff as he grabbed for another along the cliff's edge.

The sword chopped into the stone cliff, striking sparks from the high iron ore content just as Darrick's hands closed around the small ledge he'd pushed up from last. His body slammed hard against the mountainside.

"I told you I saw somebody out here," a man said as he drew his sword back again and stepped with care along the cliff's edge. His hobnailed boots scraped stone.

"Yeah," the second man agreed, joining the first in the pursuit of Darrick.

Scrambling, holding tight to the edge of the cliff, Darrick pressed his boots against the stone and tried in vain to find suitable purchase to allow him to push himself up. He gave thanks to the Light that the pirates were almost as challenged by the terrain as he was. His boot soles scraped and slid as he tried to pull himself up.

"Cut his fingers off, Lon," the man in back urged. He was a short, weasel-faced man with an ale belly pressing against his frayed shirt. Maniacal lights gleamed in his eyes. "Cut his fingers off, and watch him fall on the others down there. Before they can make it up, we can nip on down to the bonfire and warn Captain Raithen they's coming."

Darrick filed the name away. During his years as part of the Westmarch Navy, he'd heard of Raithen. In fact, Captain Tollifer had said that the Captain's Table, the quarterly meeting of chosen ships' captains in Westmarch, had suggested Raithen as a possible candidate for the guilty party in the matter of the pirate raids. It was good to know, but staying alive to relate the news might prove difficult.

"Stand back, Orphik," Lon growled. "You keep a-buzzing around me like a bee, and I'm gonna stick you myself."

"Shove off, Lon. I'll do for him." The little man's voice tittered with naked excitement.

"Damn you," Lon cursed. "Get out of the way."

Quick as a fox in a henhouse, Orphik ducked under his companion's outstretched free arm and dashed at Darrick with long-bladed knives that were almost short swords in their own right. He laughed. "I've got him, Lon. I've got him. Just sit you back and watch. I bet he screams the whole way down."

Keeping his weight distributed as evenly as possible, going with the renewed strength that flowed through his body from the adrenaline surge, Darrick swung from hand to hand, dodging the chopping blows Orphik delivered. Still, one of the pirate's attempts slashed across the knuckle of his left hand's little finger. Pain shot up Darrick's arm, but he was more afraid of how the blood flow would turn his grip slippery.

"Damn you!" Orphik swore, striking sparks from the stone again. "Just stay still, and this will be over with in a trice."

Lon reeled back away from the smaller man. "Look out, Orphik! Someone down there has a bow!" The bigger pirate held up a sleeve and displayed the arrow that had caught on its fletchings and still hung there.

Distracted by the presence of the arrow and aware that another could be joining it at any moment, Orphik stepped back a little. He drew up a boot and lashed out at his intended victim's head.

Darrick swung to one side and grabbed for the little man's leg with his bloody hand, not wanting to trade it for the certain grip of his right. He knotted his fingers in the pirate's breeches. Even though the breeches were tucked into the hobnailed boots, there was plenty of slack to seize. Balancing his weight from one hand on the cliff, Darrick yanked hard with the other.

"Damn him! Lon, give me your hand before this bilge rat yanks me off the cliff!" Orphik reached for the other man, who caught his hand in his own. Another arrow fired from below clattered against the cliff wall behind them and caused them both to duck.

Taking advantage of the confusion, knowing he'd never get a better chance, Darrick swung his weight to the side and up. He pushed his feet ahead of him, throwing his body behind, hoping to clear the cliff's edge or he would fall. Maybe the rope tied around his loins would hold him, or maybe Mat and the other men below had forgotten it in the mad rush of events.

Arching his body and rolling toward the ledge, Darrick hit hard. He started to fall, then threw an arm forward in desperation, praying it would be enough. For a gut-wrenching moment, he teetered on the edge, then the point of balance shifted, and he sprawled facedown on the ledge.

Three

Buyard Cholik followed Nullat down through the twisting bowels of Tauruk's Port into the pockets of pestilence that remained of Ransim. Enclosed in the rock and strata that were the younger city's foundation, the harbor seemed a million miles away, but the chill that had followed the fog into the valley remained with the old priest. Aches and pains he'd managed to keep warm in his rooms now returned with a vengeance as he made his way through the tunnels.

The acolyte carried an oil torch, and the ceiling was so low that the writhing flames left immediate traces of lampblack along the granite surfaces. Filled with nervous anxiety, Nullat glanced from left to right, his head moving like a fast metronome.

Cholik ignored the acolyte's apprehensions. In the beginning, when the digging had begun in earnest all those months ago, Tauruk's Port had been plagued with rats. Captain Raithen had suggested that the rats had infested the place while trailing after the camp lines of the barbarians who came down out of the frozen north. During hard winters, and last year's was just such a one, the barbarians found warmer climes farther south.

But there was something else the rats had fed on as well after they'd reached Tauruk's Port. It wasn't until after the excavation had begun that Cholik realized the horrible truth of it.

During the Sin War, when Vheran constructed the mighty gate and let Kabraxis back into the worlds of men, spells had been cast over Tauruk's Port to protect it and hide it from the war to the east. Or maybe the city had been called Ransim at that time. Cholik hadn't yet found a solid indication of which city had been ensorcelled.

The spells that had been cast over the city had raised the dead, giving them a semblance of life to carry out the orders of the demons who had raised them. Necromancy was not unknown to most practitioners of the Arts, but few did more than dabble in them. Most people believed necromancy often linked the users to the demons such as Diablo, Baal, and Mephisto, collectively called the Prime Evils. However, necromancers from the cult of Rathma in the eastern jungles fought for the balance between the Light and the Burning Hells. They were warriors pure of heart even though most feared and hated them.

The first party of excavators to punch down through the bottom layer of Tauruk's Port had discovered the undead creatures that yet lurked in the ruins of the city below. Cholik guessed that whatever demon had razed Ransim had been sloppy with its spellwork or had been in a hurry. Ransim had been invaded, the burned husks of buildings and carnage left behind offered mute testimony to that, and all among them had been slain. Then someone with considerable power had come into the city and raised the dead.

Zombies rose from where fresh corpses lay, and even skeletons in the graveyards had clawed their way free of their earthen tombs. But not all of them had made the recovery to unlife in time to go with whatever master had summoned them. Perhaps, Cholik had thought on occasion, it had taken years or decades for the rest of the populace to rise.

But those dead had risen, their flesh frozen somehow in a nether point short of death. Their limbs had atrophied, but their flesh had only withered without returning to the earth. And when the rats had come, they'd funneled down through the cracks and the crevices of Tauruk's Port to get to the city below. Since that day, the rats had feasted, and their population had reached prodigious numbers.

Of course, when presented with prey that could still fight even though a limb was gnawed off or a human with fresh blood that would lie down and die if dealt enough injury, the rats had chosen to stalk the excavation parties. For a time, the attrition rate among the diggers had been staggering. The rats had proven a resilient and resourceful enemy over the long months.

Captain Raithen had been kept busy raiding Westmarch ships, then buying slaves with Cholik's share of the gold. More gold had gone to the mercenaries whom the priest employed to keep the slaves in line.

"Step carefully, master," Nullat said, raising the torch so the light showed the yawning black pit ahead. "There's an abyss here."

"There was an abyss there the last time I came this way," Cholik snapped.

"Of course, master. I just thought perhaps you'd forgotten because it has been so long since you were down here."

Cholik made his voice cold and hard. "I don't forget."

Nullat's face blanched, and he cut his eyes away from the priest's. "Of course you don't, master. I only—"

"Quiet, Nullat. Your voice echoes in these chambers, and it wearies me." Cholik walked on, watching as Nullat flinched from a sudden advance of a red-eyed rat pack streaming along the pile of broken boulders to their left.

As long as a man's arm from elbow to fingertips, the rats raced over the boulders and one another as they fought to get a closer view of the two travelers. They chattered and squeaked, creating an undercurrent of noise that pealed throughout the chamber. Sleek black fur covered them from their wet noses to their plump rumps, but their tails remained hairless. Piles of old bones, and perhaps some new ones as well, adorned the heaps of broken stone, crumbled mortise work, and splintered debris left from dwellings.

Nullat stopped and, trembling, held the torch out toward the rat pack. "Master, perhaps we should turn back. I've not seen such a gathering of rats in weeks. There are enough of them to bring us down."

"Be calm," Cholik ordered. "Let me have your torch." The last thing he wanted was for Nullat's ravings to begin talk of an omen again. There had been far too much of that.

Hesitating a moment as if worried Cholik might take the torch from him and leave him in the darkness with the rats, Nullat extended the torch.

Cholik gripped the torch, steadying it with his hand. He whispered words of prayer, then breathed on the torch. His breath blew through the torch and became a wave of flame that blasted across the piles of stones and debris like a blacksmith's furnace as he turned his head from one side to the other across the line of rats.

Crying out, Nullat dropped and covered his face, turning away from the heat and knocking the torch from Cholik's grasp. The torch licked at the hem of Cholik's robes.

Yanking his robes away, the priest said, "Damn you for a fool, Nullat. You've very nearly set me on fire."

"My apologies, master," Nullat whimpered, jerking the torch away. He moved it so fast that the speed almost smothered the flames. A pool of glistening oil burned on the stone floor where the torch had lain.

Cholik would have berated the man further, but a sudden weakness slammed into him. He tottered on his feet, barely able to stand. He closed his eyes to shut out the vertigo that assailed him. The spell, so soon after the one he'd used against Raithen and so much stronger, had left him depleted.

"Master," Nullat called out.

"Shut up," Cholik ordered. The hoarseness of his voice surprised even him. His stomach rolled at the rancid smell of burning flesh that had filled the chamber.

"Of course, master."

Forcing himself to take a breath, Cholik concentrated on his center. His hands shook and ached as if he'd broken every one of his fingers. The power that he was able to channel was becoming too much for his body. *How is it that the Light can make man, then permit him to wield powerful auguries, only to strip him of the mortal flesh that binds him to this world?* It was that question that had begun turning him from the teachings of the Zakarum Church almost twenty years ago. Since that time, he had turned his pursuits to demons. They, at least, gave immortality of a sort with the power they offered. The struggle was to stay alive after receiving it.

When the weakness had abated to a degree, Cholik opened his eyes.

Nullat hunkered down beside him.

An attempt to make himself a smaller target if there are any vengeful rats left, Cholik felt certain. The priest gazed around the chamber.

The magical fire had swept the underground chamber. Smoking and blackened bodies of rats littered the debris piles. Burned flesh had sloughed from bone and left a horrid stink. Only a few slight chitterings of survivors sounded, and none of them seemed inclined to come out of hiding.

"Get up, Nullat," Cholik ordered.

"Yes, master. I was only there to catch you if you should fall."

"I will not fall."

Glancing to the side of the trail as they went on, Cholik gazed down into the abyss to his left. Careful exploration had not proven there was a bottom to it, but it lay far below. The excavators used it as a pit for the bodies of dead slaves and other corpses and the debris they had to haul out of the recovered areas.

Despite the fact that he hadn't been down in the warrens beneath Tauruk's Port in weeks, Cholik had maintained knowledge of the twisting and turning tunnels that had been excavated. Every day, he scoured through all manner of things the crews brought to the surface. He took care in noting the more important and curious pieces in journals that he kept. Back in Westmarch, the information he'd recorded on the dig site alone would be worth thousands in gold. If money would have replaced the life and power he was losing by degrees, he'd have taken it. But money didn't do those things; only the acquisition of magic did that.

And only demons gave so generously of that power.

The trail they followed kept descending, dipping down deep into the mountainside till Cholik believed they might even be beneath the level of the Dyre River. The constant chill of the underground area and the condensation on the stone walls further lent to that assumption.

Only a few moments later, after branching off into the newest group of tunnels that had been made through Ransim's remains, Cholik spotted the intense glare created by the torches and campfires the excavation team had established. The team had divided into shifts, breaking into groups. Each group toiled sixteen hours, with an eight-hour overlap scheduled for clearing out the debris that had been dug out of the latest access tunnels. They slept eight hours a day because Cholik found that they couldn't be worked any more than sixteen hours without some rest and sleep and still stay healthy for any appreciable length of time.

The mortality rate had been dimmed by such action and the protective wards Cholik had set up to keep the rats and undead at bay, but it had not been eradicated. Men died as they worked there, and Cholik's only lament was that it took Captain Raithen so long to find replacements.

Cholik passed through the main support chamber where the men slept. He followed Nullat's lead into one of the new tunnels, skirting the piles of debris that fronted the entrance and the first third of the tunnel. The old priest passed the confusion with scant notice, his eyes drawn to the massive gray and green door that ended the tunnel.

Men worked on the edges of the massive door, standing on ladders to reach the top at least twenty feet tall. Hammers and chisels banged against the rock, and the sound echoed in the tunnel and the chamber beyond. Other men shoveled refuse into wheelbarrows and trundled them to the dumpsites at the front of the tunnel.

The torchlight flickered over the massive door, and it

inscribed the symbol raised there for all to see. The symbol consisted of six elliptical rings, one spaced inside another, with a twisting line threading through them in yet another pattern. Sometimes the twisting line went under the elliptical rings, and sometimes it went over.

Staring at the door, Cholik whispered, "Kabraxis, Banisher of the Light."

"Get him! Get him! He's up here with us!" Orphik screamed.

Glancing up, not wanting to leap into the path of the little man's knives as he came at him on the cliff ledge, Darrick watched the pirate start for him. The hobnailed boots scratched sparks from the granite ledge.

"Bloody bastard nearly did for me, Lon," Orphik crowed as he made his knives dance before him. "You stay back, and I'll slit him between wind and water. Just you watch."

Darrick had only enough time to push himself up on his hands. His left palm, coated in blood from his sliced finger, slipped a little and came close to going out from under him. But his fingers curled around a jutting rocky shelf, and he hurled himself to his feet.

Orphik swung his weapons in a double slash, right hand over left, scissoring the air only inches from Darrick's eyes. He took another step back as the wiry little pirate tried to get him again with backhanded swings. Unwilling to go backward farther, knowing that a misstep along the narrow ledge would prove fatal, Darrick ducked below the next attack and stepped forward.

As he passed the pirate, Darrick drew the long knife from his left boot, feeling it slide through his bloody fingers for just a moment. Then he curled his hand around the weapon as Orphik tried to spin to face him. Without mercy, knowing he'd already been offered no quarter, Darrick slashed at the man's boot. The leather parted like butter at the knife's keen kiss, and the blade cut through the pirate's hamstring.

Losing control over his crippled foot, Orphik weaved

off-balance. He cursed and cried for help, struggling to keep the long knives before him in defense.

Darrick lunged to his feet, slapping away Orphik's wrists and planting a shoulder in the smaller man's mid-section. Caught by Darrick's upward momentum and greater weight, Orphik left his feet, looking as if he'd jumped up from the ledge. The pirate also went out over the dizzying fall to the river below, squalling the whole way and flailing his arms. He missed Mat and the other sailors by scant inches, and only then because they'd all seen what had happened and had flattened themselves against the cliff wall.

Dropping to his knees and grabbing for the wall behind him, clutching the thick root from the tree on the next level of the cliffs that he spotted from the corner of his eye, Darrick only just prevented his own plunge over the cliff's side. He gazed down, hypnotized by the suddenness of the event.

Orphik missed the river's depths, though. The little pirate plunged headfirst into the shallows and struck the rocky bottom. The sickening crunch of his skull bursting echoed up the cliff.

"Darrick!" Mat called up.

Realizing the precariousness of his position, Darrick turned toward the other pirate, thinking the man might already be on top of him. Instead, Lon had headed away, back up the ledge that led to the passable areas on the mountains. He covered ground in long-legged strides that slammed and echoed against the stone.

"He's makin' for the signal fire," Mat warned. "If he gets to it, those pirates will be all over us. The life of the king's nephew will be forfeit. Maybe our own as well."

Cursing, Darrick shoved himself up. He started to run, then remembered the rope tied around his loins. Thrusting his knife between his teeth, he untied the knots with his nimble fingers. He spun and threw the rope around the tree root with a trained sailor's skill and calm in the face of a sudden squall, gazing up the rocky ledge after the running pirate. *How far away is the signal fire?*

When he had the rope secure, giving Lon only three more strides on his lead, Darrick yanked on the rope, testing it. Satisfied, he called down, "Rope's belayed," then hurled himself after the fleeing pirate.

"Get up and get dressed," Captain Raithen ordered without looking at the woman who lay beside him.

Not saying a word, having learned from past mistakes that she wasn't supposed to talk, the woman got up naked from the bed and crossed the room to the clothing she'd left on a chest.

Although he felt nothing for the woman, in fact even despised her for revealing to him again the weakness he had in controlling his own lusts, Raithen watched her as she dressed. He was covered in sweat, his and hers, because the room was kept too hot from the roaring blaze in the fireplace. Only a few habitable houses and buildings remained in Tauruk's Port. This inn was one of those. The pirates had moved into it, storing food and gear and the merchandise they'd taken from the ships they'd sunk.

The woman was young, and even the hard living among the pirates hadn't done much to destroy the slender lines and smooth muscles of her body. Half-healed cuts showed across the backs of her thighs, lingering evidence of the last time Raithen had disciplined her with a horsewhip.

Even now, as she dressed with methodical deliberation, she used her body to show him the control she still felt she had over him. He hungered for her even though he didn't care about her, and she knew it.

Her actions frustrated Raithen. Yet he hadn't had her killed out of hand. Nor had he allowed the other pirates to have at her, keeping her instead for his own private needs. If she were dead, none of the other women they'd taken from ships they raided would satisfy him.

"Do you think you're still so proud in spirit, woman?" Raithen demanded.

"No."

"You trying to rub my nose in something here, then?"

"No." Her answer remained calm and quiet.

Her visible lack of emotion pushed at the boundaries of the tentative control Raithen had over his anger. His bruised neck still filled his head with blinding pain, and the humiliation he'd received at Cholik's hands wouldn't leave him.

He thought again of the way the old priest had suspended him over the long drop from the rooms he kept in the city ruins, proving that he wasn't the old, doddering fool Raithen had believed him to be. The pirate captain reached for the long-necked bottle of wine on the small stand by the bed. Gold and silver weren't the only things he and his crew had taken from the ships they'd raided.

Taking the cork from the bottle, Raithen took a long pull of the dark red wine inside. It burned the back of his throat and damn near made him choke, but he kept it down. He wiped his mouth with the back of his hand and glanced at the woman.

She stood in a simple shift by the trunk, no shoes on her feet. After the beating he'd given her the first time, she wouldn't dream of leaving without his permission. Nor would she ask for it.

Raithen put the cork back into the wine bottle. "I've never asked you your name, woman."

Her chin came up a little at that, and for a moment her eyes darted to his, then flicked away. "Do you want to know my name?"

Raithen grinned. "If I want you to have a name, I'll give you one."

Cheeks flaming in sudden anger and embarrassment, the woman almost lost control. She forced herself to swallow. The pulse at the hollow of her throat thundered.

Grabbing the blanket that covered him, Raithen wiped his face and pushed himself from the bed. He'd hoped to drink enough to sleep, but that hadn't happened.

"Were you an important person in Westmarch, woman?" Raithen pulled his breeches on. He'd left his sword and knife within easy reach out of habit, but the woman had never looked too long at either of them. She'd known they were a temptation she could ill afford.

"I'm not from Westmarch," the woman answered.

Raithen pulled on his blouse. He had other clothing back on his ship, and a hot bath as well because the cabin boy would know better than to let the water grow cold. "Where, then?"

"Aranoch."

"Lut Gholein? I thought I'd detected an accent in your words."

"North of Lut Gholein. My father did business with the merchants of Lut Gholein."

"What kind of business?"

"He was a glassblower. He produced some of the finest glassware ever made." Her voice broke a little.

Raithen gazed at her with cold dispassion, knowing he understood where the emotion came from. Once he'd found it, he couldn't resist turning the knife. "Where is your father now?"

Her lips trembled. "Your pirates killed him. Without mercy."

"He was probably resisting them. They don't much care for that because I won't let them." Raithen raked his disheveled hair with his fingers.

"My father was an old man," the woman declared. "He couldn't have put up a fight against anyone. He was a kind and gentle soul, and he should not have been murdered."

"Murdered?" Raithen threw the word back at her. In two quick steps, he took away the distance that separated them. "We're pirates, woman, not bloody murderers, and I'll have you speak of that trade with a civil tongue."

She wouldn't look at him. Her eyes wept fearful tears, and they tracked down her bruised face.

Tracing the back of his hand against her cheek, Raithen leaned in and whispered in her ear. "You'll speak of me, too, with a civil tongue, or I'll have that tongue cut from your pretty head and let my seadogs have at you."

Her head snapped toward him. Her eyes flashed, reflecting the blaze in the fireplace.

Raithen waited, wondering if she would speak. He taunted her further. "Did your father die well? I can't remember. Did he fight back, or did he die screaming like an old woman?"

"Damn you!" the woman said. She came around on him, swinging her balled fist at the end of her right arm.

Without moving more than his arm, Raithen caught the woman's fist in one hand. She jerked backward, kicking at his crotch. Turning his leg and hip, the pirate captain caught the kick against his thigh. Then he moved his shoulders, backhanding her across the face.

Propelled by the force of the blow, the woman stumbled across the room and smacked against the wall. Dizzy, her eyes rolling back up into her head for a moment, she sank down splay-legged to her rump.

Raithen sucked at the cut on the back of his hand that her teeth had caused. The pain made him feel more alive, and seeing her helpless before him made him feel more in control. His neck still throbbed, but the humiliation was shared now even though the woman didn't know it.

"I'll kill you," the woman said in a hoarse voice. "I swear by the Light and all that's holy that if you do not kill me, I will find a way to kill you." She wiped at her bleeding mouth with her hand, tracking crimson over her fingers.

Raithen grinned. "Damn me for a fool, but you do me well, wench. Spoken like you'd looked deep inside my own heart." He gazed down at her. "See? Now, most people would think you were only talking. Running your mouth to play yourself up, to make yourself feel maybe a little braver. But I look into your eyes, and I know you're speaking the truth."

"If I live," the woman said, "you'll need to look over your shoulder every day for the rest of your life. Because if I ever find you, I *will* kill you."

Still grinning, feeling better about life in general and surprised at how it had all come about, Raithen nodded. "I know you will, woman. And if I was an overconfident braggart like a certain old priest, let's say, I'd probably make the mistake of humbling you, then leaving you alive. Most people you could probably terrify and never have to worry about."

The woman pushed herself to her feet in open rebellion.

"But you and me, woman," Raithen went on, "we're different. People judge us like we were nothing, that everything we say is just pomp and doggerel. They don't understand that once we start hating them and plotting for them to fall, we're only waiting for them to show a weakness we can exploit." He paused. "Just like you'll suffer through every indignity I pass on your way to break you, and then remain strong enough to try to kill me."

She stood and faced him, blood smearing her chin.

Raithen smiled at her again, and this time the effort was warm and genuine. "I want to thank you for that, for squaring my beam and trimming my sails. Reminds me of the true course I have to follow in this endeavor. No matter how many scraps Loremaster Buyard Cholik tosses my way, I'm no hound to be chasing bones and suffering ill use at his hands." He crossed to her.

This time she didn't flinch away from him. Her eyes peered at him as if she were looking through him.

"You have my thanks, woman." Raithen bent, moving his lips to meet hers.

Moving with speed and determination that she hadn't been showing, the woman sank her teeth into the pirate captain's throat, chewing toward his jugular.

FOUR

Darrick drove his feet against the rocky ledge, aware of the dizzying sight of the fogbound river lying below. Here and there, moonlight kissed the surface, leaving bright diamonds in its wake. His breath whistled at the back of his throat, coming hard and fast. Knowing that Mat and the other sailors were already clambering up the rope cheered Darrick a little. Plunging through the darkness and maybe into a small party of pirates encamped along the cliff wasn't a pleasant prospect.

He carried his knife in his hand but left his cutlass in its scabbard at his side. The heavy blade thumped against his thigh. Covering his face with his empty hand and arm, he managed to keep the fir and spruce branches from his eyes. Other branches struck his face and left welts.

The big pirate followed a game trail through the short forest of conifers, but he left it in a rush, plunging through a wall of overgrown brush and disappearing.

Darrick redoubled his efforts, almost overrunning his own abilities after the long, demanding climb up the mountainside. Black spots swam in his vision and he couldn't get enough air in his lungs.

If the pirates discovered them, Darrick knew he and his group of warriors had little chance of reaching *Lonesome Star* out in the Gulf of Westmarch before the pirate ships overtook them. At the very least, they'd be killed out of hand, perhaps along with the young boy who had been taken captive.

Darrick reached the spot where the pirate had lunged through the brush and threw himself after the man. Almost disoriented in the darkness of the forest, he lost his bearings for a moment. He glanced up automatically, but the thick tree canopy blocked sight of the stars, so he couldn't set himself straight. Relying on his hearing, tracking the bigger man's passage through the brush, Darrick kept running.

Without warning, something exploded from the darkness. There was just enough ambient light for Darrick to get an impression of large leathery wings, glistening black eyes, and shiny white teeth that came at him. At least a dozen of the bats descended on him, outraged at the pirate's passing. Their harsh squeals were near deafening in the enclosed space, and their sharp teeth lit fiery trails along his flesh for an instant.

Darrick lashed out with his knife and never broke stride. The grimsable bats were noted for their pack-hunting abilities and often tracked down small game. Though he'd never seen it himself, Darrick had heard that flocks of the blood-drinking predators had even brought down full-grown men and stripped the flesh from their bones.

Only a short distance ahead, with the bats searching without success behind him, Darrick tripped over a fallen tree and went sprawling. He rolled with it, maintaining his hard-fisted grasp on the knife. The cutlass smashed against his hip with bruising force. Then he was up again, alert to the shift in direction his quarry had taken.

Breath burning the back of his throat, Darrick raced through the forest. His heart triphammered inside his chest, and his hearing was laced with the dulled roaring of blood in his ears. He caught a tree with his free hand and brought himself around in a sharp turn as the bark tore loose from the trunk.

The big pirate wasn't faring well, either. His breathing was ragged and hoarse, and there was no measured cadence left to it.

Given time, Darrick knew he could run the man to ground. But he was almost out of time. Even now he could see the flickering yellow light of a campfire glimmering in the darkness through the branches of the fir and spruce trees.

The pirate burst free of the forest and ran for the camp-fire.

Trap? Darrick wondered. *Or desperation? Could be he's more afraid of Captain Raithen's rage than he is that I might overtake him.* Even the Westmarch captains showed harsh discipline. Darrick bore scars from whips in the past as he'd fought and shoved his way up through the ranks. The officers had never dished out anything more than he could bear, and one day some of those captains would regret the punishments they'd doled out to him.

Without hesitating, knowing he had no choice about try-ing to stop the man, Darrick charged from the forest, sum-moning his last bit of energy. If there were more men than the one surviving pirate, he knew he was done for. He leaned into his running stride, coming close to going beyond his own control.

The campfire was set at the bottom of a low promontory. The twisting flames scrawled harsh shadows against the hollow of the promontory. Above it, only a short distance out of easy reach, the small cauldron of pitch blend that was the intended signal pot hung from a trio of crossed branches set into the ground.

Darrick knew the signal pot was in clear view of the next post up the river. Once the pirate ignited the pitch blend, there was no way to stop the signal.

Wheezing and gasping for air, the pirate reached the campfire and bent down, grabbed a nearby torch, and shoved it into the flames. The torch caught at once, burn-ing blue and yellow because the pitch had been soaked in whale oil. Holding the torch in one hand, the big pirate started up the promontory, making the climb with ease.

Darrick threw himself at the pirate, hoping he had enough strength and speed left to make the distance. He caught the pirate knee-high with his shoulders, then slammed his face against the granite mountainside. Dazed, he felt the pirate fall back across him, and they both slid down the steep incline over the broken rock surface.

The pirate recovered first, shoving himself to his feet

and pulling his sword. Light from the campfire limned his face, revealing the fear and anger etched there. He took a two-handed hold on his weapon and struck.

Darrick rolled away from the blade, almost disbelieving when the sword missed him. Still in motion, he rolled to a kneeling position, then drew his cutlass as he pushed himself to his feet. Knife in one hand and cutlass in the other, he set himself to face the pirate almost twice his size.

New agony flared through Raithen as the woman ground her teeth in his neck. He felt his own warm blood spray down his neck, and panic welled from deep inside him, hammering at the confines of his skull like a captive tiger in a minstrel show. For one frightening moment he thought a vampire had attacked him. Maybe the woman had found a way to trade her essence to one of the undead monsters that Raithen suspected Buyard Cholik hunted through the ruins of the two cities.

Mastering the cold fear that ran rampant along his spine, Raithen tried to back away. *Vampires aren't real!* he told himself. *I've never seen one.*

Sensing his movement, the woman butted into him, striking his chin with the top of her head, and threw her arms around him, holding tight as a leech. Her lips and teeth searched out new places, rending his flesh.

Screaming in pain, surprised at her maneuver even though he'd been expecting her to do something, Raithen shook and twisted his right arm. The small throwing knife concealed in a cunning sheath there dropped into his waiting palm butt-first. He wrapped his fingers around the knife haft, turned his hand, and drove it into the woman's stomach.

Her mouth opened in a strained gasp that feathered over his cheek. She released his neck and wrapped her hands around his forearm, pushing to pull the knife from her body. She shook her head in denial and stumbled back.

Grabbing the back of her head, knotting his fingers in her hair so she couldn't just slip away from him and maybe even make it through the doorway out of the room, Raithen stepped forward and trapped the woman against the wall. She looked up at him, eyes wide with wonder as he angled the knife up and searched for her heart.

"Bastard," she breathed. A bloody rose bloomed on her lips as her blood-misted word emerged arthritically.

Raithen held her, watching the life and understanding go out of her eyes, knowing full well what he was taking from her. His own fear returned to him in a rush as blood continued to stream down the side of his neck. He was afraid she'd been successful in biting through his jugular, which meant he would bleed to death in minutes, with no way to stop it. There were no healers on board the pirate ships in Tauruk's Port, and all the priests were locked away for tonight or busy digging through the graves of Tauruk's Port. Even then, there was no telling how many healers were among them.

In the next moment, the woman went limp, her dead weight pulling at the pirate captain's arm.

Suspicious by nature, Raithen held on to the woman and his knife. She might have been faking—even with four inches of good steel in her. It was something he had done with success in the past, and taken two men's lives in the process.

After a moment of holding the woman, Raithen knew she would never move again. Her lips remained parted, colored a little by the blood that had stopped flowing. Dull and lifeless, her eyes stared through the pirate captain. Her face held no expression.

"Damn me, woman," Raithen whispered with genuine regret. "Had I known you had this kind of fire in you before now, our times together could have been spent much better." He breathed in, inhaling the sweet fragrance of the perfume he'd given her from the latest spoils, then demanded that she wear to bed. He also smelled the coppery odor of blood. Both scents were intoxicating.

The door to the room broke open.

Raithen prepared for the worst, spinning and placing

the corpse between himself and the doorway. He slipped the knife free of the dead woman's flesh and held it before him.

A grizzled man stepped into the room with a crossbow in his hands. He squinted against the bright light streaming from the fireplace. "Cap'n? Cap'n Raithen?" The crossbow held steady in the man's hands, aimed at the two bodies.

"Aim that damnfool thing away from me, Pettit," Raithen growled. "You can never trust a crossbow to hold steady."

The sailor pulled the crossbow off line and canted the metal-encased butt against his hip. He reached up and doffed his tricorn hat. "Begging the cap's pardon, but I thought ye was in some fair amount of rough water there. With all that squallering a-goin' on, I mean. Didn't know you was up here after enjoying yerself with one of the doxies."

"The enjoyment," Raithen said with a forced calm because he still wanted to know how bad the wound on his neck was, "was not all mine." He released the dead woman, and she thumped to the floor at his feet.

As captain of some of the most vicious pirates to sail the Great Sea and the Gulf of Westmarch, he had an image to maintain. If any of his crew sensed weakness, someone would try to exploit it. He'd taken his own captaincy of *Barracuda* at the same time he'd taken his former captain's life.

Pettit grinned and spat into the dented bronze cuspidor in the corner of the room. He wiped his mouth with the back of his hand, then said, "Looks like ye've about had yer fill of that one. Want me to bring another one up?"

"No." Controlling the fear and curiosity that raged within him, Raithen cleaned his bloody knife on the woman's clothes, then crossed the room to the mirror. It was cracked and contained dark gray age spots where the silver-powder backing had worn away. "But she did remind me of something, Pettit."

"What's that, cap'n?"

"That damned priest, Cholik, has been thinking of us as lackeys." Raithen peered into the mirror, surveying the wound on his neck, poking at the edges of it with his fingers. Thank the Light, it wasn't bleeding any more than it had been, and it even appeared to be stopping.

The flesh between the bite marks was raised, swollen, and already turning purple. Bits of skin and even the meat beneath hung in tatters. It would scar, Raithen knew. The thought made him bitter because he was vain about his looks. By most accounts, he was a handsome man and had taken care to remain that way. And it would give him a more colorful and acceptable excuse about how all the bruising had taken place around his neck.

"Aye," Pettit grunted. "Them priests, they get up under a man's skin with them high-and-mighty ways of theirs. Always actin' like they got a snootful of air what's better'n the likes of ye and me. There's been a night or two on watch when I'd think about goin' after one of them and guttin' him, leavin' him out for the others to find. Might put them in a more appreciatin' frame o' mind about what we're a-doin' here."

Satisfied that his life wasn't in danger unless the woman was carrying some kind of disease that hadn't become apparent yet, Raithen took a kerchief from his pocket and tied it around his neck. "That's not a bad idea, Pettit."

"Thank ye, cap'n. I'm always thinkin'. And, why, this here deserted city with all them stories o' demons and the like, it'd be a perfect place to pull something like that. Why, we'd find out who the true believers were among ol' Cholik's bunch fer damn sure." He grinned, revealing only a few straggling, stained teeth remaining in his mouth.

"Some of the men might get worried, too." Raithen surveyed the kerchief around his neck in the mirror. Actually, it didn't look bad on him. In time, when the wound scarred over properly, he'd invent stories about how he'd gotten it in the arms of a lover he'd slain or stolen from, or some crazed and passionate princess out of Kurast he'd taken for ransom then returned deflowered to her father, the king, after getting his weight in gold.

"Well, we could tell the men what was what, cap'n."

"A secret, Pettit, is kept by one man. Even sharing it between the two of us endangers it. Telling a whole crew?" Raithen shook his head and tried not to wince when his neck pained him. "That would be stupid."

Pettit frowned. "Well, somethin' has to be done. Them priests has discovered a door down there in them warrens. An' if the past behavior of them priests is anythin' to go by, they ain't a-gonna let us look at what's behind it none."

"A door?" Raithen turned to his second-in-command. "What door?"

The big pirate, Lon, attacked Darrick Lang without any pretense at skilled swordplay. He just fetched up that huge sword of his in both hands and brought it crashing down toward Darrick's head, intending to split it like an overripe melon.

Thrusting his cutlass up, knowing there was a chance that the bigger sword might shear his own blade but having no other choice for defense, Darrick caught the descending blade. He didn't try to stop the sword's descent, but he did redirect it to the side, stepping to one side as he did because he expected the sudden reversal the pirate tried. He didn't entirely block the blow, though, and the flat of the blade slammed against his skull, almost knocking him out and leaving him disoriented.

Working on sheer instinct and guided by skilled responses, Darrick managed to lock his opponent's blade with his while he struggled to hold on to his senses. His vision and hearing faded out, as the world sometimes did between slow rollers when *Lonesome Star* followed wave troughs instead of cutting through them.

Recovering a little, Lon shoved Darrick back but didn't gain much ground.

Moving with skill and the dark savagery that filled him

any time he fought, Darrick took a step forward and head-butted the pirate in the face.

Moaning, Lon stumbled back.

Darrick showed no mercy, pushing himself forward again. Obviously employing all the skill he had just to keep himself alive, the pirate kept retreating, stumbling and tripping over the broken terrain as he tried to walk up the incline behind him. Only a moment later, he went too far.

As though from a great distance, Darrick heard the man's boots scrape in the loose dirt, then the man fell, flailing and yelling, in the end wrapping his arms about his head. Ruthless and quick, Darrick knocked the pirate's blade from his hand, sending the big sword spinning through the air to land in the dense brush a dozen yards away.

Lon held his hands up. "I surrender! I surrender! Give me mercy!"

But, dazed as he was from the near miss of the sword, mercy was out of Darrick's reach. He remembered the bodies he'd seen in the flotsam left by the plunderers who had taken the Westmarch ship. Even that was hard to hang on to, because his battered mind slipped even farther back into the past, recalling the beatings his father had given him while he was a child. The man had been a butcher, big and rough, with powerful, callused hands that could split skin over a cheekbone with a single slap.

For a number of years, Darrick had never understood his father's anger or rage at him; he'd always assumed he'd done something wrong, not been a good son. It wasn't until he got older that he understood everything that was at play in their relationship.

"Mercy," the pirate begged.

But the main voice that Darrick listened to was his father's, cursing and swearing at him, threatening to beat him to death or bleed him out like a fresh-butchered hog. Darrick drew back his cutlass and swung, aiming to take the pirate's head off.

Without warning, a sword darted out and deflected Darrick's blow, causing the blade to cut into the earth only inches from the pirate's arm-wrapped head. "No," someone said.

Still lost in the memory of beatings he'd gotten at his father's hands, the present overlapping the past, Darrick spun and lifted his sword. Incredibly, someone caught his arm before he could swing and halted the blow.

"Darrick, it's me. It's me, Darrick. Mat." Thick and hoarse with emotion, Mat's voice was little more than a whisper. "It's me, damn it, leave off. We need this man alive."

Head filled with pain, vision still spotty from the pirate's blow, Darrick squinted his eyes and tried to focus. Forced out as he made his way to the present reality, memory of those past events left with reluctance.

"He's not your father, Darrick," Mat said.

Darrick focused on his friend, feeling the emotion drain from him, leaving him weak and shaking. "I know. I know that." But he knew he hadn't, not really. The pirate's blow had almost taken away his senses. He took in a deep breath and struggled to continue clearing his head.

"We need him alive," Mat said. "There's the matter of the king's nephew. This man has information we can use."

"I know." Darrick looked at Mat. "Let me go."

Mat's eyes searched his, but the grip on his swordarm never wavered. "You're sure?"

Looking over his friend's shoulder, Darrick saw the other sailors in his shore crew. Only old Maldrin didn't seem surprised by the bloodthirsty behavior Darrick had exhibited. Not many of the crew knew of the dark fury that sometimes escaped Darrick's control. It hadn't gotten away from him for a long time until tonight.

"I'm sure," Darrick said.

Mat released him. "Those times are past us. You don't ever have to revisit them. Your father didn't follow us from Hillsfar. We left him there those years ago. We left him there, and good riddance, I say."

Nodding, Darrick sheathed the cutlass and turned from them. He swept the horizon with his gaze, conscious of Mat's eyes still on him. The fact that his friend didn't trust him even after he'd said he was all right troubled and angered him.

And he seemed to hear his father's mocking laughter ringing in his ears, pointing out his helplessness and lack of worth. Despite how far he'd pushed himself, even shoving himself up through the Westmarch Navy ranking, he'd never been able to leave that voice behind in Hillsfar.

Darrick took a deep, shuddering breath. "All right, then, we'd best get at it, lads. Maldrin, take a couple men and fetch us up some water, if you please. I want this bonfire wetted so it can't go up by design or by mistake."

"Aye, sir," Maldrin responded, turning immediately and pointing out two men to accompany him. A quick search through the guards' supplies netted them a couple of waterskins. After emptying the waterskins over the pitch blend torch, they set out for the cliff's edge at once to get more water to finish the job.

Turning, Darrick surveyed the big pirate as Mat tied his hands behind his back with a kerchief. "How many of you were on guard here?" Darrick asked.

The man remained silent.

"I'll not trouble myself to ask you again," Darrick warned. "At this point, and take care to fully understand what I'm telling you here, you're a better bargain to me dead than you are alive. I don't look forward to trying to complete the rest of my mission while bringing along a prisoner."

Lon swallowed and tried to look defiant.

"I'd believe him if I were ye," Mat offered, patting the pirate on the cheek. "When he's in a fettle like this, he's more likely to have ye ordered thrown off the mountain than to keep ye alive an' hope ye know some of the answers to whatever questions he might have."

Lying on the ground as he was, Darrick knew it was hard for the pirate to feel in any way in control of the situation. And Mat's words made sense. The pirate just didn't know Mat wouldn't let Darrick act on an impulse like that. Anyway, the loss of control was behind him, and Darrick was in command of himself again.

"So, go on, then," Mat encouraged in that good-natured way of his as he squatted down beside the captive. "Tell us what ye know."

The pirate regarded them both with suspicion. "You'll let me live?"

"Aye," Mat agreed without hesitation. "I'll give ye me word on it, I will, and spit on me palm to seal the deal."

"How do I know I can trust you?" the pirate demanded.

Mat laughed a little. "Well, old son, we've done an' let ye live so far, ain't we?"

Darrick looked down at the man. "How many of you were there here?"

"Just us two," the pirate replied sullenly.

"What time's the changing of the guard?"

Hesitating, the pirate said, "Soon."

"Pity," Mat commented. "If someone happens by in the next few minutes, why, I'll have to slice your throat for ye, I will."

"I thought you said you were going to let me live," the pirate protested.

Mat patted the man's cheek again. "Only if we don't have nasty surprises along the way."

The pirate licked his lips. "New guards won't be until dawn. I just told you that so maybe you'd leave and Raithen wouldn't be so vexed at me for not lighting the torch."

"Well," Mat admitted, "it was a sound plan on your part. I'd probably have tried the same thing. But we're here on some matter of consequence, ye see."

"Sure," the pirate said, nodding. Mat's behavior, as always in most circumstances, was so gentle and understanding that it was confounding.

Immediate relief went through Darrick. Changing of the guard during the middle of the night wasn't something he would have suspected, but the confirmation let him know they still had a few hours to get the king's nephew back before the morning light filled the land.

"What about the king's nephew?" Mat asked. "He's just a boy, an' I wouldn't want to hear that anything untoward has happened to him."

"The boy's alive."

"Where?" Darrick asked.

"Cap'n Raithen has him," the pirate said, wiping blood from his lip. "He's keepin' him aboard *Barracuda*."

"And where, then, can we find *Barracuda*?" Darrick asked.

"She's in the harbor. Cap'n Raithen, he don't let *Barracuda* go nowheres unless he's aboard her."

"Good." Darrick turned east, noting that Maldrin and his crew had returned with waterskins they'd filled from the river using the rope they left behind. "Get this man up and on his feet, Mat. I'll want him gagged proper."

"Aye, sir." Mat yanked the pirate to his feet and took another kerchief from a pocket to make the gag.

Stepping close to the pirate, Darrick felt bad when the man winced and tried to move away from him, held in place only because Mat blocked him from behind. With his face only inches from the pirate's, Darrick spoke softly. "And let's be having an understanding, you and me."

When the silence between them stretched out, the pirate looked at Mat, who offered no support. Then the prisoner looked back at Darrick and nodded hopefully.

"Good," Darrick said, showing him a wintry smile. "If you try to warn your mates, which could be something you'd be interested in because you might actually be inclined favorably toward some of them, I'll slit your throat for you calm as a man gutting a fish. Nod your head if you understand."

The pirate nodded.

"I've no love of pirates," Darrick said. "There's ways for an honest man to make a living without preying on his neighbors. I've killed plenty of pirates in the Great Sea and in the Gulf of Westmarch. One more won't bump up the score overmuch, but I'd feel better about it myself. Are we clear here?"

Again, the pirate nodded, and crocodile tears showed in his eyes.

"Crystal, sir," Mat added energetically as he clapped the pirate on the shoulder. "Why, I don't think we'll be having any problems with this man at all after your kind explanation regardin' the matter."

"Good. Bring him along, but keep him close to hand." Turning, Darrick started east, following the ridgeline of the Hawk's Beak Mountains that would take them down toward Tauruk's Port.

FIVE

Standing near the dead woman's body in the inn room in Tauruk's Port, Raithen watched as Pettit reached into a pocket under his vest and took out a piece of paper.

"That's what brung me up here to see ye, cap'n," the first mate said. "Valdir sent this along just now as quick as he could after them priests found the door buried down in them ruins."

Raithen crossed the room and took the paper. Unfolding it, he leaned toward the fireplace and the lantern that sat on the mantel.

Valdir was the current spy the pirate captain had assigned to Cholik's excavation team. Raithen kept them rotated out with each new arrival of slaves. The men assigned didn't care for it, and the fact that they didn't become sickly and emaciated as the others did would draw attention from the mercenaries who remained loyal to Cholik's gold.

The paper held a drawing of a series of elliptical lines, centered one within the other, and a different line running through them.

"What is this?" Raithen asked.

Leaning, Pettit spat again, missing the cuspidor this time. He rubbed strings of spittle from his chin. "That there's a symbol what Valdir saw on that door. It's a huge door, cap'n, near to three times as tall as a man, the way Valdir puts it."

"You spoke to him?"

Pettit nodded. "Went in to talk to some of the mercenaries we're doin' business with. Ye know, to kinda keep them on our side. Took 'em a few bottles of brandy we got off that last Westmarch merchant ship we took down."

Raithen knew that wasn't the only reason Pettit had gone to see the men. Since the pirates had all the women in port, a fact that Cholik and his priests didn't much care for, the mercenaries they'd hired had to negotiate prices for the women's services with Pettit.

Being avaricious was one of the reasons Raithen had taken Pettit on as first mate. Pettit's own knowledge that his loyalty ensured not only his career but also his life kept him in place. It helped that Raithen knew Pettit never saw himself as being a captain and that his only claim to power would be serving a captain who appreciated the cruel and conniving ways he had.

"When did the priests find the door?" Raithen asked. If Cholik had known, why hadn't the priest been there? Raithen still didn't know why Cholik and his minions crawled through the detritus of the two cities like ants, but their obvious zeal for whatever they looked for had gotten him excited.

"Only just," Pettit replied. "As it turned out, cap'n, I was in them tunnels when Valdir fetched up with the news of their findin'."

Raithen's nimble mind leapt. He turned his eyes back to the crude drawing. "Where is that bastard Cholik?" They had spies on the priest as well.

"He joined the diggers."

"Cholik's there now?" Raithen's interest grew more intense.

"Aye, cap'n. An' once word of this discovery reached him, Cholik wasted no time in harin' off down there."

"And we don't have any idea what's behind this door?" Of course, Cholik didn't know about the king's nephew Raithen and his pirates were holding for ransom, either. Both sides had their secrets, only Raithen knew Cholik was hiding them.

"None, cap'n, but Valdir will be lettin' us know as soon as he's in the knowin' of it."

"If he can." Any time the priests found something that they thought would be important, they got all the slaves out of the area till the recovery was complete.

"Aye, but if'n any one man can do it, cap'n, Valdir can."

Folding the note then putting it in his pocket, Raithen nodded. "I'd rather have someone down there with the priests. Get a crew assembled. Cover it as a provisions resupply for the slaves."

"It's hardly time for that again."

"Cholik won't know. He works those slaves till they drop, then heaves them into that great, bloody abyss down there."

"Aye, cap'n. I'll get to it then."

"What of our guest aboard *Barracuda?*"

Pettit shrugged. "Oh, he's in fine keepin', cap'n. Fit as a fiddle, he is. Alive, he's worth a lot, but now, dead, cap'n?" The first mate shook his scruffy head. "Why, he's just a step removed from fertilizer, isn't he?"

With care, Raithen touched the wound on his neck beneath the kerchief. Pain rattled through his skull, and he winced at it. "That boy is the king's nephew, Pettit. Westmarch's king prides himself on his knowledge and that of his get. Priests train those children for the most part, and they concern themselves with history, things better left forgotten, I say." *Except for the occasional treasure map or account of where a ship laden with treasure went down in inhospitable seas.*

"Aye, cap'n. Worthless learnin', most of it. If'n ye're askin' me own opinion."

Raithen wasn't, but he didn't belabor the point. "What do you think the chances are that the boy we took from that last Westmarch ship knows a considerable amount about history and things a priest might be interested in? Maybe even knows about this?" He patted the breast pocket where he'd stored the paper with the symbol.

Understanding dawned in Pettit's rheumy eyes. He scratched his bearded chin and grinned, revealing the few straggling teeth stained by beetle-juice. "Me, cap'n? Why, I'd say there was considerable chances, I would."

"I'm going to talk to the boy." Raithen took up his plumed hat from the trunk at the foot of the bed and clapped it onto his head.

"Ye might have to wake him," Pettit said. "An' he ain't none too sociable. Little rapscallion liked to tore ol' Bull's ear off when he went in to feed him this e'ening."

"What do you mean?"

"Ol' Bull, he up and walks into the hold where we're a-keepin' the boy like it was nothin'. That young'un, he come out of the rafters where'd he'd been a-hidin' and dropped down on ol' Bull. Walloped ol' Bull a few good licks with a two-by-four he'd pried loose from the wall of the hold. If'n ol' Bull's head hadn't been as thick as it was, why he'd have been damn near knocked to death, he would. As it was, that boy nearly got his arse offa *Barracuda* for certain."

"Is the boy hurt?" Raithen asked.

Pettit waved the possibility away. "Nah. Mighta picked him up a couple of knots on his head fer his troubles, but nothin' what's gonna stay with him more'n a day or two."

"I don't want that boy hurt, Pettit." Raithen made his voice harsh.

Pettit cringed a little and scratched at the back of his neck. "I ain't gonna let any o' the crew hurt him."

"If that boy gets hurt before I'm done with him," Raithen said, stepping over the dead woman sprawled on the floor, "I'm going to hold you responsible. And I'll take it out of your arse."

"I understand, cap'n. An' trust me, ye got no worries there."

"Get that supply crew together, but no one moves until I say."

"It'll be as ye say, cap'n."

"I'm going to speak with that boy. Maybe he knows something about this symbol."

"If I may suggest, cap'n, while ye're there, just mind ye keep a sharp watch on yer ears. That boy's a quick one, he is."

*   *   *

Buyard Cholik stared at the huge door that fronted the wall. In all the years of knowing about Kabraxis and of knowing the fate of Ransim buried beneath Tauruk's Port, he'd never known how he would feel once he stood before the door that hid the demon's secret. Even months of planning and work, of coming down to the subterranean depths on occasion to check on the work and inspire fear or reprisal in the acolytes who labored under his design, had left him unprepared.

Although he had expected to feel proud and exuberant about his discovery, Cholik had forgotten about the fear that now filled him. Quavers, like the tremor of an earthquake hidden deep within a land, ran through his body. He wanted to shriek and call on Archangel Yaerius, who first brought the tenets of Zakarum to men. But he did not. Cholik knew he had long passed the line of forgiveness that would be offered by any who followed the ways of Light.

And what good would forgiveness do a dying old man? The priest taunted himself with that question as he had for the past few months and stiffened his resolve. Death was only another few years into the future for him, nothing worthwhile left during that distance.

"Master," Brother Altharin whispered, "are you all right?" He stood to Cholik's right, two steps back as respect and the older priest's tolerance dictated.

Letting his irritation burn away the traces that were left from his own anger and resentment at his approaching mortality, Cholik said, "Of course, I am all right. Why would I not be?"

"You were so quiet," Altharin said.

"Contemplation and meditation," Cholik said, "are the two key abilities for any priest to possess in order that he may understand the great mysteries left to us by the Light. You would do well to remember that, Altharin."

"Of course, master." Altharin's willingness to accept rebuke and toil at a relentless pace had made him the natural candidate for being in charge of the excavation.

Cholik studied the massive door. *Or should I think of it as a gate?* The secret texts he'd read had suggested that Kabraxis's door guarded another place as well as the hidden things the demon lord had left behind.

The slaves continued to labor, loading carts with broken rock with their bare hands by lantern light and torchlight. Their chains clinked and clanked against the hard stone ground. Other slaves worked with pickaxes, standing on the stone surrounding the door or atop frail scaffolding that quivered with every swing. The slaves spoke in fearful tones to one another, but they also hurried to finish uncovering the door. Cholik thought that was because they believed that they would be able to rest. If something behind the great door didn't kill them, the old priest thought, perhaps for a time they would rest.

"So much of the door is uncovered," Cholik said. "Why was I not called earlier?"

"Master," Altharin said, "there was no indication that we were so close to finding the door. We came upon another hard section of the dig, the wall that you see before you, which hid the door. I only thought that it was another section of cavern wall. So many times the path that you chose for us has caused us to punch through walls of the existing catacombs."

The city's builders had constructed Ransim to take advantage of the natural caverns in the area above the Dyre River, Cholik remembered from the texts. The caves had provided warehouse area for the goods they trafficked in, natural cisterns of groundwater they could use in event of a siege—which had happened several times during the city's history—and as protection from the elements because harsh storms often raced down from the summits of the Hawk's Beak Mountains. Tauruk's Port, founded after the destruction of Ransim, hadn't benefited from access to the caverns.

"When we started to attack this wall," Altharin continued, "it fell out in large sections. That's why so much rubble remains before the door."

Cholik watched the slaves loading huge sections of broken stone into the carts, then pushing the carts up to the dump sites. Other slaves filled large buckets with smaller debris and filled more carts. The ironbound wheels creaked on dry axles and grated against the floor.

"The work to uncover the door went quickly," Altharin said. "As soon as I knew we had found it, I sent for you."

Cholik strode toward the door, drawing on the remaining dregs of his strength. His legs felt like lead, and his heart hammered against his ribs. He'd pushed himself too far. He knew that. The confrontation with Raithen and the spell he'd summoned to destroy the rats had shoved him past his limits. His breath felt tight in his chest. Using magic no longer came easy to the aged and infirm sometimes. Spellwork had its own demands and often left those too weak to handle the energies warped and broken. And he'd come into the spells late in life after wasting so many years in the Zakarum Church.

The ground inclined toward the door, and Cholik's steps hastened of their own accord. Slaves noticed him coming and cleared the way, yelling at one another to get out of the way.

Hammers rose and fell as more slaves put additional scaffolding into place, climbing higher up against the door. In their haste, part of the scaffolding fell, swinging like a pendulum from a fixed point, and four men fell with it. A lantern shattered against the stone floor and spilled a pool of oil that caught fire.

One of the fallen men screamed in pain, clasping a shattered leg. The torchlight revealed the gleam of white bone protruding through his shin.

"Get that fire put out," Altharin ordered.

A slave threw a bucket of water over the fire but only succeeded in splashing it toward the huge door, spreading the flames into little pockets.

One of the mercenaries stepped forward and cut the ragged shirt from a slave with quick flicks of his dagger. He dipped the shirt into another bucket of water, then plopped the soaked garment on top of the fire. Sizzling, the fire died.

Cholik strode forward through the fire, unwilling to show any fear of it. He summoned a small shield to protect him from the fire and walked through it unscathed. The act created the effect he wanted, drawing the slaves' attention from their fear of the door and replacing it with their fear of him.

The door was a threat, but a toothless one. Cholik had proven on several occasions that he had no compunctions about killing them and having their bodies thrown into the abyss. Gathering himself, standing now despite the weakness that filled him only because he refused to let himself falter, he turned to the slaves.

All their frantic whispering stopped except for the groaning man nursing the broken leg. Even he hid his face in the crook of his arm, whimpering and no longer crying out.

Knowing he needed more strength to face whatever lay on the other side of Kabraxis's door, Cholik spoke words of power, summoning the darkness to him that he had feared decades ago, only begun to dabble in a few years ago, and had grown strong in of late.

The old priest held up his right hand, fingers splayed. As he spoke the words, forbidden words to those of the Zakarum Church, he felt the power leech into him, biting through his flesh and sinking into his bones with razored talons. If the spell did not work, he was certain he would fall and risk becoming comatose until his body recovered.

A purple nimbus flared around his hand. A bolt shot out and touched the slave with the broken leg. When the purple light spread over him and invisible hands grabbed him, the man screamed.

Cholik continued speaking, feeling stronger as the spell bound the man to him. His words came faster and more certain. The invisible hands spread-eagled the slave on the ground, then lifted him up, dangling him in the air.

"No!" the man screamed. "Please! I beg you! I will work! I will work!"

Once, the man's fear and his pleading might have

touched Cholik. Those things did not touch Cholik intimately, for the old priest could never remember a time
when he'd placed the needs of another above his own. But
there had been times he'd gone with the Zakarum Church
missionaries in the past to heal the sick and tend to
wounded men. The recent trouble between Westmarch and
Tristram had been rife with those incidents.

"Nooooo!" the man screamed.

The other slaves drew back. Some of them called to the
afflicted man.

Cholik spoke again, then closed his fist. The purple nimbus turned dark, like the bruised flesh of a plum, and sped
along the length of the beam that held the slave.

When the darkness touched the slave, his body con-
torted. Horrible crunching echoed in the cavern as the
man's arms and legs shattered their sockets. He screamed
anew, and despite the agony that must have been coursing
through him, he remained alert and conscious.

A few of the priests who had left Westmarch with Cholik
but who had not yet abdicated the ways of the Zakarum
Church knelt and pressed their faces against the cavern floor.
The teachings of the church held only tenets of healing and
hope, of salvation. Only the Hand of Zakarum, the order of
warriors consecrated by the church, and the Twelve Grand
Inquisitors, who sought out and combated demonic activity
within the populace of the church, used the blessings Yaerius
and Akarat had given to those who had first chosen to follow.

Buyard Cholik was neither of those things. The priests
who had put their faith in him had known that, had
believed that he could make them more than what they
were, but only now saw what they could become. Cholik,
feeding off the slave's fear and life as they came back to
him through the conduit of the spell, was aware that some
of his followers regarded him with fear while others
looked at him hungrily.

Altharin was one of those horrified.

Bracing himself, not knowing for sure what to expect,
Cholik spoke the final word of the spell.

The slave screamed in anguish, but the scream stopped in the middle. The spell ripped the man apart. The explosion of blood painted the frightened faces of the nearby men crimson and extinguished two torches as well as the residual pools of flame from the shattered lantern.

A moment more, and the desiccated remains of the slave plopped against the cavern floor.

Even though he'd expected something, Cholik hadn't expected the sudden rush of euphoria that filled him. Pain echoed within him as well, sweet misery as the vampiric spell worked the restorative effects. The lethargy that had descended upon him after using the spells earlier lifted. Even some of the arthritic pains that had started to blossom in his joints faded. Part of the stolen life energy went to him, to borrow and use as he saw fit, but the spell transferred some of it to the demon worlds as well. Spellcraft designed and given by the demons always benefited them.

Cholik stood straighter as the magical nimbus around him lightened from near black to purple again. Then the hellish light drew back inside him. Refreshed, senses thrumming, the old priest regarded his audience. What he'd done here tonight would trigger reaction in the slaves, the mercenaries, Raithen's pirates, and even the priests. Some, Cholik knew, would not be there come morning.

They would be afraid of him and of what he might do.

The realization made Cholik feel good, powerful. Even when he was a young priest of the Zakarum Church and holding a position in Westmarch, only the truly repentant and those without hope who wished to believe in something had clung to his words. But the men in the cavern watched him as canaries watched a hawk.

Turning from the dead slave, Cholik walked toward the door again. His feet moved with comfort and confidence. Even his own fears seemed pushed farther back in his mind.

"Altharin," Cholik called.

"Yes, master," Altharin responded in a quiet voice.

"Have the slaves get back to work."

"Yes, master." Altharin gave the orders.

Trained survivalists themselves, knowing they offered no blood allegiance, the mercenaries showed the greatest haste in getting the slaves back to work. Slaves secured the fallen scaffolding, and work began again. Pickaxes tore at the cavern wall covering the gray and green door. Sledges pounded huge sections of rock into pieces small enough for men to carry to the waiting carts. The steady thump and crack of the mining tools created a martial cadence that echoed within the cavern.

Mastering his impatience, Cholik watched the progress of the slaves. As the slaves worked, whole sheets of rock fell, crashing against the floor or piles of debris that were already there. The mercenaries stayed among the slaves, lashing out with their whips and leaving marks and cuts against sweat-soaked skin. At times, the mercenaries even aided in shoving the laden carts into motion.

The work went faster. In moments, one of the door's hinges came into view. Only a short time after that, further work revealed another hinge. Cholik studied them, growing more excited.

The hinges were large, gnarled works of metal and amber as Cholik had been expecting from the texts he'd read. The metal was there because man had made it, worked by smiths to hold back and constrain, but the amber was in place because it held the essence of the past trapped within the stirred golden depths.

When enough debris was removed to make a path to the door, Cholik walked forward. The energy he'd taken from the slave wouldn't last long, according to the materials he had read. Once depleted, he would be left in worse condition than he had been in unless he reached his rooms and the potions that he kept there to renew himself.

As he neared the door, Cholik sensed the power that was contained within. The powerful presence surged in his brain, drawing him on and repelling him at the same time. Reaching into his robe, he removed the carved box made from a flawless black pearl.

He held the box in his hands, felt it cold as ice against his palms. Finding the box had required years of work. The secret texts concerning it and Kabraxis's door had been hidden deep in the stacks kept in the Westmarch church. Keeping the box secret had required murder and treachery. Not even Altharin knew of it.

"Master," Altharin said.

"Back," Cholik demanded. "And take your rabble with you."

"Yes, master." Altharin moved back, whispering to the men.

Gazing into the polished surface of the black pearl box, Cholik remained aware of the mass exodus from him and the gate. The old priest breathed deeply. During the years the box had been in his possession, while he'd researched and learned where Ransim had been hidden and devel-oped the courage for such an undertaking and desperation strong enough to allow him to deal with the demon he'd have to confront to take what he wanted, he'd never been able to open the box. What the contents of the box were remained to be seen.

Breathing out, concentrating on the box and the door, Cholik spoke the first Word. His throat ached with the pain of it, for it was not meant for the human tongue. As the Word left his lips, deafening thunder cannonaded in the cavern, and a wind rose up, though no wind should have existed within the stone walls.

The elliptical design on the dark gray-green surface of the door turned deep black. A humming noise echoed through the cavern over the thunder and the gusting wind.

Closing his left hand over the black pearl box, Cholik strode forward, feeling the chill of the metal. He spoke the second Word, harder to master than the first.

The amber pieces in the huge hinges lit with unholy yellow light. They looked like the fires trapped in a wolf's eyes reflecting torchlight at night.

The wind strengthened in intensity, picking up powdery-fine particles that stung flesh when they hit. Prayers echoed within the cavern, all of them to the holy Light, not demons. It was almost enough to make Cholik smile, except that a small part of him was just as afraid as they were.

At the third Word, the black pearl box opened. A gossamer sphere, glowing three different colors of green, lifted from the box. The sphere rolled in front of Cholik's eyes. According to the materials he'd read, the sphere was death to touch.

And if he faltered now, the sphere would consume him, leaving only smoking ash in its wake. Cholik spoke the fourth Word.

The sphere started growing, swelling in size like the eels some fishermen took from the Great Ocean. Prized as an exotic delicacy, the flesh of the eels brought a narcotic bliss when prepared with proper care, but it brought death on occasion even when served by a master. Cholik had never eaten of the eels, but he knew how the men and women who did must have felt.

For a moment, Cholik was certain he had killed himself.

Then the glowing green sphere flew away from him and slammed into Kabraxis's door. Amplified to titanic proportions, the *boom!* of magic contacting the door manifested itself as a physical presence that knocked rock from the edges of the door and slammed stalactites from the cavern ceiling.

The stalactites crashed down among the huddled slaves, mercenaries, and fallen Zakarum priests. Cholik somehow retained his own footing while everyone around him toppled. Glancing over his shoulder, the priest saw three men screaming in agony but heard no sound. He felt as though spun cotton filled his head. One of the mercenaries carried on a brief, macabre dance with a stalactite that had transfixed him, then fell over. He spasmed as his life drained away.

In the silent stillness that had descended upon the cavern, Cholik spoke the fifth and final Word. The elliptical design ignited on the top, outside ring. From its starting point, a blood-red bead traced the ellipses, making them all glow as it hopped from one completed ring to another.

Then it darted to the line that ran through them all, moving faster and faster.

When it reached the end of the design, the bead burst in scarlet glory.

The massive gray-green doors opened, and sound returned to the cavern in a rush. The door shoveled the remaining debris from in front of it.

Cholik watched in disbelieving horror as death poured through the open door from some forgotten corner of the Burning Hells.

Six

Darrick peered down at Tauruk's Port, cursing the clouded moon that had proven beneficial only a short time before. Even nestled in the lower reaches of the Hawk's Beak Mountains, the darkness that filled the city made it hard to discern details.

The Dyre River ran mostly east and west, flowing through the canyon time had cut through the mountains. The ruins of the city lay on the north bank of the river. The widest part of the city fronted the river, taking advantage of the natural harbor.

"In its day," Mat said in a low voice, "Tauruk's Port must have done all right by itself. Deep harbor like that, on a river that covers a lot of miles, an' wide enough to sail upstream, those people who lived here must have enjoyed the good life."

"Well, they ain't here no more," Maldrin pointed out.

"Wonder why that is?" Mat asked.

"Somebody up an' come along and stomped their city down around their damned ears," the first mate said. "Thought a bright one like yerself woulda seen that without the likes of me needin' to say it."

Mat took no insult. "Wonder who did the stomping?"

Ignoring the familiar bickering of the two men, which at times was tiresome and at other times proved enjoyable, Darrick took a small spyglass from the bag at his waist. It was one of the few personal possessions he had. A craftsman in Kurast had built the spyglass, but Darrick had purchased it from a merchant in Westmarch. The brass body made the spyglass almost indestructible, and clever design rendered it collapsible. He extended the spyglass and studied the city closer.

Three ships sat in the harbor. All of them held lights from lanterns carried by pirates on watch.

Darrick followed the sparse line of pirates and lanterns ashore, focusing at last on a large building that had suffered partial destruction. The building sat under a thick shelf of rock that looked as if it had been displaced by whatever had destroyed the city.

"Got themselves a hole made up," Maldrin said.

Darrick nodded.

"Prolly got it filled with women and wine," the first mate went on. "By the Light, lad, I know we're here for the king's nephew an' all, but I don't like the idea of leavin' them women here. Prolly got 'em all from the ships they looted and scuppered. Wasn't no way to get a proper body count on them what got killed, on account of the sharks."

Darrick gritted his teeth, trying not to think of the abuse the women must have endured at the coarse hands of the pirates. "I know. If there's a way, Maldrin, we'll be after having them women free of all this, too."

"There's a good lad," Maldrin said. "I know this crew ye picked, Darrick. They're good men. Ever last one of them. They wouldn't be above dyin' to be heroes."

"We're not here to die," Darrick said. "We're here to kill pirates."

"An' play hell with 'em if'n we get the chance." Mat's grin glimmered in the darkness. "They don't look as though they're takin' the business of guard duty too serious down here in the ruins."

"They've got all them spotters along the river," Maldrin agreed. "If we'd tried bringin' *Lonesome Star* upriver, why, we'd be sure to be caught. They ain't been thinkin' about a small force of determined men."

"A small force is still a small force," Darrick said. "But while that allows us to move around quick and quiet, we're not going to be much for standing and fighting. A dozen men we are, and that won't take long for killing if we go at this thing wrong and unlucky." Moving the spy-glass on, he marked the boundaries of the ruined city in his mind. Then he returned his attention to the docks.

Two small docks floated in the water, buoyed on water-tight barrels. From the wreckage thrust up farther east of the floating docks, Darrick believed that more permanent docks had once existed there. The broken striations of the land above the river indicated that chunks had cracked off in the past. The permanent docks probably resided in the harbor deep enough that they posed no threats to shallow-drawing ships.

Two block-and-tackle rigs hung from the lip of the river-bank thirty feet above the decks of the three cogs. Stacks of crates and hogshead barrels occupied space beside the block-and-tackles. A handful of men guarded the stores, but they were occupied in a game of dice, all of them hunkered down to watch the outcome of every roll. Every now and again a cheer reached Darrick's ears. They had two lanterns between them, placed at opposite ends of the gaming area.

"Which one of 'em do ye think is *Barracuda?*" Maldrin asked. "That's the ship that pirate said the boy was on, right?"

"Aye," Darrick replied, "and I'm wagering that *Barracuda* is the center ship."

"The one with all the guards," Mat said.

"Aye." Darrick collapsed the spyglass and put it back into his waist pouch, capping both ends. Glass ground as well as the lenses he had in the spyglass was hard to come by out of Kurast.

"Are ye plannin', then, Darrick?" Mat asked.

"As I ever am," Darrick agreed.

Looking more sober, Mat asked, "This ain't after bein' as much of a bit of a lark as we'd have hoped, is it, then?"

"No," Darrick agreed. "But I still think we can get her done." He rose from the hunkered position. "Me and you first, then, Mat. Quick and quiet as we can. Maldrin, can you still move silent, or have you got too broad abeam from Cook's pastries?"

Lonesome Star had a new baker, and the young man's culinary skills were the stuff of legend within the Westmarch Navy. Captain Tollifer had called in some markers to arrange to have the baker assigned to their ship. Every sailor aboard *Lonesome Star* had developed a sweet tooth, but Maldrin had been the first to realize the baker actually wanted to learn how to sail and had capitalized on giving him time at the steering wheel in exchange for pastries.

"I may have put on a pound or three in the last month or two," Maldrin admitted, "but I'll never get so old or so fat that I can't keep up with ye young pups. If'n I do, I'll tie a rope around me neck and dive off the fo'c'sle."

"Then follow along," Darrick invited. "We'll see if we can't take over that stockpile."

"Whatever for?" Maldrin grumped.

Darrick started down the grade, staying along the edge of the river. The block-and-tackles and the guards were nearly two hundred yards away. Brush and small trees grew along the high riverbank. Raithen's pirates had been lazy about clearing more land than necessary.

"Unless I misread those barrels," Darrick said, "they contain whale oil and whiskey."

"Be better if they contained some of them wizard's potions that explode," Maldrin said.

"We work with what we get," Darrick said, "and we'll be glad about it." He called for Tomas.

"Aye," Tomas said, drawing up out of the dark shadows.

"Once we give the signal," Darrick said, "bring the rest of the men in a hurry. We'll be boarding the middle ship to look for the king's nephew. When we find him, I'll be having him off that ship soon as we're able. Make use of one of those block-and-tackles. Understand?"

"Aye," Tomas replied. "We'll fetch him up."

"I'll be wanting him in one piece, Tomas," Darrick threatened, "or it'll be you explaining to the king how his nephew got himself hurt or dead."

Tomas nodded. "A babe in arms, Darrick, that's how

we'll be treatin' the boy. As safe as his own mother would have him."

Darrick clapped Tomas on the shoulder and grinned. "I knew I was asking the right man about the job."

"Just ye be careful down there, an' don't go gettin' too brave until we get down there with ye."

Darrick nodded, then started down the mountainside toward the riverbank. Mat and Maldrin followed him, as silent as falling snow in the winter.

Raithen followed the steps cut into the riverbank overlooking the boats. When the steps had first been cut from the stone of the mountains, they'd doubtless been of an even keel. Now, after the damage that had been done to the city, they canted to one side, making the descent a tricky one. Since Raithen's crew had been holed up at Tauruk's Port, more than one drunken pirate had ended up in the water below, and two of them had been swept away in the current and likely drowned by the time they reached the Gulf of Westmarch.

He carried a lantern to light the way, and the golden glow played over the striations in the mountainside. In the day, the stone shone blue and slate gray, different levels marked by a deepening of color till the rock looked almost charcoal gray before disappearing beneath the river's edge. The fog maintained a soft presence around him, but he saw the three cogs through it without problem.

Pirates assigned to guard duty squared their shoulders and looked alert as he passed. They deferred to him with politeness he'd beaten into some of them.

A sudden shrill of rope through pulleys alerted him to activity above.

"Look alive, ye great bastards," a rough voice called down. "I've got ye a load of victuals, I have."

"Send it on down," a man called on the cog to Raithen's right. "Been waitin' on it a dog's age. Feel like my stomach's been wrappin' itself around me backbone."

Pressing himself against the mountainside, Raithen

watched as a short, squat barrel was let go. The pulleys slowed the barrel's descent, proving that the load was light. The scent of salted pork passed within inches of Raithen.

"Got you a bottle of wine in there, too," the man called.

"An' ye damn near hit Cap'n Raithen with it, ye lummox," the guard only a few feet from the pirate captain yelled out.

A muttered curse followed. "Excuse me, cap'n," the man said in a contrite voice. "Didn't know it was ye."

Raithen held the lantern up so the man could plainly see his features. "Hurry up."

"Aye, sir. Right away, sir." The pirate raised his voice. "Ye lads heave off with that barrel. We need another, I'll fetch it up later."

The pirates aboard the first cog threw off the lines, and they were hauled back up the block-and-tackle.

As soon as the way was clear, Raithen walked to the first of the small temporary docks floating on the black water. He climbed the cargo net tossed over the side of the cog and stepped to the cog's deck.

"Evenin', cap'n," a scar-faced pirate greeted. A half-dozen other pirates did the same but didn't slow in their efforts to take the food from the barrel.

Raithen nodded at the man, feeling the pain in his wounded throat. When the ships were in port, he made certain the men stayed out of ships' stores. All of the cogs stayed fully loaded at all times, in case they had to flee out to deep water. His other ships lay a few days away, anchored off the north coastline in a bay that could be treacherous to an understaffed ship.

Planks spanned the distance between the ships. The river current was gentle enough that the cogs didn't fight the tether while they lay at anchorage. On board *Barracuda*, the ship kept between the other two, he saw Bull sitting in the prow puffing on a pipe.

"Cap'n," Bull acknowledged, taking the pipe from between his teeth. He was a big man, seemingly assembled from masts. A scarf tied around his head bound his

wounded ear, but bloodstains were visible down the sides
of his neck.

"How's the boy, Bull?" Raithen asked.

"Why, he's fine, cap'n," Bull replied. "Any reason he
shouldn't be?"

"I heard about your ear."

"This little thing?" Bull touched his wounded ear and
grinned. "Why, it ain't nothing for ye to be worryin' over,
cap'n."

"I'm not worrying over it," Raithen said. "I figure any
pirate who gets taken in by a boy isn't worth the salt I pay
him to crew my ship."

Bull's face darkened, but Raithen knew it was out of
embarrassment. "It's just that he's such an innocent-
lookin' thing, cap'n. Didn't figure him for no shenanigans
like this. An' that two-by-four? Why, he like to took me
plumb by surprise. I'm right tempted to keep him fer
myself if'n the king don't ransom him back. I'm tellin' ye
true, cap'n, we've done a lot worse than take on somebody
like this boy for crew."

"I'll keep that in mind," Raithen said.

"Aye, sir. I weren't offerin' outta nothin' but respect for
ye and that mean-spirited little lad down in the hold."

"I want to see him."

"Cap'n, I swear to ye, I ain't done nothin' to him."

"I know, Bull," Raithen said. "My reasons are my own."

"Aye, sir." Bull took a massive key ring from his waist
sash, then knocked the contents of his pipe into the river.
No fires except the watch's lanterns were allowed down in
the hold, and those were taken there seldom.

Bull walked into the small cargo hold. Raithen followed,
inhaling the familiar stink. When he'd been with the
Westmarch Navy, ships were not allowed to stink so.
Sailors had been kept busy cleaning them out, dosing them
with salt water and vinegar to kill any fungus or mold that
tried to leach into the wood.

The boy was kept in the small brig in the stern of
the cog.

After unlocking the brig door, Bull shoved his big head in, then pulled it out just as quickly. He reached up and caught a board aimed at his face, then tugged on it.

The boy flopped onto the ship's deck, landing hard on his belly and face. Quick as a fish taken out of water, the boy tried to get to his feet. Bull pinned him to the ship's deck with one massive boot.

Incredibly, the boy revealed a huge knowledge of vituperative name-calling.

"Like I said, cap'n," Bull said with a grin, "this 'un here, why, he'd make for a fine pirate, he would."

"Captain?" the boy squalled. Even trapped under Bull's foot, he craned his head around and tried to gaze up. "You're the captain of this pigsty? Why, if I was you, I'd sew a bag for my head and only leave myself one eyehole out of embarrassment."

In the first real amusement he'd felt that night, Raithen glanced down at the boy. "He's not afraid, Bull?"

"Afraid?" the boy squealed. "I'm afraid I'm going to die of boredom. You've had me for five days now. Three of them spent here in this ship. When I get back to my da and he speaks with his brother, the king, why, I'll come back here and help wallop you myself." He clenched his fists and beat the deck. "Let me up, and give me a sword. I'll fight you. By the Light, I'll give you the fight of your life."

Truly taken aback by the boy's demeanor, Raithen studied him. The boy was lean and muscular, starting to lose his baby fat. Raithen guessed he was eleven or twelve, possibly even as much as thirteen. A thick shock of dark hair crowned the boy's head, and the lantern light revealed that he had gray or green eyes.

"Do you even know where you're at, boy?" Raithen asked.

"When the king's navy pays you off or tracks you down," the boy said, "I'll know where you are. Don't you think that I won't."

Squatting down, holding the lantern close to the boy's face, Raithen shook the dagger sheathed along his arm free again. He rammed the point into the wooden deck only an inch from the boy's nose.

"The last person to threaten me tonight," Raithen said in a hoarse voice, "died only minutes ago. I won't mind killing another."

The boy's eyes focused on the knife. He swallowed hard but remained silent.

"I'll have your name, boy," Raithen said.

"Lhex," the boy whispered. "My name is Lhex."

"And you are the king's nephew?"

"Yes."

Raithen turned the knife blade, catching the lantern light and splintering it. "How many sons does your father have?"

"Five. Counting me."

"Will he miss one of them?"

Lhex swallowed again. "Yes."

"Good." Raithen raised the lantern, getting it out of the boy's eyes and letting him see the smile on his face. "This doesn't have to go hard for you, boy. But I mean to have the information I came here for tonight."

"I don't know anything."

"We'll see." Raithen stood. "Get him up, Bull. I'll talk to him in the brig."

Bending down, keeping his foot in place, Bull caught the boy's shirt in one massive hand and lifted him. Without apparent effort, he carried the boy back into the small brig. With exaggerated gentleness, Bull placed the boy against the far wall, then stood by him.

"You can leave, Bull," Raithen said.

"Cap'n," Bull protested, "maybe ye ain't yet figured out exactly what this little snot is capable of."

"I can handle a small boy," Raithen said, hanging the lantern on a hook on the wall. He took the key from Bull and sent the pirate on his way with a look. Gripping the bars of the door with one hand, Raithen closed the door. The clang of metal on metal sounded loud in the enclosed space.

Lhex started to get to his feet.

"Don't stand," Raithen warned. "If you insist on standing, I'll use this dagger and nail you to the wall behind you by one hand."

Freezing halfway to his feet, Lhex looked at Raithen. The look was one of childhood innocence and daring, trying to ascertain if the pirate captain had meant what he'd said.

Raithen maintained his icy stare, knowing he'd carry out the action he'd threatened.

Evidently, Lhex decided he would, too. Grimacing, the boy sat, but he did so with stubbornness, keeping his knees drawn up and placing his back securely against the wall behind him.

"You must think you're something," Lhex snarled. "Menacing a kid like that. What'd you do for breakfast? Kick a puppy?"

"Actually," Raithen said, "I had one beheaded and rendered out to serve you for breakfast chops. They tell me it fried up like chicken for your noonday meal."

Horror flirted with Lhex's eyes. He remained silent, watching Raithen.

"Where did you get such an attitude, boy?" the pirate captain asked.

"My parents blame each other," Lhex said. "I think I get it from them both."

"Do you think you're going to get out of here alive?"

"Either way," the boy said, "I'm not getting out of here scared. I've done that till I'm sick of it. I threw up the first three days."

"You're a most unusual boy," Raithen said. "I wish I'd gotten to know you sooner."

"Looking for a friend?" Lhex asked. "I only ask because I know most of these pirates are afraid of you. They're not here because they like you."

"Fear is a far better tool for command than friendship," Raithen responded. "Fear is instant, and it is obeyed without question."

"I'd rather have people like me."

Raithen smiled. "I'd wager to say that Bull doesn't like you."

"Some people I can live without."

"Wise lad," Raithen said. He paused, feeling the cog shift slightly in the river current.

The boy shifted with the ship automatically, just like a sailor.

"How long have you been at sea, Lhex?" Raithen asked.

The boy shrugged. "Since Lut Gholein."

"You were there?"

"The ship came from Lut Gholein," Lhex said, narrowing his eyes and watching Raithen with a thoughtful expression. "If you didn't know that, how did you find the ship?"

Raithen ignored the question. The information had come from Buyard Cholik's spies within Westmarch. "What were you doing in Lut Gholein?"

Lhex didn't answer.

"Don't trifle with me," Raithen warned. "I'm in an ill mood as it is."

"Studying," Lhex answered.

That, Raithen decided, sounded promising. "Studying what?"

"My father wanted me to have a good education. As the king's younger brother, he was sent abroad and learned from sages in Lut Gholein. He wanted the same for me."

"How long were you there?"

"Four years," the boy said. "Since I was eight."

"And what did you study?"

"Everything. Poetry. Literature. Marketing. Forecasting profits, though the whole thing with chicken gizzards was quite disgusting and not any better than just guessing."

"What about history?" Raithen asked. "Did you study history?"

"Of course I did. What kind of education would you get if you didn't study history?"

Raithen dug in his blouse for the paper Pettit had given him. "I want you to look at this paper. Tell me what it means."

Interest flickered in the boy's eyes as he regarded the paper. "I can't see it from here."

Hesitant, Raithen took the lantern from the wall. "If you try anything, boy, I'll have you crippled. If your father persuades the king to ransom you back, you'll have to hope the healers can make you whole again, or you'll drag yourself around like a circus freak."

"I won't try anything," Lhex said. "Bring the paper here. I've stared at walls for days."

Until you worked the bed support loose and attacked Bull, Raithen thought. He stepped forward, respecting the boy's skills and focus. Most boys Lhex's age would have been sniveling wrecks by now. Instead, the king's nephew had busied himself with planning escape, conserving energy, and eating to keep himself healthy and strong.

Lhex took the paper Raithen offered. His quick eyes darted over the paper. Hesitantly, he traced the design with his forefinger.

"Where did you get this?" Lhex asked in a quiet voice.

The cog shifted in the river, and water slapped against the hull, echoing throughout the ship. Raithen rode out the change in the ship without much thought. "It doesn't matter. Do you know what it is?"

"Yes," the boy said. "This is some kind of demon script. That symbol belongs to Kabraxis, the demon who supposedly constructed the Black Road."

Raithen drew back and scoffed. "There are no such things as demons, boy."

"My teachers taught me to have an open mind. Maybe demons aren't here now, but that doesn't mean that they were never here."

Raithen peered at the paper, trying to make sense of it. "Can you read it?"

Lhex made a rude noise. "Do you know anyone who can read demon script?"

"No," Raithen said. "But I've known some who sold parchments they said were treasure maps to demon hoards." He'd bought and sold a few of those himself as his belief in such creatures had risen and fallen.

"You don't believe in demons?" the boy asked.

"No," Raithen said. "They're only good for stories best told in taverns or over a slow campfire when there's nothing else to do." Still, the boy's words had intrigued him. *The priest is here hunting a demon?* He couldn't believe it. "What else can you tell me about this design?"

A trail scarred the mountainside, running parallel to the Dyre River. Darrick was certain Raithen's pirate crew used it when changing the guard. He stayed off it, choosing the slower path through the brush.

Mat and Maldrin followed him, staying to the path he chose.

As they neared the riverbank's edge overlooking the three pirate vessels, wisps of silver fog threaded through the brush. Tobacco smoke itched Darrick's nose. Though Captain Tollifer didn't allow smoking on *Lonesome Star*, Darrick had been around a number of men who smoked in ports they patrolled and traded with. He'd never acquired the habit himself and thought it was repugnant. And it reminded him of his father's pipe.

The brush and treeline ended twenty yards short of the area the pirates had been using to shift their stolen goods. Shadows painted the stacks of crates and barrels, giving him more cover to take advantage of.

One of the pirates walked away from the group of five who played dice. "That ale's gettin' the best of me. Hold my place. I'll be back."

"As long as ye have money," one of the other pirates said, "we'll stand ye to a place in this game. This is yer unlucky night and our lucky one."

"Just be glad Cap'n Raithen's been keepin' us headed toward fat purses," the pirate said. He walked around to the side of the crates where Darrick hid in the brush.

Darrick thought the man was going to relieve himself over the side of the riverbank and was surprised to see him dig in the bag at his side frantically once he was out of sight of the others. Pale moonlight touched the dice that tumbled out into the man's waiting palm.

The pirate grinned and closed his fist over the dice. Then he started to relieve himself.

Moving with catlike grace, Darrick crept up behind the pirate. Picking up a stone loose on the ground, Darrick fisted it and stepped behind the pirate, who was humming a shanty tune as he finished. Darrick recognized the tune as "Amergo and the Dolphin Girl," a bawdy favorite of a number of sailors.

Darrick swung the stone, felt the thud of rock meeting flesh, and wrapped an arm around the unconscious pirate to guide him to the ground. Leaving the fallen pirate out of sight from the others, Darrick slid to the riverbank's edge. He peered down, seeing that all three cogs did lie at anchorage beneath the overhang as he'd thought.

He drew back, put his shoulders to the crate behind him, slid his cutlass free, and waved to Maldrin and Mat. They crossed, staying low.

"Hey, Timar," one of the pirates called, "ye comin' back tonight?"

"Told ye he had too much to drink," another pirate said. "Probably start cheatin' any minute now."

"If'n I see them loaded dice of his one more time," another pirate said, "I swear I'm gonna cut his nose off."

Darrick glanced up the slight rise of land toward the ruins of Tauruk's Port. No one came down the trail that wound through the wreckage.

"Four men left," Darrick whispered. "Once one of them makes a noise, there'll be no more hiding here for us."

Mat nodded.

Maldrin slitted his eyes and ran a thumb across the knife in his fist. "Better they not have a chance to make noise, then."

"Agreed," Darrick whispered. "Maldrin, hold the steps. They'll come from below as soon as we announce ourselves.

And we will be announcing ourselves. Mat, you and I are going to see about setting the ships on fire below."

Mat raised his eyebrows.

"Barrels of whale oil," Darrick said. "Shouldn't be that hard to get them over the edge of the riverbank. They'll fall straight to the ships below. Get them on the decks of the one port of *Barracuda,* and I'll target the one starboard of her."

Smiling, Mat nodded. "They'll be busy tryin' to save their ships."

"Aye," Darrick said. "We'll use the confusion to get aboard *Barracuda* and see to the king's nephew."

"Be lucky if'n ye don't get yerselves killed outright," Maldrin groused. "An' me with ye."

Darrick smiled, feeling cocky as he always did when he was in the thick of a potentially disastrous situation. "If we live, you owe me a beer back at Rik's Tavern in Westmarch."

"I owe ye?" Maldrin looked as though he couldn't believe it. "An' how is it ye're a-gonna buy me one?"

Shrugging, Darrick said, "If I get us all killed, I'll stand you to your first cool drink in the Burning Hells."

"No," Maldrin protested. "That's not fair."

"Speak up first next time, and you can set the terms," Darrick said.

"Timar!" one of the pirates bellowed.

"He's probably fallen in," another pirate said. "I'll go look for him."

Darrick rose slowly, looking over the stack of crates as one of the pirates peeled off from the game. He held his cutlass in his hand, signaling Mat and Maldrin to stand down. If fortune was going to favor them with one more victim before they set to, so be it.

When the man stepped around the crates, Darrick grabbed him, clapped a hand over the pirate's mouth, and slit his throat with the cutlass. Darrick held the man as he bled out. A look of horror filled Mat's face.

Darrick looked away from the accusation he found in

his friend's eyes. Mat could kill to save a friend or a ship-mate in the heat of battle, but killing as Darrick had just done was beyond him. To Darrick, there was no remorse or guilt involved. Pirates deserved death, whether by his hands or by the hangman's noose in Westmarch.

As the pirate's corpse shuddered a final time, Darrick released it and stepped away. Blood coated his left arm and warmed him against the chill wind. Knowing they were working on borrowed time, Darrick caught the edge of the crates in front of him and hauled himself around them. He lifted his knees and drove his feet hard against the ground, sprinting toward the three men still occupied with the dice game.

One of the men glanced up, attracted by the flurry of motion coming toward them. He opened his mouth to yell a warning.

SEVEΠ

"Kabraxis is the demon who created the Black Road," Lhex said.

"What is the Black Road?" Raithen asked.

The boy shrugged, bathed in the golden light of the lantern the pirate captain held. "It's all just legend. Old stories of demons. There's talk that Kabraxis was just an elaborate lie."

"But you said if a demon was involved," Raithen said, "it was all truth once."

"I said it was based on something that was supposed to be the truth," Lhex replied. "But so many stories have been told since the Vizjerei started *supposedly* summoning demons from other worlds. Some of the stories are based on incidents that might have or might not have involved demons, but many are total fabrications. Or a story has been fractured, retold, and made more current. Old wives' tales. Harsus, the toad-faced demon of Kurast—if he even existed—has become four different demons in the local histories. The man who taught me history told me there are sages at work now trying to piece together different stories, examining them for common links that bind them and make only one demon exist where two had stood before."

"Why would they bother with something like that?"

"Because there were supposed to be other demons loose in the world according to all those simpleminded myths," Lhex said. "My teacher believed that men spent so much time trying to name the demons in mythology the better to hunt them down instead of waiting for them to act. To pursue their quarry, the demon hunters need to know how many demons were in our world and where to find them. Sages research those things." The boy snorted. "Personally, I think demons were all named so that a *wise and wizened* sage could recommend employing demon hunters. Of course, that sage would get a cut of the gold paid to rid a place or a city or a kingdom of a demon. It was a racket. A well-thought-out scary story to tell superstitious people and separate them from their gold."

"Kabraxis," Raithen reminded, growing impatient.

"In the beginning years," Lhex said, "when the Vizjerei first began experimenting with demon summoning, Kabraxis was supposed to be one of those demons summoned over and over again."

"Why?"

"Because Kabraxis operated the mystical bridges that stretched from the demon worlds to our world more easily than many did."

"The Black Road is a bridge to the Burning Hells?" Raithen asked.

"Possibly. I told you this was all a story. Nothing more." Lhex tapped the drawing of the elliptical lines threaded through by the solitary one. "This drawing represents the power Kabraxis had to walk between the Burning Hells and this world."

"If the Black Road isn't the bridge between this world and the Burning Hells," Raithen asked, "what else could it be?"

"Some have said it was the path to enlightenment." Lhex rubbed his face as if bored, then smothered a yawn.

"What enlightenment?" Raithen asked.

"Power," Lhex said. "Is there anything else that the legends would offer?"

"What kind of power?"

Lhex frowned at him, faking a yawn and leaning back comfortably against the wall behind them. "I'm tired, and I grow weary of telling you bedtime stories."

"If you want," Raithen suggested, "I can have Bull come back and tuck you in."

"Maybe I'll get his other ear," Lhex suggested.

"You're an evil child," Raithen said. "I can imagine why your father shipped you away to school."

"I'm willful," Lhex corrected. "There is a difference."

"Not enough of one," Raithen warned. "I've got gold enough that I can do without your ransom, boy. Making the king pay is only retribution for past indignities I've suffered at his hands."

"You know the king?" Lhex's eyebrows darted up.

"What power can Kabraxis offer?" the pirate captain demanded.

The river current shifted *Barracuda* again. She floated high, then slithered sideways a moment before settling in. The rigging slapped against the masts and yardarms above.

"They say Kabraxis offers immortality and influence," Lhex replied. "Plus, for those brave enough, and I can't imagine there being many, there is access to the Burning Hells."

"Influence over what?"

"People," Lhex said. "When Kabraxis last walked this world—according to the myths I've read in the philosophy studies I did—he chose a prophet to represent him. A man named Kreghn, who was a sage of philosophy, wrote about the teachings of Kabraxis. And I tell you, that was a very ponderous tome. It bored my arse off."

"The demon's teachings? And it wasn't a banned book?"

"Of course it was," Lhex answered. "But when Kabraxis first walked this world then, no one knew he was a demon. That's the story we've all been told, of course, and there's no proof of it. But Kabraxis was better thought of than some of the demons of legend."

"Why?"

"Because Kabraxis wasn't as bloodthirsty as some of the other demons. He bided his time, getting more and more followers to embrace the tenets he handed down through Kreghn. He taught his followers about the Three Selves. Have you heard of that concept?"

Raithen shook his head. His mind buzzed steadily,

gaining speed as he tried to figure out what Buyard Cholik was doing seeking out remnants of such a creature.

"The Three Selves," Lhex said, "consist of the Outer Self, the way a person portrays himself or herself to others; the Inner Self, the way a person portrays himself or herself to himself or herself; and the Shadow Self. The Shadow Self is the true nature of a man or woman, the part of himself or herself that he or she most fears—the dark part every person struggles hardest to hide. Kukulach teaches us that most people are too afraid of themselves to face that truth."

"And people believed that?"

"The existence of the Three Selves is known," Lhex said. "Even after Kabraxis was supposedly banished from this world, other sages and scholars carried on the work Kreghn began."

"What work?"

"The study of the Three Selves." Lhex grimaced as if displeased at Raithen's listening skills. "The legend of Kabraxis first developed the theory, but other scholars— such as Kukulach—have made our understanding of it whole. It just sounds better couched in terms that led the superstitious to believe this was one of the bits of wisdom we needed to save from the demons. Fairy tales and mechanisms to define social order, that's all they were."

"Even so," Raithen said, "there's no power in that."

"The followers of Kabraxis reveled in the exposure of their Shadow Selves," the boy said. "Four times a year, during the solstices and the equinoxes, Kabraxis's worshippers came together and partied, reveling in the darkness that dwelt within them. Every sin known to man was allowed in Kabraxis's name during the three days of celebration."

"And afterward?" Raithen asked.

"They were forgiven their sins and washed again in the symbolic blood of Kabraxis."

"That belief sounds stupid."

"I told you that. That's why it's a myth."

"How did Kabraxis get here?" Raithen asked.

"During the Mage Clan Wars. There was some rumor that one of Kreghn's disciples had managed to open a portal to Kabraxis again, but that was never confirmed."

Has Cholik confirmed it? Raithen wondered. *And did that trail lead here, to the massive door that is located beneath the ruins of Tauruk's Port?*

"How was Kabraxis banished from this world?" Raithen asked.

"According to legend, by Vizjerei warriors and wizards of the Spirit Clan," Lhex replied, "and by those who stood with them. They eradicated the temples to Kabraxis in Vizjun and other places. Only wreckage of buildings and broken altars remain where the demon's temples once stood."

Raithen considered that. "If a man could contact Kabraxis—"

"And offer the demon a path back into this world?" Lhex asked.

"Aye. What could such a man expect?"

"Wouldn't the promise of immortality be enough? I mean, if you believed in such nonsense."

Raithen thought of Buyard Cholik's body bent with old age and approaching infirmity. "Aye, maybe it would at that."

"Where did you find that?" Lhex asked.

Before Raithen could respond, the door opened, and Bull stepped inside.

"Cap'n Raithen," the big pirate said, holding a lantern high. Concern stretched his features tight. "We're under attack."

Only a few steps short of the pirate about to scream out, Darrick leapt into the air. The other two pirates who had been playing dice reached for their weapons as Darrick's feet slammed into the pirate's head.

Caught by surprise and by all of Darrick's weight, almost too drunk to stand, the pirate flew over the steep side of the riverbank. He didn't even scream. The hard thump told Darrick that the pirate had struck the wooden deck of the ship below instead of the river.

"What the hell was that?" a pirate called out from below.

Darrick landed on the bare stone ground, bruising his hip. He clutched his cutlass and swiped at the nearest pirate's legs, slashing both thighs. Blood stained the man's light-colored breeches.

"Help!" the stricken pirate yelled. "Ahoy the ship! Damn it, but he's cut me deep!" He stumbled backward, trying to pull his sword free of its sash but forgetting to release the ale bottle he already held.

Pushing himself up and drawing the cutlass back again, Darrick drove the pirate backward, close to the riverbank's edge. He whipped the cutlass around and chopped into the pirate's neck, cleaving his throat in a bloody spray. The cutlass blade lodged against the man's spine. Lifting his foot, Darrick shoved the dying man over the riverbank. He turned, listening to the splash as the pirate hit the water only a moment later, and saw Mat engaging the final pirate on guard at the supply station.

Mat's cutlass sparked as he pressed his opponent's guard. He penetrated the pirate's guard easily, hesitating about drawing blood.

Cursing beneath his breath, knowing that they had precious little time to rescue the boy and that they didn't know for sure if he was aboard the ship waiting below, Darrick stepped forward and brought his cutlass down in a hand-and-a-half stroke that split the man's skull. A cutlass wasn't a fancy weapon; it was meant to hack and cleave because shipboard battles on vessels riding the waves tended to be messy things guided mostly by desperation and strength and luck.

Blood from the dead man splashed over Mat and onto Darrick.

Mat looked appalled as the pirate dropped. Darrick knew his friend didn't approve of the blow dealt from behind or while the pirate had already been engaging one opponent. Mat believed in fighting fairly whenever possible.

"Get the barrels," Darrick urged, yanking his sword from the dead man's head.

"He didn't even see you comin'," Mat protested, looking down at the dead man.

"The barrels," Darrick repeated.

"He was too drunk to fight," Mat said. "He couldn't have defended himself."

"We're not here to fight," Darrick said, grabbing Mat's bloody shirtfront. "We're here to save a twelve-year-old boy. Now, *move!*" He shoved Mat at the oil barrels. "There's plenty of fair fights left down there if you're wanting for them."

Mat stumbled toward the oil barrels.

Thrusting his cutlass into his waist sash, Darrick listened to the hue and cry taken up from the ships below. He glanced at the top of the stone steps carved into the side of the overhang.

Maldrin had taken up a position at the top of the steps. The first mate held a war hammer with a metal-shod haft in both hands. The hammer took both hands to wield, but the squared head promised crushed skulls, broken bones, or shattered weapons.

" 'Ware arrows, Maldrin," Darrick called.

A sour grin twisted the first mate's mouth. " 'Ware yer own arse there, skipper. Ain't me gonna be goin' after that there boy."

Darrick kicked a barrel over onto its side. The thick liquid inside glugged. Working with haste, he got behind the barrel and used his hands to roll it toward the riverbank's edge. The downward slope favored the rolling barrel.

After he got it started, he knew he couldn't have easily stopped the barrel's momentum. Giving the barrel a final shove, he watched it roll over the edge and disappear. He stopped at the edge, teetering for a moment, and gazed down, spotting the falling barrel just as it smashed against the ship's deck below. Wisps of fog slid over the deck, but silvery patches showed through where the whale oil reflected the lantern lights of the pirate guards on watch.

Another smash caught Darrick's attention. Glancing to the side, he saw that Mat had succeeded in landing an oil barrel on the other cog. Pirates ran out onto the deck and lost their footing, skidding across the wooden surface.

"Oil!" a pirate cried out. "They've done an' rolled a barrel of oil onto us!"

Hustling back to the stacked barrels, Darrick kicked over two more containers and started them rolling for the riverbank. The thunderous clatter of the wooden barrels slamming against the stone surface echoed around him. He took up one of the lanterns the men on guard had carried.

Mat joined him, grabbing another lantern. "Them men down there, Darrick, they ain't going to have many places to run once we up and do this."

"No," Darrick agreed, looking into his friend's troubled face, "and we aren't going to have much running room, either, once we have the boy. I don't want to have to look over my shoulder for those ships, Mat."

Nodding grimly, Mat turned and sprinted for the riverbank.

Darrick paused only long enough to see the rest of the crew from *Lonesome Star* racing from the mountainside. "Help's coming, Maldrin," he shouted as he ran for the river.

"I got what I got here," Maldrin growled.

At the edge of the river, Darrick marked his spot, judged the rise and fall of the cog on the river current, and threw the lantern. Protected by the glass, the flame remained alive and burning brightly in the lantern. It flew, twisting end over end till it smashed against the ship's deck in the center of the spreading oil pool.

For a moment, the wick sputtered and almost drowned in the oil. Then the flames rose up across the oil like an arthritic old hound rising for one last hunt. Blue and yellow flames twisted into a roiling mass as they fed on the wind as well as the oil.

"Fire!" a pirate yelled.

A flurry of action filled the ship's deck as the pirates

gathered from belowdecks. Only a skeleton crew remained aboard.

"Save those ships!" another pirate roared. "Cap'n Raithen will kill ye if'n these ships go down!"

Darrick hoped all the ships burned down to the waterline. If they did, he knew there was a chance Captain Tollifer would be able to sail *Lonesome Star* to Westmarch and return with more ships and warriors in time to catch Raithen and his crew crossing overland to wherever the pirate captain had left his main flotilla.

Glancing to the ship Mat had dropped the barrel on, Darrick saw that it had caught fire as well. Evidently Mat's barrel had caught the wheelhouse, too, giving the flames the reach they needed to get into the sails. Fire blazed along the main mast, threading up through the rigging in a rush.

"Mat," Darrick called.

Mat looked at him.

"Are you ready?" Darrick asked.

Looking only a little unsure of himself, Mat nodded. "As I ever was."

"Going to be me and you down there," Darrick said. "I need you to stand with me." He hurried toward the middle of the riverbank, aiming himself at the middle ship, stretching out his stride.

"I'll be there for you," Mat answered.

Without pausing, Darrick took a final step at the edge of the riverbank overhang, hurling himself toward the cog's railing, hoping he could make the distance. If he fell to the ship's deck, he was certain to break something. Escape would be out of the question.

Even as Darrick's hands reached for the rigging, fingers outspread to hook into the ropes, the riverbank overhang shattered, shrugging off a section of heavy rock that dropped toward the burning ships and the whole one.

"Under attack from whom?" Raithen demanded, turning toward the door. Automatically, he started walking toward the door. His head was so filled with the sheer impossibility of the attack that he didn't recognize the rustle of clothing for what it was until it was too late. He turned, knowing Lhex had chosen that moment to make his move.

"Don't know," Bull said. "They done went an' set fire to the cogs on either side of us."

Fire? Raithen thought, and there wasn't a more fearsome announcement that could be made aboard a ship. Even if a vessel were holed, a crew might be able to pump the hold dry and keep her afloat till they reached port, but an unchecked fire quickly took away the island of wood and canvas a sailing man depended on.

As close to Bull as he was and with the announcement so new, Raithen's and the big man's attention was on each other, not the boy. Lhex was up behind Raithen in a twinkling. As the pirate captain turned to grab the boy, the young captive bent low, stepped in hard against Raithen to knock him against Bull, and was through the door before anyone could stop him.

"Damn it," Raithen swore, watching the boy speed through the darkness in the hold and run for the stairs leading up to the deck. "Get him, Bull. But I'll want him alive when you bring him back."

"Aye, cap'n." Bull took off at once, closing the distance swiftly with his long stride.

Raithen followed the pirate, his left hand tight on his sword hilt. Already he could see the bright light of a large fire through the cargo hold above them. Gray tendrils of smoke mixed with the fog clinging to the river.

He'd been right. Someone had trailed them for a time through the Gulf of Westmarch. But was it other pirates, or was it the king's navy? Were there only a few men out there, or was there a small armada choking down the river?

The ladder to the main deck quivered and shook in Raithen's hands as Bull climbed it. He was at the bigger man's heels and had just reached the top when the riverbank's overhang cracked and sheared off thirty feet above them. He gazed upward in disbelief as sections of the overhang plummeted down like catapult loads.

A huge granite block dropped onto *Barracuda*'s prow. The impact cracked timbers and tore sections of railing free. *Barracuda* rocked as if she'd been seized in a fierce gale.

A lantern tumbled loose from the hand of a pirate who had been knocked from his feet. Skidding across the wooden deck, the lantern swapped ends several times before disappearing over the ship's side.

Gaining the deck, keeping his knees bent to ride out the violent tossing of *Barracuda* fighting her mooring ropes, Raithen looked at the other two ships. Both cogs were fast on their way to becoming pyres. Flames already twisted through the rigging of the port ship, and the starboard ship wasn't far behind.

Who the hell has done this?

Ahead of him, the boy had almost used up all his running room. He stood with his back to the edge of the swaying ship's deck. The look he gave the black water around the ship indicated that he was in no hurry to try his luck with a swim.

Bull closed on the boy, yelling filth at him, ordering him to stay put.

Raithen yelled at his crew, ordering them to break out buckets and attempt to save both burning cogs. If their hiding place had been discovered, he wanted all of the ships so he could haul away as much as he could.

Kegs and crates floated in the river around *Barracuda*, but some of them sank only a moment later. Feeling the fat-assed way the cog sat in the river, Raithen knew she was taking on water. The impact that had struck the prow must have ruptured the ship as well. At least part of the damage was below the waterline.

Surveying the cracked riverbank overhang high overhead, Raithen knew the destruction wasn't a natural occurrence. Something had happened to cause it. His mind

immediately flew to Buyard Cholik. The ruins the priests
poked through were underground. The pirate captain had
a fleeting thought, wondering if the old priest had survived his own greed.

Then movement in the rigging caught Raithen's eye,
and he knew someone was up there. He turned, lifting his
sword.

EIGHT

Steadying himself in the rigging of the pirate ship *Barracuda*, Darrick reached for a ratline just as Mat landed beside him. Despite the sudden explosion that had taken out the line of supplies perched on the cliff's edge, he'd landed aboard the pirate vessel. His hands still ached from grabbing the coarse hemp rope.

"You made it," Darrick said, cutting the ratline free.

"Barely," Mat agreed. "An' where is that fabulous luck of mine ye were braggin' about earlier? That damned cliffside blew up."

"But not us with it," Darrick argued. The brief glance he had of the two burning cogs gave him a chance to feel proud of their handiwork. He checked the stone steps and saw Maldrin pushing himself to his feet. The explosion had knocked the first mate from his feet.

"There's the boy," Mat said.

Darrick scanned the deck below and saw the small figure chased into the broken prow by the huge man who followed him. He had little doubt that the boy was the king's nephew. There couldn't be many boys on the pirate vessels.

"Darrick!"

Looking up, Darrick saw Tomas standing on the cliffside near the surviving block-and-tackle rig. The other had gone down with the explosion that had restructured the riverbank.

Tomas waved.

"Get it down here," Darrick ordered. He took hold of the ratline and swung himself from the rigging. Even with the

ship foundering in the river—taking on water, he judged—
he arced out past the big man cornering the small boy.
Reaching the end of his swing, he started back, aiming
himself at the big man.

"Bull!" a pirate behind the big man yelled in warning.

The big man glanced around instead of up, though,
never seeing Darrick until it was too late.

Bending his knees a little to absorb the shock better,
Darrick drove both feet into the big man, catching him
across the shoulders. Even then, Darrick felt his knees
strain with the impact, and for a moment he didn't think
the man was going to budge and was going to smash up
against him like a wave shredding over a reef.

But the big man tore free of the deck, sprawling forward,
unable to stop himself.

Hurting and winded from the impact, Darrick released
the ratline and dropped to the deck only a few feet from
the boy. Scrambling to his feet immediately, Darrick drew
his cutlass.

"Get him," a tall man in black chainmail ordered.

Darrick got set in time to meet two pirates who rushed
him. He slapped their weapons aside with the flat of the cutlass, then stepped in, turned, and elbowed one of the pirates
in the face. The man's nose broke with a savage snap. It
wasn't the honorable thing to do, but Darrick knew he
wasn't up against honorable opponents. The pirates would
shove a blade into his back as quickly as he'd do it to them.

The pirate with the broken nose staggered to one side,
blood smearing his face. But he didn't go down.

Still in motion, Darrick plucked a dagger from his boot,
spun, and shoved it between the pirate's ribs, ripping it
through the man's chest and planting it in the heart
beneath. He kept moving, getting his cutlass up to parry
the other pirate's clumsy attack and riposting.

Mat landed on the ship's deck only a heartbeat later.

"Get the boy," Darrick ordered. Then he raised his voice.
"Tomas!"

"Aye, skipper," Tomas called from above. "On its way."

Darrick defended against the pirate's attempt to skewer him, aware that the mountain of a man was getting to his feet as well. From the corner of his eye, Darrick saw the block-and-tackle lower, a small cargo net at the end of it.

"Lhex," Mat said, holding up his empty hands and offering no threat. "Be easy, boy. Me friend *an'* I, why, we're in the king's navy, come here to see you to home safe. If you'll allow us."

The cargo net hit the bucking ship's deck in a loose sprawl of hemp.

"Yes," the boy said.

"Good." Mat smiled at him, reaching for the cargo netting and dragging it toward the boy. "Then let's be away." He raised his voice. "Darrick."

"In a minute," Darrick replied, bracing himself for the coming battle. He flicked the pirate's sword aside with his cutlass, then nipped in with a low blow, ducked and caught the pirate under the arm with his shoulder, and used his strength to lever the man over the ship's side.

"Get over here," the man in black chainmail ordered pirates on the starboard vessel.

Darrick turned to confront the big man, noticing the bandage that covered the side of his head. When he parried the man's blade, testing his strength, Darrick found the man uncommonly strong.

The big man grinned, filled with confidence.

Ducking beneath the big man's blow, Darrick stepped to one side and drove a foot into the side of his opponent's knee. Something popped, but the big man somehow remained on his feet, turning again with a sword cut that would have taken Darrick's head from his shoulders if it had struck.

Moving as swiftly as a striking serpent, Darrick kicked the man in the groin. When the man bent over in pain, Darrick performed a spinning back kick that caught the big man on the wounded side of his head. He howled in agony and went down, holding his head.

The man in black chainmail stepped forward, raising his

blade into the *en garde* position. He set to without a word, his sword flashing before him with considerable skill. "I am Raithen, captain of this ship. And you're one breath away from being a dead man."

Without warning, the swordfight took on a deadly earnestness. As skilled as he was, Darrick was hard pressed to keep the pirate captain's blade from finding his throat, eyes, or groin. Nothing was off-limits for the man's sword. Dead, blind, or unmanned, it appeared Captain Raithen would take Darrick any way he could get him.

Still howling in furious pain, the big man rose from the ship's deck and rushed at Darrick. The scarf over the man's head had turned dark with fresh blood. Darrick knew he hadn't caused the wound, only aggravated a fresh one.

"Bull!" Raithen commanded. "No! Stay back!" Enraged and hurting, the big man didn't hear his cap-tain or ignored him. He ran at Darrick, sweeping his big sword behind him, preparing a blow that completely lacked finesse. Bull interfered with his captain's attack, causing Raithen to draw back before he overexposed himself.

Giving ground before the big man, Darrick noticed that Mat had the boy secure and safe in the cargo net. "Tomas, pull them up."

"Darrick," Mat called.

Shadows spun with wild abandon across the ship's deck as nearby lanterns shifted with the ship's rise and fall on the river current. The crews aboard the other two cogs were fighting losing battles; the flames were going to claim them both within minutes. The heat rolled over Darrick as Tomas and his crew started pulling on the ropes, hauling the cargo net up to the cliffside.

"Darrick!" Mat called, concern thick in his voice.

"Stay with the boy," Darrick ordered. "I want him clear of this." He threw himself back from the big man's blow, sliding across the ship's deck in a rolling rush, coming once more to his feet as Bull bore down on him.

Aware that the cargo netting was quickly rising and that the crew on the other cog had succeeded in spanning the distance between the ships with an oak plank, Darrick took two running steps forward, guessing the distance between himself and Bull. He leapt forward, tucking his chin into his chest, and hurled himself into a front flip just as the big man started his blow.

Upside down, in the middle of the flip, Darrick watched as Bull's cutlass blade passed within inches of him. The pirate's blow pulled Darrick off-balance, causing him to bend over slightly. Darrick landed on his feet on Bull's shoulders and back, got his balance between heartbeats to manage a standing position, and leapt up.

Keeping one hand on his cutlass, stretching his arm as far as he could, Darrick focused on the cargo net being hauled up above him. He tried to curl his fingers in the cargo net, missed by inches.

Then Mat caught him, closing a powerful hand around his wrist, refusing to let him fall even as gravity pulled at him. "I've got ye, Darrick."

Hanging by his arm, Darrick watched as Raithen shook his hand. Something metallic glinted in the pirate captain's hand as he drew his arm back to throw. When the pirate's arm snapped forward, Darrick spotted the slender form of the throwing knife hurtling at him with unerring accuracy. Torchlight splintered along the razor-sharp length. Moving before he had time to think, knowing he couldn't dodge, Darrick swung the cutlass.

Metal rang as the cutlass blade knocked the throwing knife away. Darrick's breath locked at the back of his throat.

"Damn, Darrick," Mat said, "I've never seen the like."

"It's your luck," Darrick said, looking down into the angry face of the pirate captain who was powerless to stop them. Feeling cocky and damn fortunate to be alive, Darrick saluted Raithen with his sword blade. "Another time."

Raithen turned from him, yelling orders to his crew, getting them organized.

Spinning under the cargo net as it continued up, Darrick

saw the stone steps where Maldrin encountered a pirate. With a short series of sweeps with the war hammer, the first mate knocked the pirate clear of the steps and sent him plunging down into the river harbor.

Then hands grabbed onto the cargo netting and pulled it to the cliffside.

Darrick caught the cliff edge and hauled himself up as Mat sliced through the cargo net with his sword, spilling himself and the king's nephew out onto the cracked stone surface.

The boy pushed himself to his feet. Blood oozed from cuts on his forehead, his nose, and the lobe of one ear as he took in all the destruction of the cliffside. He swung his head to face Darrick. "Did you and your men do this?"

"No," Darrick said, scanning the ruins. All of them seemed to have changed and shifted. The building they had noticed being used by the pirates had disappeared under a pile of rubble.

The boy pushed away from Mat, who had been checking him over to make certain he was not badly wounded. Cold wind poured down through the Hawk's Beak Mountains, ruffling the boy's hair.

"What have they done?" the boy asked in a dry voice. "Kabraxis is only a myth. The gate to the Burning Hells is only a myth." He looked up at Darrick. "Isn't it?"

Darrick had no answer for the boy.

A horde of demonic flying insects flew out of the yawning mouth of the demon's door toward Buyard Cholik.

Lifting his arms, speaking over the dreadful moaning of the insects' wings, and trying not to give in to the stark fear that nearly overwhelmed him, the old priest spoke the words of a protection spell. He didn't know if it would have an effect on the creatures, but he knew he couldn't hope to run in the shape he was in.

The insects passed Cholik by. A streaming mass of turquoise and bottle-green carapaces and wings illuminated by the torches and lanterns used to light the work area cut through the still air of the cavern. Reaching the front line of slaves, the insects shot into the victims like arrows, burying deeply into their bodies, ripping through clothing to get at the flesh beneath.

The slaves screamed, but their agony was scarcely heard over the drone of insect wings.

Curious and appalled, hoping they would prove to be enough of a sacrifice to a demon, Cholik watched as the slaves jerked up from their hiding places. The insects writhed within the slaves' flesh, looking like dozens of growths and abscesses. Insane with pain and the horror of their situation, the slaves tried to run. Most didn't take more than three or four steps before their bodies burst open and they dropped to the cavern floor. Several torches fell with them, leaving individual fires burning in a line back toward the entrance.

In seconds, more than half of the slaves, mercenaries, and priests lay dead, their bones picked clean by the demonic insects, bloody white skeletons gleaming in the torchlight. While the demonic insects stripped victims of their flesh, it looked as if a blood mist had dawned in the air. Abandoning the dead, the insects flew up to the cavern roof and took refuge among the stalactites. Their buzzing quieted only somewhat as they became spectators to the next events.

Buyard Cholik stared into the dark recesses of the open door ahead of him. Fear settled bone-deep into him, but it wasn't fear of what lay ahead of him. True, there was some fear of the unknown. But the greatest fear he had was that the power he found on the other side of that door wouldn't be enough to take away all the damage that the sands of time had wrought.

Or, possibly, that the power on the other side of the door would find him lacking or wouldn't want him.

Being rejected by a demon after stepping away from the Zakarum Church was horrible to contemplate.

"Master," Altharin whispered. Somehow the man had escaped the destruction that had stricken most of the people around Cholik. "Master, we should go."

"Then go," Cholik said without looking at the man.

"This is an evil place," Altharin said.

"Of course it is." Cholik pulled his robes around himself, took a final breath, and marched toward the door to meet his fate.

Even at the open doorway, all Cholik could see was the unending darkness stretching before him. He paused for an instant at the threshold, tempted to call out. Would a demon answer if he spoke? He didn't know. The texts he'd read that had given him the information to come this far had not suggested anything past this point.

Somewhere ahead, if the texts were right, Kabraxis waited for the man who would free him into the world again.

A cold breeze whipped out of the yawning space before the old priest. Perhaps he would have turned around then, but the cold only reminded Cholik of the chill awaiting him in a grave. It was better to die suddenly tonight than to have to live with all his hopes shattered and stillborn.

But even better than that would be to live with the success of his efforts.

He stepped forward and entered the dark room. Immediately, the steady drone of the insects hidden against the cavern roof dimmed. He knew it wasn't because he'd simply entered another cavern in the cave systems beneath Ransim and beneath Tauruk's Port. The noise dimmed because in that one step he moved a long way from the cavern.

The chill burned into Cholik's flesh, but his fear and his determination to stave off death drove him on. With the lighted cavern behind him, he could see the narrow walls of the tunnel on either side of him as he passed but still nothing of what lay ahead.

You are a man, a deep voice boomed inside the priest's head.

Surprised, Cholik almost faltered. "Yes," he said.

Only a weak man. And you seek to face a demon? The voice sounded amused.

"Humans have slain demons," Cholik said, continuing forward through the narrow tunnel.

Not slain them, the deep voice insisted. *Merely succeeded in binding demons from your world. But only for a time. Diablo has returned. Others were never forced away. Still others remain in hiding, not even known of.*

"You were forced away," Cholik said.

Do you taunt me, human?

"No," Cholik said, gathering all his courage. The ancient texts hadn't suggested anything about what would transpire on this side of the door, but he knew from other readings that demons despised fear. It was a tool, like a blacksmith's hammer, that was used to bend and shape the human lives they controlled. Meeting a demon meant controlling the fear.

Don't lie to yourself, human. You fear me.

"As I would fear falling from a high cliff," Cholik agreed. "Yet to climb, a man must face the fear of falling and overcome it."

And have you overcome your fear?

Cholik licked his lips. All the aches and pains of his advanced years settled into him again, letting him know the spell he'd worked to strip the life energy from the slave was being undone. "I have more to fear from living my life trapped in a failing shell of a body than I do of dying suddenly."

I am a demon, Buyard Cholik. Don't you know that you risk dying for centuries?

Cholik stumbled a little in the darkness. He hadn't thought about that. In the years he'd studied Kabraxis and the Black Road, he'd only pursued knowledge. After winning Raithen over to his side to supply him with slaves and provide transport, he had thought only of digging the ruins of Ransim out to discover the door.

Cholik made his voice strong. "You seek a way out of your prison, Lord Kabraxis. I can be that way."

You? As frail and weak and near to death as you are? The demon laughed, and the hollow booming noise trapped in the tunnel sounded caustic and vibrated through Cholik's body.

"You can make me whole and strong again," Cholik said. "You can return my youth to me. I've read that you have that power. You need a man young in years to help you regain the power that you once had in my world." He paused. "You can make me that man."

Do you believe that?

"Yes." And Buyard Cholik believed in the demon's power as much as he'd believed in anything the Zakarum Church had taught him. If one was false, then it all was false. But if it was true—

Then come, Buyard Cholik, once priest of the Zakarum Church and friend to no demon. Come and let us see what can be made of you.

Nervous fear and anticipation welled up inside the old priest. Sickness coiled inside his stomach, and for a moment he thought he was going to throw up. He centered himself, using all the techniques he'd learned while serving the church, and forced his tired, aching body forward.

A star dawned in the darkness before him, spreading gossamer silver light in all directions. The stone walls on either side melted away, revealing only the darkness of the night. He was not enclosed; he stood on a trail suspended over the longest drop he had ever seen. Visibility ended below the path he walked on, and only then did he realize that he was no longer standing on a stone floor but on a swaying bridge of human bones.

Arm bones, leg bones, and ribs made up the bridge, intermixed with the occasional skull that was complete or damaged. Cholik slowed, feeling the bridge shift dizzyingly beneath him. A skull slid out of place ahead, then bumped and rattled and rolled down the bridge, finally striking a hip bone and bouncing over the bridge's side.

Cholik watched the skull fall, the broken jaw hanging askew as if it were screaming. The skull fell for a long time, tumbling end over end, finally disappearing from the reach of the silver star that waited at the end of the bridge. Only then did Cholik realize the bones were not mortared together; they lay crisscrossed, interlocking to provide support for anyone who crossed the bridge.

Would you go back, Buyard Cholik?

Before he could stop himself, Cholik glanced back along the bridge. Some distance behind him, how far he couldn't tell, the rectangular doorway that opened back into the cavern under the ruins of Ransim gaped. The torches and lanterns flickered inside the cavern, and the stripped skeletons lay on the uneven floor. Thoughts of returning to the apparent safety of the cavern wound through Cholik's mind.

An explosion shook the bridge, and Cholik watched in dismay as a section of crossed bones blew high above the bridge. The displaced bones fell through the darkness like leaves, drifting and spinning.

The gap left in the bridge was too far for Cholik to leap. The old priest realized he was trapped on the bridge.

Let that be your first lesson, the demon said. *I will be your strength when you have no strength of your own.*

Knowing he was doomed, Cholik turned and glanced back up the bone bridge. The silver star glowed brighter, revealing more of the path. The bridge of bones continued to lead up, but it zigzagged back and forth. What seemed to be trees occupied the elbows of the zigzags.

Cholik hesitated, trying to muster more strength but knowing that his body had none left to give.

Come, Buyard Cholik, the demon taunted. *You made your choice when you stepped through that doorway. You only had the illusion of being able to change your mind along the way.*

Cholik felt as though a great hand squeezed his chest, squeezing the breath from him. Was it his heart, then? Was it finally going to fail him? Or was this Zakarum's vengeance for abandoning the church?

Of course, Kabraxis said, *you could throw yourself from the bridge.*

Cholik was tempted, but only for a moment. The temptation came not out of fear but out of rebellion. But that was just a momentary spark. The fear in him of death was a raging bonfire. He lifted a foot and went on.

As he neared the first of the trees, he saw that they bore fruit. When he was closer, he saw the fruits on the tree were tiny human heads. The small faces were filled with fear. Their lips moved in pleading that only then became audible to him. Although he couldn't understand their words, Cholik understood their agony. The sound was an undercurrent, a rush of pain and despair that was somehow horribly melodic.

Tormented voices, Kabraxis said. *Isn't it the sweetest sound you've ever heard?*

Cholik kept walking, finding another bend and another tree and another chorus of hopelessness and hurt. His breath burned inside his chest and he felt as if iron bands constricted his chest.

He faltered.

Come, Buyard Cholik. It's only a little farther. Would you die there and become one of the fruits on the tree?

Pain blurred the old priest's vision, but he lifted his head after the next turn and saw that the bridge remained straight to a small island that floated in the middle of the darkness. The silver star hung behind the shoulder of a massive humanoid shape sitting on a stone throne.

Gasping, no longer able to do more than sip air, knowing he was only inches from death, Cholik made the final ascent and stopped in front of the massive figure on the throne. Unable to stand in front of the demon, the old priest dropped to his hands and knees on the abrasive black rock that made up the island. He coughed, weakly; the coppery taste of blood filled his mouth, and he saw the scarlet threads spray onto the black rock. He watched in stunned horror as the rock absorbed the blood, drinking it in till the rock was once more dry.

Look at me.

Wracked by pain, certain of his death, Cholik lifted his head. "You had best work quickly, Lord Kabraxis."

Even seated, the demon was taller than Cholik standing

up. The old priest guessed that Kabraxis was twice as tall as a man, perhaps even as much as fifteen feet tall. The demon's massively broad body was black flesh, marbled with blue fire that burned and ran through him. His face was horrid, crafted of hard planes and rudimentary features: two inverted triangle eyes, no nose but black pits that were nostrils, and a lipless gash of a mouth filled with yellowed fangs. Writhing, poisonous vipers sprouted from his head, all of them beautiful, cool crystal colors of a rainbow.

Do you know of the Black Road? the demon asked, leaning close. All the taunting had left his voice.

"Yes," Cholik gasped.

Are you prepared to face what lies on the Black Road?

"Yes."

Then do so. Kabraxis reached forward, taking Cholik's head between his huge three-fingered hands. The demon's talons bit into the old priest's head, driving into his skull.

Cholik's senses swam. His eyes teared as he stared into the demon's monstrous visage and tasted Kabraxis's foul breath. Before he knew he was doing it, Cholik screamed.

The demon only laughed, then breathed fire over him.

Πίπε

Glaring out into the harbor of Tauruk's Port, Raithen knew two of the three cogs were lost. The flames ran up the masts, too well established in the rigging and the sails to be beaten back.

He strode *Barracuda*'s deck with grim determination. "Get off that ship," he yelled to the pirates who had feared him more than they had feared the fire and had fought to save it. The effort to raise his voice hurt his wounded throat.

The pirates obeyed at once, showing no remorse at abandoning the vessel. If losing a few of the pirates would have meant saving the ship, Raithen would have done it, but losing the ship and more men was unacceptable.

Raithen leapt onto the plank that led to the narrow shoreline below the overhanging cliff. Rocks and boulders littered the narrow strip of stone that provided a walkway to the steps cut into the cliffside. Dead pirates sprawled across the steps as well, victims of the Westmarch Navy rescue crew who had taken the boy from him. Other pirates had fallen into the river and been swept away. The old man with the war hammer had become death incarnate while holding the steps. Westmarch archers among the rescue group had wreaked havoc among the pirates for a long minute or two until the pirates had no longer tried to storm the steps to the clifftop.

Raithen knew that the Westmarch sailors had gone, taking the boy with them. The pirate captain walked to the burning cog downstream from *Barracuda*, stopped in front of the mooring rope that held the ship in place, and cut it with one mighty blow from the ax he'd carried from *Barracuda*.

With the thick mooring rope severed, the burning cog slid out into the river, caught in the current, and floated away. It wasn't a vessel anymore; it was a pyre.

"On board *Barracuda*," Raithen ordered his men. "Prepare poles, and let's keep that damn burning tub from her." He crossed to the cog upstream from *Barracuda*, waited until pirates lined the cog's railing, then chopped through the hawser line.

The river carried the burning cog into *Barracuda*. The pirates strove to keep the burning ship from the vessel Raithen hoped to salvage. *Barracuda's* hull might be split or merely leaking, but he planned on saving her. Without the cog, it would be a long walk back to the rendezvous point where he kept the main ships of his pirate fleet.

Raithen cursed his pirates, finally giving up, returning to *Barracuda* himself, and taking up a pole. He felt the blaze's heat against his face, but he yelled at his pirates. Slowly, propelled by the poles, the burning ship bumped and butted around *Barracuda*.

The pirates started cheering.

Angry, Raithen grabbed the two men nearest him in quick succession and heaved them over *Barracuda's* railing. The other pirates pulled back at once, knowing they'd all feel their captain's wrath if they stayed near him. Bull was one of the first to step out of reach, knocking over three men in his haste.

Raithen drew his sword, and it gleamed. He faced his men. "You damn stupid louts. We just lost two of our ships, our hidden port, and cargo we aren't going to be able to freight out of here—and you stand there cheering like you done something?"

Smoke stained the pirates' faces, and no few of them bore burns and injuries from the brief battle with the Westmarch sailors.

"I want a crew here to pump this vessel out and see to the repairs," Raithen yelled. "We'll sail at dawn. Those damned Westmarch sailors can't get the river's mouth closed by then. Bull, bring the rest of the men with me."

"Where to, cap'n?" Bull asked.

"We're going to find that damned priest," Raithen said. "If he can persuade me to let him, I'll suffer him to live and take him out of here, too. For a price." He touched his wounded throat. "If not, I'll see him dead before I quit this port, and I'll rob whatever treasures he's scavenged from that buried city as well."

"But, Cap'n Raithen," one of the pirates said, "that explosion what took out the cliffside and flattened the ruins came from the priests' digs. I come from there when them buildings fell on us. Them priests were probably all killed."

"Then we'll be robbing dead men if we can find them," Raithen said. "I've no problem with that." He turned and walked toward the cliffside. As he climbed the crooked stone steps, he shoved debris and dead men from his path. At the least, he intended to get his vengeance on Buyard Cholik—unless the old priest had been killed in the mysterious blast.

"I won't go! I won't go, I tell you!"

Darrick Lang watched the young boy struggle and fight against Mat and one of the other sailors who pulled him toward the Hawk's Beak Mountains, escape, and *Lonesome Star* in the Gulf of Westmarch.

"Please!" the boy yelled. "Please! You've got to listen to me!"

Frustrated, Darrick waved Mat and the other sailor to halt. They were far enough up the mountainside that he had a clear view of the harbor and the city ruins. The second burning cog was passing beside them out on the river far below. A straggling line of pirates still extricated themselves from the ruins and made their way toward the cliffside harbor, but the line of lanterns and torches streaming up the stone steps announced that the pirates weren't ready to abandon the port yet.

"Listen to you about what?" Darrick asked.

"The demon," the boy said. His breath came in ragged gasps because they had pushed him hard after getting him to the top of the cliff. He was too big to carry and run, so Darrick had grabbed the boy's clothing and pushed and pulled him up the mountainside till he couldn't run anymore.

"What demon?" Mat asked, dropping to one knee to face the boy squarely.

After all those years with his younger brothers and sisters in the burgeoning Hu-Ring household, Darrick knew Mat had far more patience with children than he did.

"We don't need any talk of damn demons," Maldrin snarled. The old mate was covered in blood, but little of it was his own. Despite the battle he'd fought while holding the top of the stone steps until archers among the group could kill or chase away pirates eager to die, he still had stamina. Every hand aboard *Lonesome Star* believed that the crusty old mate could walk any sailor who shipped with him to death, then lace up his boots and walk another league or more. "We've been blessed with no bad luck thus far, an' I wouldn't have it any other way."

"The pirate captain," Lhex said. "He showed me a sign of Kabraxis."

"An' this Kabraxis," Mat said, "he'd be the demon you're referrin' to, would he?"

"Yes," Lhex said, turning and gazing back toward the ruins of Tauruk's Port. "The door to Kabraxis's Lair must be somewhere in that. I heard the pirates talking about the priests who were digging there."

"What sign?" Mat persisted.

"Captain Raithen showed me Kabraxis's sign," Lhex said.

"And how is it, then," Darrick asked in a sharp manner, "that you'd be knowing so much about demons?"

Lhex rolled his eyes at Darrick, showing obvious disapproval. "I was sent to Lut Gholein to be priest-trained. I've spent four years in school there. Some of our main philosophy books deal with the thematic struggle between man and his demons. They aren't supposed to be real. But what if they are? What if Kabraxis is somewhere lost in the ruins of this city?"

The wind came down out of the peaks of Hawk's Beak Mountains and chilled Darrick. Sweat from his exertions matted his hair, but it lifted as he gazed at the ruins of the city. Pirates boiled along the top of the cliff overhanging the Dyre River, their lanterns and torches cutting through the stirring fog and reflecting in the river below.

"We've naught to do with demons, boy," Darrick said. "Our orders are to see you safe and home, and I mean to do that."

"We're talking of a demon here, captain," Lhex insisted.

"I'm no captain," Darrick said.

"These men follow you."

"Aye, but I'm no captain. My own captain has ordered me to bring you back, and I'm going to do that."

"And if the pirates find a demon?" Lhex asked.

"They're welcome to any foul demons they might find, says I," Maldrin offered. "Honest men don't have nothin' to do with demons."

"No," the boy said earnestly, "but demons steal the souls of honest men. And Kabraxis was one of the worst while he walked through these lands."

"Ye ain't gettin' me to believe in demons," Tomas said, his face dark with suspicion. "Stories, that's all them legends are. Just meant to give a man a laugh an' maybe a sense of unease now an' again."

"Kabraxis," Lhex said, "was also called the Thief of Hope. People died wearing his chains, chains that they wove themselves because they believed he offered them redemption from sin, wealth, privilege, and everything else mortals have ever put stock in."

Darrick nodded to the carnage left of the city. "If Kabraxis is responsible for that, I'd say the pirates and the priests aren't going to find him any too thankful to be woke up."

"Not woke up," Lhex said. "Returned to this world.

The Prime Evils helped work to seal him from this place because Kabraxis grew too powerful here."

"He was no threat to them three, I'll warrant," Maldrin declared. "Else I'd have heard tell of him, 'cause that woulda been one damned bloody battle."

The wind ruffled the boy's hair, and lightning seared the sky, painting his features the pale color of bone. "Diablo and his brothers feared Kabraxis. He's a patient demon, one who works quietly and takes his time. If Kabraxis has a way into this world, we have to know. We have to be ready for him."

"My job is to get you back to Westmarch and to the king," Darrick said.

"You'll have to carry me," Lhex said. "I won't go willingly."

"Skipper," Maldrin said, "beggin' yer pardon, but tryin' to negotiate them cliffs while carryin' a bellerin' young 'un ain't gonna make for good or safe travelin'."

Darrick already knew that. He took a deep breath, smelling the approaching storm on the wind, and hardened his voice. "Better I should leave you here and tell the king I didn't get to you in time."

The boy's dark eyes regarded Darrick for only a moment. "You won't do that. You can't."

Darrick scowled fiercely, hoping to scare the boy.

"And if you take me back without checking on the demon," Lhex threatened, "I'll tell the king that you had the chance to find out more and you didn't. After the troubles in Tristram, I don't think my uncle will take kindly to a sailor derelict in his duty to find out as much as he could." The boy raised his eyebrows. "Do you?"

Darrick held his tongue for a moment, willing the boy to back down. But even if Lhex did, Darrick knew the truth of the boy's words would weigh on him. The king *would* want to know. And despite the possibility of seeing a demon, which filled him with fear, Darrick was curious.

"No," Darrick said. "I don't think the king would take kindly to such a sailor at all." He raised his voice. "Maldrin."

"Aye, skipper."

"Can you and Mat and a couple others manage getting the waif back to the longboat on your own?" Darrick stared at the boy. "If he agrees to be his most peaceable?"

"I can do that," Maldrin said grudgingly. "If it comes to it, I'll tie him up an' lower him by a rope down the mountainside." He glared at the boy for a moment, then turned his attention back to Darrick. "I don't know that I agree that ye a-harin' off right this minute is all that bright."

"I've never been overly accused of brightness," Darrick said, but it was only bravado that he didn't feel.

"I ain't gonna be left behind," Mat said, shaking his head. "No, if it's to be demon huntin' in the offin', ye got to count me in, Darrick."

Darrick looked at his oldest and best friend in the world. "Aye. I will, and glad to have you, but we're not about to have a good time of it."

Mat smiled. "It'll be an adventure we can tell our grand-kids about whilst we dandle 'em on our knees in our dotage, me an' ye."

"I should go with you," Lhex interrupted.

Darrick looked at the boy. "No. You've pushed this as far as needs be. You leave the matter with us now. The king wouldn't be happy to hear that his nephew wasn't amenable to being rescued by men who laid down their lives for him, either. Understand?"

Reluctantly, the boy nodded.

"Now, you did yourself a good turn back on the pirate ship by getting yourself free," Darrick said. "I expect the same behavior while you're with these men I'm asking to guard you with their lives. Have we got a bargain?"

"But I can identify the demon—" the boy said.

"Boy," Darrick said, "I believe I'll know a demon should I see one."

The coming storm continued to gather strength as Darrick led the group of sailors back into the ruins of the city. The moon disappeared often behind the dark, threatening masses of storm clouds, leaving the world cluttered with black silk, then appeared again to draw harsh, long shadows against the silvered grounds. The alabaster columns and stones of the city blazed with an inner fire whenever moonlight touched them.

The sailors moved in silence, unencumbered by armor the way militiamen would be. The king's army corps seldom went anywhere without the rattle and clangor of chainmail or plate. Those things were death to a man fighting on a ship if he somehow ended up in the water.

Finding the entrance to the underground cavern in the ruins turned out to be easy. Darrick held his group back, then followed the last of Raithen's pirates down into the cleared path that led into the bowels of the earth beneath the remains of Tauruk's Port.

None of them spoke over the droning buzz that filled the cavern farther down. The dank earth blocked the wind, but it kept the wintry chill locked around Darrick. The cold made his body ache worse. The long climb up the cliff as well as the battles he'd fought had stripped him of energy, leaving him running on sheer adrenaline. He looked forward to his hammock aboard *Lonesome Star* and the few days' journey it would take to reach Westmarch.

Fog or a dusty haze filled the cavern. The haze looked golden in the dim light of the lanterns Raithen's pirates carried.

Gradually, the tunnel Darrick followed widened, and he saw the great door set into the stone wall on the other side of the immense cavern. The tunnel went no farther.

Raithen and his pirates stopped before entering the main cavern area, and their position blocked Darrick's view of what lay ahead. Several of the pirates seemed in favor of turning and fleeing, but Raithen held them firm with his harsh voice and the threat of his sword.

Hunkering down behind a slab of rock that had slid free during the excavation, Darrick stared into the cavern. Mat joined him, his breath rasping softly.

"What's wrong?" Darrick whispered.

"It's this damn dust," Mat whispered back. "Must not have settled from the explosion earlier. It's tightenin' me lungs up a mite."

Taking the sleeve of his torn shirt in one hand, Darrick ripped it off and handed it to Mat. "Tie this around your face," he told his friend. "It'll keep the dust out."

Mat accepted the garment remnant gratefully and tied it around his face.

Darrick tore the other sleeve off and tied it around his own face. It was a pity because the shirt had been a favorite of his, though it was no comparison to the Kurastian silk shirts he had in his sea chest aboard *Lonesome Star.* Still, growing up hard and without as he had, he treasured things and generally took good care of the ones he had.

Slowly and tentatively, Raithen led his pirates down into the cavern.

"Darrick, look!" Mat pointed, indicating the skeletons that lay in the cavern area. A few looked old, but most of them appeared to have been just stripped clean. Ragged clothing, torn but not aged, swaddled the skeletons.

"I see them," Darrick said, and the hair at the back of his neck lifted. He wasn't one for magic, and he knew he was looking at sure proof that magic had been recently worked. *We shouldn't be here,* he told himself. *If I had any sense, I'd leave now before any of us are hurt.* In fact, he was just about to give the order when a man in black and scarlet robes stepped through the immense doorway in the far wall.

The man in scarlet and black looked as if he was in his early forties. His black hair held gray at the temples, and his face was lean and strong. A shimmering aura flowed around him.

"Captain Raithen," the man in scarlet and black greeted, but his words held little warmth.

The droning buzz increased in intensity.

"Cholik," Raithen said.

"Why aren't you with the ships?" Cholik asked.

He crossed the cavern floor, oblivious to the carnage of freshly dead men scattered around him.

"We were attacked," Raithen said. "Westmarch sailors set fire to my ships and stole the boy we held for ransom."

"You were followed?" Cholik's anger cut through the droning noise that filled the cavern.

"Who is that man?" Mat whispered.

Darrick shook his head. "I don't know. And I don't see a demon around here, either. Let's go. It's not going to take that Cholik guy long to figure out what Raithen and his pirates are doing here." He turned and signaled to the other men, getting them ready to withdraw.

"Maybe it wasn't me who got followed," Raithen argued. "Maybe one of those men you buy information from in Westmarch got caught doing something and sold you out."

"No," Cholik said. He stopped out of sword's reach from the pirate captain. "The people who do business with me would be afraid to do something like that. If your ships were attacked, it was through your own gross ineptitude."

"Maybe we should just skip all this faultfinding," Raithen suggested.

"And then what should we do, captain?" Cholik regarded the pirate captain with contempt and cold amusement. "Get to the part where you and your murderous crew kill me and try to take whatever it is that you've imagined I've found here?"

Raithen grinned without humor. "Not a very pretty way to put it, but that's about it."

Cholik drew his robes in with imperious grace. "No. That won't be done this night."

Striding forward, Raithen said, "I don't know what kind of night you had planned for yourself, Cholik, but I aim to get what I came for. My men and I have spent blood for you, and the way we figure it, we haven't gotten much in return."

"Your greed is going to get you killed," Cholik threatened.

Raithen brandished his sword. "It'll get you killed first."

A massive shape stepped through the door in the stone wall. Darrick stared at the demon, taking in the writhing snake hair, the barbaric features, the huge three-fingered hands, and the black skin slashed through with pale blue.

Ten

Raithen and his pirates drew back from the demon, filled with fear as the nightmare from the Burning Hells strode into the cavern. Men yelled in terror and retreated quickly.

"Okay," Mat whispered, fear shining in his eyes, "we can tell the boy an' his uncle the king that the demon exists. Let's be away from here."

"Wait," Darrick said, mastering the thrumming fear that filled him at the sight of the demon. He peered over the stone slab they hid behind.

"For what?" Mat gave him a disbelieving look. He made the sign of the Light in the air before him unconsciously, like the child he'd been when they'd attended church in Hillsfar.

"Do you know how many men have seen a demon?" Darrick asked.

"An' them livin' to tell about it? Damned few. An' ye want to know why, Darrick? 'Cause they were killed by the demons they was gawkin' at instead of runnin' as any sane man should do."

"Captain Raithen," the demon said, and his voice rolled like thunder inside the cavern. "I am Kabraxis, called the Enlightener. There is no need for disharmony between yourself and Buyard Cholik. You can continue to work together."

"For you?" Raithen asked. His voice held fear and awe, but he stood before the demon with his sword in his fist.

"No," the demon replied. "Through me, you can find the true path to your future." He strode forward, stepping in front of the priest. "I can help you. I can bring you peace."

"Peace I can find in the bottom of a cup of ale," Raithen said, "but I'll not resort to serving demon scum."

Darrick thought the reply would have sounded better if the pirate captain's voice hadn't been shaking, but he didn't doubt that he would have had trouble controlling his own voice if he'd spoken to the demon.

"Then you can die," Kabraxis said, waving a hand in an intricate pattern before him.

"Archers!" Raithen yelled. "Feather that hell-spawned beast!"

The pirates were stunned by the presence of the demon and slow to react. Only a few of them nocked and released arrows. The dozen or so arrows that hit the demon glanced off, leaving no sign that they had ever touched him.

"Darrick," Mat pleaded desperately, "the others have already gone."

Glancing over his shoulder, Darrick saw that it was true. The other sailors who had accompanied them were already beating a hasty retreat.

Mat pulled at Darrick's shoulder. "C'mon. There's naught we can do here. Gettin' ourselves safe an' to home, that's our job now."

Darrick nodded, getting up from behind the stone slab just as waves of shimmering force shot out from the demon's hand.

Kabraxis spoke words Darrick felt certain no human tongue could master. The droning inside the cavern increased, and what looked at first like fireflies dropped from the stalactites above. Flashing through the torchlit cavern, the fireflies slammed into Raithen's pirates but stayed clear of the pirate captain.

Frozen with horror, Darrick watched as the insects reduced the pirates they struck to stacks of bloody bones. No sooner did the freshly flensed corpses strike the stony ground than they lurched back to their feet and took up arms against the few pirates who had survived the initial assault.

The sound of men screaming, cursing, and dying filled the cavern.

Kabraxis walked toward the survivors. "If you would live, my children, come to me. Give yourselves to me. I can make you whole again. I can teach you to dream and be more than you ever thought you could be. Come to me."

A handful of pirates rushed to the demon and supplicated themselves before Kabraxis. Gently, the demon touched their foreheads, leaving a bloody mark tattooed into their flesh, but they were saved from the insects and the skeletons.

Even Raithen went forward.

The light in the cavern dimmed as the men abandoned or lost their lanterns and torches. Darrick struggled to see clearly.

Raithen kept his sword at hand as he walked toward the demon. There was no way out of the cavern. Skeletons of his men blocked the path back to the tunnel. And even if he got past them, there were the carnivorous insects to deal with.

But Raithen wasn't a man to surrender. As soon as he was close enough, one hand extended in obeisance for the demon to take, he struck with the sword, plunging it deep into the demon's abdomen. Jewels gleamed in the hilt and the blade, and Darrick knew the sword possessed some magic. He thought just for a moment that it was a lucky thing he'd not crossed blades with the man aboard *Barracuda*. Even a small wound from an enchanted weapon could wreak havoc with a man if the blade held poison.

Raithen's blade held fire. As soon as the sword plunged into the demon's body, flames lashed out from the wound, scorching the flesh.

Kabraxis howled in pain and staggered back, clutching at the wound in his stomach. Not to be denied, Raithen stepped after the creature, twisting his sword cruelly to open the demon's stomach farther.

"You'll die, demon," Raithen snarled, but Darrick heard the panic in the man's voice. Perhaps the pirate captain thought he'd had no choice but to attack, but once committed, he had no choice but to continue.

Demons died on men's blades and by spells learned by human mages, Darrick knew, but demons could be reborn, and it took a hell of a lot to kill them. Most of the time, humans only succeeded in banishing demons from the human planes for a time, and even centuries were nothing to the demons. They always returned to prey on men again.

Raithen attacked again, plunging his sword deep into the demon's stomach. Fire belched forth again, but Kabraxis showed only signs of discomfort, not distress. Flinging out one giant hand, the demon wrapped all three fingers around Raithen's head before he could escape.

Kabraxis spoke again, and an inferno whirled to life in his hand fitted over Raithen's head and shoulders. The pirate captain never managed to scream as his body went stiff. When the demon released the pirate captain, flames had consumed Raithen's upper body, leaving a charred and blackened husk where a powerfully built man had once stood. Orange coals still gleamed in Raithen's body, and smoke rose from the smoldering burns. The pirate captain's mouth was open in a silent scream that would never be heard.

"Darrick," Mat whispered hoarsely, tugging on his friend's arm again.

Bone rasped against rock behind Darrick, alerting him to other dangers waiting in the shadows around him. He glanced up, spotting the skeleton behind Mat that lifted its short sword and aimed at Mat's back.

Darrick fisted Mat's shirt with one hand as he stood and lifted his cutlass. Yanking Mat from the skeleton, Darrick parried the short sword then snap-kicked the skeleton's skull. The undead thing's lower jaw tore loose, and broken teeth flew in all directions. The skeleton staggered back and tried to lift the sword again.

Mat swung his sword at the skeleton. The heavy blade caught the skeleton's neck and snapped the skull off.

"Get those men," the demon roared farther down in the main cavern.

"Go," Darrick yelled, pushing Mat before him. They ran together, avoiding the slow-moving skeletons that had been roused by the demon's unholy magic. Darrick had fought skeletons before, and a man could usually outrun one if he outpaced them. However, if a pack of skeletons came upon a man, they wore him down in numbers, taking hellish beatings before they were finally too damaged to continue.

The droning buzz of the insects filled the cavern behind them, then the tunnel as they zipped into that. Other skeletons rose before Darrick and Mat as they ran through the tunnels beneath the dead city. Some of the skeletons had drying blood covering the white ivory of bone, but others wore tatters of clothing that had gone out of fashion a hundred years ago. Tauruk's Port had been home to innumerable dead, and they were all coming back at the demon's call.

Darrick ran, driving his feet hard, breath whistling against the back of his throat, ignoring the pain and fatigue that filled him, fueling himself with the primordial fear that thrilled through him. "Run!" he yelled to Mat. "Run, damn it, or they'll take you!"

And if they do, it will be my fault. The thought haunted Darrick, echoed inside his skull faster even than his feet drummed the stone floor of the tunnel. *I shouldn't have come here. I shouldn't have let the boy talk me into this. And I should have had Mat clear of this.*

"They're goin' to catch us," Mat wheezed, glancing back.

"Don't look back," Darrick ordered. "Keep your eyes facing front. If you trip, you'll never get back up again in time." Still, he couldn't resist ignoring his own advice and looking over his shoulder.

The skeletons pounded after them, weapons upraised to attack. Their bony feet slapped the stone floor with hollow clacks. As Darrick watched, toes snapped off the skeletons' feet, bouncing crazily through the tunnel. But the insects buzzed by them, the drone growing louder in Darrick's ears.

They easily avoided most of the skeletons that stepped out of the shadows in front of them. The undead creatures were slow, and there was room enough, but a few of them had to be physically countered. Darrick used his sword, unable to utilize the weapon with much skill while running at full tilt, but it allowed him to turn aside swords and spears the skeletons wielded. But each contact cost him precious inches that were damned hard to replace.

How far is it to the river? Darrick tried to remember and couldn't. Now, it suddenly seemed like forever.

The buzzing grew louder, thunderous.

"They're goin' to get us," Mat said.

"No," Darrick said, forcing the words out and knowing he couldn't spare the breath it took. "No, damn it. I didn't bring you here to die, Mat. You keep running."

Suddenly, the mouth of the tunnel was before them, around a turn that Darrick had thought would be their last. Jagged streaks of white-hot lightning seared the sky and clawed away long strips of night for a moment. Hope spurred them both on. He saw it in Mat's face and took heart in it himself. Fewer skeletons darted out of the shadows at them now.

"Just a little farther," Darrick said.

"An' then that long run to the river, ye mean." Mat gasped for breath. He was always the better runner of them, always more agile and quick, almost as at home as Caron in the ship's rigging.

Darrick wondered if his friend was holding back, not running at full speed. The thought angered him. Mat should have left with the other sailors, who were long gone from the tunnels.

Miraculously, they reached the final incline to the mouth of the tunnel leading into the ruins of Tauruk's Port. The carnivorous insects stayed so close now that Darrick saw their pale green coloring out of the corner of his eye as he ran.

Outside the tunnel's mouth, as he emerged into a sudden squall of wind and rain, a stray piece of stone slithered

out from under Mat's foot. With a startled yelp, he fell sliding and flailing through the clutter and debris that had
tumbled from the ruins.

"Mat!" Darrick watched in horror, stopping his own
headlong pace with difficulty. The rain was almost blinding, stinging his face and arms. The storm wasn't a normal
one, and he wondered how much the demon's arrival in
the cavern below had affected the weather. The ground
had already turned mushy underfoot from all the rain in
the last several minutes.

"Don't ye stop!" Mat yelled, trying desperately to get
up. He spat rainwater from his mouth, the sleeve Darrick
had given him to mask out the dust below hanging around
his neck. "Don't ye dare stop on account of me, Darrick
Lang! I'll not have your death on me head!"

"And I'm not about to let you die alone," Darrick
replied, coming to a halt and taking a two-handed grip on
the cutlass. The rain cascaded down his body. He was
already drenched. The cold water ran into his mouth, carrying a rancid taste he'd never experienced before. Or
maybe it was his own fear he tasted.

Then the insects were on them. Mat was to his feet but
could only start to run as the cloud of insects closed in for
the kill.

Darrick swiped at the insects with his sword, knowing it
was ineffectual. The keen blade sliced through two of the
fat-bodied demonic bugs, leaving smears of green blood
across the steel that washed away almost immediately in
the pouring rain. In the next instant, the insects vanished
in liquid pops of emerald fire that left a sulfuric stench
behind.

Staring, Darrick watched as the rest of the insects lost
their corporeal existence in the same fashion. They continued flying at him, the haze of green flames getting so thick
it became a wall of color.

"Those foul creatures, they have trouble existin' on this
plane," Mat said in awe.

Darrick didn't know. Of the two of them, Mat had more

use for the stories of mages and legendary things. But the insects continued their assault, dying by the droves only inches from their intended victims. The cloud thinned out, and the color died down in the space of a drawn breath.

That was when Darrick saw the first of the skeletons race through the tunnel mouth, war ax uplifted. Darrick dodged the ax blow and kicked out, tripping the skeleton. The skeleton fell and slid across the mounds of muddy debris like a stone skipping across a pond, then smashed against the side of a building.

"Go!" Darrick yelled, grabbing Mat and getting him started again.

They ran, sprinting toward the river again. And the skeletons poured after them, soundless as ghosts except for the thud of feet against the rain-drenched land.

Having no reason to hide anymore, certain that any pirates who might remain between them and the river wouldn't stick around long enough to engage them, Darrick fled through the center of the disheveled city. The ragged lightning that tore at the purple sky made the terrain uncertain and tricky. But the thing that got them in the end was that they were human and fatigued. Darrick and Mat slowed, their hearts and lungs and legs no longer able to keep up with the demand. The inexorable rush of the skeletons did not waver, did not slow.

Darrick glanced over his shoulder and saw only death behind them. Black spots swam in his vision, and every drawn breath felt empty of air, as if it was all motion and nothing of substance. The rain-filled wind made it hard to breathe and slashed at his face.

Mat slowed, and they were only a hundred yards or less from the river's edge. If they could make the edge, Darrick thought, and throw themselves into the water—somehow survive the plunge without smashing up against the stone bottom of the riverbed—perhaps they had a chance. The river was deep, and skeletons couldn't swim because they had no flesh to help them remain buoyant.

Darrick ran, throwing down his cutlass, only then recognizing that it was dead weight and was slowing him. Survival didn't lie in fighting; it lay in flight. He ran another ten yards, somehow stretched into another twenty, and kept lifting his knees, driving his numbed feet against the ground even though he didn't trust his footing.

And then, all at once it seemed, they were at the edge. Mat was at his side, face pale from being winded and hurting for far too long. Then, just when Darrick felt certain he could almost throw himself into the air and trust his momentum to carry him over the edge and into the Dyre River beyond, something grabbed his foot. He fell. Senses swimming already, he nearly blacked out from his chin's impact against the ground.

"Get up, Darrick!" Mat yelled, grabbing his arm.

Instinctively, driven by fear, Darrick kicked out, freeing himself from the skeleton that had leapt at him and caught up his foot. The rest of them came on, tightly together like a rat pack.

Mat dragged Darrick to the edge, only just avoiding the outstretched hands and fingers of the skeletons. Without pause, Mat flung Darrick over the edge, then readied himself to jump.

Darrick saw all of that as he began the long fall to the whitecapped river so far below. And he saw the skeleton that leapt and caught Mat before he could get clear of the cliff.

"No!" Darrick shouted, instinctively reaching for Mat although he knew he was too far away to do anything.

But the skeleton's rush succeeded in knocking Mat over the cliff. They fell, embraced in death, and bounced from the cliffside no more than ten feet from the river's surface.

Bone crunched, and the sound reached Darrick's ears just before he plunged into the icy river. In just moments since the storm had started, the river current had picked up. What had once been a steady flow out toward the Gulf of Westmarch now became a torrent. He kicked out, his arms and legs feeling like lead, certain that he'd never break the river's surface before he filled his lungs with water.

Lightning flashed across the sky, bringing the sky sandwiched between the cliffsides out in bold relief for a moment. The intensity was almost blinding.

Mat! Darrick looked around in the water, trying desperately to find his friend. His lungs burned as he swam, pushing himself toward the surface. Then he was through, his vision wavering, and he sucked in a great draught of air.

The river's surface was lathered with whitecaps that washed over him. The fog was thicker now, swirling through the canyon between the mountains. Darrick shook the water from his eyes, searching frantically for Mat. The skeleton had gone in with Mat. Had it dragged him down?

Thunder split the night. A moment later, projectiles started plummeting into the river. Tracking the movement, Darrick saw the skeletons hurling themselves from the cliffside. They smashed into the water nearly thirty feet upriver from him, and that was when he realized how much he had moved since he'd entered the water.

He watched the surface for a moment, wondering if the skeletons had been given an ability to swim. He'd never heard of such a thing, but he'd never seen a demon before tonight, either.

Mat!

Something bumped against Darrick's leg. His immediate gut reaction was to push back from it and get away. Then one of Mat's arms floated through the water by him.

"Mat!" Darrick yelled, grabbing for the arm and pulling the other man up. Lightning seared the sky again as he held Mat's back against his chest and fought to keep both their heads above water. The waves slapped him constantly in the face. A moment later, a skeleton's head popped up in the river, letting Darrick know it still had hold of Mat's leg.

Darrick kicked at the undead thing as the river current caught them more securely in its grasp. The cliffsides holding the river on course swept by at greater speed and Mat's weight combined with the weight of the skeleton was enough to keep Darrick under most of the time. He only came up behind Mat's back for a quick gulp or two of air, then submerged again to keep up the fight to keep Mat's head out of the water. *By the Light, please give me the strength to do this!*

Twice, as the current roiled and changed, Mat was nearly torn from Darrick's grip. The water was cold enough to numb his hands, and the exhaustion he felt turned him weak.

"Mat!" he screamed in his friend's ear, then went down again. He managed to call out to Mat twice more as they raced down the river but didn't get any reaction. Mat remained dead weight in his arms.

Lightning strobed the sky again, and this time Darrick thought he spotted blood on his elbow. It wasn't his blood, and he knew it had to have come from Mat. But when the next wave hit him and he resurfaced, the blood wasn't there, and he couldn't be sure if it ever was.

"Darrick!"

Maldrin's voice came out of the night without warning.

Darrick tried to turn his head, but the effort sent him plunging below the waterline again. He kicked the water fiercely, keeping Mat elevated. When he rose again, thunder boomed.

"—rick!" Maldrin squalled again in his huge voice that could reach the top of the rigging or empty a tavern of sailors that crewed aboard *Lonesome Star.*

"Here!" Darrick yelled, spluttering, spitting water. "Here, Maldrin!" He sank, then fought his way up again. Each time was getting harder. The skeleton remained clinging to Mat's leg, and twice Darrick had to kick free of its embrace. "Hang on, Mat. Please hang on. It's only a little longer now. Maldrin's—" The current took him down again, and this time he spotted light from a lantern on his port side.

"—see them!" Maldrin roared. "Hold this damn boat, lads!"

Darrick came up again, seeing a thick black shadow rising up from behind him, then lightning split the sky and reflected from the dark water, illuminating Maldrin's homely features for a moment.

"I got ye, skipper!" Maldrin yelled above the storm. "I got ye. Just ye come back on ahead to ol' Maldrin, an' let me take some of that weight from ye."

For a moment, Darrick feared that the mate was going to miss him. Then he felt Maldrin take hold of his hair—the easiest part of a drowning victim to grab hold of—and would have screamed with agony if he hadn't been choking on water. Then, incredibly, Maldrin pulled him back toward the longboat they'd arrived in.

"Give a hand!" Maldrin yelled.

Tomas reached down and hooked his hands under Mat's arms, then leaned back and started pulling him into the longboat. "I've got him, Darrick. Let him go."

Freed from Mat's weight, Darrick's arms slid away limply. If it hadn't been for Maldrin holding him, he was sure he would have been swept away by the current. He fought to help Maldrin pull him on board, catching a glimpse of the boy, Lhex, wrapped in a blanket that was already soaked through from the rain.

"We waited for ye, skipper," Maldrin said as he pulled. "Held steady to our course 'cause we knew ye'd be here. Hadn't ever been a time ye didn't make it, no matter how bollixed up things looked like they was a-gettin'." He slapped Darrick on the shoulder. "An' ye done us proud again. We'll have stories to tell after this 'un. I'll swear to ye on that."

"Something's holdin' him," Tomas said, fighting to bring Mat onto the longboat.

"Skeleton," Darrick said. "It's holding on to his leg."

Without warning, the undead thing erupted from the water, lunging at Tomas with an open mouth like a hungry wolf. Galvanized by his fear, Tomas yanked back, pulling Mat into the longboat with him.

Calmly, as if he were reaching for a dish at a tavern, Maldrin picked up his war hammer and smashed the skeleton's skull. Going limp, the undead creature released its hold and disappeared into the whitecapped water.

Darrick's chest heaved as he sucked in huge lungfuls of air. "River's full of skeletons. They followed us in. They can't swim, but they're in the water. If they find the boat anchor—"

The longboat suddenly shuddered and swung sideways, no longer pointed into the current so that it could ride out the gorged river easier. It bucked like a mustang, throwing all the sailors aboard it around as if they were ragdolls.

"Something's got hold of the rope!" one of the sailors yelled.

Shoving the other sailors aside, Maldrin raked a knife from his boot and sawed through the anchor rope as skeletal hands grabbed the longboat's gunwales. The boat leapt into the river, cutting across the whitecaps like a thing possessed.

"Man those oars!" Maldrin bawled, grabbing one from the middle of the longboat himself. "Get this damn boat squared away afore we all go down with it!"

Struggling against the exhaustion that filled him as well as the longboat being tossed like a child's toy on the rushing river, Darrick pushed himself up and crawled over to Mat Hu-Ring. "Mat!" he called.

Lightning flashed, and thunder filled the river canyon through the Hawk's Beak Mountains.

"Mat." Tenderly, Darrick rolled Mat's head over, sickened at once by how lax and loose it was on his neck.

Mat's face kept rolling, coming around to face Darrick. The wide dark eyes stared sightlessly up, capturing the next reflection of the wicked lightning in them. The right side of Mat's head was covered with blood, and white pieces of bone stuck out from the dark hair.

"He's dead," Tomas said as he pulled on his oar. "I'm sorry, Darrick. I know ye two was close."

No! Darrick couldn't believe it—*wouldn't* believe it. Mat couldn't be dead. Not handsome and witty and funny Mat. Not Mat who could always be counted on to say the right things to the girls in the dives in the port cities they visited on their rounds. Not Mat who had helped nurse him back to health those times Darrick's punishment from his father laid him up for days in the loft above the butcher's barn.

"No," Darrick said. But his denial was weak even in his ears. He stared at the corpse of his friend.

"Like as not he went sudden." Maldrin spoke quietly behind Darrick. "He musta hit his head on a rock. Or maybe that skeleton he was fightin' with done for him."

Darrick remembered the way Mat had struck the cliff-side on the long fall from the canyon ridge.

"I knew he was dead as soon as I touched him," Maldrin said. "There wasn't nothin' ye could do, Darrick. Every man that took this assignment from Cap'n Tollifer knew what our chances was goin' in. Just bad luck. That's all it was."

Darrick sat in the middle of the longboat, feeling the rain beat down on him, hearing the thunder crash in the heavens above him. His eyes burned, but he didn't let himself cry. He'd never let himself cry. His father had taught him that crying only made things hurt worse.

"Did you see the demon?" the boy asked, touching Darrick's arm.

Darrick didn't answer. In that brief moment of learning of Mat's death, he hadn't even thought of Kabraxis.

"Was the demon there?" Lhex asked again. "I'm sorry for your friend, but I have to know."

"Aye," Darrick answered through his constricted throat. "Aye, the demon was there right enough. He caused this. Might as well have killed Mat himself. Him and that priest."

Several of the sailors touched their good luck charms at the mention of the demon. They pulled at their oars in response to Maldrin's shouted orders, but it was primarily to direct the craft. The swollen river propelled the longboat swiftly.

Upriver, lantern lights burned aboard the single cog fighting the mooring tether as the river rushed against it.

Captain Raithen's crew waited there, Darrick guessed. They didn't know the captain wasn't coming.

Giving in to the overwhelming emotion and exhaustion that filled him, Darrick stretched out over Mat's body, as if he were going to protect him from the gale winds and the rain, the way Mat used to do for him when he was racked with fever while getting well from one of his father's beatings. Darrick smelled the blood on Mat, and it reminded him of the blood that had been ever present in his father's shop.

Before Darrick knew it, he fell into the waiting blackness, and he never wanted to return.

ELEVEN

Darrick lay in his hammock aboard *Lonesome Star*, his hands folded behind his head, and tried not to think of the dreams that had plagued him the last two nights. In those dreams, Mat was still alive, but Darrick still lived with his parents in the butcher's shop in Hillsfar. Since he had left, Darrick had never gone back.

Over the years since his departure from the town, Mat had gone back to visit with his family on special occasions, arriving there by merchant ship and signing on as a cargo guard while on leave from the Westmarch Navy. Darrick had always suspected that Mat hadn't visited his home or his family as much as he had wanted to. But Mat had believed there would be plenty of time. That was Mat's nature: he never hurried about anything, took each thing in its time and place.

Now, Mat would never go home again.

Darrick seized the pain that filled him before it could escape his control. That control was rock-solid. He'd built it carefully, through beating after beating, through bald cruel things his father had said, till that control was just as strong and as sure as a blacksmith's anvil.

He shifted his head, feeling the ache in his back, neck, and shoulders from all the climbing he'd done the night before last. Turning his head, he gazed out the porthole at the glittering blue-green water of the Gulf of Westmarch. Judging from the way the light hit the ocean, it was noon— almost time.

Lying in the hammock, sipping his breaths, stilling himself and controlling the pain that threatened to overflow even the boundaries he'd put up, he waited. He tried counting his heartbeats, feeling them echo in his head, but waiting was hard when he measured the time. It was better to go numb and let nothing touch him.

Then the deck pipe played, blasting shrill and somehow sweet over the constant wave splash of the ocean, calling the ship's crew together.

Darrick closed his eyes and worked on imagining nothing, remembering nothing. But the sour scent of the moldy hay in the loft above the pens where his father kept the animals waiting to be slain and bled out filled his nose. Before Darrick knew it, a brief glimpse of Mat Hu-Ring, nine years old in clothing that was too big for him, flipped down from the rooftop and landed inside the loft. Mat had climbed the chimney of the smokehouse attached to the barn behind the butcher's shop and made his way across the roof until he was able to enter the loft.

Hey, Mat said, digging in the pockets of the loose shirt he wore and producing cheese and apples. *I didn't see you around yesterday. I thought I'd find you up here.*

In his shame, his body covered with bruises, Darrick had tried to act mad at Mat and make him go away. But it was hard to be convincing when he had to be so quiet. Getting loud enough to attract his father's attention—and let his father know someone else was aware of his punishment— was out of the question. After Mat had spread the apples and cheese out, adding a wilted flower to make it more of a feast and a joke, Darrick hadn't been able to keep up the pretense, and even embarrassment hadn't curbed his hunger.

If his father had ever once found out about Mat's visits during those times, Darrick knew he would never have seen Mat again.

Darrick opened his eyes and stared up at the unmarked ceiling. Just as he would never see him again now. Darrick reached for the cold numbness that he used to cover himself when things became too much. It slipped on like armor, each piece fitting the others perfectly. No weakness remained within him.

The shrill pipe played again.

Without warning, the door to the officers' quarters opened.

Darrick didn't look. Whoever it was could go away, and would if he knew what was good for him.

"Mr. Lang," a strong, imperious voice spoke.

Hurriedly, reflexes overcoming even the pain of loss and the walls he'd erected, Darrick twisted in the hammock, fell out of it expertly even though the ship broke through oncoming waves at the moment, and landed on his feet at attention. "Aye, sir," Darrick answered quickly.

Captain Tollifer stood at the entranceway. He was a tall, solid man in his late forties. Gray touched the lamb-chop whiskers he wore surrounding a painfully clean-shaven face. The captain had his hair pulled back in a proper queue and wore his best Westmarch Navy uniform, green with gold piping. He carried a tricorn hat in his hand. His boots shone like fresh-polished ebony.

"Mr. Lang," the captain said, "have you had occasion to have your hearing checked of late?"

"It's been a while, sir," Darrick said, standing stiffly at attention.

"Then may I suggest that when we reach port in Westmarch the day after tomorrow, the Light willing, you report to a doctor of such things and find out."

"Of course, sir," Darrick said. "I will, sir."

"I only mention this, Mr. Lang," Captain Tollifer said, "because I clearly heard the pipe blow all hands on deck."

"Aye, sir. As did I."

Tollifer raised an inquisitive eyebrow.

"I thought I might be excused from this, sir," Darrick said.

"It's a funeral for one of the men in my command," Tollifer said. "A man who died bravely in the performance of his duties. No one is excused from one of those."

"Begging the captain's pardon," Darrick said, "I thought I might be excused because Mat Hu-Ring was my friend." *I was the one who got him killed.*

"A friend's place is beside his friend."

Darrick kept his voice cold and detached, glad that he felt the same way inside. "There's nothing left that I can do for him. That body out there isn't Mat Hu-Ring."

"You can stand for him, Mr. Lang," the captain said, "in front of his peers and his friends. I think Mr. Hu-Ring would expect that of you. Just as he would expect me to have this talk with you."

"Aye, sir."

"Then I'll expect you to clean yourself up properly," Captain Tollifer said, "and get yourself topside in relatively short order."

"Aye, sir." Even with all his respect for the captain and fear of his position, Darrick barely restrained the scathing rebuttal that came to mind. His grief for Mat was his own, not property of the Westmarch Navy.

The captain turned to go, then stopped at the door and spoke, looking at Darrick earnestly. "I've lost friends before, Mr. Lang. It's never easy. We perform the funerals so that we may begin letting go in a proper fashion. It isn't to forget them but only to remind ourselves that some closure is given in death and to help us mark an eternal place for them in our hearts. A few good men are born into this world who should never be forgotten. Mr. Hu-Ring was one of those, and I feel privileged to have served with him and known him. I won't be saying that in the address topside because you know I stand on policy and procedure aboard my ship, but I wanted you to know that."

"Thank you, sir," Darrick said.

The captain placed his hat on his head. "I'll give you a reasonable amount of time to get ready, Mr. Lang. Please be prompt."

"Aye, sir." Darrick watched the captain go, feeling the pain boiling over inside him, turning to anger that drew to it like a lodestone all the old rage he'd kept bottled up for so long. He closed his eyes, trembling, then released his pent-up breath and sealed the emotions away.

When he opened his eyes, he told himself he felt nothing.

He was an automaton. If he felt nothing, he couldn't be hurt. His father had taught him that.

Mechanically, ignoring even the aches and pains that filled him from that night, Darrick went to the foot of his hammock and opened his sea chest. Since the night at Tauruk's Port, he hadn't been returned to active duty. None of the crew had except Maldrin, who couldn't be expected to lie abed on a ship when there was so much to do.

Darrick chose a clean uniform, shaved quickly with the straight razor without nicking himself too badly, and dressed. There were three other junior officers aboard *Lonesome Star*; he was senior among them.

Striding out on deck, pulling on the white gloves that were demanded at ceremonial occasions, Darrick looked past the faces of the men as they stared at him. He was neutral, untouchable. They would see nothing on him today because there was nothing to see. He returned their crisp salutes proficiently.

The noonday sun hung high above *Lonesome Star*. Light struck the sea, glittering in the blue-green troughs between the white rollers like a spray of gemstones. The rigging and canvas sheets above creaked and snapped in the wind as the ship plunged toward Westmarch, carrying the news of the pirate chieftain's death as well as the unbelievable return of a demon to the world of man. The men aboard *Lonesome Star* had talked of little else since the rescue crew's return to the ship, and Darrick knew all of Westmarch would soon be buzzing with the news as well. The impossible had happened.

Darrick took his place beside the three other junior officers at the forefront of the sailors. All three of the officers were much younger than he, one of them still in his teens and already knowing command because his father had purchased a commission for him.

A momentary flicker of resentment touched Darrick's heart as they stood beside Mat's flag-covered body on the plank balanced on the starboard railing. None of the other officers deserved those positions; they had not been true sailing men like Mat. Darrick had chosen to follow his own career and become an officer when offered, but Mat never had. Captain Tollifer had never seen fit to extend a commission to Mat, though Darrick had never understood why. As a rule, such a promotion wasn't done much, and hardly ever was it done aboard the same ship. But Captain Tollifer had done just such a thing.

The officers standing beside Darrick had never known a bosun's lash for failing to carry out a captain's orders or for failing to carry them out to their full extent. Darrick had, and he'd borne those injuries and insults with the same stoic resolve his father had trained him to have. Darrick hadn't been afraid to take command in the field even when under orders. In the beginning, such behavior had earned him floggings under hard captains who refused to acknowledge his reinterpretation of their commands, but under Captain Tollifer, Darrick had come into his own.

Mat had never been interested in becoming an officer. He'd enjoyed the hard life of a sailor.

During their years aboard the ships of the Westmarch Navy, Darrick had often thought that he had been taking care of Mat, looking out for his friend. But looking at the sheet-draped body in front of him, Darrick knew that Mat had never been that interested in the sea.

What would you have done? Where would you have gone if I had not pulled you here? The questions hung in Darrick's mind like gulls riding a favorable wind. He pushed them away. He wouldn't allow himself to be touched by pain or confusion.

Andregai played the pipes, standing at Captain Tollifer's side on the stern castle. The wind whipped the captain's great military cloak around him. The boy—Lhex, the king's nephew—stood at the captain's side. When the pipes finished playing and the last echoing sad note faded away, the captain delivered the ship's eulogy, speaking with quiet dignity of Mat Hu-Ring's service and devotion to the Westmarch Navy and that he gave his life while rescuing the king's nephew. Despite the scattering of facts, the address was formal, almost impersonal.

Darrick listened to the drone of words, the call of gulls sailing after *Lonesome Star* and hoping for a trail of scraps to be left behind on the water. *Slain while rescuing the king's nephew. That's not how it was. Mat was killed while on a fool's errand, and for worrying about me. I got him killed.*

Darrick looked at the ship's crew around him. Despite the action two nights ago, Mat had been the only one killed. Maybe some of the crew believed, as Maldrin said he did, that it was all just bad luck, but Darrick knew that some of them believed it was he who had killed Mat by staying too long in the cavern.

When Captain Tollifer finished speaking, the pipes played again and the mournful sound filled the ship's deck. Maldrin, clad in sailor's dress whites that were worn only on inspection days or while at anchorage in Westmarch, stepped up on the other side of Mat's flag-covered body on the plank. Five more sailors joined him.

The pipes blew again, a going-away tune that always wished the listeners a safe trip. It was known in every maritime province Darrick had ever visited.

When the pipes finished, Maldrin looked to Darrick, a question in his old gray eyes.

Darrick steeled himself and gave an imperceptible nod.

"All right, then, lads," Maldrin whispered. "Easy as ye does it, an' with all the respect ye can muster." The mate grabbed the plank and started it up, tilting it on its axis, and the other five men—two on one side with him and three on the other—lifted together. Maldrin kept a firm grip on the Westmarch flag. Maybe they covered the dead given to the sea, but the flags were not abandoned.

As one, Darrick and the other officers turned to the starboard side, followed a half-second later by the sailors, all of them standing at rigid attention.

"For every man who dies for Westmarch," the captain spoke, "let him know that Westmarch lives for him."

The other officers and the crew repeated the rote saying.

Darrick said nothing. He watched in stony silence and kept himself dwindled down to a small ember. Nothing touched him as Mat's shroud-wrapped body slid from under the Westmarch flag and plummeted down the ship's side to the rolling waves. The ballast rocks wrapped into the foot of the shroud to weight the body dragged it down into the blue-green sea. For a time, the white of the funeral shroud kept Mat's body visible.

Then even that disappeared before the ship sailed on and left it behind.

The pipes blew the disassembly, and the men drifted away.

Darrick walked to the railing, easily riding the rise and fall of the ship that had once made him so sick in the beginning. He peered out at the ocean, but he didn't see it. The stink of the blood and the soured hay in his father's barn filled his nose and took his mind away from the ship and the sea. His heart hurt with the roughened leather strokes his father had used to punish him until only the feel of his fists against Darrick's body would satisfy him.

He made himself feel nothing at all, not even the wind that pushed into his face and ruffled his hair. He had lived much of his life numb. It had been his mistake to retreat from that.

That night, having not eaten at all during the day because it would have meant taking mess with the other men and dealing with all the unasked questions each had, Darrick went down to the galley. Cook usually left a pot of chowder hanging over a low fire during the dogwatches.

Darrick helped himself to the chowder, catching the young kitchen apprentice half dozing at the long table where the crew supped in shifts. Darrick filled a tin plate with the thick chowder. The young kitchen apprentice fidgeted, then got to wiping the table as if he'd been doing that all along.

Without speaking, ignoring the young man's embarrassment

and concern that his laxness at his duties might be reported, Darrick carved a thick hunk of black bread from one of the loaves Cook had prepared, then poured himself a mug of green tea. Tea in one hand, thick hunk of bread soaking in the chowder in the tin plate, Darrick headed back up to the deck.

He stood amidships, listening to the rustle and crackle of the canvas overhead. With the knowledge they carried and the fact that they were in clear waters, Captain Tollifer had kept the sails up, taking advantage of the favorable winds. *Lonesome Star* sloshed through the moon-kissed rollers that covered the ocean's surface. Occasional light flickers passed by in the water that weren't just reflections of the ship's lanterns posted as running lights.

Standing on the heaving deck on practiced legs, Darrick ate, managing the teacup and the tin plate in one hand— plate on the cup—and eating with his other hand. He let the black bread marinate in the chowder to soften it up, otherwise he'd have had to chew it for what seemed like forever to break it down. The chowder was made from shrimp and fish stock, mixed with spices from the eastern lands, and had thick chunks of potatoes. It was almost hot enough to burn the tongue even after being dipped on bread and cooled by the night winds.

Darrick didn't let himself think of the nights he and Mat had shared dogwatches together, with Mat telling wildly improbable stories he'd either heard somewhere or made up then and there and swore it was gospel. It had all been fun to Mat, something to keep them awake during the long, dead hours and to keep Darrick from ever thinking back to the things that had happened in Hillsfar.

"I'm sorry about your friend," a quiet voice said.

Distanced as he was from his emotions, Darrick wasn't even surprised to recognize Lhex's voice behind him. He kept gazing out to sea, chewing on the latest lump of black bread and chowder he'd put into his mouth.

"I said—" the boy began again in a slightly louder voice.

"I heard you," Darrick interrupted.

An uncomfortable silence stretched between them. Darrick never once turned to face the boy.

"I wanted to talk to you about the demon," Lhex said.

"No," Darrick replied.

"I am the king's nephew." The boy's tone hardened somewhat.

"And yet you are not the king, are you?"

"I understand how you're feeling."

"Good. Then you'll understand if I trouble you for my own peace while I'm standing watch."

The boy was silent for a long enough time that Darrick had thought he'd gone away. Darrick thought there might have been some trouble with the captain in the morning over his rudeness, but he didn't care.

"What are those lighted patches in the water?" Lhex asked. Irritated and not even wanting to feel that because long years of experience had shown him that even the smallest emotion could snowball into the feelings of entrapment that put him out of control, Darrick turned to the boy. "What the hell are you still doing up, boy?"

"I couldn't sleep." The boy stood on the deck in bare feet and a sleeping gown he must have borrowed from the captain.

"Then go find a new way of amusing yourself. I'll not have it done at my expense."

Lhex wrapped his arms around himself, obviously chilled in the cool night air. "I can't. You're the only one who saw the demon."

The only one alive, Darrick thought, but he stopped himself before he could think too far. "There were other men in that cavern."

"None of them stayed long enough to see the things you saw."

"You don't know things I saw."

"I was there when you talked with the captain. Everything you know is important."

"And what matter would it be of yours?" Darrick demanded.

"I've been priest-trained for the Zakarum Church and guided my whole life by the Light. In two more years, I'll test for becoming a full priest."

"You're no more than a boy now," Darrick chided, "and you'll be little more than a boy then. You should spend your time worrying about boy things."

"No," Lhex said. "Fighting demons is to be my calling, Darrick Lang. Don't you have a calling?"

"I work to keep a meal between my belly and my spine," Darrick said, "to stay alive, and to sleep in warm places."

"Yet you're an officer, and you've come up through the ranks, which is both an admirable and a hard thing to do. A man without a calling, without passion, could not have done something like that."

Darrick grimaced. Evidently Lhex's identity as the king's nephew had drawn considerable depth in Captain Tollifer's eyes.

"I'm going to be a good priest," the boy declared. "And to fight demons, I know I have to learn about demons."

"None of this has anything to do with me," Darrick said. "Once Captain Tollifer hands my report to the king, my part in this is finished."

Lhex eyed him boldly. "Is it?"

"Aye, it is."

"You didn't strike me as the kind of man who'd let a friend's death go unavenged."

"And who, then, am I supposed to blame for Mat's death?" Darrick demanded.

"Your friend died by Kabraxis's hand," Lhex said.

"But not till you made us go there after I told you all I wanted to do was leave," Darrick said in a harsh voice. "Not till I waited too long to get out of that cavern, then couldn't outrun the skeletons that pursued us." He shook his head. "No. If anybody's to blame for Mat's death, it's you and me."

A serious look filled the boy's face. "If you want to blame me, Darrick Lang, then feel free to blame me."

Vulnerable, feeling his emotions shudder and almost slip from his control, Darrick looked at the boy, amazed at the way he could stand up to him in the dark night. "I do blame you," Darrick told him.

Lhex looked away.

"If you choose to fight demons," Darrick went on, giving in to the cruelty that ran within him, "you'll have a short life. At least you won't need a lot of planning."

"The demons must be fought," the boy whispered.

"Not by the likes of me," Darrick said. "A king with an army, or several kings with armies, that's what it would take. Not a sailor."

"You lived after seeing the demon," Lhex said. "There must be a reason for that."

"I was lucky," Darrick said. "Most men meeting demons don't have such luck."

"Warriors and priests fight demons," Lhex said. "The legends tell us that without those heroes, Diablo and his brothers would still be able to walk through this world."

"You were there when I gave Captain Tollifer my report," Darrick said. The boy hadn't shown any reluctance to throw his weight around with the captain, either, and Tollifer had reluctantly allowed him to sit in during the debriefing the morning before. "You know everything I know."

"There are seers who could examine you. Sometimes when great magic is worked around an individual, traces of it remain within that individual."

"I'll not be poked and prodded," Darrick argued. He pointed to the patches of light gliding through the sea. "You asked what those were."

Lhex turned his attention to the ocean, but his expression revealed that he'd rather be following his own tack in the conversation.

"Some of those," Darrick said, "are fire-tail sharks, named so because they glow in such a manner. The light attracts nocturnal feeders and brings them within striking distance of the sharks. Other light patches are Rose of

Moon jellyfish that can paralyze a man unlucky enough to swim into reach of their barbed tentacles. If you want to learn about the sea, there's much I can teach you. But if you want to talk about demons, I'll have no more of it. I've learned more than I ever care to know about them."

The wind changed directions slightly, causing the great canvas sheets overhead to luff a little, then to snap full again as the crew managed the change.

Darrick tasted his chowder but found it had grown cold.

"Kabraxis is responsible for your friend's death," Lhex said quietly. "You're not going to be able to forget that. You're still part of this. I have seen the signs."

Darrick pushed his breath out, feeling trapped and scared and angry at the same time. He felt exactly the way he had when he had been in his father's shop when his father had chosen to be displeased with him again. Working hard to distance himself, he waited until he had control back, then whirled to face the boy, intending—even if he was the king's nephew—to vent some of his anger.

But when Darrick turned, the deck behind him was empty. In the moonlight, the deck looked silver white, striped by the shadows of the masts and rigging. Frustrated, Darrick turned back and flung his plate and teacup over the ship's side.

A Rose of Moon jellyfish caught the tin plate in its tentacles. Lightning flickered against the metal as the barbs tried to bite into it.

Crossing to the starboard railing, Darrick leaned on it heavily. In his mind's eye, he saw the skeleton dive at Mat, sweeping him from the cliff's edge, then witnessed again the bone-breaking thump against the wall of stone. A cold sweat covered Darrick's body as memory of those days in his father's shop stole over him. He would not go back there—not physically, and not in his mind.

Twelve

Darrick sat at a back table in Cross-Eyed Sal's, a tavern only a couple of blocks back from Dock Street and the Mercantile Quarter. The tavern was a dive, one of the places surly sailors of meager means or ill luck ended up before they signed ship's articles and went back to sea. It was a place where the lanterns were kept dim of an evening so the wenches there looked better if they weren't seen as well, and the food couldn't be inspected closely.

Money came into Westmarch through the piers, in the fat purses of merchants buying goods and selling goods, and in the modest coin pouches of sailors and longshore-men. The money spilled over to the shops scattered along the docks and piers first, and most of it stopped there. Little of it slopped over into the businesses crowded in back of the shops and tradesmen's workplaces and the finer inns and even not-so-fine inns.

Cross-Eyed Sal's featured a sun-faded sign out front that showed a buxom red-haired woman served up on a steaming oyster shell with only her tresses maintaining her modesty. The tavern was located in part of the decaying layer that occupied the stretch of older buildings that had been built higher up on the hillside fronting the harbor. Over the years as Westmarch and the harbor had existed and grown, nearly all of the buildings nestled down by the sea had been torn down and rebuilt.

Only a few older buildings remained as landmarks that had been shored up by expert artisans. But behind those businesses that seined up most of the gold lay the insular layer of merchants and tavern owners who barely made their monthly bills and the king's taxes so they could stay open. The only thing that kept them going was the desperate times endured by out-of-work sailors and longshoremen.

Cross-Eyed Sal's had a rare crowd and was filled near to capacity. The sailors remained separate from the longshoremen because of the long-standing feud between the two groups. Sailors looked down on longshoremen for not having the guts to go to sea, and longshoremen looked down on sailors for not being a true part of the community. Both groups, however, stayed well away from the mercenaries who had shown up in the last few days.

Lonesome Star had returned to Westmarch nine days ago and still awaited new orders. Darrick drank alone at the table. During his leave from the ship, he'd remained solitary. Most of the men aboard *Lonesome Star* had hung around him because of Mat. Blessed with his good humor and countless stories, Mat had never lacked for company, friendship, or a full mug of ale at any gathering.

None of the crew had made an attempt to spend much time with Darrick. Besides the captain's frowning disapproval of an officer's fraternization with crew, Darrick had never proven himself to be good company all the time. And with Mat dead now, Darrick wanted no company at all.

During the past nine days, Darrick had slept aboard the ship rather than in the arms of any of the many willing women, and he'd marked time in one dive after another much like Cross-Eyed Sal's. Normally, Mat would have dragged Darrick into any number of festive inns or gotten them invitations to events hosted by the lesser politicos in Westmarch. Somehow, Mat had managed to meet several wives and courtesans of those men while investigating Westmarch's museums, art galleries, and churches—interests that Darrick had not shared. Darrick had even found the parties annoying.

Darrick found the bottom of his mulled wine again and looked around for the tavern wench who had been serving him. She stood three tables away, in the crook of a big mercenary's arm. Her laughter seemed obscene to Darrick, and his anger rose before he could throttle it.

"Girl," he called impatiently, thumping the tin tankard against the scarred tabletop.

The wench extricated herself from the mercenary's grasp, giggling and pushing against him in a manner meant to free herself and be seductive at the same time. She made her way across the packed room and took Darrick's tankard.

The group of mercenaries scowled at Darrick and talked among themselves in low voices.

Darrick ignored them and leaned back against the wall behind him. He'd been in bars like this before countless times, and he'd seen hundreds of men like the mercenaries. Normally he was among ship's crew, for it was Captain Tollifer's standing order that no crewman drink alone. But since they'd been in port this time, Darrick had only drunk alone, making his way back to the ship each morning before daybreak any time he didn't have an early watch.

The wench brought back Darrick's filled tankard. He paid her, adding a modest tip that drew no favoring glance. Normally Mat would have parted generously with his money, endearing himself to the serving wenches. Tonight, Darrick didn't care. All he wanted was a full tankard till he took his leave.

He returned his attention to the cold food on the wooden serving platter before him. The meal consisted of stringy meat and scorched potatoes, covered with flecks of thin gravy that looked no more appetizing than hound saliva. The tavern could get away with such weak fare because the city was burgeoning with mercenaries feeding at the king's coffers. Darrick took a bit of meat and chewed it, watching as the big mercenary got up from his table, flanked by two of his friends.

Under the table, Darrick pulled his cutlass across his lap. He'd made a practice of eating with his left hand, leaving his right hand free.

"Hey there, swabbie," the big mercenary growled, pulling out the chair across the table from Darrick and seating himself uninvited. The way he pronounced the term let Darrick know the man had meant the address as an insult.

Although the longshoremen rode the sailors about being visitors to the city and not truly of it, the mercenaries were even less so. Mercenaries touted themselves as brave warriors, men used to fighting, and when any sailor made the same claim, the mercenaries tried to downplay the bravery of the sailors.

Darrick waited, knowing the encounter wasn't going to end well and actually welcoming it all the same. He didn't know if there was a single man in the room who would stand with him, and he didn't care.

"You shouldn't go interrupting a young girl what's going about her business the way that young wench was," the mercenary said. He was young and blond, broad-faced and gap-toothed, a man who had gotten by on sheer size a lot of the time. The scars on his face and arms spoke up for a past history of violence as well. He wore cheap leather armor and carried a short sword with a wire-wrapped hilt at his side.

The other two mercenaries were about the same age, though they showed less experience. Darrick guessed that they were following their companion. Both of them looked a little uneasy about the confrontation.

Darrick sipped from the tankard. A warm glow filled his belly, and he knew only part of it was from the wine. "This is my table," he said, "and I'm not inviting company."

"You looked lonely," the big man said.

"Have your eyesight checked," Darrick suggested.

The big man scowled. "You're not an overly friendly sort."

"No," Darrick agreed. "Now, you've got the right of that."

The big man leaned forward, thumping his massive elbows on the table and resting his square shelf of a chin over his interlaced fingers. "I don't like you."

Darrick gripped his cutlass beneath the tabletop and leaned back, letting the wall behind him brace his shoulders. The flickering candle flame on a nearby table drew hollows on the big man's face.

"Syrnon," one of the other men said, pulling at his friend's sleeve. "This man has officer's braid on his collar."

Syrnon's big blue eyes narrowed as he glanced at Darrick's neckline. An oak leaf cluster was pinned to Darrick's collar, two garnets denoting his rank. Putting it on had gotten to be such a habit he'd forgotten about it.

"You an officer on one of the king's ships?" Syrnon asked.

"Aye," Darrick taunted. "You going to let fear of the king's reprisal for attacking a ship's officer in his navy cow you?"

"Syrnon," the other man said. "We'd be better off taking our leave of this man."

Maybe the man would have left then. He wasn't too drunk to forget about listening to reason, and Westmarch dungeons weren't rumored to be hospitable.

"Go," Darrick said softly, giving in to the black mood that filled him, "and don't forget to tuck your tail between your legs as you do." In the past, Mat had always sensed when Darrick's black moods had settled on him, and Mat had always found a way to cajole him out of the mood or get them into areas where that self-destructive bent wouldn't completely manifest itself.

But Mat wasn't there tonight, and hadn't been around for nine long days.

Howling with rage, Syrnon stood and reached across the table, intending to grab Darrick's shirt. Darrick leaned forward and head-butted the big mercenary in the face, breaking his nose. Blood gushed from Syrnon's nostrils as he stumbled back.

The other two mercenaries tried to stand.

Darrick swung his cutlass, catching one of the men alongside the temple with the flat of the blade and knocking him out. Before the unconscious man had time to drop,

Darrick swung on the other man. The mercenary fumbled for the sword sheathed at his waist. Before his opponent could get his weapon clear, Darrick kicked him in the chest, driving the mercenary from his feet and back onto a nearby table. The mercenary took the whole table down with him, and four angry warriors rose to their feet, cursing the man who had landed upon the table, and they cursed Darrick as well.

Syrnon pulled his short sword and drew it back, causing nearby men to duck and dodge way. Curses and harsh oaths followed his movement.

Vaulting to the table, Darrick leapt over Syrnon's sword blow, flipped forward—feeling his senses spin for a moment from all he'd had to drink—and landed on his feet behind the big mercenary. Syrnon spun, his face a mask of crimson from his broken nose, and spat blood as he cursed Darrick. The big mercenary swung his short sword at Darrick's head.

Darrick parried the man's attack with the cutlass. Steel rang against steel inside the tavern. Holding the man's blade trapped, Darrick balled his left fist and slammed it into Syrnon's head. Flesh split along the mercenary's cheek. Darrick hit his opponent twice more and felt immense satisfaction with his efforts. Syrnon was bigger than him, as much bigger as his father had been in the back of the butcher's shop. Only Darrick was no longer a frightened boy too small and too unskilled to defend himself. He hit Syrnon one more time, driving the big man backward.

Syrnon's face showed abuse. His right eye promising to swell shut, a split lip and a split ear joined the split over his cheekbone.

Darrick's hand throbbed from the impacts, but he barely took notice of it. The darkness within him was loose now, in a way he'd never seen it. The emotion rattled inside him, growing stronger. Syrnon flailed out unexpectedly, catching Darrick in the face with a hard-knuckled hand. Darrick's head popped backward, and his senses reeled for a moment as the coppery taste of blood filled his mouth and the sour stench of straw filled his nose.

Nobody thinks you look like me, boy! The voice of Orvan Lang crescendoed through Darrick's head. *Why is it, do you think, that a boy don't look like his father? Everybody's tongue's wagging. And me, I love your mother, damn me for a fool.*

Parrying the mercenary's desperate attack again, Darrick stepped forward once more. His sword skill was known throughout the Westmarch Navy by any who had faced him or stood at his side when he'd fought pirates or smugglers.

For a time after he and Mat had arrived in Westmarch from Hillsfar, Darrick had trained with a fencing master, exchanging work and willingness for training. For six years, Darrick had repaired and sanded the fencing room floor and walls and chopped wood, and in turn began the training of others while pursuing a career in the Westmarch Navy.

That training had kept Darrick balanced for a time, until Master Coro's death in a duel with a duke over a woman's honor. Darrick had tracked the two assassins down, as well as the duke, and killed them all. He'd also gotten the attention of the commodore of the Westmarch Navy, who had known about the duel and the assassination. Master Coro also trained several of the ship's officers and practiced with captains. As a result, Darrick and Mat had been assigned berths on their first ship.

After Master Coro was no longer around, the tightfisted control aboard the navy ship had granted Darrick a kind of peace, providing a structured environment. Mat had helped.

Now, with this battle at hand, Darrick felt right. Losing Mat and then waiting for days to be given some kind of meaningful assignment had grated on his nerves. *Lonesome Star*, once a home and a haven, was now a reminder that Mat was gone. Guilt mortared every plank aboard the ship, and Darrick longed for action of any kind.

Darrick played with the mercenary, and the darkness stirred inside his soul. Several times during the years that had passed since he'd escaped Hillsfar, he had thought about going back and seeing his father—especially when Mat had returned to visit his family. Darrick felt no pull toward his mother; she had allowed the beatings his father had given him to go on because she had her own life to live, and being married to one of the town's successful butchers had accommodated her lifestyle.

Darrick had chosen to keep the darkness inside him walled up and put away.

There was no stopping it now, though. Darrick beat back the big mercenary's defenses, chasing the man steadily backward. Syrnon called out for help, but even the other mercenaries appeared loath to step into the fray.

A whistle shrilled in warning.

Part of Darrick knew the whistle signaled the arrival of the king's Peacekeepers. All of the Peacekeepers were tough men and women dedicated to keeping the king's peace inside the city walls.

The mercenaries and few sailors inside the tavern gave way at once. Anyone who didn't recognize a Peace-keeper's authority spent a night in the dungeon.

Caught up in the black emotions that had taken hold of him, Darrick didn't hesitate. He kept advancing, beating the big mercenary back till there was nowhere to run. With a final riposte, Darrick stripped the man of his weapon, knocking it away with a practiced twist of his wrist.

The mercenary flattened against the wall, standing on his toes, with Darrick's cutlass at his throat. "Please," he whispered in a dry croak.

Darrick held the man there. There didn't seem to be enough air in the room. He heard the whistle blasts behind him, one of them closing in.

"Put the sword away," a woman's calm voice ordered him. "Put it away now."

Darrick turned, bringing his cutlass around, intending to back the woman off. But when he attempted to parry the staff she held, she reversed the weapon and thumped it into his chest.

A wild electrical surge rushed through Darrick, and he fell.

Morning sunlight streamed through the bars of the small window above the bunk chained to a stone wall. Darrick blinked his eyes open and stared at the sunlight. He hadn't been taken to the dungeon proper. He was grateful for that, though much surprised.

Feeling as though his head were going to explode, Darrick sat up. The bunk creaked beneath him and pulled at the two chains on the wall. He rested his feet on the floor and gazed out through the bars that made up the fourth wall of the small holding cell that was an eight-foot by eight-foot by eight-foot box. Sour straw filled the thin mattress that almost covered the bunk. The material covering the mattress showed stains where past guests had relieved themselves and thrown up on it.

Darrick's stomach whirled and revolted, threatening to empty. He lurched toward the slop bucket in the forward corner of the holding cell. Sickness coiled through him, venting itself in violent heaves, leaving him barely enough strength to hang on to the bars.

A man's barking laughter ignited in the shadows that filled the building.

Resting on his haunches, not certain if the sickness was completely purged, Darrick glared across the space between his cell and the one on the other side.

A shaggy-haired man dressed in warrior's leathers sat cross-legged on the bunk inside that cell. Brass armbands marked him for an out-of-town mercenary, as did the tribal tattoos on his face and arms.

"So how are you feeling this morning?" the man asked.

Darrick ignored him.

The man stood up from the bunk and crossed to the bars of his own cell. Gripping the bars, he said, "What is it about you, sailor, that's got everybody in here in such an uproar?"

Lowering his head back to the foul-smelling bucket, Darrick let go again.

"They brought you in here last night," the shaggy-haired warrior continued, "and you was fighting them all. A madman, some thought. And one of the Peacekeepers gave you another taste of the shock staff she carried."

A shock staff, Darrick thought, realizing why his head hurt so much and his muscles all felt tight. He felt as if he'd been keelhauled and heaved up against the barnacle-covered hull. Several of the Peacekeepers carried mystically charged gems mounted in staffs that provided debilitating jolts to incapacitate prisoners.

"One of the guards suggested they cave your head in and be done with it," the warrior said. "But another guard said you was some kind of hero. That you'd seen the demon everybody in Westmarch is so afraid of these days."

Darrick clung to the bars and took shallow breaths.

"Is that true?" the warrior asked. "Because all I saw last night was a drunk."

The ratchet of a heavy key turning in a latch filled the holding area, drawing curses from men and women held in other cells. A door creaked open.

Darrick leaned back against the wall to one side of the bars so he could peer out into the narrow aisle.

A jailer clad in a Peacekeeper's uniform with sergeant's stripes appeared first. Dressed in his long cloak, Captain Tollifer followed him.

Despite the sickness raging in his belly, Darrick rose to his feet as years of training took over. He saluted, hoping his stomach wouldn't choose that moment to purge again.

"Captain," Darrick croaked.

The jailer, a square-built man with lamb-chop whiskers and a balding head, turned to Darrick. "Ah, here he is, captain. I knew we were close."

Captain Tollifer eyed Darrick with steel in his gaze. "Mr. Lang, this is disappointing."

"Aye, sir," Darrick responded. "I feel badly about this, sir."

"As well you should," Captain Tollifer said. "And you'll

feel even worse for the next few days. I should not ever have to get an officer from my ship from a situation such as this."

"No, sir," Darrick agreed, though in truth he was surprised to learn that he really cared little at all.

"I don't know what's put you in such dire straits as you find yourself now," the captain went on, "though I know Mr. Hu-Ring's death plays a large part in your present predicament."

"Begging the captain's pardon," Darrick said, "but Mat's death has nothing to do with this." He would not bear that.

"Then perhaps, Mr. Lang," the captain continued in frosty tones, "you can present some other excuse for the sorry condition I currently find you in."

Darrick stood on trembling knees facing the ship's captain. "No, sir."

"Then let's allow me to stumble through this gross aberration in what I've come to expect from you on my own," Captain Tollifer said.

"Aye, sir." Unable to hold himself back anymore, Darrick turned and threw up into the bucket.

"And know this, Mr. Lang," the captain said. "I'll not suffer such behavior on a regular basis."

"No, sir," Darrick said, so weak now he couldn't get up from his knees.

"Very well, jailer," the captain said. "I'll have him out of there now."

Darrick threw up again.

"Maybe in a few more minutes," the jailer suggested. "I've got a pot of tea on up front if you'll join me. Give the young man another few minutes to himself; maybe he'll be more hospitable company."

Embarrassed but with anger eating away at his control, Darrick listened to the two men walking away. Mat would have at least joined him in the cell, laughing it up at his expense but not deserting him.

Darrick threw up again and saw the skeleton take Mat from the harbor cliff one more time. Only this time as they fell, Darrick could see the demon standing over them, laughing as they headed for the dark river below.

"You can't take him yet," the healer protested. "I've got at least three more stitches needed to piece this wound over his eye together."

Darrick sat stoically on the small stool in the healer's surgery and stared with his good eye at Maldrin standing in the narrow, shadow-lined doorway. Other men passed by outside, all of them wounded, ill, or diseased. Somewhere down the hallway, a woman screamed in labor, swearing that she was birthing a demon.

The first mate didn't look happy. He met Darrick's gaze for just a moment, then looked away.

Darrick thought maybe Maldrin was just angry, but he believed there was some embarrassment there as well. This wasn't the first time of late that Maldrin had been forced to come searching for him.

Darrick glanced at the healer's surgery, seeing the shelves filled with bottles of potions and powders; jars of leaves, dried berries, and bark; and bags that contained rocks and stones with curative properties.

The healer was located off Dock Street and was an older man whom many sailors and longshoremen used for injuries. The strong odors of all the salves and medicants the thin man used on the people he gave care to filled the air.

Fixing another piece of thin catgut on the curved needle he held, the healer leaned in and pierced the flesh over Darrick's right eye. Darrick never moved, never even flinched or closed his eye.

"Are you sure you wouldn't like something for the pain?" the healer asked.

"I'm sure." Darrick stepped away from the pain, placing it in the same part of his mind that he'd built all those years ago to handle the hell his father had put him through. That special place in his mind could hold a whole lot more than the discomfort the healer handed out. Darrick looked up at Maldrin. "Does the captain know?"

Maldrin sighed. "That ye got into another fight an' tore up yet another tavern? Aye, he knows, skipper. Caron is over there now, seein' about the damages an' such ye'll owe. Seein' as how much damage ye been payin' for lately, I don't know how ye've had the wherewithal to drink."

"I didn't start this fight," Darrick said, but the protest was dulled by weeks of using it.

"So says ye," Maldrin agreed. "But the captain, he's heard from near to a dozen other men that ye wouldn't walk away when the chance presented itself."

Darrick's voice hardened. "I don't walk away, Maldrin. And I damn sure don't run from trouble."

"Ye should."

"Have you ever known me to retreat from a fight?" Darrick knew he was trying to put everything he'd done that night into some kind of perspective for himself. His struggles to find something right about the violence that he constantly got himself into during shore leave had only escalated.

"A fight," Maldrin said, folding his big arms over his broad, thick chest. "No. I've never seen ye back down from action we took together. But ye got to learn when to cut yer losses. The things them men say in them places ye hang out, why, that ain't nothin' to be a-fightin' over. Ye know as well as I that a sailin' man picks his battles. But ye—by the blessed Light, skipper—ye're just fightin' to be fightin'."

Darrick closed his good eye. The other was swollen shut and filled with blood. The sailor he'd fought in Gargan's Greased Eel had fought with an enchanted weapon and snapped into action quicker than Darrick had thought.

"How many fights have ye had in the last two months, skipper?" Maldrin asked in a softer voice.

Darrick hesitated. "I don't know."

"Seventeen," Maldrin said. "Seventeen fights. All of 'em partly instigated by yer own self."

Darrick felt the newest suture pull as the healer tied it.

"The Light must be favorin' ye is all that I can tell,"

Maldrin said, "for they ain't nobody what's been killed yet. An' ye're still alive to tell of it yer own self."

"I've been careful," Darrick said, and regretted trying to make an excuse at once.

"A man bein' careful, skipper," Maldrin said, "why, he'd never get in them fixes ye been into. Hell's bells, most of the trouble ye're in, a man what's got a thought in his damned head would think maybe he should ought not be in them places."

Darrick silently agreed. But the portent of trouble in those places had been exactly what had drawn him there. He wasn't thinking when he was fighting, and he wasn't in danger of thinking on things too long or too often when he was drinking and waiting for someone to pick a fight with.

The healer prepared another stitch.

"What about the captain?" Darrick asked.

"Skipper," Maldrin said in a quiet voice, "Cap'n Tollifer appreciates everythin' ye done. An' he ain't about to forget it. But he's a prideful man, too, an' him havin' to deal with one of his own always fightin' while in port during these edgy times, why, it ain't settin' well with him at all. An' ye damn sure don't need me tellin' ye this."

Darrick agreed.

The healer started in with the needle again.

"Ye need help, skipper," Maldrin said. "Cap'n knows it. I know it. Crew knows it. Ye're the only one what seems convinced ye don't."

Taking a towel from his knee, the healer blotted blood from Darrick's eye, poured fresh salt water over the wound, and started putting in the final stitch.

"Ye ain't the only man what's lost a friend," Maldrin croaked.

"I didn't say I was."

"An' me," Maldrin went on as if he hadn't heard Darrick, "I'm near to losin' two. I don't want to see you leave *Lonesome Star*, skipper. Not if'n there's a way I can help."

"I'm not worth losing any sleep over, Maldrin," Darrick said in a flat voice. The thing that scared him most was that he felt that way, but he knew it was only his father's words. They were never far from his mind. He'd found he could escape his father's fists, but he'd never been able to escape the man's harsh words. Only Mat had made him feel differently. None of the other friendships he'd made helped, nor did remembering any of the women he'd been with over the years. Not even Maldrin could reach him.

But he knew why. Everything Darrick touched would eventually turn to dung. His father had told him that, and it was turning out true. He'd lost Mat, and now he was losing *Lonesome Star* and his career in the Westmarch Navy.

"Mayhap ye ain't," Maldrin said. "Mayhap ye ain't."

Darrick ran, heart pounding so hard that the infection in his week-old eye wound thundered painfully. His breath came in short gasps as he held his cutlass at his side and dashed through the alleys around the Mercantile Quarter. Reaching Dock Street, he turned his stride toward Fleet Street, the thoroughfare that went through the Military District where the Westmarch Navy harbor was.

He saw the navy frigates in the distance, tall masts thrust up into the low-lying fog that hugged the gulf coastline. A few ships sailed out over the curve of the world, following a favorable breeze away from Westmarch.

So far, Raithen's pirates had presented no real threat to the city and may even have disbanded, but other pirates had gathered, preying on the busy shipping lanes as Westmarch brought in more and more goods to support the navy, army, and mercenaries. With almost two and a half months gone and no sighting of Kabraxis, the king was beginning to doubt the reports *Lonesome Star* had brought back. Even now, the main problems in Westmarch had become the restlessness of the mercenaries at not having a goal or any real action to occupy them and the dwindling food stores that the city had not yet been able to replace since the action against Tristram.

Darrick cursed the fog that covered the city in steel gray.

He'd woken in an alley, not knowing if he'd gone to sleep there or if he'd been thrown there from one of the nearby taverns. He hadn't awakened until after cock's crow, and *Lonesome Star* was due to sail that morning.

He damned himself for a fool, knowing he should have stayed aboard ship. But he hadn't been able to. No one aboard, including the captain and Maldrin, talked with him anymore. He had become an embarrassment, something his father had always told him he was.

Out of breath, he made the final turn toward Spinnaker Bridge, one of the last checkpoints where nonnaval personnel were turned back from entering the Military District. He fumbled inside his stained blouse for his papers.

Four guards stepped up to block his way. They were hard-faced men with weapons that showed obvious care. One of them held up a hand.

Darrick stopped, breathing hard, his injured eye throbbing painfully. "Ship's Officer Second Grade Lang," he gasped.

The leader of the guards looked at Darrick doubtfully but took the papers Darrick offered. He scanned them, noting the captain's seal embossed upon the pages.

"Says here you sail with *Lonesome Star*," the guard said, offering the papers back.

"Aye," Darrick said, raking the sea with his good eye. He didn't recognize any of the ships sailing out into the gulf as his. Maybe he was in luck.

"*Lonesome Star* sailed hours ago," the guardsman said.

Darrick's heart plummeted through his knees. "No," he whispered.

"By rights with you missing your ship like you have," the guardsman said, "I ought to run you in and let the commodore deal with you. But from the looks of you, I'd say getting beaten up and robbed will stand as a good excuse. I'll make an entry of it in my log. Should stand you in good stead if you're called before a naval inquest."

You'd be doing me no favors, Darrick thought. Any man caught missing from his ship for no good reason was hung for dereliction of duty. He turned and gazed out to sea, watching the gulls hunting through the water for scraps carried out by the tide. The cries of the birds sounded mournful and hollow, filtering over the crash of the surf against the shore.

If Captain Tollifer had sailed without him, Darrick knew there no longer remained a berth for him aboard *Lonesome Star.* His career in the Westmarch Navy was over, and he had no idea what lay ahead of him.

He wanted nothing more than to die, but he couldn't do that—he wouldn't do that—because it would mean that his father would win even after all these years. He walled himself off from his pain and loss, and he turned away from the sea, following the street back into Westmarch. He had no money. The possibility of missing meals didn't bother him, but he knew he'd want to drink again that night. By the Light, he wanted to drink right now.

Thirteen

"Master."

Buyard Cholik looked up from the comfortable sofa that took up one long wall of the coach he traveled in. Drawn by six horses on three axles, the coach had all the amenities of home. Built-in shelves held his priestly supplies, clothing, and personal belongings. Lamps screwed into the walls and fluted for smoke discharge through the sides of the coach provided light to read by. Since leaving the ruins of Tauruk's Port and Ransim almost three months ago, almost all of his time had been spent reading the arcane texts Kabraxis had provided him and practicing the sorcery the demon had been teaching him.

"What is it?" Cholik asked.

The man speaking stood outside on the platform attached to the bottom of the coach. Cholik made no move to open one of the shuttered windows so that he might see the man. Since Kabraxis had changed him, altering his mind and his body—in addition to removing decades from his age—Cholik felt close to none of the men who had survived the demon's arrival and the attack of Raithen's pirates. Several of them were new, gathered from the small towns the caravan had passed through on its way to its eventual destination.

"We are approaching Bramwell, master," the man said. "I thought you might want to know."

"Yes," Cholik replied. He could tell by the level ride of the coach that the long, winding, uphill trek they'd been making for hours had passed.

Cholik marked his place in the book he'd been reading with a thin braid of human tongues that had turned leathery over the years. Sometimes, with the proper spell in place, the tongues read aloud from profane passages. The book was writ in blood upon paper made from human skin and bound in children's teeth. Most of the other books Kabraxis had provided over the past months were crafted in things that Cholik in his past life as a priest of the Zakarum Church would have believed to be even more horrendous.

The bookmarker made of tongues whispered a sibilant protest at being put away, inciting a small amount of guilt in Cholik as he felt certain Kabraxis had spelled them to do. Nearly all of his days were spent reading, yet it never seemed enough.

Moving with the grace of a man barely entering his middle years, Cholik opened the coach's door, stepped out onto the platform, then climbed the small hand-carved ladder that led up to the coach's peaked, thatched roof. A small ledge was rather like a widow's walk on some of the more affluent houses in Westmarch where merchanter captains' wives walked to see if their husbands arrived safely back from sea.

The coach had been one of the first things Cholik had purchased with the gold and jewels he and his converted priests had carted out of the caverns with Kabraxis's blessing. In its past life, the coach had belonged to a merchant prince who specialized in overland trading. Only two days before Cholik had bought the coach, the merchant prince had suffered debilitating losses and a mysterious illness that had killed him in a matter of hours. Faced with certain bankruptcy, the executor of the prince's goods had sold the coach to Cholik's emissaries.

Standing on the small widow's walk, aware of the immense forest around him, Cholik looked over the half-dozen wagons that preceded the coach. Another half-dozen wagons, all loaded down with the things that Kabraxis had ordered salvaged from Tauruk's Port, trailed behind Cholik's coach.

A winding road cut through the heart of the forest. Cholik couldn't remember the forest's name at the moment, but he had never seen it before. His travels from Westmarch had always been by ship, and he'd never been to Bramwell as young as he now was.

At the end of the winding road lay the city of Bramwell, a suburb north-northwest of Westmarch. Centuries ago, situated among the highlands as it was, the city had occupied a position of prominence that competed with Westmarch. Bramwell had been far enough away from Westmarch that its economy was its own. Farmers and fishermen lived in the tiny city, descendants of families that had lived there for generations, sailing the same ships and plowing the same lands as their ancestors had. In the old days, Bramwell's sailors had hunted whales and sold the oil. Now, the whaling fleets had become a handful of diehard families who stubbornly got by in a hardscrabble existence more with pride and a deep reluctance to change than out of necessity.

Almost ancient, Bramwell was constructed of buildings two and three stories tall from stones cut and carried down from the mountains. Peaked roofs crafted with thatching dyed a dozen different shades of green mimicked the forest surrounding the city on three sides. The fourth side fronted the Gulf of Westmarch, where a breakwater had been built of rock dug from the mountains to protect the harbor from the harsh seasons of the sea.

From atop the coach and atop the mountains, Cholik surveyed the city that would be his home during the first of Kabraxis's conquests. An empire, Cholik told himself as he gazed out onto the unsuspecting city, would begin there. He rode on the platform, rocking back and forth as the heavy-duty springs of the coach compensated for the road's failings, watching as the city drew closer.

Hours later, Cholik stood beside the Sweetwater River that fed Bramwell. The river ran deep and true between broad, stone-covered banks. The waterway also provided more harbor space for smaller craft that plied the city's trade farther inland and graced the lands with a plenitude of wells and irrigation for the farms that made checker-boards outside the city proper.

At the eastern end of the city where the loggers and craftsmen gathered and where shops and markets had sprung up years ago, Cholik halted the caravan in the campgrounds that were open to all who hoped to trade with the Bramwell population.

Children had gathered around the coach and the wagons immediately, hoping for a traveling minstrel show. Cholik didn't disappoint them, offering the troupe of entertainers he'd hired as the caravan had journeyed north from Tauruk's Port. They'd taken the overland route, a long and arduous event compared with travel by sea, but they had avoided the Westmarch Navy as well. Cholik doubted that anyone who had once known him would recognize him since his youth had been returned, but he hadn't wanted to take the chance, and Kabraxis had been patient.

The entertainers gamboled and clowned, performing physical feats that seemed astounding and combining witty poems and snippets of exchanges that had the gathering audience roaring with laughter. The juggling and acrobatics, while pipes and drums played in the background, drew amazed comments from the families.

Cholik stood inside the coach and watched through a covered window. The festive atmosphere didn't fit with how he'd been trained to think of religious practices. New converts to the Zakarum Church weren't entertained and wooed in such a manner, although some of the smaller churches did.

"Still disapproving, are you?" a deep voice asked.

Recognizing Kabraxis's voice, Cholik stood and turned. He knew the demon hadn't entered the coach in the conventional means, but he didn't know from where Kabraxis had traveled before stepping into the coach.

"Old habits are hard to break," Cholik said.

"Like changing your religious beliefs?" Kabraxis asked.

"No."

Kabraxis stood before Cholik wearing a dead man's

body. Upon his decision to go among the humans and look for a city to establish as a beachhead to begin their campaign, Kabraxis had killed a merchant, sacrificing the man's soul to unforgiving darkness. Once the mortal remains of the man were nothing more than an empty shell, Kabraxis had labored for three days and nights with the blackest arcane spells available, finally managing to fit himself into the corpse.

Although Cholik had never witnessed something like that, Kabraxis had assured him that it was sometimes done, though not without danger. When the host body was taken over a month ago, it had been that of a young man who had not yet seen thirty. Now the man looked much older than Cholik, like a man in his twilight years. The flesh was baggy and loose, wrinkled and crisscrossed by hair-fine scars that marred his features. His black hair had gone colorless gray, his eyes from brown to pale ash.

"Are you all right?" Cholik asked.

The old man smiled, but it was with an expression Cholik recognized as Kabraxis's. "I've put many harsh demands on this body. But its use is almost at an end." He stepped past Cholik and peered out the window.

"What are you doing here?" Cholik asked.

"I came to watch you observe the festivities of the people coming to see you," Kabraxis said. "I knew that this many people around you, and so many of them happy and needing diversion, would prove unnerving for you. Life goes much easier for you if you can maintain a somber vigilance over it."

"These people will know us as entertainers," Cholik said, "not as conduits to a new religion that will help them with their lives."

"Oh," Kabraxis said, "I'll help them with their lives. In fact, I wanted to have a word with you about how this evening's meeting will go."

Excitement flared within Cholik. After two months of being on the road, of planning to found a church and build a power base that would eventually seek to draw its constituency from the Zakarum Church, it felt good to know that they were about to start.

"Bramwell is the place, then?"

"Yes," Kabraxis said. "There is old power located within this town. Power that I can tap into that will shape your destiny and my conquest. Tonight, you will lay the first stone in the church we have discussed for the past month. But it won't be of stone and mortar as you think. Rather, it will be of believers."

The comment left Cholik cold. He wanted an edifice, a building that would dwarf the Zakarum Church in Westmarch. "We will need a church."

"We will have a church," Kabraxis said. "But having a church anchors you in one spot. Although I've tried to teach you this, you've still not learned. But a belief—Buyard Cholik, First Chosen of the Black Road— a belief transcends all physical boundaries and leaves its mark on the ages. That's what we want."

Cholik said nothing, but visions of a grand church continued to dance in his head.

"I've given you an extended life," Kabraxis said. "Few humans will ever achieve the years that you've lived so far without the effects of my gift. Would you want to spend all the coming years in one place, looking only over the triumphs you've already wrought?"

"You are the one who has spoken of the need for patience."

"I still speak of patience," Kabraxis insisted, "but you will not be the tree of my religion, Buyard Cholik. I don't need a tree. I need a bee. A bee that flits from one place to another to collect our believers." He smiled and patted Cholik on the shoulder. "But come. We start here in Bramwell with these people."

"What do you want me to do?" Cholik asked.

"Tonight," Kabraxis said, "we will show these people the power of the Black Road. We will show them that anything they may dream possible can happen."

*　　　*　　　*

Cholik walked out of the coach and toward the gathering area. He wore his best robe, but it was of a modest style that wouldn't turn away those who were poor.

At least three hundred people ringed the clearing where the caravan had stopped. Other wagons, some of them loaded with straw, apples, and livestock, formed another ring outside Cholik's. Still more wagons, empty of any goods, made seating areas beneath the spreading trees.

"Ah," one man whispered, "here comes the speechmaker. The fun and games are over now, I'll warrant."

"If he starts lecturing me on how to live my life and how much I should tithe to whatever religion he's shilling for," another man whispered, "I'm leaving. I've spent two hours watching performers that I didn't have time to lose and will never get back."

"I've got a field that needs tending."

"And the cows are going to be expecting an early morning milking."

Aware that he was losing part of the audience the performers had brought in for him, knowing not to make any attempt to speak to them of anything smacking of responsibility or donations, Cholik walked to the center of the clearing and brought out the metal bucket containing black ash that Kabraxis had made and presented to him. Speaking a single word of power that the audience couldn't hear, he threw out the ashes.

The ashes roiled from the bucket in a dense black cloud that paused in midair. The long stream of ash twisted like a snake on a hot road as it floated on the mild breeze wafting through the clearing. Abruptly, the ash thinned and shot forward, creating whorls and loops that dropped over the ground. In places, the lines of ash crossed over other lines, but the lines didn't touch. Instead, the loops and whorls stayed ten feet away, creating enough distance that a man might walk under.

The sight of the thin line of ash hanging in the air caught the attention of the audience. Perhaps a mage might be able to do something like that, but not a typical priest. Enough curiosity was created that most people wanted to see what Cholik would do next.

When the line of ash ended its run, it glowed with deep violet fire, competing just for a moment with the deepening twilight darkening the eastern sky and the embers of the sunset west over the Gulf of Westmarch.

Cholik faced the audience, his eyes meeting theirs. "I bring you power," he said. "A path that will carry you to the dreams you've always had but were denied by misfortune and outdated dogma."

An undercurrent of conversation started around the clearing. Several voices rose in anger. The populace of Bramwell clung to their belief in Zakarum.

"There is another way to the Light," Cholik said. "That path lies along the Way of Dreams. Dien-Ap-Sten, Prophet of the Light, created this path for his children, so that they might have their needs met and their secret wishes answered."

"I've never heard of yer prophet," a crusty old fisherman in the front shouted back. "An' ain't none of us come here to hear the way of the Light maligned."

"I will not malign the way of the Light," Cholik responded. "I came here to show you a clearer way into the beneficence of the Light."

"The Zakarum Church already does that," a grizzled old man in a patched priest's robe stated. "We don't need a pretender here digging into our vaults."

"I didn't come here looking for your gold," Cholik said. "I didn't come here to take." He was conscious of Kabraxis watching him from inside the coach. "In fact, I will not allow the gathering of a single copper coin this night or any other that we may camp in your city."

"The Duke of Bramwell will have something to say to you if you try staying," an elderly farmer said. "The duke don't put up with much in the way of grifters and thieves."

Cholik pushed aside his stung pride. That chore was made even harder by the knowledge that he could have blasted the life from the man with one of the spells he'd learned from Kabraxis. After he'd become one of Zakarum's priests and even while he was wearing the robe of a novice, no one had dared challenge him in such a manner.

Crossing the clearing, Cholik stopped in front of a large family with a young boy so crippled and wasted by disease that he looked like a stumbling corpse.

The father stepped up in front of Cholik protectively. The man gripped the knife sheathed at his waist.

"Good sir," Cholik said, "I see that your son is afflicted."

The farmer gazed around self-consciously. "By the fever that come through Bramwell eight years ago. My boy ain't the only one that was hurt by it."

"He hasn't been right since the fever."

Nervously, the farmer shook his head. "None of them has. Most died within a week of getting it."

"What would you give to have one more healthy son to help you work your farm?" Cholik asked.

"I ain't going to have my boy hurt or made fun of," the farmer warned.

"I will do neither," Cholik promised. "Please trust me."

Confusion filled the man's face. He looked at the short, stocky woman who had to be the mother of the nine children who sat in their wagon.

"Boy," Cholik said, addressing the young boy, "would you stay a burden to your family?"

"Hey," the farmer protested. "He ain't no burden, and I'll fight the man that says he is."

Cholik waited. As an ordained priest of the Zakarum Church, he'd have had the father penalized at once for daring to speak to him in such a manner.

Wait, Kabraxis whispered in Cholik's mind.

Cholik waited, knowing the audience's full attention was upon him. It would be decided here, he told himself, whether the audience stayed or went.

Something lit the boy's eyes. His head, looking bulbous on his thin shoulders and narrow chest, swiveled toward his father. Reaching up with an arthritic hand with fingers that had to have been painful to him all the time and could barely be expected to enable him to feed himself, the boy tugged on his father's arm.

"Father," the boy said, "let me go with the priest."

The farmer started to shake his head. "Effirn, I don't know if this is right for you. I don't want you to get your hopes up. The healers at the Zakarum Church haven't been able to cure you."

"I know," the boy said. "But I believe in this man. Let me try."

The farmer glanced at his wife. She nodded, tears flashing diamondlike in her eyes. Looking up at Cholik, the farmer said, "I hold you accountable for what happens to my son, priest."

"You may," Cholik said politely, "but I assure you the healing that young Effirn will shortly enjoy shall be the blessing of Dien-Ap-Sten. I am not skilled enough to answer this boy's wish to be healed and whole." He glanced at the boy and offered his hand.

The boy tried to stand, but his withered legs wouldn't hold him. He folded his hand with its twisted and crooked fingers inside Cholik's hand.

Cholik marveled at the weakness of the boy. It was hard to remember when he'd been so weak himself, but it had been only scant months ago. He helped the boy to his feet. Around the clearing almost every voice was stilled.

"Come, boy," Cholik said. "Place your faith in me."

"I do," Effirn replied.

Together, they walked across the clearing. Not quite to the nearest end of the long rope of black ash that still sparked with violent fire, the boy's legs gave out. Cholik caught Effirn before he could fall, overcoming his own discomfort at handling the disease-ridden child.

Cholik knew that every eye in the clearing was upon him and the child. Doubt touched Cholik as he gazed up at the tall trees around the clearing. If the boy died along the path of the Black Road, perhaps he could hold the townspeople off long enough to get away. If he didn't get away, he was certain he'd be swinging by a noose from one of those branches overhead. He'd heard about the justice meted out by the people of Bramwell to bandits and murderers among their community.

And Cholik intended to help them suckle a serpent to their breasts.

At the beginning of the black ash trail, Cholik helped the boy stand on his own two feet.

"What do I do?" Effirn whispered.

"Walk," Cholik told him. "Follow the trail, and think about nothing but being healed."

The boy took a deep, shuddering breath, obviously rethinking his decision to follow a path so obviously filled with magic. Then, tentatively, the boy released his grip on Cholik's hands. His first steps were trembling, tottering things that had Cholik's breath catching at the back of his throat.

With agonizing slowness, the boy walked. Then his steps came a little smoother, although the swaying gait he managed threatened to tear him from the path.

No sound was made in the clearing as the audience watched the crippled boy make his way around the black ash trail. His feet kicked violet sparks from the black ash with every step he took, but it didn't take long for the steps to start coming more sure, then faster. The boy's shoulders straightened, and his carriage became more erect. His thin legs, then his arms, then his body swelled with increased muscle mass. No longer did his head look bulbous atop his skeletal frame.

And when the black ash trail rose up in the air to pass over a past section, the boy stepped up into the air after it. Before, even omitting the impossibility of following such a thin line of ash into the air, the boy would not have been able to meet the challenge of the climb.

Conversations buzzed around Cholik, and he gloried in the amazement the audience had for what was taking place. While serving at the Zakarum Church, he would never have been allowed to take credit for such a spell. He turned to face the audience, moving so that he faced them all.

"This is the power of the Way of Dreams," Cholik crowed, "and of the generous and giving prophet I choose to serve. May Dien-Ap-Sten's name and works be praised. Join me in praising his name, brothers and sisters." He raised his arms. "Glory to Dien-Ap-Sten!"

Only a few followed his example at first, but others joined. Within a moment, the tumultuous shout rose above the clearing, drowning out the commonplace noise that droned from the city downriver.

Buyard Cholik!

The voiceless address exploded in Cholik's mind with such harshness that he momentarily went blind with the pain and was nauseated.

Beware, Kabraxis said. *The spell is becoming unraveled.*

Gathering himself, Cholik glanced back at the maze created by the line he'd cast, watching as the starting point of the line suddenly burst into violet sparks and burned rapidly. The small fire raced along the length of the line of ash. As the fire moved, it consumed the ash, leaving nothing behind.

The fire raced for the boy.

If the fire reaches the boy, Kabraxis warned, *he will be destroyed.*

Cholik walked to the other end of the line of ash, watching as the fire swept toward the boy. He thought furiously, knowing he couldn't show any fear to the cheering audience.

If we lose these people now, Kabraxis said, *we might not get them back. If a miracle occurs, we will win believers, but if a disaster happens, we could be lost. It will be years before we can come back here, and maybe even longer before these people will forget what happened tonight to let us attempt to win them over again.*

"Effirn," Cholik called.

The boy looked up at him, taking his eyes from the path for a moment. His steps never faltered. "Look at me!" he cried gleefully. "Look at me. I'm walking."

"Yes, Effirn," Cholik said, "and everyone here is proud of you and grateful to Dien-Ap-Sten, as is proper.

However, there is something I need to know." Glancing back at the relentless purple fire pursuing the boy, he saw that it was only two curves back from Effirn. The end of the ash trail was still thirty feet from the boy.

"What?" Effirn asked.

"Can you run?"

The boy's face worked in confusion. "I don't know. I've never tried."

The violet fire gained another ten feet on him.

"Try now," Cholik suggested. He held his arms out. "Run to me, Effirn. Quickly, boy. Fast as you can."

Tentatively, Effirn started running, trying out his new muscles and abilities. He ran, and the violet fire burning up the ash trail chased him, still gaining, but by inches now rather than feet.

"Come on, Effirn," Cholik cheered. "Show your da how fast you've become now that Dien-Ap-Sten has shown you grace."

Effirn ran, laughing the whole way. The conversation of the audience picked up intensity. The boy reached the trail's end, sweeping down the final curve to the ground, and was in Cholik's arms just as the violet blaze hit the end of the trail and vanished in a puff of bruised embers.

Feeling as though he'd just escaped death again, Cholik held the boy to him for a moment, surprised at how big Effirn had gotten. He felt the boy's arms and legs tight against him.

"Thank you, thank you, thank you," Effirn gasped, hugging Cholik with strong arms and legs.

Embarrassed and flushed with excitement at the same time, Cholik hugged the boy back. Effirn's health meant nothing but success for him in Bramwell, but Cholik didn't understand how the demon had worked the magic.

Healing is simple enough, Kabraxis said in Cholik's mind. *Causing hurt and pain are separate issues, and much harder if it's going to be lasting. In order to learn how to injure someone, the magic is designed so that first a person learns to heal.*

Cholik had never been taught that.

There are a number of things you haven't been taught,

Kabraxis said. *But you have time left to you. I will teach you. Turn, Buyard Cholik, and greet your new parishioners.*

Easing the boy's grip from him, Cholik turned to face the parents. No one thought to challenge him about why the ash trail had burned away.

Released, wanting to show off his newfound strength, the boy raced across the clearing. His brothers and sisters cheered him on, and his father caught him up and pulled him into a fierce hug before handing him off to his mother. She held her son to her, tears washing unashamedly down her face.

Cholik watched the mother and son, amazed at the way the scene touched him.

You're surprised by how good you feel at having had a hand in healing the boy? Kabraxis asked.

"Yes," Cholik whispered, knowing no one around him could hear him but that the demon could.

It shouldn't. To know the Darkness, a being must also know the Light. You lived your life cloistered in Westmarch. The only people you met were those who wanted your position.

Or those whose positions I coveted, Cholik realized.

And the Zakarum Church never allowed you to be so personal in the healing properties they doled out, the demon said.

"No."

The Light is afraid to give many people powers like I have given you, Kabraxis said. *People who have powers like this get noticed by regular people. In short order, they become heroes or talked-about people. In only a little more time, the tales that are told about them allow them to take on lofty mantles. The stewards of the Light are jealous of that.*

"But demons aren't?" Cholik asked.

Kabraxis laughed, and the grating, thunderous noise echoing inside Cholik's head was almost painful. *Demons aren't as jealous as the stewards of Light would have you believe. Nor are they as controlling as the stewards of Light. I ask you, who always has the most rules? The most limitations?*

Cholik didn't answer.

Why do you think the stewards of Light offer so many rules?

Kabraxis asked. *To keep the balance in their favor, of course. But demons, we believe in letting all who support the Darkness have power. Some have more power than others. But they earn it. Just as you have earned that which I'm giving you the day you faced your own fear of dying and sought out the buried gateway to me.*

"I had no choice," Cholik said.

Humans always have choices. That's how the stewards of Light seek to confuse you. You have choices, but you can't choose most of them because the stewards of Light have decreed them as wrong. As an enlightened student of the Light, you're supposed to know that those choices are wrong. So where does that really leave you? How many choices do you really have?

Cholik silently agreed.

Go to these people, Buyard Cholik. You'll find converts among them now. Once they have discovered that you have the power to make changes that will let them attain their goals and desires, they will flock to you. Next, we must begin the church, and we must find disciples among these people who will help you spread word of me. For now, give the gift of health to those who are sick among these before you. They will talk. By morning, there won't be anyone in this city who hasn't heard of you.

Glorying in the newfound respect and prestige he'd gained by healing the boy, Cholik went forward. His body sang with the buzzing thrill of the power Kabraxis channeled through him. The power drew him to the weak and infirm in the crowd.

Laying hands on the people in the crowd as he came to them, Cholik healed fevers and infections, took away warts and arthritis, straightened a leg that had grown crooked after being set and healing, brought senses back to an elderly grandmother who had been addled for years according to the son who cared for her.

"I would like to settle in Bramwell," Cholik said as the Gulf of Westmarch drank down the sun and twilight turned to night around them.

The crowd cheered in response to his announcement.

"But I will need a church built," Cholik continued. "Once a permanent church is built, the miracles wrought by Dien-Ap-Sten will continue to grow. Come to me that I may introduce you to the prophet I choose to serve."

For a night, Buyard Cholik was closer to lasting renown than he'd ever been in his life. It was a heady feeling, one that he promised himself he would get to know more intimately.

Nothing would stop him.

Fourteen

"Are you a sailor?" the pretty serving wench asked.

Darrick looked up at her from the bowl of thick potatoes and meat stew and didn't let the brief pang of loss her words brought touch him. "No," he replied, because he hadn't been a sailor for months.

The serving girl was a raven-haired beauty scarcely more than twenty years old if she was that. Her black skirt was short and high, revealing a lot of her long, beautiful legs. She wore her hair pulled back, tied at the neck.

"Why do you ask?" Darrick held her eyes for a moment, then she looked away.

"Only because your rolling gait as you entered the door reminded me of a sailor's," the wench said. "My father was a sailor. Born to the sea and lost to the sea, as is the usual course for many sailors."

"What is your name?" Darrick asked.

"Dahni," she said, and smiled.

"It's been nice meeting you, Dahni."

For a moment, the wench gazed around the table, trying to find something to do. But she'd already refilled his tankard, and his bowl remained more than half full. "If you need anything," she offered, "let me know."

"I will." Darrick kept his smile in place. He'd learned in the months since losing his berth aboard *Lonesome Star* that smiling politely and answering questions but asking none ended conversations more quickly. If people thought he was willing to be friendly, they didn't find his lack of conversation as threatening or challenging. They just thought he was inept or shy and generally left him alone. The ruse had kept him from a number of fights lately, and the lack of fighting had kept him from the jails and fines that often left him destitute and on the street again.

Tilting his head, he glanced briefly at the four men playing dice at the table next to his. Three of them were fishermen, he knew that from their clothing, but the fourth man was dressed a little better, like someone who was putting on his best and hoping to impress. It came off as someone down on his luck and getting desperate. That appearance, Darrick knew, was an illusion.

He ate hungrily, trying not to act as if he hadn't eaten since yesterday. Or perhaps it was the day before. He was no longer certain of time passing. However few meals he'd had, he'd always managed to make enough money to drink. Drinking was the only way to keep distanced from the fears and nightmares that plagued him. Almost every night, he dreamed of the cliffside in Tauruk's Port, dreamed that he almost saved Mat from the skeleton's clutches, from the awful thump against the cliffside that had broken Mat's skull.

The tavern was a dive, another in a long string of them. They all looked alike to him. When he finished with his work, wherever he was, he ate a meal, drank until he could hardly walk, then hired a room or bedded down in a stable if the money hadn't been enough to provide drink and a proper bed.

The clientele was mostly fishermen, hard-faced men with callused hands and scars from nets, hooks, fish, the weather, and years of disappointment that ran bone-deep. They talked of tomorrows that sounded much better than the morning would bring, and what they would do if someday they escaped the need to climb aboard a boat every day and pray the Light was generous.

Merchants sat among the fishermen and other townspeople, discussing shipments and fortunes and the lack of protection in the northern part of the Great Ocean since Westmarch was keeping its navy so close to home these days still. There still had been no sign of the demon whom the Westmarch sailors had seen at Tauruk's Port, and many of the merchants and sailors north of Westmarch believed that the pirates had made up the story to lure the king into pulling his navy back.

Dissent grew among the northern ports and cities because they depended on Westmarch to help defend them. With the Westmarch Navy out of the way, men turned to piracy when they couldn't make the sea pay any other way. Although most pirates weren't acting together, their combined raiding had hurt the economies of several independent ports and even cities farther inland. Westmarch diplomacy, once a feared and treasured and expansive thing, had become weak and ineffective. Northern cities no longer curried favor with Westmarch as much.

Darrick sopped a biscuit through the stew and popped it into his mouth. The stew was thick and oily, seasoned with grease and spices that made it cloying and hot, a meal that finished off a hardworking man's day. Over the last months, he'd lost weight, but his fighting ability had stayed sharp. For the most part, he stayed away from the docks for fear that someone might recognize him. Although the Westmarch Navy and guardsmen hadn't made a strong effort to find him, or other sailors who had intentionally jumped ship, he remained leery of possible apprehension. Some days death seemed preferable to living, but he couldn't make that step. He hadn't died as he'd grown up under his father's fierce hands, and he didn't intend to die willingly now.

But it was hard to live willingly.

He glanced across the room, watching Dahni as she talked and flirted with a young man. Part of him longed for the companionship of a woman, but it was only a small part. Women talked, and they dug at the things that bothered a man, most of them wanting only to help, but Darrick didn't want to deal with that.

The big man sitting at the end of the bar crossed the floor to Darrick. The man was tall and broad, with a nose flattened and misshapen from fights. Scars, some freshly pink and webbed with tiny scabs, covered his knuckles and the heels of his palms. An old knife scar showed at his throat.

Uninvited, he sat across from Darrick, his truncheon lying across his knees. "You're working," the man said.

Darrick kept his right hand in his lap where his cutlass was. He gazed at the man. "I'm here with a friend."

To his right, the gambler who had hired Darrick for an evening's protection after they had come in on the trade caravan together praised the Light for yet another good turn. He was an older man, thin and white-haired. During an attack by bandits only yesterday, Darrick had learned that the man could handle himself and carried a number of small knives secreted on his person.

"Your friend's awfully lucky tonight," the big man said.

"He's due," Darrick said in a level voice.

The big man eyed Darrick levelly. "It's my job to keep the peace in the tavern."

Darrick nodded.

"If I catch your friend cheating, I'm throwing you both out."

Darrick nodded again, and he hoped the gambler didn't cheat or was good at it. The man had gamed with others on the caravan as they had wound their way back from Aranoch and trading with a port city that supplied the Amazon Islands.

"And you might have a care when you step out of here tonight," the bouncer warned, nodding at the gambler. "You got a demon's fog that's rolled up outside that won't burn off till morning. This town isn't well lighted, and some folks that gamble with your friend might not take kindly to losing."

"Thank you," Darrick said.

"Don't thank me," the bouncer said. "I just don't want either of you dying in here or anywhere near here." He stood and resumed his position at the end of the bar.

The serving wench returned with a pitcher of wine, a hopeful smile on her face.

Darrick covered his tankard with a hand.

"You've had enough?" she asked.

"For now," he answered. "But I'll take a bottle with me when I leave if you'll have one ready."

She nodded, hesitated, smiled briefly, then turned to walk away. The bracelet at her wrist flashed and caught Darrick's eye.

"Wait," Darrick whispered, his voice suddenly hoarse.

"Yes?" she asked hopefully.

Darrick pointed at her wrist. "What is that bracelet you wear?"

"A charm," Dahni replied. "It represents Dien-Ap-Sten, the Prophet of the Way of Dreams."

The bracelet was constructed of interlinked ovals separated by carved amber and rough iron so that none of the ovals touched another. The sight of it sparked memory in Darrick's mind. "Where did you get it?"

"From a trader who liked me," Dahni answered. It was a cheap attempt to make him jealous.

"Who is Dien-Ap-Sten?" That name didn't ring a bell in Darrick's memory.

"He's a prophet of luck and destiny," Dahni said. "They're building a church down in Bramwell. The man who gave me this told me that anyone who had the courage and the need to walk the Way of Dreams would get whatever his or her heart desires." She smiled at him. "Don't you think that's a bit far-fetched?"

"Aye," Darrick agreed, but the story troubled him. Bramwell wasn't far from Westmarch, and that was a place he'd promised himself he wouldn't be any time too soon.

"Have you ever been there?" Dahni asked.

"Aye, but it was a long time ago."

"Have you ever thought of returning there?"

"No."

The serving wench pouted. "Pity." She shook her wrist, making the bracelet spin and catch the lantern light. "I should like to go there someday and see that church for myself. They say that when it is finished, it will be a work of art, the most beautiful thing that has ever been built."

"It's probably worth seeing, then," Darrick said.

Dahni leaned on the table, exposing the tops of her breasts for his inspection. "A lot of things are worth seeing. But I know I won't get to see them as long as I stay in this town. Perhaps you should think about returning to Bramwell soon."

"Perhaps," Darrick said, trying not to offer any offense.

One of the fishermen called Dahni away, raising his voice impatiently. She gave Darrick a last, lingering look, then turned in a swirl of her short skirt and walked away.

At the next table, the gambler had another bit of good fortune, praising the Light while the other men grumbled.

Pushing thoughts of the strange bracelet from his mind, Darrick returned his attention to his meal. Swearing off wine for the rest of the gambler's turn at the gaming table meant the nightmares would be waiting on Darrick when he returned to his rented room. But the caravan would be in town for another day before the merchants finished their trading. He could drink until he was sure he wouldn't be able to dream.

Fog rolled through the streets and made the night's shadows seem darker and deeper as Darrick followed the gambler from the tavern two hours later. He tried to remember the man's name but wasn't surprised to find that he couldn't. Life was simpler when he didn't try to remember everything or everyone. On the different caravans he hired onto as a sellsword, there were people in charge, and they had a direction in which they wanted to go. Darrick went along with that.

"I had a good night at the table tonight," the gambler confessed as they walked through the street. "As soon as I get back to my room, I'll pay you what we agreed on."

"Aye," Darrick said, though he couldn't remember what amount they had agreed on. Usually it was a percentage against a small advance because a true gambler could never guarantee that he would win, and those who could were cheats and would guarantee a fight afterward.

Darrick gazed around at the street. As the tavern bouncer had said, the town had poor lighting. Only a few lamps, staggered haphazardly and primarily centered near the more successful taverns and inns as well as the small dock lit the way. The heavy fog left a wet gleam on the cobblestones. He looked for a sign, some way of knowing where he'd ended on this journey, not really surprised that he didn't know where he was, and not truly caring, either. Many of the towns he'd been to in the last few months had tended to blur into each other.

The sound of the gambler's in-drawn breath warned Darrick that something was wrong. He jerked his head around to the alley they'd just passed. Three men bolted from the alley, hurling themselves at Darrick and the gambler. Their blades gleamed even in the fog-dulled moonlight.

Darrick drew his cutlass, dropping the jug of wine he carried under one arm. By the time the ceramic jug shattered across the poorly fit cobblestones, he had his cutlass in hand and parried a blow aimed to take off his head. Fatigued as he was, with the wine working within him, it was all Darrick could do to stay alive. He stumbled over the uneven street, never seeing the fourth man step out behind him until it was too late.

The fourth man swung a weighted shark's billy that caught Darrick over his left ear and dropped him to his knees. Almost unconscious from the blow, he smashed his face against the cobblestones, and the sharp pain brought him back around. He fought to get to his knees. From there, he felt certain that he could make it to his feet. After that, perhaps he'd even be able to fight. Or at least earn the money the gambler had paid to protect him.

"Damn!" one of the thieves shouted. "He cut me with a hide-out knife."

"Watch out," another man said.

"It's okay. I got him. I got him. He won't be sticking anybody else ever again."

Warm liquid poured down the side of Darrick's neck.

His vision blurred, but he saw two men taking the gambler's purse.

"Stop!" Darrick ordered, finding his cutlass loose on the cobblestones and picking it up. He lurched toward them, lifting the blade and following it toward one of the men. Before he reached his intended target, the other man whirled around and drove a hobnailed boot into Darrick's jaw. Pain blinded him as he fell again.

Struggling against the blackness that waited to take him, Darrick pushed his feet, trying in vain to find purchase that would allow him to stand. He watched in helpless frustration as the men vanished back into the shadows of the alley.

Using the cutlass as a crutch to keep his feet, Darrick made his way to the gambler. Darrick peered through his tearing eyes, listening to the thundering pain inside his head, and stared at the gambler.

A bone-hilted knife jutted from the gambler's chest. A crimson flower blossomed around the blade where it was sunk into flesh to the cross-guard.

The man's face was filled with fear. "Help me, Darrick. Please. For the Light's sake, I can't stop the bleeding."

How can he remember my name when I can't remember his? Darrick wondered. Then he saw all the blood streaming between the man's hands, threading through his fingers.

"It's okay," Darrick said, kneeling beside the stricken gambler. He knew it wasn't going to be okay. While serving aboard *Lonesome Star*, he'd seen too many fatal wounds not to know that this one was fatal as well.

"I'm dying," the gambler said.

"No," Darrick croaked, pressing his hands over the gambler's hands in an attempt to stem the tide of his life's blood. Turning his head, Darrick shouted over his shoulder. "Help! I need help here! I've got an injured man!"

"You were supposed to be there," the gambler accused. "You were supposed to look out for this kind of thing for me. That's what I paid you for." He coughed, and bright blood flecked his lips.

From the blood on the gambler's lips, Darrick knew the knife had penetrated one of his lungs as well. He pressed his hands against the gambler's chest, willing the blood to stop.

But it didn't.

Darrick heard footsteps slap against the cobblestones just as the gambler gave a final convulsive shiver. The gambler's breath locked in his throat, and his eyes stared sightlessly upward.

"No," Darrick croaked in disbelief. The man couldn't be dead; he'd been hired to protect him, still had a meal he'd paid for from his advance in his belly.

A strong hand gripped Darrick's shoulder. He tried to fight it off, then gazed up into the eyes of the tavern bouncer.

"By the merciful Light," the bouncer swore. "Did you see who did it?"

Darrick shook his head. Even if he saw the men responsible for the gambler's murder, he doubted that he could identify them.

"Some bodyguard," a woman's voice said from somewhere behind Darrick.

Looking at the dead gambler, Darrick had to agree. *Some bodyguard.* His senses fled, making his aching head too heavy to hold upright. He fell forward and didn't even know if he hit the street.

The silver peal of the bells in the three towers called the citizens of Bramwell to worship at the Church of Dien-Ap-Sten. Most were already inside the warren of buildings that had been erected over the last year since the caravan's arrival in the city. Foundations for still more buildings had been laid, and as soon as they were completed, they would be added to the central cathedral. Beautiful statuary, crafted by some of the best artisans in Bramwell as well as other artists in Westmarch, Lut Gholein, and Kurast and beyond the Sea of Light, sat at the top of the buildings.

Buyard Cholik, called Master Sayes now, stood on one of

the rooftop gardens that decorated the church. Staring down at the intersection near the church, he watched as wagons carrying families and friends arrived. In the beginning, he remembered, the poorer families were the first to begin worship at the church. They'd come for the healing and in hopes of having a lifelong dream of riches or comfort answered.

And they came wishing to be chosen that day to walk on the Way of Dreams. Only a few were allowed to walk the Way of Dreams, generally only those afflicted with physical deformities or mental problems. People with arthritis and poorly mended broken limbs were nearly always admitted. Kabraxis achieved those miracles of healing with no difficulty. Every now and again, the demon rewarded someone with riches, but there was always a hidden cost none of the population could know about. As the Church of Dien-Ap-Sten had grown, so had the secrets it kept.

The church had been built high on a hill overlooking the city of Bramwell proper. Quarried from some of the best limestone in the area, which was generally shipped off to other cities while plain stone was used for the local buildings, the church gleamed in the morning light like bone laid clean from under the kiss of a knife. No one in the city could look southeast toward Westmarch and not see the church first.

The forest had been cleared on two sides of the church to accommodate the wagons and coaches that arrived during the twice-a-week services. All the believers in Bramwell came to both services, knowing the way would be made clear to the Way of Dreams where the miracles could take place.

Special, decorated boats tied up in front of the church at the newly built pilings. Boatmen in the service of the church brought captains and sailors from the ships that anchored out in the harbor. Word of the Church of Dien-Ap-Sten had started spreading across all of Westmarch, and it brought the curious as well as those seeking salvation.

High in their towers, the three bells rang again. They would ring only once more before the service began. Cholik glanced down in front of the church and saw that, as usual, only a few would be late to the service.

Cholik paced through the rooftop garden. Fruit trees and flowering plants, bushes, and vines occupied the rooftop, leaving a winding trail over the large building. Pausing beside a strawberry plant, Cholik stripped two succulent fruits from it, then popped them into his mouth. The berries tasted clean and fresh. No matter how many he took, there were always more.

"Did you ever think it would be this big?" Kabraxis asked.

Turning, the taste of the berries still sweet in his mouth, Cholik faced the demon.

Kabraxis stood beside a trellis of tomato vines. The fruits were bright cherry red, and more tiny yellow flowers bloomed on the vines, promising an even greater harvest to come. An illusion spell, made strong by binding it to the limestone of the building, kept him from being seen by anyone below. The spell had been crafted so intricately that he didn't even leave a shadow to see for anyone not meant to see him.

"I had hopes," Cholik answered diplomatically.

Kabraxis smiled, and the effect on his demonic face was obscene. "You're a greedy man. I like that."

Cholik took no offense. One of the things he enjoyed about the relationship with the demon was that he had to offer no apologies for the way he felt. In the Zakarum Church, his temperament always had to be in line with accepted church doctrine.

"We're going to outgrow this town soon," Cholik said.

"You're thinking of leaving?" Kabraxis sounded as though he couldn't believe it.

"Possibly. It has been in my thoughts."

"You?" Kabraxis scoffed. "Who thought only of the building of this church?"

Cholik shrugged. "We can build other churches."

"But this one is so big and so grand."

"And the next one can be bigger and more grand."

"Where would you build another church?"

Cholik hesitated, but to know the demon was to speak his mind. "Westmarch."

"You would challenge the Zakarum Church?"

Cholik answered fiercely, "Yes. There are priests there whom I would see humbled and driven from the city. Or sacrificed. If that is done, and this church is positioned to look as though it can save all of Westmarch from great evil, we could convert the whole country."

"You would kill those people?"

"Only a few of them. Enough to scare the others. The survivors will serve the church. Dead men can't fear us and properly worship us."

Kabraxis laughed. "Ah, but you're a willing pupil, Buyard Cholik. Such bloodthirstiness is so refreshing to find in a human. Usually you are all so limited by your own personal desires and motivations. You want revenge on this person who wronged you or that person who has been fortunate enough to have more than you. Petty things."

A curious pride moved through Cholik. Over the year and some months of their acquaintance, he had changed. He hadn't been lured over to the Darkness as so many priests he'd known had feared for those they sought to save. Rather, he'd reached inside himself and brought it all forward.

The Zakarum Church taught that man was of two minds as well, constantly fighting an inner war between the Light and the Darkness.

"But my plan to move into Westmarch is a good one?" Cholik asked. He knew he was currying the demon's favor, but Kabraxis liked to give it.

"Yes," the demon answered, "but it is not yet time. Already, this church has earned enmity from the Zakarum Church. Gaining the king's permission to build a church within the city would be hard. The tenets between the king and the church are too tight. And you forget: Westmarch still seeks the demon that was seen with the pirates. If we move too quickly, we will draw more suspicion."

"It has been more than a year," Cholik protested.

"The king and the people have not forgotten," Kabraxis said. "Diablo has left his mark upon them after the subterfuge he ran at Tristram. We must first win their trust, then betray them."

"How?"

"I have a plan."

Cholik waited. One thing he'd learned that Kabraxis didn't like was being questioned too closely.

"In time," Kabraxis said. "We have to raise an army of believers before then, warriors who will go and kill anyone who stands in their way to bringing the truth to the world."

"An army to oppose Westmarch?"

"An army to oppose the Zakarum Church," Kabraxis said.

"There are not enough people in all of Bramwell." The thought staggered Cholik. Images of battlefields painted red with the blood of men flashed through his mind. And he knew those images were probably much less horrific than the actual battles would be.

"We will raise the army from within Westmarch," Kabraxis said.

"How?"

"We will turn the king against the Zakarum Church," the demon replied. "And once we make him see how unholy the Zakarum Church has become, he will create that army."

"And the Zakarum Church will be razed to the ground." Warmth surged through Cholik as he entertained the idea of it.

"Yes."

"How will you turn the king?" Cholik asked.

Kabraxis gestured toward the church. "In time, Buyard Cholik. Everything will be revealed to you in time. Diablo returned to this world only a short time ago by corrupting the Soulstone that bound him. He unleashed his power in Tristram, taking over King Leoric's son, Prince Albrecht. As you will remember, for you were privy to the machinations of the Zakarum Church at the time, Tristram and Westmarch almost warred. The human adventurers who fought Diablo thought they destroyed him, but Diablo used one of his enemies as the new vessel in which to get around these lands. As we plan for conquest and success, so Diablo plans. But demons must be cunning and crafty, as we are being now. If we grow too quickly, we will attract the attention of the Prime Evils, and I'm unwilling to deal with them at the moment. For now, though, you have a service to give. I promise you a miracle today that will bring even more converts."

Cholik nodded, stilling the questions that flooded into his brain. "Of course. By your leave."

"Go with Dien-Ap-Sten's blessings," Kabraxis said, intoning the words that they had made legendary throughout Bramwell and beyond. "May the Way of Dreams take you where you want to go."

Fifteen

The service passed with liquid ease.

Standing in the shadowed balcony that overlooked the parishioners, Buyard Cholik watched as the crowd fidgeted and waited through the singing and the addresses of the young priests speaking of Dien-Ap-Sten's desires for each and every man, woman, and child in the world of men to rise and succeed to their just rewards. The young priests stood on the small stage below Cholik's balcony. Mostly, though, the young priests' messages intoned the virtues of serving the Prophet of the Light and sharing profits with the church so that more good work could be done.

But they were all truly waiting on the Call to the Way of Dreams.

After the last of the priests finished his message and the final songs were sung, songs that Kabraxis had written himself, which echoed of drumbeats like a hammering heart and melodic pipes that sounded like blood rushing through a man's ears, a dozen acolytes stepped up from the pit in front of the small stage with lighted torches in their hands.

The drums hammered, creating an eerie crescendo that resounded among the rafters of the high-vaulted ceiling. Cymbals crashed as the pipes played.

Frenzy built within the crowd. There still, Cholik saw, were not enough seats in the church. They'd just opened the upper floor of the church three weeks ago, and the membership had more than filled the cathedral again. Many of the worshippers were from other cities up and

down the coastline, and a number of them were from
Westmarch. They made pilgrimages from the other cities
by hired caravan or by paying ship's passage.

Some ships' captains and caravan masters made small
fortunes out of operating twice-weekly round-trips to
Bramwell. Many people were willing to pay passage for
the chance to walk the Way of Dreams, for health reasons
or in hopes of gaining their heart's desire.

Once Cholik had discovered the startup of the lucrative
business, he'd sent word to the captains and caravan masters that they would be expected to bring offerings in the
way of building materials for the church with each trip.
Only two ships had gone down and one caravan was
destroyed by a horde of skeletons and zombies before the
tribute asked of them started getting delivered on a regular
basis. More caravans were starting up from Lut Gholein
and other countries to the east.

The crowd shouted, "Way of Dreams! Way of Dreams!"
Their manner would not have been permitted in the
Zakarum Church, and they bordered on the fringe of
becoming an unruly crowd.

Guards Cholik had chosen from the warriors who
believed in Dien-Ap-Sten lined the cathedral walls and
stood in small raised towers in the midst of the congrega-
tion. For the most part, the guards carried cudgels that
bore the elliptical rings that were Kabraxis's sign cleverly
worked into the wire-bound hilt. Other guards carried
crossbows that had been magically enchanted by mystic
gems. The guards dressed in black chainmail with stylized
silver icons of the elliptical rings on their chests. All of
them were hard men, warriors who had ventured down
the Black Road, as the Way of Dreams was called by initiates, and had been imbued with greater strength and
speed than normal men.

The dozen acolytes touched their torches to different
spots on the wall that held the stage and Cholik's balcony.
Cholik watched as the flames leapt up the whale-oil-fed
channels and came straight up to him.

The flames, aided by a ward that was laid upon the wall, raced around Cholik and lifted the balcony and the design from the wall, exposing the flaming face of the cowled snake that had been designed by black stones intermixed with white. The flames danced along the black stones and lit in the pits of the snake's eyes.

The audience quieted waiting expectantly to see what would occur. But Cholik sensed the violence in the room that was on the cusp of breaking out. The guards moved at their posts, reminding everyone they were there.

"I am Master Sayes," Cholik said into the sudden silence that filled the cathedral. "I am the Wayfinder, designated so by the hand of Dien-Ap-Sten, Prophet of the Light."

Polite applause followed Cholik's words as it was supposed to, but the expectant air never left the room. Believers though they were, the people waited like jackals at a feast, knowing that as soon as the larger predators left the area, they would have what was left.

Cholik scattered powder around him that ignited in great gouts of green, red, violet, and blue flames that stopped short of the closest parishioners. The scents of honeysuckle, cinnamon, and lavender filled the cathedral. He spoke, unleashing the spell that held the gateway to the wall.

In response to the spell, the flaming cowled snake's head lunged from the wall, hanging out over the crowd and opening its mouth. Cholik rode the balcony that stood out over the snake's eyes. The snake's mouth was the entrance to the Black Road, leading to the gateway where a black marble trail wound over and under and through itself, winding around to bring the traveler back to the snake's mouth bearing the gifts Kabraxis had seen fit to bestow.

"May the Way of Dreams take you where you want to go," Cholik said.

"May the Way of Dreams take you where you want to go," the audience roared back.

Beneath the hood of his robe, Cholik smiled. It felt so right to be in charge of all this, to be so powerful. "Now," he said, knowing they hung on his every word, "who among you is worthy?"

It was a challenge, and Cholik knew it, reveled in the knowledge.

The group went wild, screaming and yelling, announcing their needs and wants and desires. The crowd became a living, feral thing, on the brink of lashing out at itself. People had died within the church, victims of their friends and neighbors and strangers over the past year, and the limestone floor had drunk down their blood, putting down crystal roots into the ground beneath that Kabraxis had one day shown Cholik. The roots looked like cones of weeping blood rubies, never quite solid and seeming to ooze into the earth more with every drop that was received.

Undulating, taking Cholik with it, the fiery snake head reached out over the crowd, over the first tier of people, then over the second. People held their ill and diseased children above them, calling out to Dien-Ap-Sten to bless them with a cure. The wealthier people among the audience hired tall warriors to hold them on their shoulders, putting them that much closer to the entrance to the Black Road.

The snake's tongue flicked out, a black ribbon of translucent obsidian that was as fluid as water, and the choice was made.

Cholik gazed at the child who had been held up by his father, seeing that it wasn't one child but two somehow grown together. The children possessed only two arms and two legs attached to two heads and a body and a half. They looked no more than three years of age.

"An abomination," a man in the audience cried out.

"It should never have been allowed to live," another man said.

"Demon born," still another said.

The dozen acolytes with the torches raced forward, aided by the guards till they reached the chosen one.

There has to be some mistake, Cholik thought as he stared at the afflicted children knitted together of their own flesh and bone. He couldn't help feeling that Kabraxis had betrayed him, though he could think of no reason the demon would do that.

Children so severely deformed usually died during childbirth, as did the women who bore them. Their fathers put the children who didn't die to death, or it was done by the priests. Cholik had executed such children himself, then buried them in consecrated earth in the Zakarum Church. Other deformed children's bodies were sold to mages, sages, and black marketers who trafficked in demonic goods.

The acolytes surrounded the father and the conjoined children, filling the area with light. The chainmail-clad guards shoved the crowd back from the father, making more room.

Cholik looked at the man and had to force himself to speak. "Will your sons follow the Black Road, then?"

Tears ran down the father's face. "My sons can't walk, Wayfinder Sayes."

"They must," Cholik said, thinking that was perhaps the way to break the moment. Some who wanted to walk the Black Road gave in to their own fears at the last minute and did not go. The chance to walk the Black Road was never offered again.

Unbidden, the snake's obsidian tongue flicked out and coiled around the twin boys. Without apparent effort, the snake pulled the boys into its fanged mouth. They screamed as they approached the curtain of flames that hugged the huge head.

Standing on the platform over the ridge of the snake's heavy brow and peering through the fire, Cholik only saw the two boys disappear beneath him and couldn't see them anymore. He waited, uncertain what would happen, afraid that he was about to lose all that he had invested in.

Meridor stood at her mother's side, watching as the massive stone snake licked her little brothers into its huge, gaping maw. Mikel and Dannis passed so close to the flames that light the snake's face—she knew they didn't actually have faces because her father told her that, and her older brothers made fun of her when she mentioned it—that she felt certain they were going to be cooked.

Her uncle Ramais always told stories about children getting cooked and eaten by demons. And sometimes those children were baked into pies. She always tried to figure out how a child pie would look, but whenever she asked her mother, her mother would always tell her she needed to stay away from her uncle and his terrible stories. But Uncle Ramais was a sailor for the Westmarch Navy and always had the best stories. She was old enough that she knew she couldn't believe all of her uncle's stories, but it was still fun making believe that she did.

Meridor really didn't want her younger brothers baked or broiled or burned in any manner. At nine years of age and the youngest girl in a household of eight children, she was the one who watched and cleaned Mikel and Dannis the most. Some days she got tired of them because they were always cranky and uncomfortable. Da said it was because each of her brothers was a tight fit living in one body. Sometimes Meridor wondered if Mikel's and Dannis's other arms and legs were somehow tucked up into the body they shared.

But even though they were troublesome and cranky, she didn't want them eaten.

She watched, staring at the stone snake head as it gulped her brothers down. Since no one was listening to her, she prayed the way she'd been taught to in the small Zakarum Church. She felt guilty because her da had told her that the new prophet was the only chance her brothers had of living. They were getting sicker these days, and they were more aware that they weren't like anybody else and couldn't walk or move the way they wanted to. She thought it must be pretty horrible. They couldn't be happy with each other or anyone else.

"Way of Dreams! Way of Dreams!" the people around her yelled, shaking their fists in the air.

The yelling always made Meridor uncomfortable. The people always sounded so angry and so frightened. Da had always told her that the people weren't that way; it was just that they were all so hopeful. Meridor couldn't understand why anyone would want to walk down into the stone snake's belly. But that was where the Way of Dreams was, and the Way of Dreams—according to Da—could accomplish all kinds of miracles. She had seen a few of them over the past year, but they hadn't mattered much. No one she knew had ever been chosen by Dien-Ap-Sten.

On some evenings, when the family gathered around their modest table, everyone talked about what they would wish for if they had the chance to walk the Way of Dreams. Meridor hadn't added much to the conversation at those times because she didn't know what she wanted to be when she grew up.

Lying on the snake's tongue, Meridor's brothers wailed and screamed. She saw their tiny faces, tears glittering like diamonds on their cheeks as they screamed and wept.

Meridor looked up at her mother. "Ma."

"Shhh," her mother responded, knotting her fists in the fancy dress she'd made to go to the Church of the Prophet of the Light. She'd never worn anything like that to the Zakarum Church, and she'd always said that being poor wasn't a bad thing in the eyes of the church. But Da and Ma both insisted that everybody be freshly bathed and clean both nights a week that they went to the new church.

Scared and nervous, Meridor fell silent and didn't talk. She watched as Mikel and Dannis rolled in the snake's mouth toward the Way of Dreams housed in its gullet. Over the months of their visits to the church, she had seen people walk into the snake's mouth, then walk back out again, healed and whole. But how could even Dien-Ap-Sten heal her brothers?

The snake's mouth closed. Above it on the platform over the snake's fiery eyes, Master Sayes led the church in prayer. The screams of the two little boys echoed through the cathedral. Knotting her fists and pressing them against her chin as she listened to the horrid screams, Meridor backed away and bumped into the man standing beside her.

She turned at once to apologize because many adults in the church were short-tempered with children. Children got chosen a lot by Dien-Ap-Sten for healing and miracles, and most of the adults didn't feel they deserved it.

"I'm sorry," Meridor said, looking up. She froze when she saw the monstrous face above her.

The man was tall and big, but that was somewhat hidden beneath the simple woolen traveling cloak he wore. His clothing was old and patched, showing signs of hard usage and covered over with road dust and grit. The frayed kerchief at his neck was tied by a sailor's knot that Uncle Ramais had showed her. The man stood like a shadow carved out of the crowd.

But the most horrible thing about him was his face. It was blackened from burning, the skin crisp and ridged as it had pulled together from the heat. Fine, thin cracks showed in the burned areas, and flecks of blood ran down his face like sweat. Most of the damage was on the left side of his face and looked like an eclipse of the moon. There had been one of those the night Mikel and Dannis had been born.

"It's all right, girl," the man said in a hoarse voice.

"Does it hurt?" Meridor asked. Then she clapped a hand over her mouth when she remembered that many adults didn't like being asked questions, especially about things they probably didn't want to talk about.

A small smile formed on the man's cracked and blistered mouth. New blood flecks appeared on his burned cheek, and pain shone in his eyes. "All the time," he answered.

"Are you here hoping to get healed?" Meridor asked, since he seemed to be open to questions.

"No." The man shook his head, and the movement

caused the hood of his traveling cloak to shift, baring his head a little and revealing the gnarled stubble of burned hair that poked through the blackened skin.

"Then why are you here?"

"I came to see this Way of Dreams that I had heard so much about."

"It's been here a long time. Have you been here before?"

"No."

"Why not?"

The burned man glanced down at her. "You're a curious child."

"Yes. I'm sorry. It's none of my business."

"No, it's not." The man stared at the stone snake as the drums boomed, the cymbals clashed, and the pipes continued their writhing melodies. "Those were your brothers?"

"Yes. Mikel and Dannis. They're conjoined." Meridor stumbled over the word a little. It just didn't sound right. Even after all the years of having to tell other people about her brothers, she still couldn't say it right all the time.

"Do you believe they're abominations?"

"No." Meridor sighed. "They're just unhappy and in pain."

The boys' screams tore through the cathedral again. Atop the stone snake, Master Sayes showed no sign of stopping the ritual.

"They sound like they're in pain now."

"Yes." Meridor worried about her brothers as she always did when they were out of her sight. She spent so much time taking care of them, how could she not be worried?

"You've seen others healed?" the burned man asked.

"Yes. Lots." Meridor watched the undulations of the stone snake. Were Mikel and Dannis walking the Way of Dreams now? Or were they just trapped inside the snake while truly terrible things happened to them?

"What have you seen?" the man asked.

"I've seen the crippled made whole, the blind made to see, and all kinds of diseases healed."

"I was told that Dien-Ap-Sten usually picks children to heal."

Meridor nodded.

"A lot of adults don't like that," the burned man said. "I heard them talking in the taverns in town and on the ship that brought me here."

Meridor nodded again. She had seen people get into fights in Bramwell while discussing such things. She was determined not to argue or point out that there were a lot of sick kids in the city.

"Why do you think Dien-Ap-Sten picks children most of the time?" the burned man asked.

"I don't know."

The burned man grinned as he watched the stone snake. Blood wept from his upper lip and threaded through his white teeth and over the blistered flesh of his pink lips. "Because they are impressionable and because they can believe more than an adult, girl. Show an adult a miracle, and he or she will reach for logical conclusions for why it happened. But the heart of a child . . . by the Light, you can win the heart of a child forever."

Meridor didn't completely understand what the man was talking about, but she didn't let it bother her. She'd already discovered that there were things about adults that she didn't understand, and things about adults that she wasn't meant to understand, and things that she understood but wasn't supposed to act as if she understood.

Abruptly, Master Sayes ordered silence in the cathedral. The musical instruments stopped playing at once, and the hoarse shouts of the crowd died away.

Once when she had been there, Meridor remembered, a group of rowdy men hadn't stopped making noise as Master Sayes had ordered. They'd been drunk and argumentative, and they had said bad things about the church. Master Sayes's warriors had forced their way through the crowd, sought them out, and killed them. Some said that they had killed two innocent men as well, but people stopped talking about that by the next meeting.

Silence echoed in the massive cathedral and made Meridor feel smaller than ever. She clasped her hands and fretted over Mikel and Dannis. Would the Way of Dreams simply tear off one of their heads, killing one of them to make a whole child out of what was left? That was a truly horrible thought, and Meridor wished it would leave her mind. But it would have been even worse, she supposed, if Dien-Ap-Sten had asked her da or ma to decide which child lived and which child died.

Then the power filled the cathedral.

Meridor recognized it from the other times she had experienced it. It vibrated through her body, shaking even the teeth in her head, and it made her all mixed up and somehow excited inside.

The burned man lifted his arm, the one with the hand that was completely blackened by whatever had cooked him. Crimson threads crisscrossed the cooked flesh as he worked his fingers. Flesh split open over one knuckle, revealing the pink flesh and the white bone beneath.

But as Meridor watched, the hand started to heal. Scabs formed over the breaks, then flaked away to reveal whole flesh again. However, the new flesh was still crisp, burned black. She glanced up at the burned man and saw that even the cracks in his face had healed somewhat.

Taking down his hand, the burned man gazed at it as if surprised. "By the Light," he whispered.

"Dien-Ap-Sten can heal you," Meridor said. It felt good to offer the man hope. Da always said hope was the best thing a man could wish for when dealing with fate and bad luck. "You should start coming to church here. Perhaps one day the snake will pick you."

The burned man smiled and shook his head beneath the hood of his traveling cloak. "I would not be allowed to seek healing here, girl." Crimson leaked down his cracked face again. "In fact, I'm surprised that I wasn't killed outright when I tried to enter this building."

That sounded strange. Meridor had never heard anyone speak like that.

With a sigh that sounded like a bellows blast she'd heard at the blacksmith's shop, the snake's huge lower jaw dropped open. Smoke and embers belched from the snake's belly.

Meridor stood on her tiptoes, waiting anxiously. When Mikel and Dannis had entered the snake, she'd never thought that she might not see them again. Or even that she might not see one of them again.

A boy stepped through the opening of the snake's mouth on two good legs. He gazed out at the crowd fearfully, trying in vain to hide.

Dannis! Meridor's heart leapt with happiness, but it plunged in the next moment when she realized that Mikel, little Mikel who loved her sock puppet shows, was gone. Before her first tears had time to leave her eyes or do more than blur her vision, she saw her other little brother step out from behind Dannis. *Mikel! They both live! And they are both whole!*

Da whooped with joy, and Ma cried out, praising Dien-Ap-Sten for all to hear. The crowd burst loose with their joy and excitement, but Meridor couldn't help thinking that it was because having Mikel and Dannis returned meant that another would soon be selected to journey down the Way of Dreams.

Da rushed forward and took her brothers from the fiery maw of the stone snake. Even as he pulled them into an embrace, joined by Ma, movement at Meridor's side drew her attention to the burned man.

She watched as everything seemed to slow down, and she could hear her heartbeat thunder in her ears. The burned man whipped his traveling cloak back to reveal the hand crossbow he held there. The curved bow rested on a frame no longer than Meridor's forearm. He brought the small weapon up in his good hand, extended it, and squeezed the trigger. The quarrel leapt from the crossbow's grooved track and sped across the cathedral.

Tracking the quarrel's flight, Meridor saw the fletched shaft take Master Sayes high in the chest and knock him backward. The Wayfinder plunged from the snake's neck, disappearing from sight. Screams split the cathedral as Meridor's senses sped up again.

"Someone has killed Master Sayes!" a man's voice yelled.

"Find him!" another yelled. "Find that damned assassin!"

"It came from over there!" a man yelled.

In disbelief, Meridor stood frozen as cathedral guards and robed acolytes plunged into the crowd brandishing weapons and torches. She turned to look for the burned man, only to find him gone. He'd taken his leave during the confusion, probably brushing by people who were only now realizing what he had done.

Altough the cathedral guards worked quickly, there were too many people inside the building to organize a pursuit. But one man fleeing through people determined to get out of the way of the menacing guards moved rapidly. She never saw him escape.

One of the acolytes stopped beside Meridor. The acolyte held his torch high and shoved people away, revealing the abandoned hand crossbow on the floor.

"Here!" the acolyte yelled. "The weapon is here."

Guards rushed over to join him.

"Who saw this man?" a burly guard demanded.

"It was a man," a woman in the nearby crowd said. "A stranger. He was talking to that girl." She pointed at Meridor.

The guard fixed Meridor with his harsh gaze. "You know the man who did this, girl?"

Meridor tried to speak but couldn't.

Da strode forward to protect her, she knew that he did, but one of the guards swung his sword hilt into her da's stomach and dropped him to his knees. The guard grabbed the back of her da's head by the hair and yanked his head back, baring his throat for the knife that he held.

"Talk, girl," the guard said.

Meridor knew the men were afraid as well as angry.

Perhaps Dien-Ap-Sten would take vengeance against them for allowing something terrible to happen to Master Sayes.

"Do you know the man who did this?" the burly guard repeated.

Shaking her head, Meridor said, "No. I only talked to him."

"But you got a good look at him?"

"Yes. He had a burned face. He was scared to come in here. He said Dien-Ap-Sten might know him, but he came anyway."

"Why?"

"I don't know."

Another guard rushed up to the burly one. "Master Sayes lives," the guard reported.

"Thank Dien-Ap-Sten," the burly guard said. "I would not have wanted to go where the Way of Dreams would have taken me if Master Sayes had died." He gave a description of the assassin, adding that a man with a burned face should be easy enough to find. Then he turned his attention back to Meridor, keeping a painful grip on her arm. "Come along, girl. You're coming with me. We're going to talk to Master Sayes."

Meridor tried to escape. The last thing she wanted to do was talk to Master Sayes. But she couldn't escape the grip the guard had on her arm as he dragged her through the crowd.

Sixteen

"I'm tellin' ye, I've seen it with me own two eyes, I have," old Sahyir said, looking mightily offended. He was sixty if he was a day, lean and whipcord tough, with a cottony white beard and his hair pulled back into a ponytail. Shell earrings hung from both ears. Scars showed on his face and hands and arms. He wore tarred breeches and a shirt to stand against the spray that carried across the still-primitive harbor.

Darrick sat on a crate that was part of the cargo he'd been hired to help transport from the caravel out in the bay to the warehouse on the shoreline of Seeker's Point. It was the first good paying work he'd had in three days, and he'd begun to think he was going to have to crew out on a ship to keep meals coming and a roof over his head. Shipping out wasn't something he looked forward to. The sea held too many memories. He reached into the worn leather bag he carried and took out a piece of cheddar cheese and two apples.

"I have trouble believing the part about the stone snake gulping people down, I do," Darrick admitted. He used his small belt knife to cut wedges from the half-circle of cheese and to cut the apples into quarters, expertly slicing the cores away. He gave Sahyir one of the cheese wedges and one of the sliced apples. Tossing the apple cores over the side of the barge attracted the small perch that lived along the harbor and fed on refuse from the ships, warehouses, and street sewers. They kissed the top of the water with hungry mouths.

"I seen it, Darrick," the old man insisted. "Seen a man that couldn't use his legs pull himself into that snake's gullet, an' then come up an' walk outta there on his own two legs again. Healthy as a horse, he was. It was right something to see."

Darrick chewed a piece of cheese as he shook his head. "Healers can do that. Potions can do that. I've even seen enchanted weapons that could help a man heal faster. There is nothing special about healing. The Zakarum Church does it from time to time."

"But those all come for a price," Sahyir argued. "Healers an' potions an' enchanted weapons, why, they're all well an' good for a man what's got the gold or the strength to get 'em. And churches? Don't get me started. Churches dote on them that put big donations in the coffers, or them what's got the king's favor. Churches keep an eye on the hands what feed 'em, I says. But I ask ye, what about the common, ordinary folk like ye and me? Who's gonna take care of us?"

Gazing across the sea, feeling the wind rush through his hair and against his face, the chill of it biting into his flesh in spite of his own tarred clothing, Darrick looked at the small village that clung tenaciously to the rocky land of the cove. "We take care of ourselves," he said. "Just like we always have." He and the old man had been friends for months, sharing an easy companionship.

Seeker's Point was a small town just south of the barbarian tribes' territories. In the past, the village had been a supply fort for traders, whalers, and seal hunters who had trekked through the frozen north. Little more than a hundred years ago, a merchant house had posted an army there meant to chase off the marauding barbarian pirates who hunted the area without fear of the Westmarch Navy. A bounty had been placed on the heads of the barbarians, and for a time the mercenary army had collected from the trading house.

Then some of the barbarian tribes had united and laid siege to the village. The trading house hadn't been able to resupply or ship the mercenaries out. During the course of one winter, the mercenaries and all those who had lived with them had been killed to the last person. It had taken more than forty years for a few fur traders to reestablish themselves in the area, and only then because they traded favorably with the barbarians and brought them goods they couldn't get on their own with any dependability.

Houses and buildings dotted the steep mountains that surrounded the cove. Pockets of unimproved land and forest stood tall and proud between some of the houses and buildings. The village slowly eroded those patches, though, taking the timber for buildings and for heat, but baring several of those places only revealed the jagged, gap-toothed, rocky soil beneath. Nothing could be built in those places.

"Why didn't you stay in Bramwell?" Darrick asked. He bit into the apple, finding it sweet and tart.

Sahyir waved the thought away. "Why, even before they up an' had all this religious business success, Bramwell wasn't for the likes of me."

"Why?"

Snorting, Sahyir said, "Why, it's too busy there is why. A man gets to wanderin' around them streets—all in a tizzy and a bother—an' he's like to meet hisself comin' and goin'."

Despite the melancholy mood that usually stayed with him, Darrick smiled. Bramwell was a lot larger than Seeker's Point, but it paled in comparison with Westmarch. "You've never been to Westmarch, have you?"

"Once," Sahyir answered. "Only once. I made a mistake of signing on with a cargo freighter needin' a hand. I was a young strappin' pup like yerself, thought I wasn't afeard of nothin'. So I signed on. Got to Westmarch harbor and looked out over that hell-spawned place. We was at anchorage for six days, we was. An' never once durin' that time did I leave that ship."

"You didn't? Why?"

"Because I figured I'd never find my way back to the ship I was on."

Darrick laughed.

Sahyir scowled at him and looked put out. "'Tweren't funny, ye bilge rat. There's men what went ashore there that didn't come back."

"I meant no offense," Darrick said. "It's just that after making that trip down to Westmarch and through the bad weather that usually marks the gulf, I can't imagine anyone not leaving the ship when they had a chance."

"Only far enough to buy a wineskin from the local tavern and get a change of victuals from time to time," Sahyir said. "But the only reason I brought up Bramwell today was because I was talkin' to a man I met last night, an' I thought ye might be interested in what he had to say."

Darrick watched the other barges plying the harbor. Today was a busy day for Seeker's Point. Longshoremen usually had two jobs in the village because there wasn't enough work handling cargo to provide for a family. Even men who didn't take on crafts and artisan work hunted or fished or trapped when finances ran low. Sometimes they migrated for a time to other cities farther south along the coast like Bramwell.

"Interested in what?" Darrick asked.

"Them symbols I see ye a-drawin' and a-sketchin' now an' again." Sahyir brought up a water flask and handed it to Darrick.

Darrick drank, tasting the metallic flavor of the water. There were a few mines in the area as well, but none of them was profitable enough to cause a merchant to invest in developing and risk losing everything to the barbarians.

"I know ye don't like talkin' about them symbols," Sahyir said, "an' I apologize for talkin' about 'em when it ain't no business of me own. But I see ye a-frettin' an' a-worryin' about 'em, an' I know it troubles ye some."

During the time he had known the old man, Darrick had never mentioned where he'd learned about the elliptical design with the line that threaded through it. He'd tried to put all that in the past. A year ago, when the gambler had died while under his protection, Darrick had lost himself to work and drink, barely getting by. Guilt ate at him over losing Mat and the gambler. And the phantasm of his father back in the barn in Hillsfar had lived with him every day.

Darrick didn't even remember arriving in Seeker's Point, had been so drunk that the ship's captain had thrown him off the ship and refused to let him back on. Sahyir had found Darrick at the water's edge, sick and feverish. The old man had gotten help from a couple of friends and taken Darrick back to his shanty up in the hills overlooking the village. He'd cared for Darrick, nursing him back to health during the course of a month. It had been a time, the old man had said, when he'd been certain on more than one occasion he was going to lose Darrick to the sickness or to the guilt that haunted him.

Even now, Darrick didn't know how much of his story he'd told Sahyir, but the old man had told him that he'd drawn the symbol constantly. Darrick couldn't remember doing that, but Sahyir had produced scraps of paper with the design on it that Darrick had been forced to assume were in his own hand.

Sahyir appeared uncomfortable.

"It's all right, then," Darrick said. "Those symbols aren't anything."

Scratching his beard with his callused fingers, Sahyir said, "That's not what the man said that I talked to last night."

"What did he say?" Darrick asked. The barge had nearly reached the shore now, and the men pulling the oars rested more, letting the incoming tide carry them along as they jockeyed around the other barges and ships in the choked harbor.

"He was mighty interested in that there symbol," the old man said. "That's why I was a-tellin' ye about the Church of the Prophet of the Light this mornin'."

Darrick thought about it for a moment. "I don't understand."

"I was worried some about tellin' ye that I'd done a bit of nosin' about in yer business," Sahyir said. "We been friends for a time now, but I know ye ain't up an' told me everythin' there is to know about that there symbol or yer own ties to it."

Guilt flickered through Darrick. "That was something I tried to put behind me, Sahyir. It wasn't because I was trying to hide anything from you."

The old man's eyes fixed him. "We all hide somethin', young pup. It's just the way men are an' women are, an' folks in general is. We all got weak spots we don't want nobody pokin' around in."

I got my best friend killed, Darrick thought, *and if I told you that, would you still be my friend?* He didn't believe that Sahyir could, and that hurt him. The old man was salt of the earth; he stood by his friends and even stood by a stranger who couldn't take care of himself.

"Whatever it is about this symbol that draws ye," Sahyir said, "is yer business. I just wanted to tell ye about this man 'cause he's only gonna be in town a few days."

"He doesn't live here?"

"If he had," Sahyir said with a grin, "I'd probably have talked to him before, now, wouldn't I?"

Darrick smiled. It seemed there wasn't anyone in Seeker's Point who didn't know Sahyir. "Probably," Darrick said. "Who is this man?"

"A sage," Sahyir replied, "to hear him tell it."

"Do you believe him?"

"Aye, I do. If'n I didn't, an' didn't think maybe he could do ye some good, why, we'd never be having this talk, now, would we?"

Darrick nodded.

"Accordin' to what I got from him last night," Sahyir said, "he's gonna be at the Blue Lantern tonight."

"What does he know about me?"

"Nothin'." Sahyir shrugged. "Me, young pup? Why, I done forgot more secrets than I ever been told."

"This man knows what this symbol represents?"

"He knows somewhat of it. He seemed more concerned learnin' what I knew of it. 'Course, I couldn't tell him nothin' 'cause I don't know nothin'. But I figured maybe ye could learn from each other."

Darrick thought about the possibility as the barge closed on the shoreline. "Why were you telling me about the Church of the Prophet of the Light?"

"Because this symbol ye're thinkin' about so much? That sage thinks maybe it's tied into all that what's going on down in Bramwell. And the Church of the Prophet of the Light. He thinks maybe it's evil."

The old man's words filled Darrick's stomach with cold dread. He had no doubt that the symbol denoted evil, but he no longer knew if he wanted any part of it. Still, he didn't want to let Mat's death go unavenged.

"If this sage is so interested in what's going on down in Bramwell, what is he doing here?" Darrick asked.

"Because of Shonna's Logs. He came here to read Shonna's Logs."

Buyard Cholik lay supine on a bed in the back room of the Church of the Prophet of the Light and knew that he was dying. His breath rattled and heaved in his chest, and his lungs filled with his own blood. Try as he might, he could not see the face of the man—or woman—who had so gravely wounded him.

In the beginning, the pain from the arrow embedded in his chest had felt as if a red-hot poker had been shoved into him. When the pain had begun to subside, he'd mistakenly believed it was because he hadn't been as badly hurt as he'd at first feared. Then he'd realized that he wasn't getting better; the pain was going away because he was dying. Death closing in on him robbed him of his senses.

He silently damned the Zakarum Church and the Light he'd grown to love and fear as a child. Wherever they were, he was certain that they were laughing at him now. Here he was, his youth returned to him, stricken down by an unknown assassin. He damned the Light for abandoning him to old age when it could have killed him young before fear of getting infirm and senile had settled in, and he damned it for letting him be weak enough to allow his fear to force him to seek a bargain with Kabraxis. The Light had driven him into the demon's arms, and he'd been betrayed again.

You haven't been betrayed, Buyard Cholik, Kabraxis's calm voice told him. *Do you think I would let you die?*

Cholik had believed the demon would let him die. After all, there were plenty of other priests and even acolytes who could step into the brief void that Cholik felt he would leave in his passing.

You will not die, Kabraxis said. *We still have business to do together, you and I. Clear the room that I may enter. I don't have enough power to maintain an illusion to mask myself and heal you at the same time.*

Cholik drew a wheezing breath. Fear rushed through him, winding hard and coarse as a dry-mouthed lizard's tongue. He had less room to breathe now than he had during his last breath. His lungs were filling up with his blood, but there was hardly any pain.

Hurry. If you would live, Buyard Cholik, hurry.

Coughing, gasping, Cholik forced open his heavy eyelids. The tall ceiling of his private rooms remained blurred and indistinct. Blackness ate at the edges of his vision, steadily creeping inward, and he knew if it continued it would consume him.

Do it now!

Priests attended Cholik, putting compresses on the wound in his chest. The crossbow quarrel jutted out, the shaft and feathers speckled with his blood. Acolytes stood in the background while mercenaries guarded the doorway. The room was decorated with the finest silks and hand-carved furniture. An embroidered rug from the Kurast markets covered the center of the stone floor.

Cholik opened his mouth to speak and only made a hoarse croaking noise. His breath sprayed fine crimson droplets.

"What is it, Master Sayes?" the priest beside Cholik's bed asked.

"Out," Cholik gasped. "Get out! Now!" The effort to speak nearly drained him.

"But, master," the priest protested. "Your wounds—"

"Out, I said." Cholik tried to rise and was surprised that he somehow found the strength.

I am with you, Kabraxis said, and Cholik felt a little stronger.

The priests and acolytes drew back as if watching the dead return to life. Perplexity and maybe a little relief showed on the faces of the mercenaries. A dead employer meant possibly some blame in the matter, and definitely no more gold.

"Go," Cholik wheezed. "*Now. Now,* damn you all, or I'll see to it that you're lost in one of the hell pits that surround the Black Road."

The priests turned and ordered the acolytes and the mercenaries from the room. They closed the massive oaken double doors, shutting him off from the hallway.

Standing beside the bed where he'd lain hovering between life and death, Cholik gripped a small stand that held a delicate glass vase that had been blown in the hands of a master. Flowers and butterflies hung trapped in death inside the glass walls of the vase, preserved by some small magic that had not allowed them to burn while the molten glass had been formed and cooled.

The secret door hidden at the back of the chamber opened, turning on hinges so that the section of wall twisted to reveal the large tunnel behind it. The church was honeycombed with such tunnels to make it easier for the demon to get around inside the buildings. Even as tall as the ceiling was, the demon's horns almost scraped it.

"Hurry," Cholik gasped. The room blurred further still, then abruptly seemed to spin around him. Only a moment of dizziness touched him, but he saw the rug on the floor coming up at him and knew he was falling although there was no sensation of doing so.

Before Cholik hit the floor, Kabraxis caught him in his huge, three-fingered hands.

"You will not die," the demon said, but his words took on more the aspect of a command. "We are not done yet, you and I."

Even though the demon was in his face, Cholik barely heard the words. His hearing was failing him now. His heart had slowed within his chest, no longer able to struggle against his blood-filled lungs. He tried to take a breath, but there was no room. Panic set in, but it was only a distant drumbeat at his temples, no longer able to touch him.

"No," Kabraxis stated, gripping Cholik by the shoulders.

A bolt of fire coursed through Cholik's body. It ignited at the base of his spine, then raced up to the bottom of his skull and exploded behind his eyes. He went blind for a moment, but it was white light instead of darkness that filled his vision. He felt the pain of the quarrel as it was ripped from his chest. The agony almost pushed him over the edge of consciousness.

"Breathe," Kabraxis said.

Cholik couldn't. He thought perhaps he didn't remember how or that he lacked the strength. Either way, no air entered his lungs. The world outside his body no longer mattered; everything felt cottony and distant.

Then renewed pain forked through his chest, following the path the quarrel had made and spiking into his lungs. Gripped by the pain, Cholik instinctively took a breath. Air filled his lungs—now empty of blood—and with each heaving breath he took, the incredible iron bands of pain released their hold on him.

Kabraxis guided him to the edge of the bed. Cholik only then realized that his blood smeared the bed coverings. He gasped, drinking down air as the room steadied around him. Anger settled into him then, and he glanced up at the demon.

"Did you know about the assassin?" Cholik demanded. He imagined that Kabraxis had let the assassin shoot him only to remind Cholik how much he was needed.

"No." Kabraxis crossed his arms over his huge chest. Muscles rippled in his forearms and shoulders.

"How could you not know? We built this place. You have wards everywhere around the grounds."

"I was also making your miracle happen at the time of your attack," Kabraxis said. "I made two whole boys from the conjoined twins, and that was no easy feat. People will be talking about that for years. While I was still working on that, your assassin struck."

"You couldn't save me from that arrow?" Assessing the demon's abilities and powers had been out of Cholik's reach. Did the Black Road consume Kabraxis so much that it left him weak? That knowledge might be important. But it was also frightening to realize that the demon was limited and fallible after Cholik had tied his destiny to Kabraxis.

"I trusted the mercenaries hired with the gold that I have made available to you to save you from something like this," Kabraxis answered.

"Don't make that mistake again," Cholik snapped.

Deliberately, Kabraxis twisted the bloody quarrel in his hands. Lines in his harsh face deepened. "Never make the mistake of assuming you are my equal, Buyard Cholik. Familiarity breeds contempt, but it also pushes you toward sudden death."

Watching the demon, Cholik realized that Kabraxis could just as easily thrust the bolt through his chest again. Only this time the demon could pierce his heart. He swallowed, hardly able to get around the thick lump in his throat. "Of course. Forgive me. I forgot myself in the heat of the moment."

Kabraxis nodded, dipping his horns, almost scratching the ceiling.

"Did the guards catch the assassin?" Cholik asked.

"No."

"They failed even in that? They could not protect me, and they could not get vengeance on the person who nearly killed me?"

Disinterested, the demon dropped the quarrel to the floor. "Punish the guards as you see fit, but realize that something else has come of this."

"What?"

Kabraxis faced Cholik. "Hundreds of people saw you killed today. They were certain of it. There was much weeping and wailing among them."

The thought that the crowd had lamented his apparent death filled Cholik with smugness. He liked the way the people of Bramwell curried favor with him when he passed through the city's streets, and he liked the desperate envy he saw in their eyes regarding his place in the worship of their new prophet. They acknowledged the power that he wielded, each in his or her own way.

"Those people thought the Way of Dreams was going to be denied to them as a result of your murder," Kabraxis said. "Now, however, they're going to believe that you're something much more than human, made whole again by Dien-Ap-Sten. Talk will go out past Bramwell even more, and the miracles that were seen here will grow in the telling."

Cholik thought about that. Although he would not have chosen the action, he knew that what the demon said was true. His fame, and that of Dien-Ap-Sten, would grow because of the murder attempt. Ships and caravans would carry the stories of the conjoined twins and his near assassination across the sea and the land. The stories, as they always did, would become larger than life as each person told another.

"More people will come, Buyard Cholik," Kabraxis said. "And they will want to be made to believe. We must be prepared for them."

Striding to the window, Cholik looked out at Bramwell. The city was already bursting at the seams as a result of the church's success. Ships filled the harbor, and tent camps had sprung up in the forests around Bramwell.

"An army of believers lies outside the walls of this church waiting to get in," Kabraxis said. "This church is too small to deal with them all."

"The city," Cholik said, understanding. "The city will be too small to hold them all after this."

"Soon," Kabraxis agreed, "that will be true."

Turning to face the demon, Cholik said, "You didn't think it would happen this quickly."

Kabraxis gazed at him. "I knew. I prepared. Now, you must prepare."

"How?"

"You must bring another to me whom I may remake as I have remade you."

Jealousy flamed through Cholik. Sharing his power and his prestige wasn't acceptable.

"You won't be sharing," Kabraxis said. "Instead, you will take on greater power by acquiring this person and bending him to our power."

"What person?"

"Lord Darkulan."

Cholik considered that. Lord Darkulan ruled Bramwell and had a close relationship with the King of Westmarch. During the problem with Tristram, Lord Darkulan had been one of the king's most trusted advisors.

"Lord Darkulan has let people know he's suspicious of the church," Cholik countered. "In fact, there was talk for a time of outlawing the church. He would have done it if the people hadn't stood so firmly against that, and if the opportunity for taxing the caravans and ships bringing the people from other lands hadn't come up."

"Lord Darkulan's concern has been understandable. He's been afraid that we would win the allegiance of his people." Kabraxis smiled. "We have. After today, that is a foregone conclusion."

"Why are you so sure?"

"Because Lord Darkulan was in the audience today."

Seventeen

A chill stole over Cholik at Kabraxis's announcement about Lord Darkulan's presence in the church. The man had never come there before.

"Lord Darkulan entered the church disguised," Kabraxis went on. "No one knew he was here except for his bodyguards and me. And now you."

"He may have hired the assassin," Cholik said, feeling his anger rise. He gazed down at his chest, seeing the crimson-stained robe and the hole where the quarrel had penetrated. Only unblemished flesh showed beneath now.

"No."

"Why are you so certain?"

"Because the assassin strove alone to murder you," Kabraxis said. "If Lord Darkulan had organized the murder, he would have ordered three or four crossbowmen into the church. You would have been dead before you hit the floor."

Cholik's mouth went dry. A thought occurred to him, one that he didn't want to investigate, but he was drawn to it as surely as a moth was drawn to the candle flame. "If they had killed me, would you have been able to return me to life?"

"If I'd had to do that, Buyard Cholik, you would not have recognized the true chill of death. But neither would you have known again the fiery passion of life."

An undead thing, Cholik realized. The thought almost made him sick. Images of lurching zombies and skeletons with ivory grins came to him. As a priest for the Zakarum Church, he'd been called on to clear graveyards and buildings of undead things that had once been humans and animals. And he had nearly been damned with coming back as one of them. His stomach twisted in rebellion, and sour bile painted the back of his mouth.

"You would not have been merely animated as those things were," Kabraxis said. "I would have gifted you with true unlife. Your thoughts would have remained your own."

"And my desires?"

"Your desires and mine are closely aligned at this time. There would have been little you would have missed."

Cholik didn't believe it. Demons lived their lives differently from men, with different dreams and passions. Still, he couldn't help wondering if he would have been less—or more?

"Perhaps," Kabraxis said, "when you are more ready, you'll be given the chance to find out. For now, you've learned to hang on to your life as it is."

"Then why was Lord Darkulan here?" Cholik asked.

The demon smiled, baring his fangs. "Lord Darkulan has a favored mistress dying of a slow-acting poison that was given to her by Lady Darkulan only yesterday."

"Why?"

"Why? To kill her, of course. It seems that Lady Darkulan is a jealous woman and only discovered three days ago that her husband was seeing this other woman."

"Wives have killed their husbands' mistresses before," Cholik said. Even past royal courts of Westmarch had stories about such events.

"Yes," Kabraxis replied, "but it appears that Lord Darkulan's mistress of the last three months is also the daughter of the leader of the Bramwell merchants' guild. If the daughter should die, the merchant will wreak havoc with Bramwell's trade agreements and use his influence in the Westmarch royal courts to have his daughter's murderess brought to justice."

"Hodgewell means to have Lady Darkulan brought up on charges?" Cholik couldn't believe it. He knew the merchant Kabraxis was talking about. Ammin Hodgewell was a spiteful, vengeful man who had stood against the Church of the Prophet of the Light since its inception.

"Hodgewell means to have her hanged on the Block of Justice. He's working now to bring charges against Lady Darkulan."

"Lord Darkulan knows this?"

"Yes."

"Why doesn't he enlist the aid of an apothecary?"

"He has," Kabraxis said. "Several of them, in fact, since it was discovered yesterday that his mistress is doomed to a lingering illness. None of the apothecaries or healers can save her. She has only one salvation left to her."

"The Way of Dreams," Cholik breathed. The implications of the impending murder swirled in his mind, banishing all thoughts of his near death.

"Yes," Kabraxis said. "You understand."

Cholik glanced at the demon, hardly daring to hope. "If Lord Darkulan comes to us for aid and we are able to save his mistress from the poison, save his wife from being hanged, and keep the peace in Bramwell—"

"We will claim him on the Black Road," the demon said. "Then Lord Darkulan will be ours now and forever. He will be our springboard into Westmarch and the destiny that lies before us."

Cholik shook his head. "Lord Darkulan is no young man to give into his passions with a woman of Merchantman Hodgewell's standing."

"He had no choice," Kabraxis said. "The young woman's desire for him became overwhelming. And Lord Darkulan's desires for her became strong as well."

Understanding flooded Cholik, and he gazed at the demon in wonder. "You. *You* did this."

"Of course."

"What about the poison that Lady Darkulan used? I can't believe that all of Lord Darkulan's healers and apothecaries couldn't find an antidote."

"I gave it to Lady Darkulan," Kabraxis admitted, "even as I consoled her over her husband's infidelity. Once she had the poison, she wasted no time in the administration of it."

"How much longer does Hodgewell's daughter have before the poison kills her?" Cholik asked.

"Till tomorrow night."

"And Lord Darkulan knows this?"

"Yes."

"Then today—"

"I believe he meant to come forward today after the service," Kabraxis said. "Your attempted assassination caused his bodyguards to get him clear of the church. Some of the church's guards—as well as the lord's protectors—were killed in that maneuver, which helped cover the real assassin's escape."

"Then Lord Darkulan will still come," Cholik said.

"He must," Kabraxis agreed. "He has no choice. Unless he wishes to see his mistress dead by nightfall tomorrow and witness his wife's hanging shortly after that."

"Lord Darkulan might take his wife and try to run."

Kabraxis grinned. "And leave his riches and power behind? For the love of a woman he betrayed? A woman who can no longer love him back in the same manner as before? No. Lord Darkulan would see them both dead before he would willingly abdicate his position here. But even that won't save him. If all of this comes to light and the women die—"

"Especially when the people believe he could have saved them both by turning to the Church of the Prophet of the Light as they have all done with their own problems," Cholik said, halfway stunned by the devious simplicity of Kabraxis's scheme, "Lord Darkulan will fall out of favor with the populace."

"You do see," Kabraxis said.

Cholik stared at the demon. "Why didn't you tell me any of this?"

"I did," Kabraxis explained. "As soon as you needed to know."

Part of Cholik's upbringing in the Zakarum Church whispered into the back of his mind. *Demons can influence men, but only if those men are willing to listen.* At any point, Kabraxis's multitiered scheme might have come apart.

The mistress might not have fallen for the lord. The lord might not have betrayed his lady or might have broken the relationship off and confessed his indiscretions. And the lady might have taken a lover out of vengeance rather than poison the woman who took her husband.

If the plan had not worked, Cholik would never have known, and the demon's pride would have been intact.

"I humbled them all," Kabraxis said, "and I have brought these lands under our control. And we will have some of the most powerful people here as our allies. Lord Darkulan will be thankful for the salvation of his mistress, just as Merchantman Hodgewell will be grateful for the salvation of his daughter."

Cholik examined the plan. It was bold and cunning and duplicitous—exactly what he would have expected from a demon. "We have it all," he said, looking back at Kabraxis.

"Yes," the demon replied. "And we will have more."

Someone knocked on the chamber doors.

"What?" Cholik said with some annoyance.

"Master Sayes," the priest called from the other side, "I only wanted to know that you were all right."

"Go to them," Kabraxis said. "We will talk again later." He retreated to the back of the room and passed through the secret door.

Cholik strode to the door and flung it open. The priests, acolytes, and mercenaries stepped back. One of the mercenaries held a small girl before him, one hand clapped over her mouth as she struggled to get free.

"Master," the head priest said, "I beg your forgiveness. Only my worry over you prompted me to interrupt you."

"I am fine," Cholik said, knowing the priest would continue to excuse himself out of his own fear.

"But the arrow went so deep," the priest said. "I saw it for myself."

"I was healed by the grace of Dien-Ap-Sten." Cholik pulled his robe open, revealing the unmarked flesh beneath the bloody clothing. "Great is the power of the Prophet of the Light."

"Great is the power of the Prophet of the Light," the priests replied at once. "May Dien-Ap-Sten's mercies be eternal."

Cholik pulled his robe back around himself. He looked at the struggling girl in the mercenary's hands. "What is this child doing here?"

"She is the sister to the boys that Dien-Ap-Sten made whole today," the mercenary said. "She also saw the assassin."

"This child did, and yet you and your men did not?" Cholik's voice held the unforgiving edge of bared steel.

"She stood beside him when he loosed his shaft at you, Master Sayes," the mercenary replied. He looked uncomfortable.

Cholik stepped toward the man. The priests and the other mercenaries moved back, as if expecting Cholik to summon down a lightning bolt to reduce the mercenary leader to ash. The thought, Cholik had to admit, was tempting. He looked away from the quaking mercenary and at the girl. The resemblance between the girl and the conjoined twins was striking.

Tears leaked from the girl's eyes as she shuddered and cried. Her fear had turned her pale.

"Release her," Cholik said.

Reluctantly, the mercenary removed his big, callused hand from the girl's mouth. She drew in a deep, quaking breath. Tears continued to trickle down her face as she glanced around, seeking some way to escape.

"Are you all right, child?" Cholik asked in a soft voice.

"I want my da," the girl said. "I want my ma. I didn't do anything."

"Did you see the man who shot me?" Cholik asked.

"Yes." Her tear-filled eyes gazed up at Cholik. "Please, Master Sayes. I didn't do anything. I would have screamed, but he was too fast. He shot you before I could think. I didn't think he was going to do it. I wouldn't hurt you. You saved my brothers. Mikel and Dannis. You saved them. I wouldn't hurt you."

Cholik put a comforting hand on the girl's shoulder. He felt her shudder and cringe at his touch. "Easy, child. I only need to know about the man who tried to kill me. I won't hurt you, either."

She looked at him. "Promise?"

The girl's innocence touched Cholik. Promises were easy to give to the young; they wanted to believe.

"I promise," Cholik said.

The girl looked around, as if making sure the hard-faced mercenaries had heard Master Sayes's promise as well.

"They will not touch you," Cholik said. "Describe the man who shot me."

She gazed at him in big-eyed wonderment. "I thought he killed you."

"He can't," Cholik said. "I'm one of the chosen of Dien-Ap-Sten. No mortal man may take my life as long as I stay in the prophet's favor."

The girl sipped air again, becoming almost calm. "He was burned. Nearly all of his face was burned. His hands and arms were burned."

The description meant nothing to Cholik. "Is there anything else you noticed about him?"

"No." The girl hesitated.

"What is it?" Cholik asked.

"I think he was afraid that you would know him if you saw him," the girl said. "He said that he was surprised that he was let into the building."

"I've never seen a man burned so badly as you say who still lived."

"Maybe he didn't live," the girl said.

"What makes you say that?"

"I don't know. I just don't see how anyone could live after being burned so bad, is all."

Pursued by a dead man? Cholik turned the thought over in his mind for a short time.

Come, Kabraxis said in his mind. *We have things to do. The assassin is gone.*

Cholik reached into the pocket of his robe and took out a few silver coins. The amount was enough to feed a family in Bramwell for months. Once, perhaps, the money might have meant something to him. Now, it was only a bargaining tool. He placed the silver coins in the girl's hand and folded her fingers over them.

"Take this, girl," Cholik said, "as a token of my appreciation." He glanced up at the nearest mercenary. "See that she gets back to her family."

The mercenary nodded and led the little girl away. She never once looked back.

Despite the fact that more than a year had passed since he'd found Kabraxis's gateway under the remains of Tauruk's Port and Ransim, Cholik's mind wandered back to the labyrinth and the chamber where he'd released the demon back into the human world. One man had escaped that night, a Westmarch sailor who had even evaded the skeletons and zombies Kabraxis had raised to kill everyone there.

Cholik felt that no one in Bramwell would have dared attack him in the church. And if the man were burned as badly as the girl described, someone would have come forward to identify him and hope to earn a reward from Dien-Ap-Sten or himself.

So it had been an outsider. Someone not even the populace of the city had known about. Yet it had to be someone who had known Cholik from before.

Where had the man who had escaped from Tauruk's Port gone? If this was him, and it made no sense for it to be anyone else, why had he waited so long before he'd stepped forward? And why approach Cholik now at all?

It was unsettling. Especially when Cholik thought about how near the quarrel had come to piercing his heart. Thoughts churning, Cholik reentered his private chamber to plan and scheme with the demon he had freed. Whatever chance the assassin had had was now gone. Cholik would never be caught unprepared again. He consoled himself with that.

*   *   *

Back and shoulders on fire from all the lifting he'd done during the day, Darrick entered the Blue Lantern. Pipe smoke and the closing night filled the tavern with darkness. Men swapping stories and telling lies filled the tavern with noise. To the west, near where the mouth of the Gulf of Westmarch met the Frozen Sea, the sunset settled into the water, looking like dying red embers scattered from a stirred campfire.

A cold north wind followed Darrick into the tavern. The weather had changed in the last hour, just as the ships' captains and mates had been thinking it would. Come morning, Sahyir had told Darrick, there might even be a layer of ice covering the harbor. It wouldn't be enough to lock the ships in, but that time wasn't far off, either.

Men looked up as Darrick walked through the small building. Some of the men knew him, and some were from the ships out in the harbor. All of their eyes were wary. Seeker's Point wasn't a big village, but the numbers swelled when ships were in the harbor. And if a man wanted trouble in the village, the Blue Lantern was where he came.

There was no table space in the tavern. Three men Darrick knew slightly offered their tables with their friends. Darrick thanked them but declined, passing on through the tables till he spotted the man Sahyir had talked about earlier that day.

The man was in his middle years, gray showing in his square-cut beard. He was broad-shouldered and a little overweight, a solid man who had seen an active life. His clothing was second-hand, worn but comfortable-looking, and warm enough against the cool winds blowing in from the north. He wore round-lensed spectacles, and Darrick could still count on the fingers of both hands how many times he'd seen such devices.

A platter of bread and meat sat to the sage's left. He wrote with his right hand, pausing every now and again to dip his quill into an inkwell beside the book he worked in. A whale-oil lantern near the book provided him more light to work by.

Darrick stopped only a short distance from the table, uncertain what he should say.

Abruptly, the sage looked up, peering over his spectacles. "Darrick?"

Startled, Darrick said nothing.

"Your friend Sahyir named you," the sage said. "He told me when he talked to me last night that you might be stopping by."

"Aye," Darrick said. "Though I must confess I don't truly know what I'm doing here."

"If you've seen that symbol as Sahyir seems inclined to believe that you have," the sage said, "it's probably marked you." He gestured to the book before him. "The Light knows that the pursuit of knowledge about it has marked me. Much to my own detriment, according to some of my mentors and peers."

"You've seen the demon?" Darrick asked.

Renewed interest flickered in the sage's deep green eyes. "You have?"

Darrick paused, feeling that he'd admitted more than he should have.

An irritable look filled the sage's face. "Damnation, son. If you're going to talk, then sit. I've been working hard for days here, and weeks and months before that in other places. Looking up gets hellaciously tiresome for me." He pointed at a chair across from him with the quill, then closed his book and put it aside.

Still feeling uncertain, Darrick pulled out the chair and sat. Out of habit, he laid his sheathed cutlass across his thighs.

The sage laced his fingers together and rested both elbows on the tabletop. "Have you eaten tonight?"

"No." Unloading imported goods from the ship and then loading exported goods had filled the day. Darrick had only eaten what he'd carried along in the food bag, which had been empty for hours.

"Would you like to eat?"

"Aye."

The sage gestured to one of the serving wenches. The young woman went to get the order immediately.

"Sahyir told me you were a sailor," the sage said.

"Aye."

"Tell me where you saw the demon," the sage suggested.

Darrick held himself in check. "I never said that I saw such a thing, now, did I?"

A frown deepened the wrinkles over the sage's eyes. "Are you always this churlish?"

"Sir," Darrick stated evenly, "I don't even know your name."

"Taramis," the sage replied. "Taramis Volken."

"And what is it that you do, Taramis Volken?" Darrick asked.

"I gather wisdom," the man replied. "Especially that pertaining to demons."

"Why?"

"Because I don't like them, and usually the things that I learn can be used against them."

The serving wench returned with a platter of goat's meat and shrimp and fish, backed by fresh bread and portions of melon that had shipped up that day. She offered mulled wine.

The temptation was there only for a moment for Darrick. For the last year he had tried to bury his life and his pain in wine and spirits. It hadn't worked, and only old Sahyir had seen fit to save him from himself. But as the old man had told him, saving himself was a day-to-day job, and only one man could do that.

"Tea," Darrick said. "Please."

The wench nodded and returned with a tall tankard of unsweetened tea.

"So," Taramis said, "about your demon—"

"Not my demon," Darrick said.

A fleeting smile touched the sage's lips. "As you will. Where did you see the demon?"

Darrick ignored the question. He dipped his finger into the gravy on his plate and drew out the ellipses with the single line threading through them. He even drew the symbol so that the line went under and over the appropriate ellipses.

The sage studied the gravy symbol. "Do you know what this is?"

"No."

"Or whom it belongs to?"

Darrick shook his head.

"Where did you see this?" the sage asked.

"No," Darrick replied. "You'll get nothing from me until I'm convinced I'm getting something from you."

The sage reached into the worn lizard-hide traveler's pack in the chair beside him. Thoughtfully, he took out a pipe and a bag. After shoving the bowl full of tobacco, he set his pipe ablaze with the lantern. He smoked in silence, a hazy wreath forming around his head. He never blinked as he stared at Darrick.

Fresh-shaved that morning, Darrick hadn't seen a more fiercely demanding gaze since the mirror then. Even the Westmarch ships' officers paled by comparison. But he ate, savoring the hot food. By the working standards he was accustomed to in Seeker's Point, the meal was an extravagance. The cargo handling he'd done for the day might have to feed him for two weeks in order to keep him from hunting meager game in the forest with winter soon to be breathing down their necks.

Taramis reached back into his traveler's pack and took out another book. Flipping through the tome, he stopped at a page, laid the book on the table, spun it around, and pushed it across the table toward Darrick. The sage moved the lantern so it shone on the pages more directly.

"The demon that you saw," Taramis said. "Did it look anything like this?"

Darrick glanced at the page. The illustration was done by hand and in great detail.

The picture was the demon he'd seen at Tauruk's Port, the one who had summoned the undead creatures responsible for Mat Hu-Ring's death.

Not entirely responsible, Darrick told himself, feeling his appetite ebb. He owned the majority of that responsibility. He kept eating mechanically, knowing it would be days or weeks before he had the chance to eat so well again.

"What do you know about the symbol?" Darrick asked, not answering the sage's question.

"You're a hard sell, aren't you, boy?" Taramis asked.

Darrick broke a piece of bread and slathered honey butter onto it. He started eating while Taramis tried to wait him out.

Finally giving up, Taramis replied, "That symbol is the one that was longest associated with a demon called Kabraxis. He is supposed to be the guardian of the Twisted Path of Dreams and Shadows."

"The Way of Dreams?" Darrick asked, remembering the stories Sahyir had been telling about Bramwell that morning.

"Interesting, isn't it?" the sage asked.

"Sahyir told me he'd gone to church in Bramwell," Darrick said. "There's a new church there called the Church of the Prophet of the Light. They also mention the Way of Dreams there."

Taramis nodded. "They worship a prophet there named Dien-Ap-Sten."

"Not Kabraxis?"

"It would be pretty stupid for a demon to be going around telling people to call him by his rightful name, now, wouldn't it?" Taramis grinned. "I mean, the whole bit of anonymity would be right out the window if that was the case. Most people wouldn't worship a demon by choice, although there are some."

Darrick waved a hand over his platter. "I appreciate this fine meal you went and bought me, I really do. But I have to tell you, if this story hasn't picked up some by the time I finish, I'm out of here."

"Patience isn't one of your virtues, is it?"

"No." Darrick felt no shame in admitting such.

"Kabraxis is an old and powerful demon," Taramis said.

"He's been around, in one form or another, since the beginning of recorded history. He's been known by dozens, possibly hundreds, of names."

Darrick pointed to the gravy-rendered symbol on the tabletop. "And this is his symbol?"

Taramis puffed on his pipe. The coals in the pipe bowl glowed orange. "I believe this is the demon's primary symbol. Did you see this in Bramwell?"

"I've not been to Bramwell in years," Darrick answered. It had been too close to Westmarch.

"Then where did you see the demon?" The sage's interest was intense.

"I never said I did," Darrick reminded.

"Your friend told me—"

"He told you that I knew about this symbol."

"That's all you've ever told him?"

Darrick sipped his tea and ignored the question. He pointedly returned his attention to his meal. The plate steadily emptied.

"Do you know the meaning of the symbol?" Taramis asked.

"No."

"It's supposed to represent the layers of man. The facets of a man that a demon may prey on."

"I don't understand," Darrick said.

The sage seemed surprised. "You've had no priest's training?"

"No."

"And yet you know of Kabraxis's most potent symbol without training?"

Darrick said nothing as he used his knife to spear a potato chunk.

Taramis sighed. "All right, then. You intrigue me, and that's the only reason I'm going to continue, because I will not tolerate being treated in such a cavalier manner." He tapped the ellipses. "These are the layers of man as divined by Kabraxis, Banisher of the Light."

"Why is he called Banisher of the Light?" Darrick asked.

He glanced around them, making sure none of the sailors or longshoremen was taking much interest in their conversation. In some communities, the discussion of demons was enough to get a man strung up or, at the least, tested by a dunking chair or a red-hot poker.

"Because Kabraxis's main objective in the world of man is to eclipse and replace Zakarum. Kabraxis worked during the Sin War to keep Zakarum from being brought forth by the Archangel Yaerius through his disciple Akarat."

"What of the Archangel Inarius?" Darrick asked, remembering the old stories he'd been told of the Sin War. "It was Inarius who first built a Cathedral of Light in this world."

"Inarius grew overconfident and destroyed Mephisto's temple, and Inarius was enslaved and returned with the Seraph to Hell to be tortured for all time. Kabraxis aided in Inarius's downfall by winning them over to the demon's side."

"I don't remember that," Darrick said.

"The war was primarily between Mephisto and Inarius," Taramis said. "Only a sage or someone who has had priest training would know of Kabraxis's part in the Sin War. The Banisher of Light is a conniving demon. Kabraxis works in the shadows, stretching their boundaries till they cover the Light. Most men who have worshipped him over all those years have never known his true name."

"But you believe he is in Bramwell?" Darrick asked.

"At the Church of the Prophet of the Light." The sage nodded. "Yes. And there he is known as Dien-Ap-Sten."

Darrick tapped the symbol. "What of this?"

"Again," Taramis said, "those ellipses represent the layers of man as Kabraxis perceives them. It is through those layers that he is able to reach into a man's soul, twist it, bend it, and finally possess it. He is not by nature a confrontational demon as are Diablo, Mephisto, and Baal."

Darrick shook his head. "You can't go about just dropping

the names of all those demons like that. They aren't real. They can't be all real."

"The Prime Evils are real."

A chill threaded through Darrick, but even after everything he'd seen—even after everything he'd lost after seeing the demon in Tauruk's Port—he struggled to believe that the worlds of the demons, the Burning Hells, were real and not just stories.

"Have you seen the Church of the Prophet of the Light?"

"No."

"It is huge," Taramis said. "In less than a year, the Church of the Prophet of the Light has become one of the most prominent structures in Bramwell."

"Bramwell isn't a big city," Darrick said. "Mainly fishermen and farmers live there. Westmarch barely keeps a garrison of guards there, and it's mostly a show of support because no invading army would attack Westmarch through Bramwell. The roads are too harsh and uncertain."

"Kabraxis takes generations to build his power," Taramis said. "That's why even the unholy trinity of brothers learned to fear him. Where they waged war and fought with human armies with their own demonic ones, Kabraxis won believers to him."

"Through the layers of man."

"Yes." The sage tapped the outermost ellipse. "First is the fear mankind has of demons. People who fear Kabraxis will acknowledge his leadership, but they will break away at the first chance." He tapped the next ellipse. "Next comes greed. Through the Church of the Prophet of the Light, Kabraxis and the high priest known as Master Sayes, also called the Wayfinder have granted gifts to their worshippers. Good fortune in business, money, an unexpected inheritance. Then he moves closer to the heart." He tapped the next ellipse. "Covetousness. Do you secretly want your neighbor's wife? His land? Worship Kabraxis, and it will be yours in time."

"Only if the man you want those things from doesn't worship Kabraxis as well."

"Not true." Taramis paused to relight his pipe. "Kabraxis weighs and judges those who serve him. If one man—more powerful in the community than another—will better serve Kabraxis's purposes, the Banisher of the Light rewards the more powerful man."

"What of the worshipper who loses whatever the other man wants?"

The sage waved the question away. "Simple enough. Kabraxis tells everyone that the man who lost his lands or his wife or his family wasn't strong in his faith. That he played Kabraxis—or, in this case, Dien-Ap-Sten—falsely and deserved what he got."

Sour bile rumbled in Darrick's stomach. Every word the sage spoke had the ring of truth in it.

Taramis moved to the next ellipse. "From that point, Kabraxis seeks out those people with greater fears. Sickness in your family? Come to the church to be healed. Your father is becoming senile? Come to the church, and have clarity returned to him."

"Kabraxis can do these things?"

"Yes," Taramis said. "And more. Demons have many powers. In their own way, they offer salvation to those who serve them. You've heard of the gifts Diablo, Baal, and Mephisto have given their own champions in the past. Enchanted armor, mystical weapons, great power to raise armies of dead. The Prime Evils rule through fear and destruction, always aiming for subjugation."

"Kabraxis has no interest in that?"

"Of course he does," Taramis said. "He's a demon, after all. Even archangels want those who worship them to fear them just a little bit. Otherwise, why would they choose such fearsome forms and act the way they do?"

Darrick considered the question and supposed it was true. Still, all this talk of demons was foreign to him, something he didn't even want to invest in. Yet he felt he had no choice.

"Archangels for the Light threaten man with being tortured by demons for the rest of his eternal life, and they promise dire vengeance for any who worship and aid the demons." Taramis shook his head. "Archangels are warriors, just as demons are."

"But they have a more generous view of how man is supposed to fit into this world with them."

"That," the sage said, "depends on your belief, doesn't it?"

Darrick sat quietly.

"There are some who believe this world should be cleansed of demons and angels, that there should be no Light or Darkness, and men should find their own way in life."

"What do you believe?" Darrick asked.

"I believe in the Light," Taramis replied. "That's why I hunt demons and expose them for what they are. I've killed eight lesser demons in the last twenty years. Not all of them are the likes of the Prime Evils."

Darrick knew that, but he'd only seen the one demon, and it had been a truly horrifying creature. "What are you going to do to Kabraxis?"

"Kill him if I can," the sage stated. "If not, I mean to see him exposed for what he is, his priest slain, and his church razed to the ground."

The man's words drew Darrick in, and he took comfort in them. Taramis made doing such an incredible thing sound possible.

"You've lost someone to the demon," Taramis whispered.

Darrick drew back.

"Don't bother to deny it," the sage said. "I see the truth in your eyes. You wear your pain like a chevron for anyone who has been through the same thing." He paused, his eyes sliding from Darrick's for a moment. "I lost my family to a demon. Twenty-three years ago. I was a priest. Such a thing wasn't supposed to happen to me. But a demon's hand took my wife and my three children from me."

The lantern light flickered on the table.

"I was young then and full of my studies as a Vizjerei

mage. I taught in one of the outlying schools in my home-lands. A stranger came to our door. We lived in back of the school, just my family and I. This man told us that he had no place to sleep and had eaten nothing for two days. Fool that I was and full of my new position, I let him in. During the night, he killed my family. Only I lived, though most thought I would not." He pulled back the sleeves of his shirt, revealing the long, wicked scars across his flesh. "I have more scars over the rest of my body." He tilted his head back, revealing the thick scar that curved around half of his neck and across his throat. "The priests who saved me had to piece me back together. All of the healers told me later that I should have died. The Light knows I wanted to."

"But you lived," Darrick whispered, drawn into the horror of the story.

"Yes." Taramis knocked ash from his pipe and put it away. "For a time, I resented my life. Then I came to realize that it was a more focused one. The demon that had killed my family would go on to kill other families. I resolved to get well, mentally and physically. And I did. It took me three years to heal and nine years to track down the demon that took my family from me. I had killed two other demons by that time and revealed four others."

"And now you hunt Kabraxis?"

"Yes. When the Church of the Prophet of the Light first came into being, I became suspicious. So I began research-ing it and found enough similarities between the healing and the changes wrought within the worshippers to lead me in the direction of Kabraxis."

"Then why come here?" Darrick asked.

"Because," the sage said, "Kabraxis was once here. For a time, the barbarian tribes worshipped him when they warred against the people of the southern lands. During that time he was known as Iceclaw the Merciless. He suc-ceeded in uniting some of the more powerful barbarian tribes, creating a great horde that landed between the Twin Seas, the Great Ocean, and the Frozen Sea."

Darrick considered the implications. The stories about the barbarian horde went so far back that they were considered only tales to frighten children with. The barbarians had been depicted as cannibalistic warriors who filed their teeth and filled their bellies from the bodies of women and children. "Until Hauklin came with his great sword, Stormfury, and slew Iceclaw during a battle that took six days."

Taramis grinned. "You've heard the stories."

"Aye," Darrick replied. "But that doesn't answer why you're here."

"Because Stormfury is still here," the sage answered. "I came for the sword because it is the only thing that can slay Kabraxis."

"It didn't slay him the first time," Darrick pointed out.

"The texts I read said that Kabraxis fled before the devastating might of Stormfury. Only in the stories of men was the demon reported dead. But I believe the sword has the power to kill Kabraxis. If you can track him back into the Burning Hells with it."

"If you knew all of this, why did you bother to talk to me?"

The sage's eyes searched Darrick. "Because I am one man, Darrick Lang, and I'm not as young as I used to be."

"You know my name?"

"Of course." Taramis waved at the books before him. "I am a learned man. I heard the stories of the discovery of the demon at Tauruk's Port more than a year ago while I was down in Westmarch. And I heard of the young navy officer who lost his best friend while carrying out a mission given him by the king's nephew."

"Then why go through all this subterfuge?"

"So that I could convince you of my cause," Taramis said softly, "and perhaps your destiny."

"What destiny?" Darrick immediately felt trapped.

"You're tied to this thing somehow," the sage said. "You lost blood to Kabraxis, so perhaps that's it. Or maybe there is something more that binds you to the demon."

"I want nothing more to do with that demon," Darrick

said. But even as he said it, he felt uncertain, and with that uncertainty came a harsh wave of fear.

"Really? Then how is it you've ended up here? Where the weapon that will cut Kabraxis down is?"

"I've been drunk most of the past year," Darrick said. "I lost my post in the Westmarch Navy. Drunk and destitute most of the time, I only drifted from town to town, finding enough work to keep myself alive and away from Westmarch. I didn't know I was here till I woke up damn near freezing to death. I knew nothing of that sword until you told me just now. I haven't been following a demon's trail."

"No?" Taramis glanced at the elliptical symbol drawn in gravy on the tabletop. "Then what are you doing here now? Unless you've only come for a free meal."

"I don't know," Darrick admitted.

"You already knew who that symbol belonged to before you spoke to me," Taramis said. "Now that you know the demon is in Bramwell, hiding behind the mystical auguries of the Church of the Prophet of the Light, can you truly walk away from this? From any of this?"

Unbidden, the memory of Mat plunging over the cliffside to his doom trickled through Darrick's mind in slow motion again. The pain, once blinded and muffled by drink for the past year, twisted within him again as if it were new and fresh. Anger raged within him, but somehow he managed to keep it under control.

"The Light has guided you here, Darrick," the sage said in his quiet voice. "It has guided you here to this place and at this time, and made it possible for us to meet, because you have a stake in this. Because you can make a difference. My question is whether you're ready to take up the battle that awaits you."

Darrick hesitated, knowing that either answer he gave—and, perhaps, even giving no answer at all—would doom him.

"You believe the sword can kill Kabraxis?" Darrick asked in a hoarse whisper.

"Yes," Taramis answered. "But only here in the final layer." He tapped the elliptical symbol again. "Two layers yet remain that we've not spoken of. The outermost is where Kabraxis takes initiates to forge them into something more than mere men. Here they must face the fears of a demon world, walk the Twisted Path of Dreams and Shadows. The Black Road."

"The Black Road?" Darrick asked.

"As Kabraxis calls it. He's had several names for it during his campaigns here in the world of men, but its true and proper name is the Twisted Path of Dreams and Shadows. Once facing the demonic world, Kabraxis's chosen must give themselves to him, mind and body and soul, for now and forever. Many fail, and they are cast into the Burning Hells to die and die again for all eternity."

"How are the men changed?"

"They become faster and stronger than normal men," the sage replied. "Harder to kill. And some of them are given an understanding of demonic magic."

"You make getting to Kabraxis sound impossible."

"Not with Stormfury," Taramis said. "And I'm not without magic of my own."

"What if I chose not to go?"

"Then I would go alone." The sage smiled. "But you can't deny this, can you, Darrick? This has become too much a part of you. Perhaps a year ago you would have been able to turn your back on me and walk away. But not now. You've tried to live around what happened to your friend and what happened to you. It's nearly destroyed you." He paused. "Now you must find the strength to live through this."

Darrick looked at the elliptical drawing. "What lies in the final layer?"

Hesitating, Taramis shook his head. "I don't know. The texts that I've read regarding Kabraxis have no answer. It has been referred to as the layer of the greatest fear, but I have no idea what that is."

"It might be good to know what is there."

"Perhaps we can find out together," the sage suggested.

Darrick locked eyes with the man, wishing he were strong enough to say no, that he wouldn't go. But he couldn't do that because he was tired of trying to live half a life and avoid the guilt. He should have died with Mat. Perhaps the only way to escape was to die now.

"Aye," Darrick whispered. "I'll go with you."

Eighteen

Buyard Cholik stood on the platform above the snake's head and awaited the arrival of his guest. Anticipation filled Cholik as he surveyed the empty pews around him. That morning, he had been enthused to see the large room overflowing with people. Every day the service was larger than the day before. There was no longer seating for all those in attendance. Even building as quickly as they were able, the construction crews weren't able to keep pace with the growth.

Yet tonight there was only one person in attendance, and Cholik's elation soared even higher. He remained silent as Lord Darkulan paused at the great central entrance.

Around the lord, a score of armored guards held lanterns and bared weapons. The lantern light glinted from scale mail and keen-edged steel. Voices whispered, and in their barely heard words Cholik detected fear and hostility.

Lord Darkulan was a young man of thirty. His regal bearing showed the regimen he used to stay in shape as a warrior as well as a leader of men. An open-faced helmet with fierce curved horns framed his lean, hawklike features. A mustache followed the sneering curve up his mouth. He wore a dark green cloak that blended with his black breeches and tunic over a dark green shirt. Although it was hidden, Cholik was certain the lord wore the mystical chainmail armor beneath the tunic.

Impatiently, Lord Darkulan waved to one of his warriors.

The man nodded and stepped into the main area of the cathedral. His metal-shod boots clanked as he crossed the stone floor into the cathedral proper.

Cholik raised his voice, knowing from the way the room was constructed that it would be easily heard. "Lord Darkulan, this meeting time was set aside for you. No one else may enter this part of the church."

The warriors swung their lanterns in Cholik's direction. Some of the lanterns had bull's-eye construction and lit on Cholik directly.

Cholik squinted against the blinding light but did not raise his hand to shield his eyes.

"These are only my personal bodyguards," Lord Darkulan responded. "They will offer you no harm. In fact, after the episode today, I thought you would appreciate their presence."

"No," Cholik said. "You requested this meeting, and I acceded to it. We will keep it like that."

"And if I insist?" Lord Darkulan asked.

Cholik spoke words of power and thrust his hands straight out. Flames leapt from his fingertips and ignited the oil-filled channels around the snake's head. Alive once more, the snake's head leapt from the stone wall toward the guard.

Unnerved, the guard threw himself backward. His metal-shod boots scraped sparks from the stone floor as he hurried to rejoin the other guards. The warriors clustered around Lord Darkulan, trying to draw him back to safety. Lanterns swirled like a cloud of fireflies in the main entrance.

"Would you have your mistress die?" Cholik asked as he rode the swaying snake's head. "Would you have your lady hung by the neck? Would you have your own good name dragged through the mud and dung of this city? Especially when I can change all that?"

Lord Darkulan cursed his men and fought them off him. Reluctantly, the warriors stepped away from him. Their leaders talked quickly to their lord, trying to get him to listen to their reason.

The lord paused at the mouth of the entrance and stared at Cholik atop the stone snake's head. Below Cholik, fire clung to the snake's jaws, and he knew it must be a horrific sight in the middle of the dark cathedral.

"They said you were killed this morning," Lord Darkulan said.

Cholik spread his arms, enjoying the role he played. "Do I look like a dead man, Lord Darkulan?"

"More like he's a zombie," one of the guards muttered.

"I'm no zombie," Cholik said. "Come closer, Lord Darkulan, that you may hear my heartbeat. Perhaps, should you truly not believe, I'll let you bleed me. Zombies and dead things don't bleed as the living do."

"Why can't my men accompany me?" Lord Darkulan asked.

"Because if I am to save the people in your life whom you wish saved—if I am to save *you*, Lord Darkulan—you must trust me." Cholik waited, trying not to act as though he had as much depending on the lord's decision as he did. He wondered if Kabraxis were watching, then realized that wasn't the proper question. The proper question was from where the demon watched.

Lord Darkulan took a lantern from one of his men, steeled himself for a moment, then strode into the cathedral. "How is it that you know so much about my business and the affairs of state?" he demanded.

"I am the Wayfinder," Cholik declared. "Chosen of Dien-Ap-Sten himself. How could I not know?"

"A few among those who counsel me suggest that somehow you and this church are behind the troubles that plague me."

"Do you believe that, Lord Darkulan?" Cholik asked.

The lord hesitated. "I don't know."

"This morning you saw me dead, slain by a quarrel from the hand of a treacherous assassin. Yet here I stand. I am whole and alive and ready to help you in your hour of need, my lord. Or perhaps I should turn from you as you have turned from Dien-Ap-Sten and this church since we first began our sojourn among you." Cholik paused. "I could do that, you know. There are some among my own counsel who believe the assassin who tried to kill me today was hired by you and that you are jealous of my own rise to power within your community."

"Those are lies," Lord Darkulan responded. "I have never been one to skulk around."

"And does Lady Darkulan still feel that is a fair assessment of you?" Cholik asked softly.

Lord Darkulan's hand dropped to the hilt of his saber. His voice turned gruff and hard. "Don't press your luck, priest."

"I stared death in the eye today, Lord Darkulan. Your threats won't carry much weight with me. I know that I walk hand-in-hand with Dien-Ap-Sten."

"I could have you driven from this church," Lord Darkulan said angrily.

"There are more citizens and visitors here who wouldn't allow that to happen than you have army or navy to get it done."

"You don't know—"

"No," Cholik interrupted, causing the stone snake's head to rear up above the lord. "You don't know what you're dealing with."

The snake opened its fanged jaws and spewed fire against the stone floor in front of the guards and drove them back.

"You need me," Cholik told Lord Darkulan. "And you need the salvation that Dien-Ap-Sten can offer. If your mistress is saved, your wife will be saved. If both women are saved, your power will be saved."

"Letting you stay here was a mistake," Lord Darkulan said. "I should have had you banished from the city."

"After the first night of miracles here," Cholik said, "you wouldn't have been able to do that. Dien-Ap-Sten and the Way of Dreams bring power to people. Wealth and privilege. Both are for the taking. Health for the sick and infirm and dying." He silently commanded the snake's head to the ground where it lay prone.

Lord Darkulan stepped backward, but the flame still

roiled where it had struck the stone floor. He was separated from his men, but Cholik was also grimly aware that
some of the guards had bows, and even knives could be
thrown that distance.

"You did the only thing you could in coming here
tonight," Cholik said. He walked down the platform cir-
cling the stone snake's neck.

The snake lay quiet and still, but the fiery eyes
darted and watched. Its tongue, smoldering and steaming,
flicked out rapidly, scenting the air. Deep orange embers
swirled through the still air inside the dark cathedral,
turning to black ash shortly before reaching the ceiling.
Waves of heat rolled off the stone snake.

Cholik stopped in front of the snake, knowing the animated creature outlined him, making him seem like a dark
shadow in front of a dreadful beast.

"Perhaps you think you have sealed your doom by coming here tonight, Lord Darkulan," Cholik said softly.

The lord said nothing. Fear etched deep shadows into
his face despite the light given off by his lantern and the
snake.

"I assure you," Cholik said, "that the opposite is true: you
have sealed your future." He gestured at the snake, feeling
the furnace blast of heat as the creature opened its jaws.
"Walk with me, Lord Darkulan. Give your worries and fears
over to Dien-Ap-Sten that he may make them go away."

Lord Darkulan stood his ground.

"You were here today," Cholik said. "You witnessed the
miracle that Dien-Ap-Sten performed on the Black Road
by separating the two boys locked in each other's flesh.
Have you ever seen such a thing done before?"

"No," the lord replied in a quaking voice.

"Have you even heard of such a thing?"

"Never."

"With Dien-Ap-Sten at his side," Cholik promised, "a
man who ventures down the Way of Dreams may do anything." He held out his hand. "Come with me that I may
show you even more miracles."

Hesitation showed on Lord Darkulan's face.

"By morning," Cholik said, "it will be too late. The poison will have claimed the life of your mistress. Her father will demand the life of your wife in return."

"How am I supposed to save them by going with you?"

"On the Way of Dreams," Cholik said, "all things are made possible. Come."

Trying not to show his fear, Lord Darkulan stepped forward and allowed Cholik to take his arm and guide him.

"Be brave, Lord Darkulan," Cholik advised. "You are going to see wonders seldom seen by human eyes. Step into the snake's mouth, and all your fear will be taken from you if you but believe."

Lord Darkulan followed a half-step behind Cholik. They stepped over the stone snake's sharp teeth and followed the black, smoldering ribbon of tongue down into the snake's throat, where it became a black road that wound down into a long hallway.

"Where are we?" Lord Darkulan asked.

"On the Way of Dreams," Cholik replied. "We're going to find your destiny. It takes a strong man to follow the teachings of Dien-Ap-Sten. You will become an even stronger man."

The hallway widened and changed a number of times, but the Black Road remained constant beneath Cholik's feet. He'd talked to several parishioners who had ventured along the Black Road to be healed or receive a blessing, and all of them had described the path differently. Some had said they'd journeyed down familiar hallways, while others were taken through places they'd never seen and hoped they would never see.

A green sun dawned in the hallway before them, and suddenly they were no longer in a hallway. Now the Black Road clung to a cliffside. The path they followed was so high that clouds obscured the view below. Still, the harsh mountain range towered above. Ice glinted on the peaks only a little farther up.

Lord Darkulan stopped. "I want to go back."

"You can't," Cholik replied. "Look." He turned and pointed back along the way they had come.

Flames clung to the Black Road, twisting and curling three times the height of a man.

"The only way open to you is forward," Cholik said.

"I've made a mistake," Lord Darkulan announced.

"This was not the first," Cholik replied.

Spinning abruptly, Lord Darkulan raised his sword, bringing it to within inches of Cholik's unprotected throat. "You will let me out of here now, or I'll have your head from your shoulders!"

Secure in the knowledge that Kabraxis watched over him, Cholik grasped the sword. The sharp edges cut into the flesh of his hand. Blood trickled down the blade and dripped to the Black Road, giving birth to fist-sized fires at their feet.

"No," Cholik said, "you won't." Power coursed through him, turning the sword red-hot in a heartbeat.

Screaming in pain, Lord Darkulan released his weapon and stumbled back. He held his burned hand in disbelief.

Cholik ignored the sizzling pain of his own burning hand, ignored the stink of scorched flesh and the smoke that curled up. Much worse things had happened to him during the trips down the Black Road that Kabraxis had led him on. He could still occasionally feel the demon's talons rooting around inside his brain, scraping against his skull.

Swiveling, Cholik flung the lord's sword over the cliff's edge. He held out his burned and bleeding hand for inspection.

"You're insane," Lord Darkulan said in disbelief.

"No," Cholik stated calmly. "I believe in Dien-Ap-Sten and the power of the Way of Dreams." He held his hand up. Even as he watched, the cuts knitted together, and the burns healed and went away. In less than a moment, his hand was completely healed. "You can believe, too. Hold out your hand, and accept what I am telling you."

Trembling, afraid, and hurting, Lord Darkulan held his hand up.

"Believe," Cholik said softly. "Believe, and you will be given the power to heal yourself and end your misery."

Lord Darkulan concentrated. Sweat popped out on his brow. "I can't," he whispered hoarsely. "Please, I beg you. Make the pain go away."

"I can't," Cholik said. "That is for you to do. Just come to Dien-Ap-Sten willingly. Only a little faith is needed. Trust that."

Slowly, then, Lord Darkulan's hand began to heal. The burns scabbed over, and only a moment or two after that, smooth flesh remained where the horrible burns had been.

"I've done it." Lord Darkulan gazed at his uninjured hand in disbelief. His fingers still trembled.

"Yes," Cholik said. "But the worst is yet to come."

Without warning, the ledge broke away, dropping them into the abyss over the clouds.

Lord Darkulan screamed.

Cholik controlled his own fear. He was on the Black Road now. The warriors and priests who had become part of his inner circle had all experienced much worse than this. All of those men who had reached this point had to relive a horrific nightmare that was their deepest secret.

The bottom of the long fall through the cottony clouds wasn't the bone-breaking stop against jagged rocks that Cholik had expected. Instead, he landed light as a feather in the midst of a moon-dappled bog under a clear night sky.

Lord Darkulan plummeted into the bog, disappearing with a huge splash that threw black mud in all directions.

Cholik grew worried after a time that something had gone wrong. Initiates had died along the way of the Black Road, but generally Kabraxis was selective about who was brought into the inner circle.

"He's fine," the demon said. "Give him a moment more. I found this place and this event in a tight secret place that he seldom goes to these days. Pay attention."

Cholik waited, amazed that he could stand on the bog's surface tension.

Then Lord Darkulan shoved an arm up through the bog, clapped it onto a semi-submerged tree trunk that had fallen a long time ago. Mud covered his head and face, stripping away the regal look and leaving only the frightened man behind.

Lord Darkulan reached toward Cholik. "Help me! Hurry!"

"What is he afraid of?" Cholik asked Kabraxis. Neither of them made a move toward the struggling lord. "The bog is not so deep that he will drown."

"He fears the past," the demon said. "And he should."

Fearfully, Lord Darkulan gazed over his shoulder at the swamp. Naked and dead trees stood out from the loose mud. Dead brush with ashy, curling leaving lined the shore. Skeletons of small creatures, some of them recently dead so that patches of fur clung to them, lay partially submerged in the swamp and on the shore. Dead birds clung upside down by their claws from naked tree branches. Frog corpses floated in the bog.

Lord Darkulan screamed, then was pulled under the bog by something strong and fierce. Bubbles erupted from the mud.

"Is he going to die here?" Cholik asked.

"He will," Kabraxis answered, "if I don't save him. He can't fight this nightmare. It's too strong for him."

The man's arm shot out of the bog again, found the tree trunk, and succeeded in pulling himself out of the muck. When he appeared, a skeleton clung to his back.

Years of submersion in the bog had turned the dead woman's skin to leather, and it sank in tightly to her skull. Once, Cholik knew, she might have been pretty, but there was no way to know that now. The soft blue dress that might once have hidden womanly curves now clung to the emaciated form of the horror that rode Lord Darkulan's back. The dead woman bent close to him, teeth showing through her ruined flesh. She licked out a dead, leathery tongue that caught his ear, then drew it back between her broken teeth. When she bit down, crushing the earlobe like a grape, crimson sprayed.

Lord Darkulan screamed in pain and flailed, trying desperately to shove the dead woman from him and haul himself onto the tree trunk.

"Help me!" the lord called out.

"Who is the woman?" Cholik asked.

"Once," Kabraxis said, "she was his lover. It was during the early years before his marriage. She was a common girl named Azyka, a shopkeeper's daughter. Before the marriage, she told Lord Darkulan she was going to have his child. Knowing he couldn't allow that, Lord Darkulan killed her and left her body in this bog outside Bramwell."

"The girl was never found?" Cholik asked.

"No."

Cholik watched the horrified lord fighting to maintain his grip on the moss-encrusted tree trunk. The dead woman's weight steadily bore him under. Cholik was not amazed by Kabraxis's story. As a priest of the Zakarum Church, he was no stranger to the special privileges invoked by royalty. In Westmarch's history, several murders had been forgotten about and the murderers absolved by special dispensation from the church.

"Help me!" Lord Darkulan screamed.

Kabraxis strode forward. His large feet left only small ripples on the bog water and never once became wet. "Lord Darkulan," the demon called.

The lord glanced up, seeing the demon for the first time. For a moment, Lord Darkulan froze, but the dead woman chewing his ear into ragged, bloody bits caught his attention again. He fought against her, losing his grip on the tree trunk and plunging into the bog up to his chin. The dead woman's hair floated on the bog water.

"Lord Darkulan," the demon said. "I am Dien-Ap-Sten. I am your salvation."

"You're no salvation," Lord Darkulan cried. "You're a demon."

"And you're a drowning man," Kabraxis stated. "Accept me or die."

"I'll not be tricked by one of your illusions—"

The dead woman reached up behind Lord Darkulan and knotted her skeletal fingers in his hair. When she yanked, Lord Darkulan vanished beneath the black muck of the bog.

Kabraxis stood patiently waiting.

For a moment, Cholik believed it was done and that the lord had died in the bog with the specter of the girl he had murdered so long ago. The chill of the swamp blew through Cholik, and he wrapped his arms around himself. As many times as he had ventured down the Black Road, he had never gotten used to the experience. Each time was unique, each fear different.

Lord Darkulan's hand broke the surface, and Kabraxis's hand was there to catch it. Effortlessly, the demon hauled the lord from the muck and the mire with the dead woman still riding him.

"Live or die," Kabraxis offered calmly. "The choice is yours."

Lord Darkulan hesitated only a moment. "Live. May the Light forgive me, I want to live."

A cruel smile carved Kabraxis's horrendous face. "*I* forgive you," the demon mocked. He continued pulling the muddy, bloody lord from the swamp. The dead woman still clung to Lord Darkulan's back, biting his mangled ear and scratching his face with the claws of her free hand.

Kabraxis backhanded the dead woman from Lord Darkulan's back. When he finished hauling the man up, Cholik found that they all once more stood on the solid ground of the Black Road twisting through the high mountains. The swamp was nowhere to be seen.

Lord Darkulan gave in to his fear, shaking and shivering before the demon's wrath. "Don't kill me," the lord pleaded.

"I won't kill you," Kabraxis said, pushing the man to his knees before him, humbling him. "I am going to give you your life."

Shuddering, Lord Darkulan stayed still before the demon.

"You are weak." Kabraxis spoke in deep tones. "I will be

your strength." The demon wrapped one of his large hands around Lord Darkulan's head. "You are unguided. I will be your design." The fingers elongated into sharp spikes. "By your own hand and childish desires of flesh, you are unmade. I will make you a man and a leader of men." With a quick snap of his wrist, the demon drove his spiked fingers through Lord Darkulan's skull. Blood leaked down his face, threading through the mud that clung to his features. "Mind, body, and soul, you are *mine!*"

Lightning flashed through the dark sky above the mountains, followed immediately by the rumbling roar of thunder that shattered all other sounds. The Black Road trembled beneath Cholik's feet, and for a dreadful moment he thought the whole mountain range was going to fall.

Then the lightning and the thunder faded, and Kabraxis withdrew his spiked fingers from Lord Darkulan's skull.

"Rise," the demon ordered, "and begin the new life that I have given you."

Lord Darkulan rose, and as he did the mud and fatigue and blood vanished from him. He stood straight and tall, clear-eyed and calm. "I hear and obey."

"Only one thing yet remains," Kabraxis said. "You must bear my mark that I may keep watch over you."

Without hesitation, Lord Darkulan stripped away his tunic, chainmail shirt, and blouse beneath to bare his chest. "Here," he offered. "Over my heart that I may keep you close to me."

Kabraxis placed his palm over Lord Darkulan's chest. When he removed his hand, the tattoo that was the demon's mark marred the lord's flesh.

"You are in my service," the demon said.

"Till the end of my days," Lord Darkulan said.

"Go then, Lord Darkulan, and know that you have the power to heal your mistress and prevent your wife's hanging. Draw a bit of your blood, mix it in wine, and have her drink it to cure her."

Lord Darkulan agreed and offered his undying loyalty to the demon once more, then followed the Black Road back out of the stone snake's mouth. At the other end of the Black Road, Cholik once more saw the interior of the great cathedral.

"So now you have him," Cholik said, watching as Lord Darkulan rejoined his guards.

"We have him," Kabraxis agreed.

Surprised that the demon didn't sound more satisfied, Cholik looked at him. "Is something wrong?"

"There is a man I have learned of," the demon said. "Taramis Volken. He's a demon hunter, and he has picked up my trail."

"How?"

"It doesn't matter. After tonight, he will no longer be a concern to me. But after the burned man attempted to kill you today, which I did not see coming, I think you should tighten security around the church." Kabraxis paused. "Lord Darkulan should be more than willing to aid you with that."

"There's no way to tighten security completely in the church," Cholik objected. "We admit too many people, and many of them we can't identify, to screen everyone."

"Do it better," Kabraxis snapped.

"Of course," Cholik said, bowing his head and watching as the demon vanished from sight. Cholik's thoughts rushed, scrambling over one another in his head. Who was this demon hunter Kabraxis feared? In their year and more together, Cholik had never seen the demon concerned about anything. The matter was puzzling and more than a little unsettling, even after Kabraxis's assurances that the matter was taken care of.

And how was it that Kabraxis had taken care of the man who hunted him?

Nineteen

Although he'd ridden horses a few times while working with overland trade caravans, Darrick had never grown used to their lurching gait. Even a ship's deck riding the crests of a storm-tossed sea felt more certain than the beast beneath him as it picked its way down the forested hillside.

Luckily, the animal followed Taramis Volken's mount along the narrow trail and required no real guidance from him. He only wished he could sleep in the saddle as some of the other men accompanying them seemed able to do.

Last night at the Blue Lantern tavern, Darrick would not have guessed that Taramis headed the small army of men encamped outside Seeker's Point. But after witnessing their professionalism and dedication to their quest, he understood how they could have escaped notice.

All of the warriors rode in single file along the trail. Two riderless horses testified to the fact that scouts ranged on foot ahead of the group. The men rode with hardly any noise, their gear carefully padded so that nothing clinked or clanked. They were hard-eyed men, like wolves that hunted in a pack. The wintry wind and the leaden, overcast sky of morning further brought that appearance out.

Darrick straightened in the saddle, trying to find a comfortable position. Since leaving the Blue Lantern last evening, he'd ridden all night. A few times he'd dozed in the saddle, exhaustion finally overcoming his fear of falling off the horse, but that had been reawakened after only a moment or two when he woke and found himself sliding.

A birdcall sounded in the quiet of the forest.

Darrick's sharp ears picked the sound out, recognizing that it was false only because he'd heard the same cry earlier. The call came from one of the two scouts ahead. During the night, they'd used owl calls to communicate, but this morning they emulated a small ruby-throated wren that sailors sometimes took on board sailing ships to raise.

One of the scouts stepped from the forest and loped alongside Taramis Volken's mount, matching the long-limbed animal with ease. The scout and the sage talked briefly, then the scout disappeared again.

Taramis appeared unconcerned, so Darrick tried to relax. His muscles were stiff and sore from hauling cargo the day before and the long ride during the night. More than anything, he wanted off the horse, and he wished he'd stayed in Seeker's Point. He had no business among these men. They all seemed to be veteran warriors, and the few words that Darrick had overheard them say alluded to past battles with demons, though none of them was as powerful as Kabraxis.

Darrick pushed his breath out, watching it fog briefly in the chill of morning. He couldn't imagine why Taramis had asked him to come along when there were already so many warriors.

A little farther on, the trail they followed led out into a cleared space. Among a littering of tree stumps sat a small house with a thatched roof. The land to the south of the house had been cleared for gardening. The current crop appeared to be onions and carrots, but there were stands where vine crops had grown during the summer. In back of the garden was a door set into a small hill that Darrick believed would lead to a root cellar. A well occupied the space between the garden and the small barn.

An old man and a young boy came out of the barn. They looked enough alike that Darrick believed they were family, probably grandfather and grandson.

The old man carried a pitchfork and a milking pail.

He handed the pail to the boy and waved him back into the barn. The old man was bald and had a long gray beard. He wore deerskin outer garments, but the neck of a purple blouse showed under the jacket.

"May the Light bless you," the old man said, holding the pitchfork in both hands. A little fear showed in his eyes, but the confident manner in which he wielded the pitchfork told Darrick that the old man was prepared for trouble.

"And may the Light bless you," Taramis said, reining his horse in at a respectful distance from the old man. "My name is Taramis Volken, and if I got your directions right, you'd be Ellig Barrows."

"Aye," the old man said, keeping his stance open. His bright blue eyes roved over the warriors and Darrick. "And if you're who you says you are, I've heard of you."

"I am," Taramis said, swinging down from his horse with easy grace. "I've got papers that prove it right enough." He reached inside his blouse. "They bear the king's mark."

The old man held up a hand. A light sapphire glow enveloped Taramis. For a moment a ruby glow surrounded the sage and kept the sapphire glow from him. Then the ruby light faded and vanished entirely.

"Sorry," Taramis apologized. "Wooten told me you'd be a cautious man."

"You're no demon," Ellig Barrows said.

"No," Taramis agreed. "May the Light blind them and bind them and burn them forever." He spat.

"I bid you welcome to my home," Ellig said. "If you and your men have not eaten, I'll have a simple breakfast out soon enough if you'll have it."

"We wouldn't want to impose," Taramis said.

"It's not imposition," the old man assured him. "As you can tell from the trail you followed up, we seldom have company here."

"I need you to know something further," Taramis said.

Ellig regarded him. "You've come for the sword. I knew

that from the reading I took of you. Come on inside the house, and we'll talk. Then we'll see if you get it or not."

Taramis waved to his men to dismount, and Darrick dismounted with them. The wind whistled through the trees overhead.

Cholik found Kabraxis in one of the rooftop gardens. The demon faced north, his arms folded over his broad chest. The illusion spell he maintained over the garden prevented anyone in the street below from seeing him.

Pausing, Cholik peered over the roof's side, spotting the steady stream of worshippers pouring into the building.

"You sent for me?" Cholik asked, coming to a halt behind the demon. Kabraxis had, of course, because Cholik wouldn't have heard the demon's voice in his head while he was preparing for the morning service otherwise.

"Yes," Kabraxis said. "In dealing with the man I'd learned of, I found out something else interesting."

"Taramis Volken?" Cholik asked. He remembered the demon hunter's name from the previous night's conversation.

"Yes. But there is another man that I recognize with Taramis Volken's group. I wanted you to look at him as well."

"Of course."

Kabraxis turned and crossed the rooftop to one of the small pools in the garden. Passing a hand over the pool, the demon stepped back. "Look."

Moving forward, Cholik knelt and gazed into the pool. Ripples passed over the water's surface, then settled out again. For a moment, Cholik only saw the reflected blue of the sky.

Then the image formed, showing a small house tucked away under the embrace of tall fir, maple, and oak trees. Warriors sat outside the small house, all of them rough-looking and hard traveled. Cholik knew at once that there were too many of them to live at the house. They were visitors, then, but he didn't recognize the house.

"Do you see him?" Kabraxis demanded.

"I see many men," Cholik replied.

"Here." Kabraxis gestured impatiently.

The pool rippled and clouded for a moment, then cleared once more and focused on a wan young man with reddish hair pulled back into a queue. Seated at the base of a big oak tree, a cutlass across his knees, the young man appeared to sleep with his back to the tree. A ragged scar marred one of his eyebrows.

"Do you recognize him?" Kabraxis asked.

"Yes," Cholik replied, recognizing the man now. "He was at Tauruk's Port."

"And now he is with Taramis Volken," Kabraxis mused.

"They know each other?"

"Not that I was aware of. For all I know, Taramis Volken and this man, Darrick Lang, met each other in Seeker's Point last evening."

"You have spies watching the demon hunter?" Cholik asked.

"When I am not watching the man myself, of course. Taramis Volken is a dangerous human, and the quest he's on pertains to us. If he is given what he seeks at this farmer's house, his next move will be to come for us."

"What is it he seeks?"

"Stormfury," Kabraxis replied.

"The mystic sword that turned the barbarian horde hundreds of years ago?" Cholik asked. His nimble mind searched for the reasons Kabraxis would be interested in the sword and why he would think that the demon hunter would turn his sights on them.

"The same." A grimace twisted the demon's hideous face.

Cholik thought then that Kabraxis was afraid of the sword and what it might do, but he also knew he dared not mention that. Desperately, he tried to eradicate the errant thought from his mind before the demon sensed it.

"The sword can be a problem," Kabraxis said, "but I have minions that are even now closing in on Taramis

Volken and his band. They won't escape, and if the sword is there, my minions will retrieve it."

Cholik thought and worked to couch his words carefully. "How is the sword a problem?"

"It is a powerful weapon," Kabraxis said. "A blacksmith imbued with the power of the Light forged the sword hundreds of years ago to use against the barbarian horde and the dark force they worshipped."

Understanding dawned in Cholik. "They worshipped you. You were Iceclaw."

"Yes. And the humans used the sword to drive me from this world then."

"Can it be used against you again?" Cholik asked.

"I am more powerful now than I was then," Kabraxis said. "Still, I will see to it that the sword is destroyed forever and always after this day." The demon paused. "But the presence of this other man troubles me."

"Why?"

"I have cast auguries to show the portents of the things we have done concerning Lord Darkulan," Kabraxis said. "This man keeps turning up in them."

Cholik considered that. Spies he had placed inside the lord's keep had relayed that Darkulan's mistress was already better and on her way back to a full recovery. Lord Darkulan had visited her immediately after leaving the church last evening.

"When did you see this man again after Tauruk's Port?" Cholik asked.

"Only moments ago," Kabraxis said. "When I summoned the lezanti and set them upon the hunt for Taramis Volken and his warriors. I had to scry upon the group to set the lezanti upon the scent."

A shudder passed through Cholik when he considered the lezanti. He'd always believed the creatures to be truly the stuff of legends and myth.

According to the tales he'd been told, the lezanti were created by the blending of a human female's corpse, a freshly slain wolf, and a lizard, creating a fast and ferocious chimera that possessed super-animal cunning, a partially upright physique, and an ability to take a lot of damage and grow limb replacements after amputation.

"If you've only just now seen this man," Cholik said, "how do you know he was the one you saw in your auguries?"

"Do you distrust my abilities, Buyard Cholik?" the demon demanded.

"No," Cholik replied quickly, not wanting Kabraxis to vent the cold rage that filled him. "I just wondered how you kept him separate from Taramis Volken or another of the warriors with him."

"Because I can," the demon replied. "Just as I robbed time of your years and returned your youth to you."

Cholik stared into the pool, looking into the young man's relaxed face. He wondered how the young man had gotten there, more than a year after the events at Tauruk's Port.

"I am concerned because of the magic that was used to open the gateway," Kabraxis said. "When demons come from the Burning Hells, so, too, come the seeds of their potential downfall. It is a balance that is kept between the Light and the Darkness. But by the same hand, no champion of the Light may burst forth without a weakness that can be exploited. It's up to the champion which propensity—strength or weakness—wins out. And it is up to the demon whether he stands against the power that would banish him from this plane again."

"And you think such power has been assigned to this man because he was there the night you came through the gateway back into our world?" Cholik asked.

"No. This man doesn't have such power. And there is a great affinity for darkness in his soul." The demon smiled. "In fact, were we able to get him here and persuade him properly, I think he could be turned to serve me. There is weakness in him as well as strength. I feel it would be no problem to exploit that weakness."

"Then why the concern?"

"The juxtaposition of all the variables," Kabraxis said.

"Taramis Volken's discovery of Stormfury is bad enough, but for this man to appear here so soon after the burned man attempted to kill you, I have to consider how threatening our situation can get. The balance between Light and Dark has always been maintained, and somewhere out there is a threat I have to recognize."

Staring into the pool of water as the view shifted and pulled back, Cholik watched the sleek forms of the lezanti cluster along the ridgeline around the small house. The lezanti stood hunchbacked and broad-shouldered on two clawed feet and legs that bent backward like a horse's rear legs. Lizard's skin hugged the body and shifted colors as quickly as a chameleon's, allowing them to blend into their surroundings with astonishing ease. Tufts of fur spread over their shoulders, crowned their heads around their small triangular ears, and covered their flanks where a hairless lizard's tail flicked and twisted. Their jaws were filled with large fangs.

The church bells rang, signaling the beginning of the morning service.

Cholik stood, waiting for the order to dismiss and return to the church. "This situation is under your control," he said. "The lezanti will leave no one alive."

"Perhaps," Kabraxis said. He gestured toward the pool.

In the image trapped in the water, the lezanti began stealthily closing in on the warriors and the little house in the forest. Hypnotized, remembering the violence the demon-formed creatures were reputed to be capable of, Cholik watched while the cathedral below them continued to fill.

Darrick sat under the spreading oak tree a short distance from the house and held the deep wooden plate he'd been given in his hands. He wished the house had been bigger or that there had been fewer men. The dark chimney smoke pouring into the air let him know there was a fire inside. He wasn't truly cold, but a chance to sit by the fire for a few moments to break the chill that covered him would have been welcome.

The generosity Ellig Barrows showed his unexpected guests was amazing. It was one thing for the old man to have been willing to care for such a large group, but it was even more surprising that he was able to. Breakfast consisted of simple fare: eggs, stringy venison chops, potato mush, thick brown gravy, and fat wedges of bread. But it was all warm and welcome.

As it turned out, both of Taramis's scouts had taken deer in the forest and dressed them out to replace the meat they ate from the old man's larder. There was no replacing the bread, though, and Darrick guessed that the old man's wife would be busy for several days baking to replace what they'd consumed that morning.

Darrick sopped up the last of the gravy and eggs with his remaining piece of bread and drank from his waterskin. Setting the plate to one side for the moment, he enjoyed the sensation of being full and off the horse. He pulled a blanket from his pack and wrapped it around his shoulders.

Winter was coming, marching down from the harsh northlands. Soon enough, mornings would be filled with frost and cold that made a man's bones ache. Darrick kept to himself, watching the other warriors break up into small groups and talk among themselves. As they ate, the warriors also relieved the guards posted in the forest, making sure everyone was fed and rested.

Ellig Barrows and Taramis Volken talked on the covered porch in front of the house. Each man seemed intent on taking the measure of the other. Taramis wore orange-colored robes with silver designs worked into them. During his travels, Darrick had heard descriptions of the Vizjerei robes, but he had never seen them before. The enchanted robes offered protection from spells and demonic creatures.

Darrick knew that Taramis sought to persuade the old man to give him Stormfury, the sword from the old legend. Although he'd seen a number of things in his life as a sailor for Westmarch even before he'd seen the demon at Tauruk's Port, Darrick had never seen anything as legendary as the sword. His mind played with the idea of it, what it might look like and what powers it might hold. But again and again, his thoughts insisted on coming back to why Taramis would believe he belonged with them on this quest.

"Darrick," Taramis called a few minutes later.

Rousing from near slumber, regretting the need to move when he'd finally gotten comfortable against the tree, Darrick glanced at the sage.

"Come with us," Taramis requested, standing and following the old man across the yard.

Reluctantly, Darrick got to his feet and carried the plate to the porch, where it was taken by the old man's grandson. Darrick followed Taramis and Ellig Barrows into the root cellar built into the hillside.

The old man took a lantern from the root cellar's wall inside, lit it with a coal he'd carried from the house, and followed the short flight of earthen stairs down into the small root cellar.

Darrick hesitated in the doorway. The cloying smell of dank earth, potatoes, onions, and spices filled his nostrils. He didn't like the darkness of the cellar or the closed-in feeling he got from the racks of foods canned in jars or the wine bottles. For a house in the middle of nowhere along the Frozen Sea coast, Ellig Barrows and his family had a large larder.

"Come on," Taramis said, following the old man to the back of the cellar.

Darrick crossed the uneven floor dug from the earth and covered with small rock. The cellar's ceiling was so low his head scraped a couple of times, and he kept hunkered down.

A huge stone surface blocked the other end of the cellar. The lantern Ellig Barrows carried clanked against the stone as he stood next to it.

"I was given care of the sword," the old man said, turning to face Taramis, "along with the power to do so by my grandfather, as he was given the power to care for it by his grandfather. I teach this responsibility and power to my own grandson now. For hundreds of years, Stormfury has been in the possession of my family, awaiting the time when the demon would rise again and it would be needed."

"The sword has been needed before now," Taramis said gravely. "But Kabraxis is a cunning demon and doesn't ever use the same name twice. If it were not for Darrick's encounter with the demon in Tauruk's Port more than a year ago, we would not know which one we faced now."

"Iceclaw was a fierce and evil beast," the old man said. "The old stories tell of all the murder and carnage he wrought while he was in our world."

"There were two other times Kabraxis was in the world," Taramis said. "Both times before, Diablo and his brothers sought him out and returned him to the Burning Hells. Only the sword now offers a chance against the demon."

"You know why the sword has never been taken from my family before," Ellig Barrows said. The lantern light deepened the hollows of his eye sockets, making him look like a man days dead.

Darrick shivered at the thought.

"The sword has never allowed itself to be taken," Taramis said.

"Two kings have died trying to take this sword," the old man said.

Darrick hadn't known that. He glanced at Taramis, studying the sage's appearance in the lantern's pale yellow glow.

"They died," the sage said, "because they didn't understand the sword's true nature."

"So you say," Ellig Barrows replied. "There are mysteries about the sword that I don't know. That my grandfather before me didn't know, and his grandfather before him. Yet you come to my house and tell me you know more than all of them."

"Show me the sword," Taramis said, "and you can see for yourself."

"We have been responsible for the sword for so long. It has not been an easy burden to bear."

"It shouldn't have been," Taramis agreed. He faced the old man. "Please."

Sighing, the old man turned to the wall. "You take your own lives in your hands," he warned. His fingers inscribed arcane symbols in the air. As soon as each one was completed, it glowed briefly, then sank into the wall.

Darrick glanced at Taramis, wanting to ask why he instead of one of the other warriors had been brought on this part of their search. Even as he started to open his mouth, the root cellar wall shimmered and turned opaque.

Ellig Barrows raised the lantern, and the light shone into the room on the other side of the opaque stone wall. Eldritch energy sparkled inside the wall, illuminated by the lantern light.

Beyond the wall, wreathed in the shadows of the hidden room, a dead man lay in a niche cut into the hillside. His snow-white beard trailed down to his chest, and he wore animal hides over crude chainmail. A visored helm hid part of the shrunken features that bound the dead man's head. His arms crossed over his chest, and his withered hands—the yellow ivory of his knuckles showing through—gripped the hilt of a long sword.

Twenty

In the hidden room in Ellig Barrows's root cellar, Darrick studied the sword Taramis Volken had come all this way to get and found the weapon was in no way like anything he'd imagined since the sage had told him of it. The sword appeared plain and unadorned, hammered from steel with a craftsman's skill but lacking the touch of an artist. The blade was an infantryman's weapon, not something that would invoke fear in demons.

"You're disappointed?" Ellig Barrows asked, looking at Darrick.

Darrick hesitated, not wanting to offend. "I had just expected something more."

"A jeweled weapon, perhaps?" the old man asked. "Something every bandit you met would want and try to steal? A weapon so unique and striking-looking that everyone would mark its passage and know it for what it was?"

"I hadn't thought of it like that," Darrick admitted. But he also wondered if someone had stolen the real sword a long time ago and left the barbaric piece in its stead. He immediately felt guilty for that, because it would have meant the old man's life had been spent doing useless guard duty.

Ellig Barrows stepped through the opaque wall. "The smith who forged this weapon did think of those things. Perhaps Stormfury isn't an elegant weapon, but you'll never find a truer one. Of course, you'll only know that if you're able to take it."

Taramis followed the old man through the wall.

After a moment, Darrick stepped through the mystical wall as well. A cold sensation gripped him as he passed through, and it felt as if he were walking through the thickest forest growth, having to fight his way through.

"The sword is protected from interlopers," Ellig Barrows said. "No man may touch it or take it if Kabraxis is not within this world."

"And if any try?" Darrick asked.

"The sword can't be taken," the old man said.

"What of the kings who died?"

"One slew members of my family," Ellig Barrows said. "He and all his warriors died less than a day later. The Light is not evil as the demons are, but it is vengeful against those who transgress against it. Another tried to drag Hauklin's body from its resting place. He rose that time and slew them all."

Standing in the crypt carved from the root cellar, Darrick felt afraid. Although the caverns under Tauruk's Port were larger and the huge doorway had seemed more threatening, the dead man lying with the sword clasped in his hands seemed just as deadly. Darrick would have gladly left the crypt and been satisfied never to see anything more of a magical nature.

He glanced at Taramis. "Why did you want me here?"

"Because you are tied to this," the sage said. "You have been since you witnessed Kabraxis's arrival on this plane." He looked at the dead man. "I think that you are the one who can take Hauklin's sword to use against the demon."

"Why not you?" Darrick demanded. For a moment he wondered if the sage was only using him, willing to risk his life in the effort to recover the sword.

Taramis turned and reached for the sword. His hand halted, quivering, in the air several inches from the weapon. The effort he made to reach the weapon corded muscle along his arm. Pain showed on his features. Finally, in disappointed disgust, he drew his arm back.

"I can't take it," the sage said. "I am not the one." He turned to Darrick. "But I believe that you are."

"Why?"

"Because the Light and the Darkness balance each other,"

Taramis said. "Any time power is passed into this world from the Light or the Darkness, a balance must be made. Demons come into this world, and a means of defeating them is also created. If the Light tries to upset the balance by introducing an object of power that can be used against the Darkness, the powers of Darkness intercede to make the balance whole again. Ultimately, the true threat to the balance, whether the Light or the Darkness has the greater power in our world, is left up to us. The people. Just as when the Prime Evils appeared in this world during the time that came to be known as the Dark Exile, the Angel Tyreal gathered the magi, warriors, and scholars in the East and formed the Brotherhood of the Horadrim. Those people would never have come together with such power if the demons had not been loosed in our world. If Tyreal had tried to do this before the Prime Evils had arrived here, Darkness would have found a means to strike a balance."

"That doesn't explain why you think I can pick up that sword," Darrick said. He made no move to try.

"I heard the stories about you when I arrived in Westmarch," Taramis said. "And I began looking for you. But by the time I'd arrived, you'd vanished. I caught up with your ship, but no one knew where you were. I couldn't tell many that I was searching for you, because that might have alerted Kabraxis's minions, and your life could have become forfeit." He paused, locking his gaze with Darrick's. "As for the sword, perhaps I'm wrong. If I am, it will prevent you from taking it. You have nothing to lose."

Darrick glanced at Ellig Barrows.

"Over the years before the sword was hidden away," the old man said, "many tried to take it just as Taramis has. If there was no true evil in their hearts, they were only prevented from removing the sword."

Darrick looked at the corpse and the plain sword it held. "Has Hauklin's sword ever been taken?"

"Never," Ellig Barrows said. "Not once from his hand. Not even I can remove it. I have only been made their protector. As my grandson shall be after me."

"Try," Taramis urged. "If you can't take up the sword, then I've come on a fool's quest and uncovered secrets best left hidden."

"Yes," Ellig Barrows said. "No one has ever come for the sword in my lifetime. I had begun to think the world had forgotten about it. Or that the demon Kabraxis had been permanently banished from this world."

Taramis put his hand on Darrick's shoulder. "But the demon is back," the sage said. "We know that, don't we? The demon is back, and the sword should come free."

"But am I the one?" Darrick asked in a hoarse voice.

"You must be," Taramis said. "I can think of no other. Your friend died in that place. There has to be a reason you were spared. It's the balance, Darrick. The needs of the Light must always be balanced against the power of the Darkness."

Darrick gazed at the sword. The stink of the barn behind his father's butcher shop returned to him. *You'll never amount to anything!* his father had shouted. *You're dumb, and you're stupid, and you're going to die dumb and stupid!* Days and weeks and years of that rolled through Darrick's head. Pain tingled through his body again, reminding him of the whippings he'd endured and somehow survived. His father's voice had often haunted him during the past year, and he'd tried to drown it in wine and spirits, in hard work and bleak disappointment.

And in the guilt over Mat Hu-Ring's death.

Hadn't that been punishment enough? Darrick stared at the simple sword clasped in the dead man's hands.

"And if I can't take the sword?" Darrick asked in a ragged voice.

"Then I will search out the true secret," Taramis said. "Or I will find another way to battle Kabraxis and his accursed Church of the Prophet of the Light."

But the sage believed in him, and Darrick knew that. It was almost too much to bear.

Pushing away his own fears, going numb and dead inside the way he had when he'd faced his father in that small barn in Hillsfar, Darrick stepped toward the dead man. He reached for the sword.

Inches from the blade's hilt, his hand froze, and he found he was unable to go any farther.

"I can't," Darrick said, refusing to give in, wanting desperately to be able to pick up the sword and prove his worth even if only to himself.

"Try," Taramis said.

Darrick watched his hand shake with the effort he was making. It felt as if he were pushing against a stone wall. Pain welled up inside him, but it had nothing to do with the sword.

You're stupid, boy, and you're lazy. Not worth the time or the trouble or the food to keep you.

Darrick fought the barrier, willing his hand to pass through. He pressed his whole body against it now, feeling it support most of his weight.

"Ease off," Taramis said.

"No," Darrick said.

"C'mon, lad," Ellig Barrows said. "It's not meant to be."

Darrick strained for the sword, wanting even another fraction of an inch if he could get it. It felt as if his finger bones were going to pass through the flesh. Pain raced up his arm, and he clenched his teeth against it.

I should have knocked you in the head the day you were born, boy. That way you wouldn't have lived to be such a disgrace.

Darrick reached, in agony now.

"Give it up," Taramis said.

"No!" Darrick said in a loud voice.

The sage reached for him, gripping him by the shoulder and trying to pull him away.

"You're going to get hurt, lad," Ellig Barrows said. "You can't force this thing."

Pain dimmed Darrick's hearing. Images of Mat falling from the cliffside spun through his brain again. Guilt filled Darrick, echoed by the worthlessness he felt from his father's oft-repeated words. For a moment, he thought the pain was going to destroy him, melt him down where he stood. He was locked in the pursuit of the sword, didn't think he could pull back if he wanted to.

And where would he go from here after failing this? He had no answers.

Then a calm, cool voice holding just a hint of mocking amusement filled his head. *Take up the sword, skipper.*

"Mat?" Darrick said aloud. He was so surprised at hearing Mat's voice that he didn't even realize at first that he had fallen across the corpse, bruising his knees against the earthen floor. Instinctively, his hand curled around the sword's hilt, but he glanced around the shadows of the crypt looking for Mat Hu-Ring.

Only Taramis and Ellig Barrows stood there.

"By the Light," the old man whispered. "He has taken the sword."

Taramis smiled in triumph. "As I told you he would."

Darrick gazed down at the dead man so close to him. The corpse felt unnaturally cold.

"Take the sword, Darrick," the sage urged.

Slowly, disbelieving, not knowing if he'd truly heard Mat's voice or it had been part of some spell that opened the ward protecting the sword or a delusion of his own, Darrick pulled the sword away from the dead warrior. Despite its length and unfamiliar style, the sword felt comfortable in Darrick's hand. He stood, holding it out before him.

Something in the scarred and dark metal caught the light of Ellig Barrows's lantern, glinting dulled silver.

Tentatively, Taramis reached for the sword, but his hand stopped inches away. "I still cannot touch the sword."

The old man tried to touch the weapon as well but with the same results. "Nor can I. None in my family has ever been able to touch the sword. Whenever we moved it, we had to move Hauklin's body as well." A note of sadness sounded in the old man's voice.

For the first time, Darrick realized that taking the sword would leave the old man and his grandson with nothing to care for or protect. Darrick gazed at the old man. "I'm sorry," he whispered.

Ellig Barrows nodded. "All of us who have defended the sword have prayed that this day would come, this day when we would be free of our burden, but to see it actually happen—" Words failed him.

"Taramis!" one of the men shouted from outside.

Even as the sage started for the magical door, the sound of inhuman and monstrous yips and growls cascaded into the root cellar.

Darrick followed the sage, bolting through the racks of foodstuffs and wines, trailed by Ellig Barrows with the lantern. The weak gray daylight pouring through the root cellar door marked the entrance.

The noise of men fighting, their curses and yells, as well as the growls and howls of the creatures they fought, pummeled Darrick's ears as he raced up the earthen steps. He was on Taramis's heels as they burst from the root cellar.

The clearing around the house, which had moments ago been peaceful and restful, was now filled with battle. Taramis's warriors formed a quick skirmish line against the bloodthirsty beasts that raged against them from the forest.

"Lezanti," Taramis breathed. "By the Light, Kabraxis has found us out."

Darrick recognized the demon-forged beasts, but only from tales he'd been told aboard ship. Even in all of his travels, he'd never before encountered the creatures.

The lezanti stood a little less than five feet tall. They were human-shaped, but they possessed the reverse-hinged knees of a wolf and the thick hide of a lizard. The head was lizard-shaped as well, bearing an elongated snout filled with serrated teeth and flat, flaring nostrils. The eyes were close-set under a hank of wooly hair and surprisingly human. The hands and feet were oversized, filled with huge claws. Lizards' tails, barbed on the ends, swung around behind them.

"Archers!" Taramis cried hoarsely as he stood his ground and began weaving his hands through the air, inscribing symbols that flared to flaming life.

Four warriors took up longbows, stood behind swordsmen,

and drew back shafts. They had two arrows away each, dropping the lezanti in their tracks, before the first wave of the creatures reached them. Then the swordsmen held them back with their shields, staggered by the lezantis' speed, strength, and weight. The clang of flesh meeting steel boomed in the clearing.

"Darrick," Taramis said, his hands still moving, "hold the door to the house. There are women and children inside. Hurry."

Darrick ran, trusting the line of warriors to protect his back as he made for the small house.

Taramis unleashed a wave of shimmering force that hit the center of the lezanti pack, scattering them and showering them with flame. Several of the smoldering bodies hung in the trees or landed with bone-breaking thumps against the ground. Only a few of them tried to get up. The archers calmly nocked more shafts and fired again, as cool as any crew Darrick had ever seen. The clothyard shafts drilled into the eyes and throats of their foes, putting them down. But the odds were not in the favor of the warriors. They numbered twenty-six men, including Darrick, and there had to be at least eighty of the lezantis.

We're going to die, Darrick thought, but he never once considered running. Hauklin's mystical sword felt calm and certain in his hand despite the unaccustomed length.

A scrabbling sound alerted Darrick. He swung around in time to see the lezanti on the roof of the house leap at him, its claws reaching for him.

Darrick ducked beneath the creature's attack, set himself as it thudded against the ground. Not dazed even for a moment, the lezanti came up snarling and snapping. The elongated snout shot at Darrick's head. He parried the head with the sword, then drove a boot into the lezanti's stomach, doubling it over.

Still moving, Darrick stepped to the side and brought the sword down in a hand-and-a-half grip that powered the blade into the creature's side. To his surprise, the sword sliced through the lezanti, dropping it to the ground in halves. The body parts quivered and jerked, then lay still. Blue energy crackled along the sword's length, and the lezanti's blood dried and flaked away, leaving the steel clean of it again.

Men cursed and fought out in the clearing, striving to hold back the merciless horde of creatures. Two men were down, Darrick saw, and others were wounded. Taramis unleashed another bolt of mystical energy, and two of the lezantis were covered in ice, frozen in place, shattering beneath the blades of the warriors who took advantage of their weakness.

Racing into the house, Darrick surveyed the small room filled with carvings and a few books. Ellig Barrows's wife, as gray-haired and gaunt as the old man was, stood in the center of the room with her hands over her chest.

Darrick glanced around at the wide windows in the front wall of the room as well as one of the side walls. There was too much open space; he could never hope to guard the old man's family there.

The grandson tugged at a heavy rug that covered the floor. "Help me!" he cried. "There is a hiding place beneath."

Understanding, Darrick grabbed the rug in one hand and yanked, baring the trapdoor beneath the material. Many of the homes along the border where the barbarian tribes often crossed over and raided were constructed with security holes. Families could lock themselves beneath the houses and live for days on the food and water stored there.

The boy's clever fingers found the hidden latch, and the trapdoor popped up.

Darrick slid the sword under the trapdoor's edge and levered it up, revealing the ladder beneath.

The boy took a lantern from the floor and reached for the old woman. "Come on, Grandmother."

"Ellig," the old woman whispered.

"He would want you to be safe," Darrick told her. "Whatever may come of this."

Reluctantly, the old woman allowed her grandson to lead her into the hiding place.

Darrick waited until they were both inside, then closed the trapdoor and dragged the rug back over it. Glass shattered behind him. He rose with the sword in his hand as the lezanti howled in through the broken window and threw itself at him.

There was little room to work with inside the house. Darrick reversed the sword in his right hand, gripping it so that it ran down his arm to his elbow and beyond. He kept his left hand back but ready, allowing his body to follow the line of the sword.

The lezanti reached for him. Darrick swung the sword, not allowing it to drift out beyond his body, keeping it in nice and tight as he'd been trained by Maldrin, who had been one of the best Darrick had ever seen at dirty infighting.

Darrick slapped the lezanti's claws to one side with the blade, then whipped his body back the other way, reversing the sword still along his arm, and slashed the creature across the face. The lezanti stumbled back, one hand to its ruined eye and crying out in pain. Darrick stepped in, keeping the sword close, and slashed at the creature's face again. Before it could retreat, he cut the head from its shoulders.

Even as the decapitated head rolled across the hardwood floor, another lezanti crashed through the door, and a third came through the window overlooking the well and the barn.

Breath rasping in his throat but feeling calm and centered, Darrick parried the spear the first creature wielded with surprising skill, caught the spear haft under his left arm, and caught it in his left hand. Holding the spear-carrying lezanti back by holding on to the spear, Darrick wheeled, dropped his sword, turned his hand over, caught the weapon in a regular grip before it fell, and chopped an arm from the other lezanti.

The spear-carrying lezanti shoved forward, trying to drive Darrick backward over a cushioned bench. Darrick pushed the spear out so that the point dug into the wall behind him and halted the lezanti. Releasing the spear, he stepped forward, knowing the one-armed lezanti was closing in on him from behind again. He sliced the lezanti in front of him, shearing its head and one shoulder away, amazed at the sharpness of the sword. With the sword still in motion, he reversed his grip and drove the blade through the chest of the lezanti behind him.

Energy crackled along the blade again. Before Darrick could kick the lezanti free of the sword, blue flames erupted from where the blade pierced the creature's chest and consumed it in a flash. Ash drifted to the ground before Darrick's stunned eyes.

Before he could recover, another lezanti hurled itself through the broken window on the barn's side. Darrick succeeded in escaping the fist full of claws the lezanti threw at him but caught the brunt of the creature's charge. He flew backward, stumbling back through the door, unable to get his balance, and landed on the porch. He flipped to his feet as the lezanti charged again. Ducking this time, Darrick slashed the blade across the creature's thighs, chopping both legs off. The lezanti's torso hurtled by overhead and landed in the dirt in front of the porch.

"They're after the sword, Darrick!" Taramis called. "Run!"

Even as he realized what the sage said was true, Darrick knew he couldn't run. After losing Mat at Tauruk's Port, and himself for most of the past year, he couldn't run anymore.

"No," Darrick said, rising to his feet. "No more running." He took a fresh grip on the sword, feeling renewed strength flow through him. For the moment, all uncertainty drained away from him.

Several of the lezanti tore past the sprawling bodies of the warriors who had fought them. Nearly half of Taramis's group lay on the ground. Most of them, Darrick felt certain, wouldn't rise again.

Darrick waited on the charging creatures, lifting the sword high in both hands. Seven of them came at him, getting in one another's way. Energy flickered along the sword's blade. He slashed at his foes as they came into reach, cutting into them, then stepping through the gap that was filled with the swirling ash the mystical flames left behind. Three had died in that attack, but the other four came around again.

Regrouping, moving the sword around in his hands as if he'd trained with it all his life, Darrick cut at them, taking off a head, two arms, and a leg, then thrusting into two more creatures and reducing them to swirling ash as well. He stepped over to the creatures he had maimed, piercing their hearts with the enchanted blade and watching them burst into pyres that left the ground scorched.

Rallied by Darrick's show of power against the lezantis, the warriors drew up their steel and their courage, and attacked their foes with renewed vigor. The price was high, for men dropped where they stood, but the lezanti died faster. Taramis's and Ellig Barrows's spells took their toll among the demon-forged creatures as well, burning them, freezing them, twisting them into obscene grotesqueries.

Darrick continued battling, drawn by the bloodlust that fired him. It felt good to be so certain and sure of himself, of what he was doing, of what he needed to do. He hacked and slashed and thrust, cleaving through the lezantis that seemed drawn to him.

From the corner of his eye, he saw the lezanti rush toward Ellig Barrows from the side, giving the old man no warning. Knowing he'd never reach the old man in time to prevent the creature's attack, Darrick reversed his grip on the sword and threw it like a spear without thinking about what he was doing, as if it were something he'd done several times.

The sword flashed across the distance and embedded itself in the lezanti's chest. The blade halted the creature, then quivered in its chest as the eldritch scarlet energies gathered again. With a sudden fiery flash, the lezanti crisped to ash. The sword dropped point-first to the ground and stuck.

Out of reflex, Darrick thrust his hand out for the blade.

The weapon quivered again, then yanked free of the earth and flew back to his hand.

"How did you know to do that?" Taramis asked.

Shocked himself, Darrick shook his head. "I didn't. It just—happened."

"By the Light," Ellig Barrows said, "you were the one destined for Hauklin's sword."

But Darrick remembered Mat's voice in his head. If Mat hadn't been there, somehow, Darrick felt certain that he'd never have been able to pick up the weapon. He turned and gazed across the battleground, not believing the carnage that he'd somehow survived almost completely unmarked.

"Come on," Taramis said, walking to help his men. "We can't stay here. Somehow Kabraxis has discovered us. We've got to leave as soon as we're able."

"And then what?" Darrick asked, sheathing the sword in his belt and catching the bag of medicants the sage tossed his way.

"Then we make for Bramwell," Taramis replied over the moans of the wounded warriors. "Kabraxis knows we have Stormfury now, and I've never been one to hide. Besides, now that we have the sword, the demon has every reason to fear us."

Even though he knew the sage's words were meant to be reassuring, and even though the power contained in the sword inspired a lot of confidence, Darrick knew the quest could still take them all to their deaths. The warriors who had fallen today and wouldn't get back up were grim reminders of that. He opened the medicants bag and tried to help those who still lived.

But confusion dwelt in his thoughts as well. *If I was the one meant for Hauklin's sword, then why couldn't I pick it up immediately? And where did Mat's voice come from?* He felt those questions were important but had no clue what the answers were. Grimly, he set to work, trying desperately not to think too far ahead.

Twenty-one

Perched high on a northern hill overlooking Bramwell and the Church of the Prophet of the Light to the south, Darrick scanned the imposing edifice with the spyglass he'd managed to hang on to even over the worst of the past year. A quarter-mile distant, the church was lighted, festooned with lanterns and torches as worshippers continued their pilgrimage into the structure.

Farther out into the harbor, several ships remained lighted as well. Along with the influx of worshippers wanting to try their luck at getting to walk along the Way of Dreams, smugglers had also seen opportunities to reap financial gain by supplying the populace with black market goods. Guards stayed with the ships during all watches, and it still wasn't unusual for some of them to be attacked and raided by pirates. Thieves picked the pockets of worshippers and robbed them in the alleys.

Bramwell was fast becoming one of the most dangerous port cities on the Gulf of Westmarch.

Darrick lowered the spyglass and rubbed his aching eyes. It had taken the group almost three weeks to reach Bramwell as they journeyed down from the north. It seemed that winter had followed on their heels, blowing in on cold gusts.

Seven men had died at Ellig Barrows's home, and two more had been permanently crippled during the attack of the lezantis and couldn't continue. Seventeen men remained of Taramis Volken's original group of demon hunters.

Seventeen, Darrick mused as the cold air cut through the forest around him, *against hundreds and maybe thousands that Kabraxis has inside the church.* The odds were overwhelming, and their chances of success seemed nonexistent. *Even an army wouldn't stand a chance.*

And yet Darrick couldn't turn away. There was no fear left in him, and no anticipation, either. For the last three weeks, his father's voice had been inside his head—during his waking moments as well as his sleep—telling him how worthless he was. His dreams had been nightmares, looping segments of events that had transpired in the small barn behind the butcher's shop. Worst of all had been the memories of Mat Hu-Ring bringing him food and medicines, being there to let Darrick know he wasn't alone—yet all the while he had been trapped. Until he had made his escape.

Brush stirred behind Darrick. He shifted slightly, his hand dropping to the hilt of the long sword across his thighs. The blade was naked and ready as he faded into the long shadows of the approaching night.

A dim sunset, a thin slice of ocher and amber, like grapes smeared through pale ale, hung in the west. The last dregs of the day managed to cast a silvery sheen over the harbor, making the ships and boats look like two-dimensional black cutouts on the water. The light barely threaded through the city and seemed not to touch the Church of the Prophet of the Light.

Darrick released his breath slowly so it wouldn't be heard, emptying his lungs completely so he could draw in a full breath if he needed to go into action. The demon hunters had camped within the forest high in the mountains for the last two days and not been disturbed. In the higher reaches where they were, where the cold could reach them, game had been chased up from the foothills by the tent city that had sprung up outside Bramwell and was plentiful.

Maybe it was only a deer, Darrick thought. Then he dismissed the possibility. The sound he'd heard had been too calm, too measured.

"Darrick," Rhambal called.

"Aye," Darrick said in a low voice.

Tracking the sound of Darrick's voice, Rhambal crept closer. The warrior was a big man but moved as quietly as a woodlands creature through the forest. A square-cut beard framed his broad face, and he had a cut across his nose and beneath his left eye from a lezanti claw that hadn't quite healed during the past three weeks. Exposure to the harsh weather and not being able truly to rest had slowed the healing. Several of the other warriors bore such marks as well.

"I've come to get you," Rhambal said.

"I'd prefer to stay out here," Darrick said.

The big man hesitated.

Despite the fact that Darrick was the only one among them who could carry Hauklin's enchanted blade, Darrick's lack of interest in getting to know the other warriors had made him suspect to them. If it hadn't been for Taramis Volken's leadership, Darrick thought the warriors would have abandoned him or forced him to leave.

Of course, without Taramis Volken, the quest to break into the Church of the Prophet of the Light would have been abandoned. Only Taramis's charisma and his own unflinching courage kept them moving forward.

"Taramis has returned from the town," Rhambal said. "He wants everyone to gather and talk. He thinks he has a way into the church for us."

Darrick had known that the demon hunter had returned. He'd watched Taramis come up the mountainside less than an hour before.

"When do we go?" Darrick asked.

"Tonight."

The answer didn't surprise Darrick.

"And I for one am ready to do this thing," Rhambal said. "Crossing all this distance from the north and haunted by nightmares the way we've been, I'm ready to get shut of it all one way or another."

Darrick didn't reply. The nightmares had been a constant in all their lives. Even though Ellig Barrows and

Taramis had carefully constructed a warding around the group that prevented Kabraxis's scrying on them, they all knew their lives were forfeit if they were caught. The demon had identified them. Several times during the last few weeks, they'd barely escaped patrols of warriors as well as herds of demonic-forged creatures that hunted them.

The group hadn't been able to escape the nightmares, though. Taramis had said that he was certain the night terrors were inspired by an insidious spell that they hadn't been able to escape. Not a warrior among the group avoided them, and the three weeks of sleepless nights and private hells had taken their toll. A few of the warriors had even suggested that the nightmares were a curse, that they'd never be free of them.

Palat Shires, one of the oldest warriors among them, had tried to leave the group, unable to bear whatever it was that had haunted him. Darrick had heard whispers that Palat had once been a pirate, and as vicious a killer as any might fear to meet, till Taramis had exorcised the lesser demon that had crawled into Palat's mind from the enchanted weapon he carried and almost driven him insane with bloodlust. Still, even though he knew it had been the demon's possession of him that had caused him to do such horrible things, Palat had never been truly able to forgive himself for the murders and maiming he had committed. But he had sworn himself to Taramis's cause.

Three days after he'd left the group, Palat had returned. All knew from his haggard look that he had failed to escape the nightmares. Two days later, in the still hours near dawn, Palat had slashed his wrists and tried to kill himself. Only one of the other warriors, unable to sleep, had prevented Palat's death. Taramis had healed the old warrior as much as he could, then they'd holed up for four days to weather out a rain squall and let Palat regain his lost strength.

"Come on," Rhambal said. "There's stew still in a pot back there, and Taramis brought up loaves of bread and honeyed butter. There's even a sack of apple cakes because he was in such a generous mood." A wide grin split the warrior's face, but it didn't get past the fatigue that showed there.

"What about a sentry?" Darrick asked.

"We've been here two nights before this," Rhambal said. "Hasn't anyone come close to us in all that time. There's no reason to think it's going to happen in the next hour."

"We're leaving in the next hour?"

Rhambal nodded and squinted toward the dimming of the day. "As soon as true night hits and before the moon comes into full. Only a fool or a desperate man would be out in the chill of this night."

Reluctantly, because it meant being around the warriors and seeing the damage the harsh journey and the sleepless nights had wrought on them, Darrick stood and crept through the forest, heading higher up the mountainside. The heavy timber blocked most of the north wind that ravaged the mountain.

The campsite was located in a westward-facing cul-de-sac of rock near the peak of the mountain. The cul-de-sac was a small box of stone that stood up from the scrub brush and wind-bent pine trees.

The campfire was that in name only. No flames leapt up around piles of wood to warm the warriors gathered there. Only a heap of orange-glowing coals sheathed amid white and gray ash took the barest hint of the chill away. A pot of rabbit stew sat in the coals and occasionally bubbled.

The warriors sat around the campfire, but it was more because there was so little room in the cul-de-sac than out of any vain hope that the coals might stave off the cold. The horses stood at the back of the canyon, their breaths feathering the air with gray plumes, their long coats frosted over. The animals filled the cul-de-sac with the scent of wet horse and ate the long grass that the warriors had harvested for them earlier.

Taramis sat nearest the campfire, his legs crossed under him. The dim orange glow of the coals stripped the shadows from his face and made him look feverish. His eyes met Darrick's, and he nodded in greeting.

Holding his hands out over the coals, the sage said, "I can't guarantee you the success of our foray this night, but I will tell you that it is warmer down in Bramwell than it is up on this mountain."

The warriors laughed, but it was more out of politeness than real humor.

Rhambal took a seat beside Darrick, then picked up two tin cups from their meager store of utensils by the campfire. The big warrior dipped both cups into the stew they'd made from vegetables and leaves they could find and three unwary hares caught just before sunset. After pulling the cups back from the stewpot, Rhambal dragged a large finger along their sides to clean them, then popped his finger into his mouth.

Despite his fatigue and the feeling of ill ease that clung to him, Darrick accepted the cup of stew with a thankful nod. The warmth of the stew carried through the tin cup to his hands. He held it for a time, just soaking up the warmth, then started to drink it before it cooled too much. The bits of rabbit meat in the stew were tough and stringy.

"I've found a way into the church," Taramis announced. "A place as big as that," Palat grumbled, "it should be as full of holes as my socks." He held up one of the socks that he'd been drying on a stick near the campfire. The garment was filled with holes.

"It is full of holes," Taramis agreed. "A year ago, Master Sayes arrived in Bramwell and began the Church of the Black Road from the back of a caravan. That sprawl of buildings that makes up the church now was built in sections, but it was built well. There are secret passages honeycombing the church, used by Master Sayes and his acolytes, as well as the guards. But the church is well protected."

"What about the sewers?" Rhambal asked. "We'd talked about getting into the building through the sewers."

"Mercenaries guard the sewer entrances," Taramis answered. "They also guard the underground supply routes into the building."

"Then where's this way you're talking about?" Palat asked.

Taramis took a small, charred stick from the teeth of the dying coals. "They built the church too fast, too grand, and they didn't allow for the late-spring flooding. All the building along the shore, including new wells to feed the pools and water reservoirs inside the church, created problems."

The sage drew a pair of irregular lines to represent the river, then a large rectangle beside it. He added another small square that thrust out over the river.

"Where the church hangs out over the river here," Taramis continued, "offering grand parapets where worshippers can wait to get into the next service and look out over the city as well as be impressed by the size of the church, the river has eroded the bank and undermined the plaza supports, weakening them considerably."

Accepting the chunk of bread smothered in honey butter that Rhambal offered, Darrick listened to Taramis and ate mechanically. His mind was full of the plan that the sage sketched in the dirt, prying and prodding at the details as they were revealed.

"One of the problems they had in constructing that parapet that was more vanity than anything else," Taramis continued, "was that the pilings for the parapet had to be laid so that they missed one of the old sewer systems the church had outgrown. Though the church's exterior may look polished and complete, the land underneath hasn't improved much beyond the quagmire it was that persuaded the local populace not to build there."

"So what are you thinking?" Palat asked.

Taramis gazed at the drawing barely lit by the low orange glow of the coals. "I'm thinking that with a little luck and the theft of one of those boats out there, we'll have a way into the church tonight as well as a diversion."

"Tonight?" Rhambal asked.

The sage nodded and looked up, meeting the gaze of every man in front of him. "The men I talked to down in Bramwell's taverns this afternoon said that the church services go on for hours even after nightfall."

"That's something you don't always see," Corrigor said. "Usually a man working the field or a fishing boat, he's looking for a warm, dry place to curl up after the sun sets. He's not wanting a church service."

"Most church services," Taramis said, "aren't giving away healing or luck that brings a man love or wealth or power."

"True," Corrigor said.

"So we go tonight," Taramis said. "Unless there's someone among us who would rather wait another night." He looked at Darrick as he said that.

Darrick shook his head, and the other men all answered the same. Everyone was tired of waiting.

"We rested up last night," Rhambal said. "If I rest any more, I'm just going to get antsy."

"Good." Taramis smiled grimly, without mirth and with perhaps a hint of fear. Despite the sage's commitment to hunting demons and the loss of his family, he was still human enough to be afraid of what they were going to attempt.

Then, in a calm and measured tone, Taramis told them the plan.

A light fog shrouded the river, but lanterns and torches along the banks and aboard the ships at anchorage in front of the warehouses and taverns burned away patches of the moist, cottony gray vapor. Men's voices carried over the sound of the wind in the rigging and the loose furls of sailcloth. Other men sang or called out dirty limericks and jokes.

Stone bridges crossed the river in two places, and both of them were filled with people walking from one bank to the other in search of food or drink. Some of the people were tourists, whiling away the time till the church let out and the next service began. Others were thieves, merchants, and guardsmen. The prostitutes were the loudest, yelling offers to the sailors and fishermen aboard their boats.

Darrick followed Taramis along the shore toward the cargo ship that the sage had selected as their target. *Blue Zephyr* was a squat, ugly cargo ship that held the rancid stench of whale oil. Not a sailor worth his salt would want to crew aboard her because she was such a stinkpot, Darrick knew, but she could guarantee a small crew a decent profit for their efforts.

Three men remained on board the small cargo ship. The captain and the rest of the crew had gone into the taverns along Dock Street. But careful observation of the crew revealed that they also had a bottle on board the ship and gathered in the stern to drink it.

The thieves and smugglers in Bramwell wouldn't want *Blue Zephyr*'s cargo, Darrick knew. The barrels of whale oil were too heavy to steal easily or escape with from the harbor.

Without breaking his stride, Taramis reached the bottom of the gangplank leading up to the cargo ship. The sage started up the gangplank without pause. Darrick trailed after him, heart beating rapidly in his chest as his boots thudded against the boarding ramp.

The three sailors gathered in the cargo ship's stern turned at once. One of the men grabbed a lantern sitting on the plotting table and shined it toward them.

"Who goes there?" the sailor with the lantern asked.

The other two sailors filled their hands with swords and took up defensive positions.

"Orloff," Taramis said, walking toward the men without hesitation.

Darrick split off from the sage, surveying the rigging and deciding in the space of a drawn breath which canvases to use and how best to free them. Only four other men among the sage's warriors had any real experience aboard masted ships, and they all had considerably less than he did.

"I don't know no Orloff," the sailor with the lantern said. "Mayhap ye got the wrong ship there, mate."

"I've got the right ship," Taramis assured the man. He closed on them, walking with a confident gait. "Captain Rihard asked me to drop by with this package." He held up a leather-covered bottle. "Said it would be something to warm you up against the night's chill."

"I don't know no Cap'n Rihard," the sailor said. "Ye got the wrong ship. Ye'd best be shovin' off."

But by that time, Taramis was among them. He sketched an eldritch symbol in the air. The symbol flared to emerald-green life and flickered out of existence.

Before the last of the color died away, a shimmering wall of force exploded toward the three sailors and knocked them all over the stern railing, scattering them like leaves before a fierce gust. The sailor carrying the lantern hung on to it, arcing out over the river and falling like a comet from the heavens till he disappeared into the water with a loud splash.

At the same time, signaled by the spell Taramis had used, Rhambal set fire to the oil-soaked exterior of one of the larger warehouses on the south side of the river to create a diversion. Flames blossomed up the side of the warehouse, alerting dozens of people living in the surrounding neighborhood. In seconds, even as the three sailors were knocked from *Blue Zephyr*'s stern, the hue and cry about the fire filled the streets and the banks on both sides of the river.

When the sailors surfaced, they didn't gain much support for their troubles. Palat joined Taramis in the stern, an arrow to bowstring and the fletchings pulled back to his ear. The sailors got the message and swam for the riverbank.

"Get those sails down," Darrick ordered. Now that they were into the action, with little chance of turning back, his blood sang in his veins. A part of him came back alive after a year of trying to deaden it. He remembered times past when he and Mat had scrambled aboard a ship to prepare for battle or respond to a surprise attack.

The four warriors with sailing experience split up. One went to the stern to take the wheel, and the others scrambled up the rigging.

Darrick climbed the rigging like a monkey, all the moves coming back to him even though it had been months since he'd last climbed in a sailing ship. Hauklin's mystic sword banged against his back as he climbed. The cutlass had been short enough that he'd kept it sheathed at his side, but the long sword felt more natural slung across his shoulder.

As he climbed the rigging and reached the furled sails, he slashed through the neatly tied ropes with his belt knife. His sailor's soul resented the loss of the rope, always a prized commodity of a ship at sea, but he knew they'd have no further use of it. Thinking like that made him remember what Taramis had in store for the cargo vessel, and that made Darrick even sadder. The small ship wasn't much, but she was seaworthy and had a purpose.

At the top of the mast, all the sails cut loose below him, Darrick gazed down at the deck. The remaining eleven warriors—Rhambal would join them in a moment—busied themselves with bringing small casks of whale oil up from the hold. *Blue Zephyr* had shipped with small kegs of oil as well as the large kegs, otherwise they'd have needed a block-and-tackle to get them on deck.

Darrick slipped down through the rigging, dropping hand-over-hand to the deck. "Lash those sails in place. Hurry." He scanned the river anchorage.

The three sailors Taramis had knocked over the cargo ship's side had reached the riverbank, calling out to other sailors and city guards. For the most part they were ignored. The fire at the warehouse was more important because if it spread, the city might be in danger.

Watching the flames blaze, stretching long tongues into the sky above the warehouse, while he tied the sails fast, Darrick knew he couldn't have given the order to fire the building as Taramis had. The people who owned the warehouse had done nothing wrong, nor had the people who stored their goods there.

It had been a necessary evil, the sage had told them all. None of the warriors had exhibited any problems with the plan.

"Darrick," Taramis called from the ship's stern. He'd taken off his outer coat, revealing the orange Vizjerei robes with the silver mystic symbols.

"Aye," Darrick called back.

"Are the sails ready?"

"Aye," Darrick replied, finishing the last lashing and glancing around at the other warriors working on the canvas. They had been slower at it than he had, but it was all done. "You're clear." He glanced at the other men again. "Stand ready, boys. This is going to be a quick bit of work if we can pull it off."

Taramis spoke, and the words he used sounded like growls. No human throat was meant to use the phrases, and Darrick was certain that the sage's spell was from some of the earliest magic that had been brought into the world by the demons among the Vizjerei. Some mages and sorcerers believed that spellcraft was purer when used in the old language it had first been taught in.

A wavering reflection of the warehouse fire spread over the choppy surface of the river. Other glowing dots spread along the banks reflected on the river, too. More were in a straight line under the second bridge that lay between the cargo ship and the church. Hoarse shouts drifted, trapped and held close to the water as sound always was. A bucket brigade had started near the warehouse.

Despite his readiness, Darrick was almost knocked from his feet as Taramis's spell summoned a wild wind from the west. The canvas popped and crackled overhead as the sails filled. Her sails filled with the magically summoned wind, and the ship started forward, cutting through the river against the current.

Twenty-two

Propelled by the sudden onslaught of wind, *Blue Zephyr* nosed down into the river. The sudden action caught three of the warriors unprepared, and they fell onto the deck. The oil kegs overturned and rolled, creating a brief hazard till the ship's keel came up. One of the warriors almost rolled through the open space in the railing where the boarding ramp had fallen away, but he managed to stop himself just short of it.

"Hold what you've got!" Darrick cried out over the roaring wind to the other warriors manning the sails. He strained to hang on to the ropes, keeping the sail full into the wind. Little work was necessary on the part of the ship-trained men, though. Taramis's wind caught the cargo vessel squarely and sped her across the river.

Other nearby ships rocked at anchor, and small sailcraft that had been used to ferry goods across the river were blown down, their sails lying in the water.

"Wheel!" Darrick yelled, watching as *Blue Zephyr* closed with frightening quickness on a low barge.

"Aye," Farranan called back.

"Hard to starboard, damn it, or we're going to end up amidships," Darrick ordered.

"Hard to starboard," Farranan replied.

Immediately, the cargo ship came about. The port-side hull rubbed along the low-slung barge, coming up out of the river slightly and cracking timbers. Darrick hoped most of the cracking timbers belonged to the barge.

Hanging on to the ropes tied to the sail, he watched as the corner of the barge went under the cargo ship, the prow of the boat and the other corner coming clear of the water. Boxes and crates and longshoremen spilled into the water. Two lanterns dropped into the river as well, both of them extinguishing as soon as the water touched the flames.

Then the cargo ship was past the barge, running free through the channel in the middle of the river. The others ships were packed so close together that there wasn't much space to navigate between them. Darrick saw the surprised faces of several sailors peering over taller ships down at the small cargo vessel.

"Break that oil open," Taramis ordered.

The warriors broke the oil kegs open with hand axes, spilling the dark liquid across the prow deck. The whale oil ran thick and slow, like blood from a man almost bled out.

When the cargo ship passed under the bridge that marked the boundary of the last harbor area, Darrick glanced up in time to see Rhambal throw himself over the side of the bridge. The warrior made a desperate grab for the rigging as it passed, caught hold of it and slammed back into the web of rope, then tossed himself into the nearest sail and slid down to the deck. He landed hard and on his back.

"Are you all right?" Darrick asked, offering a hand as the wind roared around them and the ship's deck pitched.

"Nothing wounded but my pride," Rhambal said, taking Darrick's hand. The warrior clambered to his feet and winced. "And maybe my arse." He looked back at the blazing warehouse. "Now, that'll be enough of a diversion."

"It's already lasted long enough," Darrick replied, gazing at the thick, syrupy liquid that covered the prow.

"Provided we get over into the pilings that Taramis was talking about," Rhambal said.

"We'll get there," Darrick said. He raised his voice. "Hard to port."

"Hard to port!" Farranan shouted from the stern.

Darrick felt *Blue Zephyr* lunge in response, cutting back

toward the northern riverbank where the imposing mono-
lith of the Church of the Prophet of the Light stood. The
parapet stood out over the river less than three hundred
yards away, and the distance was closing fast. Two pillars
of square-cut blocks held the parapet twenty feet up from
the river surface, allowing for the rising current during the
flood season.

On both sides of the river, torches and lanterns trailed
Blue Zephyr's passage, marking the passage of the city
guards. Church guards filled the parapet as the cargo ship
sailed within a hundred yards of the overhang. Several of
them had crossbows, and the air filled with quarrels.

"Take cover!" Palat squalled, ducking down and behind
the cargo hold amidships. Quarrels slapped into the deck
around him.

Darrick heard the missiles whistle by his head within
inches of striking him. He pulled himself behind the center
mast, trusting the magical winds that Taramis had stirred
up to drive *Blue Zephyr* into the pilings. Overhead, more
quarrels ripped through the canvas sails.

"Hold the wheel!" Darrick commanded, gazing back at
the stern.

Farranan had ducked down, trying desperately to take
cover. The weak grip he kept on the wheel allowed the
ship to glide back toward the center of the river channel.

Throwing himself from the mast, Darrick charged
toward the ship's stern. His back and shoulders tightened
up as he ran across the heaving deck, expecting to feel the
unforgiving bite of a steel arrowhead at any moment.
Grabbing the stairwell railing, he hurled himself up the
short flight of steps, almost stumbling over Farranan in his
haste.

Taramis stood at the railing. "Get back from the prow!"
he yelled.

Darrick grabbed the wheel and pulled hard to port,
bringing the cargo ship back on course. The winds continued unabated, whipping the rigging and tearing the canvas where the quarrels had ripped through. The wheel

jerked in Darrick's hands as the rudder fought the river current and the mystical winds.

After inscribing a glowing seven-pointed symbol in the air, Taramis spoke a single word. Activated by the magic, the symbol spun the length of the deck and ignited the whale oil spilled over the prow. The dark liquid went up in a liquid *whoosh!* of twisting yellow and lavender flames.

A wall of heat washed back over Darrick, causing him to squint against it. Panic filled him for a moment when he realized he could no longer see the parapet because of the whirling mass of flames and flying embers. Leaping into the rigging and catching the first sail, the fire climbed the forward mast like a lumbering bear cub, testing each new resting place, then diving upward again.

He looked up, thinking for one insane moment that he could chart by the stars.

Instead, he spotted the tall bell tower atop the tallest part of the Church of the Prophet of the Light. He aimed the ship by the bell tower, figuring out where it was in relation to the parapet.

"Hold what you have," Taramis said.

Darrick nodded grimly.

Quarrels continued to fall onto the ship, sinking deep into the wood. Another caromed from the ship's wheel in Darrick's hands and bit into his left side. For a moment he thought his ribs had caught fire, then he glanced down and saw the quarrel lodged there.

Sickness twisted Darrick's stomach as he thought the shaft had penetrated his stomach or chest. Then he noticed that it had taken him low, skimming across his ribs with bruising force but not biting into muscle or an organ. The quarrel would probably have gone on through if it hadn't been for his traveling cloak.

Steeling himself, Darrick reached down and pulled the quarrel through his own flesh and tossed it over the side. His fingers gleamed crimson with his own blood.

"Look out!" Palat yelled.

For one frozen moment, Darrick saw the thick pilings

supporting the parapet before him. *We're too high,* he thought, realizing the cargo ship came up higher on the structure than they'd guessed. *The impact is going to turn us away.*

But he had forgotten about the sheer, unstoppable tonnage the wild winds drove before them. As cargo ships went, not many were loaded more compactly or more heavily than oil freighters. *Blue Zephyr* was loaded to the top with driving weight and powered by a whirling storm.

The ship slammed into the pilings, driving from their moorings against the riverbed, collapsing the parapet in a sudden stream of rubble, driving a wall of water up and into the swirling winds so that a sudden monsoon rained down. *Blue Zephyr's* starboard side took a beating as rock fell from above. Shudders ran the length of the ship, feeling like monstrous blows from a blacksmith's hammer. *Blue Zephyr* was the anvil, and just as unrelenting and uncompromising. Rock and rubble bounced from the deck, which was canted hard to starboard as it scraped along the exposed riverbank.

The church's guards fell amid the rubble as well. Darrick watched them fall, some of them dropping into the foaming river current on the starboard side of the ship and others bouncing across the deck, caught up in an avalanche of stone and mortar. Two of the guards fell into the flaming canvas on the forward mast. They screamed and dove from the rigging, candle flames burning brightly till they plunged into the river.

Releasing the wheel, knowing he could no longer attempt to hold it in place without risking dire injury, Darrick stepped back and seized the railing. He held on as the ship battled the wind and the riverbank. Pulling himself along the railing, he reached up for a ratline running to stern, caught it, and forced his way to the port side.

Blue Zephyr ground to a halt on rock.

Darrick heard the rock scraping along the ship's hull, giant's teeth worrying at a bone. He winced as he realized the amount of damage they'd done to the vessel and the countless hours of work it would take to get her seaworthy again. He gazed over the deck, wondering if, after all they'd risked, they'd accomplished what they set out to do.

Shadows clung to the fallen debris and the dark mud of the riverbank. Darrick searched the riverbed but didn't see the threatened sewer system Taramis's research had turned up. Still, despite the grimness of their situation, no real fear touched Darrick. All he felt was an anxiety and a hope that the desperate madness of guilt of the last year would soon be over. Kabraxis's church guards wouldn't let them live after the assault.

Taramis joined Darrick at the railing. The sage spoke a word and pointed to the torch he held. Flames instantly wreathed the torch, and light glared down over the ship's side.

"That torch is going to light us up for the crossbowmen," Farranan said as he stood at the railing.

"We can't stay here," Rhambal said.

Blue Zephyr continued to rub and buck against the exposed limestone of the riverbed.

"The ship's not going to be here for long, either," Darrick said. For the first time he noticed the quiet that was left after the storm winds had died away. "The current's going to dislodge us, sweep us away."

Thrusting the torch out, Taramis scanned the riverbank. More rock dropped from the broken parapet.

"They've got a boat in the water," Palat warned. Looking over the stern railing, Darrick saw a guard ship streaking for them. Lanterns lighted Lord Darkulan's flag in the stern and on the prow, marking the vessel for all to see.

"The torch is too weak," Taramis said. "But it's got to be down there." He waved the torch, reaching down as far as he could, but it was futile. The light simply wouldn't reach the riverbank properly.

Draw the sword, Mat Hu-Ring said into Darrick's mind.

"Mat?" Darrick whispered. The guilt returned full blast, disrupting the peace he thought he'd have when it became apparent there would be no escape. Accepting his own death was far easier than accepting Mat's.

Draw the sword, Mat repeated, sounding far away.

Turning, knowing he wasn't going to find his friend standing somewhere behind him the way it sounded, Darrick looked at the warriors assembling in the stern, looking toward Taramis to call their next move.

The sword, ye damned fool! Mat said. *Draw the bloody great sword. It'll help ye an' them with ye.*

Darrick reached over his right shoulder, feeling the pain along his left side where the quarrel had gone through, and gripped the hilt of Hauklin's sword. A tingle ran through his hand, and the sword seemed to spring into his grip. He held the weapon before him, a huge gray bar of sharpened steel bearing battle scars.

Taramis and the other warriors holding lanterns and torches they'd gotten from the whale-oil freighter tried to penetrate the shadows covering the riverbank.

"Maybe if someone goes down there," Rhambal suggested.

"A man going down there ain't gonna be with the ship if it leaves," Palat said. "We might need to stick with this old scow if we're going to make it out of here."

"Be better off trying our luck in the streets," Rhambal said. "Even if we made it out into the harbor without being closed in, they'd run us down. We don't have a seasoned crew working the sails and ropes."

Call out the sword's name, Mat ordered.

"Mat," Darrick whispered, hurting inside as if he'd just witnessed his friend's death. He wasn't imagining Mat's voice. It was real. It was real, and it was inside his head.

Call out the sword's name, ye great lumberin' lummox, Mat ordered.

"What are you doing here?" Darrick asked.

Same as ye, Mat replied, *only I'm a damn sight better'n ye at it. Now, call on the sword's power before ye get swept off them rocks an' back into the arms of them guards. We got a ways to go tonight.*

"How do I call on the sword?" Darrick asked.

Yell out its name.

"What is the sword's name?" In all the confusion, Darrick suddenly couldn't remember.

Stormfury, Mat replied.

"Are you alive?" Darrick said.

We ain't got time to go into that now. We're hard up against it now, an' there's still Kabraxis to contend with.

The freighter scraped rock again, shifting more violently than ever. For a moment, Darrick thought the vessel had torn free.

"Stormfury," Darrick said, holding the hilt in both hands and not knowing what to expect. The unaccustomed tingle flared through his hands again.

In an eyeblink, a cold blue light ran the length of the sword blade. As lacking as it was in heat, though, the light was bright but colored so that it didn't hurt the eyes.

The magical light given off by the blade cut through the darkness swaddling the riverbank with ease. Blue high-lights reflected on the river water pouring into the broken section of the eight-foot sewer system that ran under the church. The ship's collision with the riverbank had sheared away the parapet and the mud, revealing the sewer tunnel and cracking it open.

"There it is," Taramis said.

Darrick whispered, "Mat."

There was no answer, only the whistling sound of the normal breeze moving through the rigging.

The whale-oil freighter bucked again, sliding four or five feet backward and almost coming free of the rocks.

"We're losing the ship," Taramis said. "Move! Now!" He stepped over the railing and threw himself at the river-bank, leading the way.

Go! Mat whispered in Darrick's mind, sounding farther away than ever.

Trapped, wanting to know more about how Mat was able to talk to him, thinking perhaps his friend was actu-ally alive somewhere, Darrick climbed the railing and stepped over as the freighter shifted once more, turning slightly as the river current caught it. Another good shove like that by the current, and Darrick knew the ship would twist free. Stepping off the ship, he threw himself forward.

Darrick landed in the mud, sinking his boots up past the ankles, losing his footing and sliding out of control, ending up facedown in the cold muck. The river current washed over him, drenching him and chilling him to the bone. In contrast, the wound in his side burned as if he'd been jabbed with a red-hot poker.

The other warriors leapt after him, landing in the mud for the most part, but the last few landed in the river and were nearly washed away in the current before the others helped them. For a moment as they gathered themselves, *Blue Zephyr* acted as a defensive wall. Quarrels thunked into the ship's side from the guard ship that closed on them.

In the space of the next drawn breath, the burning ship twisted once more and was gone, following the river current. The ship full of guards managed to avoid the bigger ship, but the wash left by its passing and their efforts to get out of the way caught them and nearly capsized them. Then the freighter was by them, plunging downriver toward the ships lying at anchor, promising all manner of destruction before morning saw Bramwell again.

"Damnation," Palat swore. "We're like to burn this unfortunate town down around its ears while we're trying to save it tonight."

"If it happens," Taramis said, "the people here would be better served if it were humans doing the rebuilding instead of demons."

Slipping and sliding, Darrick followed the sage into the sewer tunnel. He only noted then that his sword had dimmed, leaving Taramis's torch and the lanterns and torches carried by the other warriors.

The sewer was halfway submerged from the problems Taramis had found out about during his foray through Bramwell's taverns. The collision with the freighter had broken through the wall as Taramis had planned, but the extent of the damage was greater than what Darrick would have believed possible. Water poured through cracks in the mortared brick wall wide enough to fit the fingers of a man's hand, sluicing in to join the waist-high deluge that rapidly deepened. Moss and slime grew on the sewer walls, and muck clung to the stone floor beneath the rancid-smelling water.

Taramis halted in the middle of the wide sewer, glancing to the left and the right.

"Which way?" Palat asked, raking an arm over his face to clear the water and mud. Smears streaked his features.

"To the left," Taramis said, and turned in that direction.

To the right, Mat said in Darrick's ear. *If ye go to the left, ye will be caught.*

Taramis waded through the rising water.

Tell them!

Hesitant, not truly trusting that Mat was speaking to him, knowing that he could have gone insane and never noticed it until now, Darrick said, "You're going the wrong way."

Taramis halted in water that was now chest deep. He peered at Darrick. "How do you know?" the sage asked.

Darrick didn't answer.

Tell him, Mat said. *Tell him about me.*

Shouts outside the sewer system echoed inside the tunnel, carried flat and hard across the water. Torchlight neared the break, and Darrick knew it wouldn't be long before the guards attacked them.

"Because Mat is telling me which way to go," Darrick said.

"Mat who?" Taramis demanded suspiciously. "Your friend who was killed at Tauruk's Port?"

"Aye," Darrick replied, knowing he wouldn't have believed his story if he'd been the one it was being told to. He could scarcely believe it now.

"How?" Taramis asked.

"I don't know," Darrick admitted. "But it was him who

got me to activate the sword's power and show us the way into this sewer."

The warriors gathered around Taramis, all of them wet and bedraggled, all of their faces filled with doubt and dark suspicion.

"What do you think?" Palat asked Taramis, taking a half-step in front of the sage to separate him further from Darrick.

Aware of the big warrior's cautionary measure, Darrick remained silent and understood. He would have thought he was mad as well if he hadn't been the one hearing Mat's voice.

Taramis held his torch higher. The flames licked at the stones overhead, charring the moss and lichens that grew there. "Every time a demon is loosed into the world of men," he quoted, "the balance must be kept. A way will be made, and only human choice can rid the world of the demon again." He smiled, but there was no mirth in the expression. "Are you certain of this, Darrick?"

"Aye."

Rhambal pointed his lantern at the wall. "We've got no choice about moving. Those damned guards are going to be on top of us in no time. And most of them are honest men, men just getting paid for enforcing the peace. I don't want to hang around and fight them if I can help it."

Taramis nodded. "To the right, then." He led the way, pushing his torch before him.

The sewer channel gradually headed up. Darrick felt the incline more because the inrushing water flooded around him and made him more buoyant, which made walking up the hill harder than it should have been. Gradually, though, the water level dropped, and Taramis's torchlight reflected in hundreds of eyes before them.

"Rats," Rhambal said, then swore.

The rats occupied the sides of the sewer, shifting and slithering against one another, islands and clots of rat flesh. Their hairless tails flipped and wriggled as they moved constantly.

The rising water lapped over the sides of the sewer tunnel, lifting small groups of tightly clustered rats free of their temporary retreat. Riding the crest of the water as it ebbed and flowed, the rats fixated on the warriors in the tunnel.

And in the next moment, they attacked.

Buyard Cholik rode the stone snake's head back to the wall as guards circulated through the crowd. The confluence of whispered voices created a din in the cathedral that made it impossible to talk.

Someone attacked the church.

The thought pounded through Cholik's mind. He didn't know who could dare such a thing. During the last month, the relationship with Lord Darkulan had become even better. Ties and agreements were beginning to be made to erect a church in Westmarch. The Zakarum Church was fighting politically to disallow the Church of the Prophet of the Light entrance to the capitol city, but Cholik knew it was only a matter of time before even that resistance went away. Through Lord Darkulan and his own observers, many of whom Cholik had entertained in the church during the last month with Lord Darkulan's help, the king had learned how much wealth the hopeful pilgrims brought to Bramwell.

But even beyond the basic wealth that the church could bring to Westmarch, there was no doubt about the miracles. Or about the man who made them happen. With more people coming to the church, Cholik had begun doing more services. He now conducted six from dawn until after dusk. A normal man, Cholik knew, a simply human man, would have dropped in his tracks from the demands, but he had reveled in them, meeting them and surpassing them. Kabraxis had given Cholik his strength, shoring him up and keeping him going.

More miracles had been worked, all of them received by those fortunate enough to be chosen to journey along the Way of Dreams. During the past months, the size and number of the miracles had increased along with the number of services. Health had been restored. Crooked limbs had been straightened. Wealth had been given. Love had been granted. Husbands and sons who had gone missing in battles had emerged from the gaping, flaming jaws of the stone snake, called from wherever they had been to the path of the Black Road. Those survivors had no memories of where they had been until the moment they stepped from the snake's mouth into the cathedral.

And three times, youth had been restored to aging parishioners.

That had all of the coastal cities along the Gulf of Westmarch talking as the story was carried by ship from port to port. Caravans picked up the stories in the port cities and carried them to the east, to Lut Gholein and possibly across the Twin Seas to Kurast and beyond.

Giving the youth back to the three men was the most difficult, Cholik knew, and required great sacrifice. Kabraxis made the sacrifice, but the demon didn't pay the price himself. Instead, Kabraxis took children from the city during the nights and sacrificed them on the Black Road, robbing them of their years so he could reward the parishioners he'd chosen with extended years. All three of those parishioners were men who could help the Church of the Prophet of the Light grow and earn the favor of the king. One of them, in fact, had been one of the king's own observers, a man—Lord Darkulan insisted—who was like a father to the king.

It was a time of miracles. Everyone in Bramwell spoke of the Church of the Prophet of the Light that way. Health, wealth, love, and a return to youth—there was nothing more a man could hope for in life.

But someone had dared attack the church.

Deep anger resonated inside Cholik as he gazed out over the filled cathedral. One of the lesser priests Cholik had groomed stepped forward into the lighted area below.

"Brothers and sisters," the priest said, "beloved of Dien-Ap-Sten, join me now in prayer to our magnificent prophet. Wayfinder Sayes goes to speak on your behalf to our prophet and ask that only a few more miracles be granted before we take leave of this service."

His words, amplified by the specially constructed stage, rolled over the church audience and quieted the whispering that had resulted from the news about the attack on the church.

Threaten to take away their chances at a miracle for themselves, Cholik mused, *and you get the attention of every person in the room.*

The priest guided the assembly in prayers to Dien-Ap-Sten, singing of the prophet's greatness, goodness, and generousness.

Once the snake's head was again locked into place on the wall and had become immobile, the flames died away, and that section of the cathedral darkened. Many worshippers screamed out Dien-Ap-Sten's name then, begging that the prophet return and grant more miracles.

Cholik stepped from the platform on the snake's back onto the third-floor balcony. A guard hidden in the shadows pulled the heavy drapes back and opened the door for him. Two crossbowmen stood behind the drapes at all times, relieved every hour during the times of service.

Stepping through the door into the hallway beyond, Cholik found a dozen members of his personal guard waiting for him. No one used this hallway except him, and it led to the secret passageways that had been honeycombed throughout the church. They held lanterns to light the darkened hallway.

"What is going on?" Cholik demanded, stopping among them.

"The church has been attacked, Wayfinder," Captain Rhellik reported. He was a hard-faced man, used to commanding mercenaries and waging small, hard-won wars or tracking bandits.

"I knew that," Cholik spat. "Who has dared attack my church?"

Rhellik shook his head. "I've not yet learned, Wayfinder.

From what I've been told, a ship smashed into the court-yard south of the church that overhung the river."

"An accident?"

"No, Wayfinder. The attack on the parapet was delib-erate."

"Why attack the courtyard there? What could they possibly hope to gain?"

"I don't know, Wayfinder."

Cholik believed the mercenary captain. When Rhellik had been brought to the church almost a year ago, he'd been dying a paraplegic, paralyzed from the neck down by a horse stepping on him during a battle with bandits while traveling from Lut Gholein. His men had bound him to a litter and brought him almost two hundred miles for healing.

At first, Cholik had seen no value in the mercenary cap-tain, but Kabraxis had insisted that they watch him. For weeks, Rhellik had stayed at every service, fed by his men and bathed in the river, and he had sung praises to Dien-Ap-Sten as best as he was able with his failing voice. Then, one day, the snake's head had lifted him from the crowd and gulped him down. A few minutes after that, the mer-cenary captain had walked back from the Way of Dreams, hale and hearty, and he had pledged his service forever to the prophet Dien-Ap-Sten and his Wayfinder.

"It doesn't make any sense," Cholik said, starting down the hallway.

"No, Wayfinder," Rhellik agreed. He raised the lantern he carried in one hand to light their way. He carried his vicious curved sword in the other hand.

"None of these people has been identified?"

"No."

"How large is the force that attacked the church?" Cholik demanded.

"No more than a couple dozen warriors," Rhellik said. "The city guards tried to turn them."

"The boat had to sail upriver to crash into that parapet." Cholik turned and followed the passageway to his right, going up the short flight of steps. He knew every hallway in the church. His robes swished as he hurried. "It couldn't have been going fast. Why didn't the city guards stop it?"

"The ship was driven by magic, Wayfinder. They had no chance to stop it."

"And we don't know who these people are?"

"I regret to say, Wayfinder, that we don't. As soon as that changes, I'll let you know."

Only a little farther on, Cholik reached the hidden door that opened into one of the main hallways on the fourth floor. He released the lock and stepped out into the hallway.

No one was in the hallway. No visitors were allowed up from the first and second floors where seating was made available in the cathedral. And none of the staff who lived there was in those rooms because they were all attending the service. The south fourth-floor wing was reserved for acolytes who had been with the church for six months or longer. It was surprising how quickly those small rooms had filled.

Cholik turned to the left and walked toward the balcony that overlooked the parapet courtyard at the river's edge below.

"Wayfinder," Rhellik said uncomfortably.

"What?" Cholik snapped.

"Perhaps it would be better if you allowed us to protect you."

"Protect me?"

"By taking you to one of the lower rooms where we can better defend you."

"You want to hide me away?" Cholik asked in exasperation. "At a time when my church is attacked, you expect me to hide away like some coward?"

"I'm sorry, Wayfinder, but it would be the safest course of action."

The mercenary's words weighed heavily on Cholik's thoughts. He had sought out Kabraxis with his mind, but the demon was nowhere to be found. The situation irritated and frightened him. As big as the church was, there was nowhere for him to go if he'd been targeted by assassins.

"No," Cholik said. "I am guarded by Dien-Ap-Sten's love for me. That will be my buckler and my shield."

"Yes, Wayfinder. I apologize for doubting."

"Doubters do not stay in the grace of the Prophet of the Light for long, captain. I would have you remember that."

"Of course, Wayfinder."

Cholik strode up the final flight of steps to the balcony. The night wind whipped over him. There was no sign of the mystical winds of which Rhellik had spoken. But Cholik's eyes settled on the burning ship loose on the river current.

Flames roiled across the entire length of the ship, twisting and shifting and racing toward the heavens. Swirls of orange and red embers leapt up from the topmost parts of the masts and rigging, dying in their suicidal race to reach the night sky. In the next moment, the ship rammed into one of the vessels anchored in the river harbor, catching the other ship broadside.

A shower of embers and flying debris from the sails blew over the line of ships beyond the two that remained locked together. Torches and lanterns marked the sailors running to deal with the fire and save the ships. As tightly packed as they were, the fire would spread rapidly if it remained unchecked.

Cholik glanced upriver, spotting the guards at the base of the river where the hanging courtyard had been torn away. He watched in confused speculation as the guards leapt from their craft and waded through the water. Only when their lanterns and torches neared the opening in the sewer did he spot it.

"They're inside the sewers," Cholik said.

Rhellik nodded. "I have already sent a runner to take some of my men there to intercept them. We have maps of the sewer systems." His mouth tightened into a grim line. "We shall protect you, Wayfinder. You need have no fear."

"I have no fear," Cholik said, turning to address the

mercenary captain. "I am chosen of Dien-Ap-Sten. I am the Wayfinder of the Way of Dreams where all miracles take place. The men who have broken into my church are dead men, whether they know it or not. If they don't die at the hands of the guards or at my own hands, then they will die at the hands of Dien-Ap-Sten. Although generous to his believers, Dien-Ap-Sten is merciless against those who would strike against him."

The guards funneled into the breached sewer tunnel. Their lantern light and torchlight made the opening glow cherry red like a wound gone bad with poisonous infection.

"Pass the word along to your men, captain," Cholik said. "I want them to watch for the burned man who attacked me last month."

"Yes, Wayfinder. I only pray that no worshipper comes here this night with such an affliction in hopes of being healed. Such a person would find only death waiting."

Cholik stared across the black river. Clusters of lights stood on either bank. More lights raced along the two bridges that connected the north and south sections of the city.

When the attackers were caught, and Cholik had every reason to believe that they would be, they would be put to death. He'd have their heads mounted on pikes at the main entrance through the church walls, and he would say that Dien-Ap-Sten had commanded that it be so, to show the enemies of the Church of the Prophet of the Light that the prophet could be fierce and unforgiving as well. It would temper the faith of those who believed, and it would be a grand story that would bring more people in to see the church and the religion.

Buyard Cholik.

Surprised by the demon's voice in his head, Cholik started. "Yes, Dien-Ap-Sten."

The mercenary captain signaled his men, waving them back away from Cholik, taking two steps himself. He touched the back of his sword hand to the tattoo that had been placed over his heart when he had sworn loyalty to the church. A rote prayer to the prophet tumbled from his lips, praying for a safe and enlightening journey that the wisdom and power of Dien-Ap-Sten be spread even farther.

Return to the services, Kabraxis said. *I will not have those disrupted. I will not be shown as weak or wanting.* The demon sounded far away.

"Who has attacked the church?" Cholik asked.

Taramis Volken and his band of demon hunters, Kabraxis said.

A worm of fear crawled through Cholik's heart. Although he had not talked to Kabraxis of the demon hunter, Cholik had read about the man. Taramis Volken had been a powerful force against demons for years. Once he had read and heard some of the stories about the man, Cholik remembered reading about him from the archives in the Zakarum Church. Taramis Volken was viewed as an inflexible man, one who would not quit. The demon hunter had proven that over the last few weeks. Ever since recovering Stormfury, Hauklin's sword, the group had vanished.

They've only been hidden, Kabraxis said. *Now they are once more in my grasp.*

But before he could stop himself, Cholik wondered if they were somehow in Taramis Volken's grasp instead. All his training in the Zakarum Church had taught him that demons didn't enter the human world without affecting the balance between Light and Darkness. Taramis Volken had proven himself to be the champion of Light on several occasions.

Taramis Volken will die in those sewers, Kabraxis growled inside Cholik's mind. *Doubt me, and you will pay, Buyard Cholik, even if you are my chosen one.*

"I don't doubt you, Dien-Ap-Sten," Cholik said.

Then go. I will deal with Taramis Volken.

"As you wish, my prophet." Cholik touched his head in benediction, then turned with a swirl of his robe.

"Wayfinder," Rhellik said, looking up, "returning to the cathedral might not be the safest thing you can do."

"It is the safest place to be," Cholik said, "when you go there with Dien-Ap-Sten's blessing." *And not going there could be the most dangerous.* But he amended that even as he thought it.

The most dangerous place to be was in the sewers beneath the Church of the Prophet of the Light.

Twenty-three

Hairless tails flicking, sharp teeth snapping, the rat packs poured toward Darrick, Taramis Volken, and the demon hunters. The pale yellow light of the warriors' lanterns and torches played over the wriggling rat bodies as they raced along the ledges and the uneven walls and swam through the murky water of the sewer mixing with the river encroaching through the break in the tunnel behind them.

For a moment, ice-cold terror thudded through Darrick's veins as he thought about being covered over in a mass of furry bodies and dragged under the water. The other warriors cursed and called out to the Light as they spread out and took up defensive positions.

Rhambal stood tall and massive at the head of the group. With a backward swipe of his shield, the warrior knocked a dozen of the leaping rats from the air. The thuds of their bodies slamming against the shield echoed in the sewer tunnel.

"Stand," Taramis ordered his warriors. "Hold them from me for only a moment more."

Rats leapt from the walls, landing on the armored helms and shoulders of the warriors. Their claws scratched against the plate and chainmail, demanding blood.

Darrick swiped at one of the foul creatures and halved it from nose to tail with Hauklin's sharp blade. The rat's blood sprayed across him, blinding him in one eye for a moment. By the time he'd wiped the blood from his face and cleared his vision, three more rats landed on him, staggering him with their sudden weight. The rats started up toward his face at once, the flickering torchlight dancing across their fangs. Cursing, Darrick knocked the rats from him. They plopped into the water and disappeared for a moment before they bobbed back to the surface.

Despite their best efforts, the warriors gave ground before the onslaught of rats. Blades and hammers flashed through the air, coming dangerously close to hitting their comrades. Blood mixed in with the dark sewer water and the white froth of the river rushing into the tunnel.

The undertow created by the pull of the river and the push of the sewer almost dislodged Darrick's tenuous stance atop the muck-lined stone floor. Darrick whipped the sword around, amazed at how easily and fluidly the weapon moved. Dead rats and pieces of dead rats flew around him, but still many managed to reach him. Their fangs cut his arms and legs where they were left uncovered by the chainmail shirt he wore.

Working quickly, Taramis inscribed magical symbols in the air. Green fire followed his fingertips, and the finished symbols glowed brightly. With another gesture, the sage sent the symbols spinning forward.

The symbols exploded in the air only a few feet away, and white light stabbed out. The light shafts speared through the rats and dropped them in their tracks, shredding the flesh from their bones till only skeletons remained.

For a moment, Darrick believed the danger had passed. The bites stung, but none of them was bad enough to slow him. Infection, however, was a concern, but only if they lived through the attack on the church.

"Taramis," Palat said, supporting one of the warriors and keeping a hand pressed over his neck. "One of the rats tore Clavyn's throat and cut the jugular vein. If we don't get the bleeding stopped, he's going to die."

Wading through the rising water to examine the warrior, Taramis shook his head. "There's nothing I can do," he whispered hoarsely. They'd not been able to find healing potions along the way and lacked gold to buy it, besides.

Palat's face turned wintry hard as the blood continued seeping between his fingers. "I'm not going to let him die, damn it," the grizzled old warrior said. "I didn't come all this way just to watch my friends die."

Shaking his head, Taramis said, "There's nothing you can do."

Horror touched Darrick, sliding past the defenses he tried to erect. If Clavyn died a quick death, they'd have to leave his body there—for the rats. And if the warrior died slowly, he'd have to die alone, because they couldn't afford to stay with him.

Since arriving in the tunnel, Darrick had stepped back into that safe place he'd first created to endure his father's beatings and harsh words. He refused to let Clavyn's death touch him.

No, Mat whispered. *He doesn't have to die, Darrick. Use the sword. Use Hauklin's sword.*

"How?" Darrick asked. Inside the tunnel, his voice cut through the splashing echoes of the water swirling into the walls on either side of him.

The hilt, Mat replied. *The hilt must be pressed to Clavyn's flesh.*

Desperate, not wanting to see the man die in such an ignoble fashion, Darrick moved forward. As he did, the sword's blade glowed fierce blue again.

Palat stepped forward, standing between Darrick and the wounded warrior. "No," Palat said. "I'll not have you ending his life."

"I'm not going to kill him," Darrick said. "I'm going to try to save him."

Still, the big warrior refused to move.

In that moment, Darrick knew that he'd never been one of them and would never be one of them. They had traveled together and eaten together and fought together, but he was apart from them. Only his ability to take Hauklin's sword had bound them to him. Anger stirred in him.

Darrick, Mat said. *Don't give in to this. You're not alone.*

But Darrick knew that wasn't true. He'd been alone all his life. At the end, even Mat had left him.

No, Mat argued. *The way ye're feelin' isn't real, Darrick.*

It's the demon. It's Kabraxis. He's down here with us. He's aware of us. Even now, there are warriors coming to intercept yer group. But Kabraxis's thoughts are within ye's. I'm tryin' to keep him from ye, but he's sortin' out yer weaknesses. Don't let the demon turn ye from these men. They need ye.

A fierce headache dawned between Darrick's temples, then throbbed with an insane beat that almost dropped him to his knees in the cold water. Black spots swam in his vision.

Use the sword, Darrick, Mat insisted. *It can save all of ye.*

"What can I do?" Darrick asked.

Believe, Mat answered.

Struggling, Darrick tried to find the key to make the magic work. It would be better if there were a magic word or something else. All he could remember was how the sword had acted and felt at Ellig Barrows's house, and how the sword had behaved when it lit the riverbank to reveal the tunnel they'd clambered through only moments before. It wasn't belief, Darrick knew, but it was something he knew to be true.

The sword shivered and glowed blue again. Calm warmth filled the tunnel and soaked into Darrick's flesh and bones as a humming sound filled the air. In stunned amazement, he watched as the blood stopped slipping between Palat's fingers.

Hesitantly, Palat removed his hand from Clavyn's neck, revealing the jagged wound that had severed the warrior's jugular. As they watched, the flesh knitted, turning back into seamless flesh with only a small scar left behind.

The humming and the warmth continued, and Darrick watched as even the wounds he'd endured healed, including the rip along his ribcage made by the arrow earlier. In less than a minute, the warriors were all healed.

"Blessed by the Light," Rhambal said, a childlike grin on his broad face. "We've been blessed by the Light."

"Or saved to be killed later," Palat growled, "if you're going to stand there flapping your lips."

Darrick reached for Mat, wanting to hear his voice.

Stay strong, Mat said. *The worst is yet to come. This is only the calm before the storm.*

"Damn," Palat swore, pointing back the way they'd come. "The guards are nearly upon us."

Head buzzing, still filled with the headache, Darrick gazed back along the tunnel.

Flickering light filled the darkness behind them, proof that the guard ship had arrived. Splashing echoed around Darrick and signaled the guards' approach.

"Forward," Taramis ordered, lifting his lantern and moving farther up the sewer.

The group started forward, fighting the water and the sewer's slick stone bottom. The darkness ahead of them retreated before the torches and the lanterns. Darting through the shadows and the water, a few rats shrilled and squeaked at their approach but made no move to attack.

Something thudded into Darrick's side, drawing his attention. He looked down, barely able to spot the short piece of ivory bone that slid through the water. At first, he thought the bone was some sore of creature with a hard carapace, then he saw that it was a leg bone from one of the rats Taramis had slain with his spell.

"Hey," Rhambal called out, reaching down and snatching a small rat's skull from the water. "These are the bones of the rats."

Before the big warrior could say any more, the skull leapt from his hand and snapped at his face, causing him to draw back. He swept his armored fist at it, but the skull was gone, dropping back into the water.

"Hold," Taramis said, taking a lantern from one of the nearby warriors and raising it. The light chased the darkness, splintering the shadows and reflecting from the tossed and uneven planes of the water.

Revealed by the lantern light, hundreds of bones slid through the water, flashing greenish white under the light.

"It's the demon's doing," Palat snarled. "The demon knows we're down here."

In the next instant, a frightening figure surged from

beneath the water. The line of warriors closest to it stepped back.

Formed of the rats' bones, the creature stood eight feet tall, built square and broad-chested as an ape. It stood on bowed legs that were whitely visible through the murky water. Instead of two arms, the bone creature possessed four, all longer than the legs. When it closed its hands, horns formed of ribs and rats' teeth stuck out of the creature's fists, rendering them into morningstars for all intents and purposes. The horns looked sharp-edged, constructed for slashing as well as stabbing. Small bones, some of them jagged pieces of bone, formed the demon's face the creature wore.

"That's a bone golem," Taramis said. "Your weapons won't do it much harm."

The bone golem's mouth, created by splintered bones so tightly interwoven they gave the semblance of mobility, grinned, then opened as the creature spoke in a harsh howl that sounded like a midnight wind tearing through a graveyard. "Come to your deaths, fools."

Taramis gestured with his free hand, inscribing a mystic symbol. Immediately, the symbol became a pumpkin-sized fireball that streaked for the incredible bone creature.

Striking the bone golem in the chest, the impact of the fireball knocked the creature back on its heels for a moment. Flames wreathed the demon-made thing, crawling through the gaps in the bones till it seemed to be burning on the inside as well. Steam welled out of the bone golem but didn't appear to do any further damage.

Opening its mouth again, the bone golem howled once more, and this time flames spat into the air as well. The ululating wail echoed the length of the sewer, so loud it was deafening. Several of the warriors put their hands to their ears, their mouths open as they screamed in pain.

Darrick never heard the warriors' screams over the spine-chilling roar. But he heard Mat's voice.

It's up to ye, Darrick, Mat said calmly. *The bone golem will kill them if it gets the chance. Only Hauklin's enchanted blade can damage the creature.*

"I'm no hero," Darrick whispered as he looked at the creature.

Perhaps not, Mat said, *but there's no place to run.* Glancing back over his shoulder, Darrick saw the line of church guards filling the sewer behind them. Retreat only offered the inevitable battle with the guards and the promise of even more waiting for them out in the harbor.

The warriors drew back beside Darrick, obviously preferring their chances against human foes instead of the bone golem. Darrick stared at the creature, pushing himself through and past his fear. There was no way out except through the bone golem.

He stepped forward, falling into a defensive position as the creature closed on him. One of the spiked fists slashed at him. Ducking beneath the blow, Darrick set himself and cut upward. Catching the bone golem's arm with the edge of his blade, Darrick tried to cut through the elbow joint. The blow missed by a couple of inches and skidded along the creature's arm.

Sensing his opponent's movement more than he saw it, Darrick dodged backward, narrowly avoiding the balled left fist that streaked for his head. The bone blades jutting from the fist slashed through the chest of his traveling leathers, then splashed into the waist-high water swirling around them.

Before the bone golem could draw its arm back, Darrick swung the enchanted blade again. This time the sword sheared through the arm, splintering it into a thousand bone shards and scattering them through the water. The bone golem threw a right fist at Darrick's face that would have carved the face from his skull if it had landed.

Desperately, Darrick threw himself backward. The razor edges of the fist slashed across his chest again, cutting through his traveling leathers but scoring on the flesh beneath this time as well. Fear rattled through Darrick, almost causing him to give up hope, but Hauklin's sword felt steady and true in his hands. He parried the bone golem's next blow, turning the huge fist from its target, stepping back as the creature followed the bony hammer into the water and bent double. Spinning, Darrick landed a blow against the bone golem's ribcage beneath the stub of its bottom left arm. Broken bone shards flew in all directions, but the creature remained whole.

Still moving, somehow keeping his footing in the water and in the muck, Darrick retreated, slashing and parrying with Hauklin's sword. Crimson stained the front of his traveling leathers as he bled. While pulling back, he tripped and fell.

The bone golem swiped at Darrick at once, aiming a fist at his face.

Then Rhambal was there, blocking the blow with his shield. The razor-sharp spikes that festooned the bone golem's fist tore through the warrior's shield less than a foot from Darrick's face. Getting his feet under him again, Darrick saw the bone golem's spike pierce Rhambal's shield and into the arm that held it. Blood spurted as the bone golem drew its fist free.

In obvious agony, Rhambal stepped back, then faltered and fell to his knees, clutching his wounded arm to his chest and leaving his head exposed.

Guilt hammered Darrick, more painful than the cuts across his chest. *It's my fault,* he told himself. *If I hadn't been able to free Hauklin's sword, they would have never come here.*

No, Mat said. *They would have come, Darrick. Even without ye an' that sword. It's the demon working inside ye. It's puttin' them thoughts there. Fillin' ye with bad thoughts an' makin' ye weak. Ye can make a difference in this, an' that's what I come back for. Now move!*

The bone golem wasted no time in setting itself and attacking the new prey it found before it. Gripping the enchanted sword in both hands, Darrick stepped forward and swung. When the blade met the bone golem's arm, the weapon shattered the limb.

Roaring with rage, the bone golem turned its attention back to Darrick, flailing after him with its two remaining arms. Darrick fended one of the blows off, then avoided the other, throwing himself into the air and flipping over the arm.

Taramis and Palat dashed forward, caught Rhambal under the arms, and dragged him back from the bone golem's reach.

Landing on his feet, Darrick blocked another sweeping roundhouse blow, feeling the impact vibrate through his wrists and arms. He almost lost his grip on the sword but clung to it tightly. Running at the wall on the left, knowing if he stopped the bone golem would swarm over him, Darrick threw himself into the air and struck the wall with his water-filled boots. Water splashed out of his boots on impact.

You're a blight on me, boy, his father's voice thundered inside his head. *An embarrassment to me. By the Light, I hate the sight of your ugly face. It ain't no face that ever belonged to me. And that red hair of yours, you'll never find it in my family. Nor in your ma's, I'll warrant.*

The words tumbled through Darrick's mind, splitting his concentration as he cushioned the impact against the wall by bending his knees and falling forward.

Don't listen to him, Mat said. *It's only the damned demon talkin' to ye. He's lookin' for yer weak spots, he is. An' yer personal business, why, it's no business of his.*

But Darrick knew that the words didn't just come from the demon. They came from that small stable in back of his father's butcher shop, and they came from years of abuse and cold hatred that he hadn't understood as a child. Even as a young man, Darrick had been powerless to defend himself against his father's harsh words. Maybe his father had learned not to be so quick with his hands when Darrick had started fighting back, but Darrick had never learned to protect himself from his father's verbal assaults and his mother's neglect.

Darrick fell forward on the wall, his forward momentum allowing him to make contact for just an instant before gravity pulled him toward the water-filled tunnel. From the corner of his eye, he saw the bone golem throwing another punch. By the time it reached the wall where he'd landed, he had pushed off with one hand—the other gripping Hauklin's sword—and flipped back toward the tunnel behind his attacker.

The bone golem's fist crunched into the wall, splitting stone and breaking loose mortar that held it together.

Darrick forced his father's words from his mind, stilled his shaking hand, and squared himself as he took a full breath of the fetid air around him. Taking a two-handed grip on the magical blade, watching the bone golem start turning to face him, Darrick saw Taramis and his warriors on the other side of the creature. Beyond them, the church guards awaited an opportunity. Crossbowman fired their weapons, but the quarrels caught on the shields of the men at the rear of the warrior group.

Do it! Mat roared in Darrick's head.

The sword blazed blue again, a true and cold blue like that found in the sea before the deep turned black. Swinging, not holding anything back, Darrick felt the enchanted weapon shatter through the bone golem's ribcage and grate to a stop embedded in the creature's spine.

The bone golem howled with pain, but its macabre voice carried laughter as well, rolling gales of it. "Now you're going to die, insect."

"No," Darrick said, feeling the power tingling through the sword. "Go back to hell, demon."

Eldritch blue flames leapt down the length of the sword and curled around the bone golem's spine as it reached for Darrick. The fire grew, enveloping the bone golem and burning away whatever magic bound the skeletal remains of the dead rats together. Flaming bones toppled into the sewer water, hissing when they struck.

For a moment, everyone—including Darrick—stood frozen in disbelief.

Run! Mat yelled.

Turning, Darrick ran, raising his knees high to clear the water level. The sword continued to glow, chasing back the shadows that filled the tunnel. Taramis and the demon hunters came after Darrick.

Less than fifty yards farther on, the tunnel ended at a T juncture. Without hesitation, the sword pulled Darrick to the right. He ran on, filmed by the condensation filling the tunnel as well as perspiration pouring from every pore. His breath burned the back of his throat, and he was convinced the stench of the place was soaking into him.

Only a short distance farther on, the tunnel ended without warning. Sometime in distant years past, the sewer had collapsed. The sword's bright blade illuminated the pile of rubble that blocked the passageway. Cloaked in the shadows and the collapse of broken rock, rats prowled the rubbish heap. Hundreds of them scampered and crept along the broken rock.

Above the rubble, a rounded dome of fallen earth peeked through. No longer shored up by the stones, the earth had collapsed inward over the years but had not completely fallen. There was no way to guess how many feet of earth and rock separated the tunnel from the surface.

"Dead end," Palat growled. "That damned sword has played us false this time, Taramis. Those guards will be down on us in another moment, and there's no place for us to run."

Taramis turned to Darrick. "What is the meaning of this?"

"I don't know," Darrick admitted.

Twenty-four

In the distance, the splash of the closing guards running through the sewer grew steadily louder in Darrick's ears. At least in this part of the tunnel, the water level was a few inches below knee-high, and the current was weak, little more than a steady flow.

Darrick felt betrayed. The voice that he'd thought had been Mat's had only been another demon-spawned trick. Staring at the sword, he knew it had been bait for an insidious trap.

No, Mat said. *This is where ye're supposed to be. Just hold yer water, I say, an' things will be revealed to ye.*

"What things?" Darrick demanded.

Taramis and the other warriors turned to watch him, and the splashing of the approaching church guards grew louder, more immediate.

There were three of us in that cavern when Kabraxis stepped through into our world, Mat answered. *The magicks that Buyard Cholik unleashed when he opened that gateway to the Burning Hells marked all of us. Them doubts in yer head, Darrick, that's just Kabraxis playing on yer fears. Just hold the course.*

"Three?" Darrick repeated. "There weren't three of us." Unless Buyard Cholik was being counted.

There was another, Mat insisted. *We all lost somethin' that night, Darrick, an' now we must stand together to get it back. Demons never enter this world without sowing the seeds of their own destruction. It's up to men to figure out what they are. Me? I been lost for a long time, an' it wasn't until ye found Hauklin's sword that I come back to meself and ye.*

Darrick shook his head, doubting all of it.

You're worthless, boy, his father's voice said. *Hardly worth the time to kill you. Maybe I'll just wait until you get a little bigger, put a little more meat on your bones, then I'll dress you out and tell everybody you up and ran away.*

The old fear vibrated through Darrick. In the shadows he thought he could almost see his father's face.

"Darrick," Taramis called.

Even though he heard the man clearly, Darrick found he couldn't respond. He was trapped by the memory and by the old fear. The stink of the stables behind the butcher's shop filled his nostrils, making the images of the men before him and the sewer tunnel around him seem dreamlike.

C'mon, Darrick! Mat called. *Pay attention, damn ye! This is the hold that Kabraxis has found over ye. Me, why, that foul demon up an' lost me out in the ghost ways, an' maybe I'd be there still if ye hadn't found Hauklin's blade the way ye done.*

Darrick felt the sword in his fist, but he blamed it for leading them into the dead end. Maybe Mat still believed the sword was a talisman of power, something to stand tall against the demons, but Darrick didn't. It was a cursed thing, like other weapons he'd talked about. Palat had owned a cursed weapon; he knew what he was talking about when he denounced Hauklin's sword.

It's the demon, Darrick, Mat said. *Be strong.*

"I can't," Darrick whispered hollowly. He watched the torchlights of the approaching guards gather at the far end of the tunnel.

"You can't what?" Taramis asked him.

"I can't believe," Darrick said. All his life he'd trained himself not to believe. He didn't believe that his father had hated him. He didn't believe that it was his father's fault that he was beaten. He'd trained himself to believe that life was one day after another at the butcher's shop and that a good day was one when a beating didn't cripple him up.

But ye escaped that, Mat said.

"I ran," Darrick whispered, "but I couldn't outrun what was meant to be."

Ye have.

"No," Darrick said, gazing at the guard.

"They're waiting," Palat said. "They figure there's too many of us for them to take without losing more than a few of their own. They're going to hold up, get more archers in here, then take us down."

Taramis stepped toward Darrick. "Are you all right?"

Darrick didn't answer. Helplessness filled him, and he struggled to push it away. The feeling settled over his chest and shoulders, making it hard for him to breathe. For this past year, he'd put his life into a bottle, into the bottom of a glass, into the cheap wine in every lowdown tavern he'd wandered through. Then he'd made the mistake of trying to sober himself up and believe there was more than futility in his life.

More than the bad luck and the feeling of being unwanted that had haunted him all his life.

Worthless, his father's voice spat.

And why had he saved himself? To die at the end of a collapsed sewer like a rat? Darrick wanted to laugh, but he wanted to cry as well.

Darrick, Mat called.

"No, Mat," Darrick said. "I've come far enough. It's time to end it."

Moving closer, holding the lantern he held up to Darrick's face, Taramis stared into his eyes. "Darrick."

"We've come here to die," Darrick said, telling Mat as well as Taramis.

"We didn't come here to die," Taramis said. "We've come here to expose the demon for what he is. Once the people here who worship him know what he is, they will turn from him and be free."

The malaise that possessed Darrick was so strong that the sage's words barely registered on him.

It's the demon, Mat said.

"Are you talking to your friend?" Taramis asked.

"Mat's dead," Darrick said in a hoarse whisper. "I saw him die. I got him killed."

"Is he here with us?" Taramis asked.

Darrick shook his head, but the movement felt distant from him, as if it were someone else's body. "No. He's dead."

"But he's talking to you," the sage said.

"It's a lie," Darrick answered.

It's not a lie, ye bloody great fool! Mat exploded. *Damn ye, ye thick-headed mullet. Ye was always the hardest to convince of somethin' ye couldn't see, couldn't touch for yerself. But if ye don't listen to me now, Darrick Lang, I'm gonna be travelin' the ghost ways forever. I'll never know no rest, never be at peace. Would ye wish that on me?*

"No," Darrick said.

"What is he saying?" Taramis asked. "Have we come to the right place?"

"It's a trick," Darrick said. "Mat says that the demon is in my head, trying to weaken me. And he's telling me he's not the demon."

"Do you believe him?" Taramis asked.

"I believe the demon is in my head," Darrick said. "I've somehow betrayed you all, Taramis. I apologize."

"No," Taramis said. "The sword is true. It came to you."

"It was a demon's trick."

The sage shook his head. "No demon, not even Kabraxis, could have power over Hauklin's sword."

But Darrick remembered how the sword had resisted him, how it hadn't come free at first down in that hidden tomb.

The sword couldn't be freed at first, Mat said. *It couldn't. It had to wait on me. It took us both, ye see. That's why I was wanderin' the ghost ways, stuck between hither an' thither. That's me part of this. An' the third man, why, he's yer way out, he is.*

"The third man is the way out," Darrick repeated dully.

Taramis studied him, moving the lantern in front of Darrick's eyes.

Despite the irritation he felt at having the light so close to his eyes, Darrick found that he couldn't move.

You ain't my son, his father roared in his mind. *Folks look at you, and they wouldn't blame me if I killed your mother. But she's bewitched me. I can't even raise a hand to her.*

Pain exploded along Darrick's cheek, but it was pain

from the memory, not something that was happening at present. The boy he'd been had landed in a heap on a pile of dung-covered straw. And his father had closed in and beaten him, causing Darrick to spend days lying in the stable with fever and a broken arm.

"Why didn't I die then?" Darrick asked. Everything would have been so much easier, so much simpler.

Mat would still have been alive, still living in Hillsfar with his family.

I chose not to be there, Mat said. *I chose to go with me friend. An' if ye hadn't given me reason to get out of Hillsfar, I'd have gotten out of there on me own. Hillsfar wasn't that big a place for the likes of ye and me. Me da knew that, just like he knew about me leavin' for ye.*

"I killed you," Darrick said.

An' if it wasn't for ye, how many times over dead would I have been by now? Before we ended up at Tauruk's Port?

In his mind, Darrick saw Mat slam into the cliff wall again, the skeleton hanging to him like a leech.

How many times did them captains we crewed with tell us that the life of a Westmarch Navy sailor wasn't worth havin'? Long hours, short pay, an' an even shorter life was it come to that, as it most likely would. The only things what made it all worthwhile was yer shipmates an' what few tavern wenches would roll their eyes at ye like ye was some kind of big damn hero.

Darrick remembered those speeches and those times. Mat had always made the best of it, always got the prettiest wenches, always had the most friends.

An' I'd be knowin' if me luck holds true in the hereafter, Mat said, *were I ever to get finished with this last bit of business we signed on for. Take up the sword, Darrick, an' stand ready. The third man is comin'.*

Part of the malaise lifted from Darrick. Only then did he realize that Taramis had gripped the front of his shirt in both fists and was shaking him.

"Darrick," the sage said. "Darrick."

"I hear you." Darrick heard the thunk of quarrels meeting the metal shields that the other warriors held up as well. Evidently the church guards had grown braver and decided to pick some of them off if they could. At the moment, the warriors were able to keep the shields overlapping so that none of the fletched missiles got through.

"What third man?" Taramis demanded.

"I don't know."

"Is there a way out of this?"

"I don't know."

Desperation creased the sage's face. "Use the sword."

"I don't know how."

Ye're waitin', Mat said.

"We're waiting," Darrick repeated dully. He'd dwindled so close inside himself that nothing mattered. His father's voice was muted, somewhere in the background. Maybe Mat had found a way to keep it quiet, but if he believed that, then Mat couldn't be the demon, and Darrick was pretty certain that the demon inside his head was Mat, too.

"There's other guards coming," Palat announced.

Without warning, stone shifted against stone.

Taramis glanced over Darrick's shoulder. "Look," the sage said. "Perhaps your friend was right."

Numbly, Darrick turned and spotted the rectangular hole that opened in the sewer ceiling above the pile of rubble. Peering closer, he realized it wasn't a door that had opened but rather a large section of rock that had been lifted up and out of the way. Light shone on the rubble and the water below.

A man shoved his head through the rectangle. "Darrick Lang," he called.

Shifting his lantern, Taramis brought the man into view.

Staring into the burned wreckage of the man's face, Darrick didn't believe for a moment that help had arrived.

"Darrick Lang," the burned man called again.

"He knows you," Taramis said at Darrick's side. "Who is he?"

Shaking his head, unable to recognize the burned man's features in the shifting of light and shadows, Darrick said, "I don't know."

Ye know him, Mat said. *That's Cap'n Raithen. From the pirates what was at Tauruk's Port. Ye fought him aboard the pirate ship.*

Amazed, knowing somehow Mat was speaking the truth, Darrick recognized the man. "But he died."

"He looks like he did," Taramis agreed in a quiet voice, "but he's offering us a way out of certain death. He's certainly mastered close escapes."

"This way," Raithen said. "If you would live, hurry. That damned demon has sent more people into the tunnel after you, and now that they've seen me open this one, they're likely to check up with the maps and figure out how I got here."

"Come on," Taramis said, taking Darrick by the arm.

"It's a trick," Darrick argued.

No, Mat said. *We're joined, the three of us. Joined in this endeavor.*

"We stay here, and we'll die like fish in a barrel," Taramis said. He shoved Darrick into reluctant movement.

As they neared the debris pile, the rats scattered, and quarrels struck the stones and sometimes the rats, but luckily the warriors all got through.

Raithen shoved his hand down toward Darrick. "Give me the sword," the pirate captain said. "I'll help you up."

Before Darrick could move the sword, Raithen reached down for it. As soon as the man's fingers touched the sword, they hissed.

Raithen yelped and yanked his hand back. Fresh steam rose from his burned fingers as he retreated into the tunnel above the sewer. He cursed and broke two more rocks free, enlarging the space so the demon hunters could more easily gain entrance.

Taramis went through first, clambering into the smaller tunnel above them. Dully, Darrick followed, taking care to watch the enchanted sword.

After introducing himself, Taramis offered his hand. The pirate captain remained out of arm's reach and ignored the hand. His gaze focused on Darrick. "Has your dead friend been in touch with you?" the pirate captain demanded.

Darrick looked at him, unwilling to answer. If anything, Darrick was ready to put Hauklin's sword through the pirate captain's heart.

A cold smile framed Raithen's lips. Cracks opened in the burned flesh, and blood beaded his mouth. "You don't have to answer," the pirate captain said. "There was no other way you'd be here if it weren't for your meddling friend."

Meddlin' friend, is it, then? Mat demanded. *Why, if I could put me hands on ye, or take a good length of steel up to do battle, I'd have the head off yer shoulders for that, ye mangy swab.*

"He's still with us, I see," Raithen said.

Surprised, Darrick asked, "You can hear him?"

"Whenever he's around, aye. He prattles on constantly. I just thank the Light that I've only listened to him these past few weeks." Raithen's gaze dropped to the sword in Darrick's hand. "He told me you'd come bearing Hauklin's mighty blade. Is that it?"

"Aye," Darrick replied.

The other warriors clambered into the small tunnel and milled around. Taramis issued quiet orders, getting men on either side of the opening in the bottom of the new tunnel.

"And that will kill Kabraxis?" Raithen demanded.

"So I've been told," Darrick replied. "Or at least drive the demon from this world back to the Burning Hells."

Spitting blood onto the tunnel floor, Raithen said, "I'd rather we gutted him and threw him to the sharks, then watched them carry him away a bite at a time."

"The church guards are coming," Palat said. "We'd best be on our way."

"Running through this tunnel with them on our heels?" Raithen asked. He grimaced, and the bloody froth at his mouth made him look demented.

He is demented, Mat said. *What Kabraxis did to him has nearly taken his sanity.*

"What are you doing here?" Darrick demanded of Raithen.

The pirate captain smiled, and more blood flecked his

lips. "The same as you, I expect. I came to be free of the demon. Although, after hearing of your friend's death and knowing what's happened to me, I'd have to say that you appear to have gotten better treatment than any of us."

Darrick didn't say anything.

Splashing sounded in the sewer below.

"Those church guards aren't going to wait for you two to finish palavering," Palat said.

Raithen stepped back and pulled a barrel from the wall beside the opening. As he yanked on the heavy barrel, the skin covering his hands split and bled. Crimson stained the barrel as Darrick and Palat lent hands, pushing the barrel toward the opening in the floor. Yanking the lid from the barrel, the pirate captain revealed the dark oil inside.

"Pour," Raithen commanded.

Together, they poured the contents of the barrel into the sewer water and over the rocks below. Rats scampered from beneath the dark liquid, and the guards held their positions warily.

Two crossbow quarrels flew through the opening in the floor. One of them splintered through the side of the barrel, and the other sliced through Raithen's right calf. Cursing with the pain, Raithen reached back to the wall and yanked a torch from the sconce there. He tossed the torch through the hole in the floor and onto the pile of debris below.

Peering cautiously over the side of the hole, Darrick watched as the oil caught fire. Flames spread over the pile of rubble, chasing the rats from their hiding places and onto the guards and into the water. The oil floating on top of the water caught fire as well. Carried by the slow current of the sewer, flames floated toward the guards, forcing them to retreat.

"That will buy us some time," Raithen said. He turned to the left and hurried along the tunnel.

"Where are you taking us?" Taramis asked.

"To the demon," Raithen said. "That's where we've got to go." He ran down the tunnel, pausing only long enough to take another torch from a sconce farther on.

The passageway was smaller than the sewer below, only wide enough for three warriors to jog abreast. Drawn by the urgency that vibrated within him, Darrick took the lead position among the demon hunters, joined quickly by Taramis and Palat.

"Who is that man?" Taramis asked, eyes locked on the fleeing figure ahead of them.

"Raithen," Darrick replied. "He is—"

Was, Mat assured him.

"—*was*," Darrick amended, "a pirate captain in the Gulf of Westmarch. A year ago, Raithen worked with Buyard Cholik."

"The Zakarum priest who opened the gateway for Kabraxis?"

"Aye."

"What happened to him?"

"He was killed by the demon in Tauruk's Port," Darrick said, knowing how strange it sounded as they watched the burned madman racing before them.

"He's not dead enough to my way of thinking," Palat said.

At the same time Raithen was killed, Mat said, *Kabraxis also cast the spell to raise the zombies an' skeletons to pursue us. The magic pervaded Raithen's corpse afterward, causin' him to rise again. After ye freed the sword, I was drawn here to him. I found I could talk to him as I talk to ye. The three of us are bound, Darrick, an' in our bindin', we present the way to end Kabraxis's reign here.*

"He's dead," Darrick explained, giving the details that Mat had given him.

"The prophecy of Hauklin," Taramis said.

"What prophecy?" Darrick asked. They trailed after Raithen, following the pirate captain around a bend in the tunnel.

"It was said that Hauklin's sword would never be taken from his tomb except to unite the Three," the sage said.

"What three?" Darrick asked.

Twenty-five

"One lost in death, one lost in life, and one lost in himself," Taramis said. "One trapped in the past, one trapped in the present, and one trapped in the future."

A cold chill of dread filled Darrick.

"Your friend Mat must be the one who is trapped in death, unreleased by his death in the past. Raithen has to be the one trapped in life, unable to die and doomed to live out the way he is through the present." He gazed at Darrick. "That leaves you."

"Why didn't you mention this earlier?" Darrick asked.

"Because not all prophecies are true," the sage answered. "All weapons and artifacts have stories that are told about them, but not all of those stories are true. When you drew the sword from Hauklin's body, I thought the prophecy was false."

Taramis's words hammered Darrick.

Aye, Mat said inside his head, *ye've been the one lost in yerself. But them sad times is behind ye. Just like Hillsfar an' that stable behind yer father's butcher shop. Just ye keep that in yer head, an' ye're gonna be all right. I'll not desert ye.*

"The prophecy goes on," Taramis said. "One will lift the sword, one will provide the way, and one will face the demon." The sage stared at Darrick. "You couldn't lift the sword at first because your friend wasn't with you then. You couldn't lift the sword till you heard Mat's voice."

Darrick knew it was true, and in a way it made sense with all the events that had transpired since.

"And he shows us the way," Taramis said, pointing at

Raithen still running before them. "That leaves you to face the demon."

"Beside the sage," Palat snorted derisively.

Darrick's face flamed in embarrassment, knowing the warrior didn't believe him strong enough or brave enough to confront the demon even with Hauklin's enchanted sword. And truth to tell, he didn't feel strong enough or brave enough himself.

Worthless, his father's voice said.

Cringing inside, Darrick desperately wanted out of the course of action left before him. He was no hero. At best, he would have made a decent Westmarch naval officer; perhaps—but only perhaps—he might have made a decent ship's captain.

But a hero?

No. Darrick couldn't accept that. But if he left, if he walked away from this confrontation to save himself, what would be left of him? Cold realization flooded him, and his footing nearly faltered. If he backed away from the coming battle, he knew he would be everything his father had ever accused him of being.

And if he did that, he would be as trapped between life and death as Mat or Raithen.

There's salvation in this for us all, Mat said.

Even if I become a martyr? Darrick wondered.

"We got men behind us," Clavyn called from the rear of the warriors.

"It's the guards," Raithen said. "I told you they'd find us. This tunnel is one of the newer ones. They use it to bring supplies into the church. Secret passageways and tunnels honeycomb these buildings. Over the last few weeks, I've ferreted out most of them."

"Where are you taking us?" Taramis asked.

"To the central cathedral," Raithen answered. "If you want to face Kabraxis, you'll find him and Cholik there."

Only a few feet farther on, the pirate captain came to a halt under a slanted section of ceiling. The door was as slanted as the ceiling, fitting into it.

"Guards sometimes wait here," Raithen said. "But they're not here now. They went below to help trap you in the sewer, not knowing the way the tunnel overlapped the sewer as I did." He pulled himself up and peered through a slit.

Darrick joined the man, keeping his sword naked in his fist. Taramis stood on the other side of him.

Gazing out through the slit, Darrick saw Buyard Cholik standing on a platform on top of a huge stone snake with a flaming face. As Darrick watched, the snake bobbed and weaved above the expectant audience. The way the audience beseeched and cried out to the snake and the man atop it left a sick knot in Darrick's stomach. He knew a few of the worshippers might know they prostrated themselves before evil, but most of them didn't. They were innocents, praying for miracles and never knowing they were being preyed on by a hell-spawned demon.

"There are hundreds, maybe thousands of people out there," Palat said in wonderment as he crowded up to the viewing slit as well. "If we step out into that, we're going to be outnumbered."

"The crowd will also give us a means of escaping," Taramis said. "The church guards won't be able to seal off all the exits and keep the crowd under control. Once we kill Buyard Cholik, there should be confusion enough to cover our retreat. After that, we'll spread the truth about Kabraxis through the city."

"You can't kill Buyard Cholik," Raithen said.

Darrick looked at the pirate captain. Aware of the pounding boots echoing down the tunnel, Darrick knew they didn't have much time.

"What do you mean?" Taramis asked.

"I tried to kill the bastard," Raithen said. "Weeks ago. I was part of the audience. I slipped a handheld crossbow past his guards and put a quarrel through his heart. I know I did. Yet a few hours later, Buyard Cholik gave another of his services. My attempt to assassinate him only made his fame grow even stronger."

It was Kabraxis, Mat said. *The demon saved him. But even the demon can't save him from Hauklin's blade.*

"We can't stay here," Palat said. "And retreat is out of the question."

Darrick swept his eyes over the demon hunters, marveling again at the small group of men who had been brave enough to walk into the church against such insurmountable odds. If he'd been asked to do such a thing, instead of being chosen by an enchanted sword and accompanied by the ghost of his dead friend, he doubted he would have accompanied them. He had no choice about being there, but they did.

Ye had a choice, Mat said. *Ye could have walked away from this.*

The sour smell of the hay in the stable behind his father's butcher shop swirled around Darrick. He could almost feel the heat of the day press against him, trapped by the small crawlspace among the rafters where the hay was kept. And where he'd lain while waiting to die or be killed the next time his father beat him.

No, Darrick told himself. There had been no choice.

Worthless, his father's voice snarled.

Steeling himself, drinking in air to keep his muscles loose and ready and energized, Darrick tried to ignore the voice.

"What's above us?" Darrick asked.

The thunder of the approaching guards' boots sounded closer, louder.

"Steps," Raithen said, "but they're counterweighted. Once I release the lock, the steps will rise."

Darrick looked at Taramis, who glanced at his men.

"If we stay here," Palat said, "we'll die. But out there, even with that stone snake moving around, we've got a chance."

Taramis nodded. "Agreed."

All the warriors readied their weapons.

"We make the attempt on Cholik," Taramis said, "then we get out of here if we can. We hope the demon will reveal himself. If not, we plan again." He glanced at Darrick. "Hauklin's sword is our best chance to get Kabraxis to come out of hiding."

"Aye," Darrick said, taking a two-handed grip on the sword hilt. He gazed out at the cathedral again, noting how the circular area beneath the shifting stone snake resembled an arena. The flames around the snake's snout blazed. Atop the serpent's neck, Buyard Cholik rode the platform with calm assurance.

"Do it," Taramis ordered Raithen.

The pirate captain reached beneath his robe and brought out a handheld crossbow. Along his burn-blackened hands, thick, crusty scabs cracked open and leaked blood. A madman's grin fitted itself to his bloody lips as he reached for a small lever overhead. He gazed at Darrick. "Don't fail me, sailor. I crossed blades with you before, aboard *Barracuda*. Be as good now as you were then. And be everything your little dead friend said you could be."

Before Darrick could respond, Raithen tripped the lever. In response, the hidden doorway built into the steps swung upward as light as a feather. Light from the cathedral invaded the small tunnel.

Taramis led the way out, his orange robes swirling.

Stepping out of the hiding place after the sage, Darrick was almost overwhelmed by the cacophony of sound that filled even the huge cathedral. Thousands of voices were lifted in praise of Dien-Ap-Sten, the Prophet of the Light.

Church guards occupied a raised area to the right. All of them spotted the secret door opening. One of the bowmen lifted his weapon and drew an arrow back to his ear. Before the guard could properly aim his shaft, Raithen extended his hand with the crossbow in it and squeezed the trigger. The small bolt left Raithen's weapon and pierced the guard's Adam's apple, nailing it to the back of his throat. The guard toppled from the raised area into the crowd, inciting a small riot and starting a wave of hoarse shouting and screaming.

The guards erupted from the checkpoint, and the demon

hunters ran to meet them. Steel rang on steel, and Darrick was in the thick of them.

On the platform attached behind the stone snake's head, Buyard Cholik brought the beast to a standstill even as the great, flaming mouth opened and disgorged a small boy who was swept up in the arms of his father.

Stand ready, Mat said into Darrick's mind. *What ye've been facin' so far is about to turn worse.*

"We can't hold this position," Palat said. Blood streaked his face, but not all of it was his own. "We need to run."

Runnin' ain't the answer, Mat said. *Ye have the power, Darrick. We have the power. Me an' Raithen, why, we done brung ye this far, but the rest of it is up to ye.*

"Worshippers of Dien-Ap-Sten," Buyard Cholik's voice thundered. "You see before you infidels, people who would see this great church torn down and stripped of its ability to house and hold the Prophet of the Light and the Way of Dreams."

Howls of fear and rage filled the cathedral.

Darrick battled for his life. Outnumbered as they were at the moment, he knew it was only going to get worse. He parried and riposted, turning a blade aside, then following through behind the point as it sank through the heart of a mercenary. Placing his foot against the dead man's chest, Darrick kicked him backward into three others who rushed to take his spot.

Hands moving with grace and speed, Taramis inscribed mystic symbols in the air. At a shouted phrase, the symbols flew toward the cathedral's peaked roof.

A black cloud formed near the high ceiling as Darrick blocked another blade. Holding the weapon trapped, Darrick stepped up and delivered an elbow and a backfist blow to a church guard who had hard pressed Rhambal, who was having trouble due to his wounded arm. The guard dropped in front of Rhambal.

"Thanks," the warrior gasped. His face looked pasty white beneath his helm.

But even though Darrick had dealt with the one opponent, others stepped up immediately to take his place. And the man Darrick had engaged had slipped his weapon free. The guard slashed at Darrick's face as the dark cloud overhead roiled and flashed. Darrick trapped the man's blade again, set himself, twisted, and drove a foot into the man's head, knocking him from his feet and back into a knot of worshippers.

Breathing hard, feeling the chill in the air now, Darrick swept the cathedral with his desperate gaze. Even now, some of the worshippers pulled belt knives and were on their way to join the fight.

They're innocents, Mat said inside Darrick's head. *Not all of 'em are evil. They're just drawn to it.*

"Where's the demon?" Darrick asked.

Inside the snake, Mat said. *Where the Black Road is. Kabraxis has returned to his place of power. He knows you have Hauklin's sword, he does.*

Darrick blocked, blocked again, parried, and riposted, putting his point through a man's throat. Scarlet bubbled at the guard's throat as he stumbled backward, dropped his sword, and wrapped both hands around his neck in an effort to stem the blood flow.

The cloud Taramis created suddenly unleashed a wintry keening. Freezing storm winds whipped up and tore through the cathedral, twisting the flames wreathing the snake's snout into a flickering frenzy. Frost formed on the great stone creature but quickly melted away as the snake belched fire. Steam shimmered around it.

Cocking its head, the snake focused on the group of demon hunters. Baleful flames danced in the snake's eyes.

Buyard Cholik is the first, Mat said. *He must die, Darrick, for he holds Kabraxis anchored to this world.*

A blizzard suddenly filled the cathedral, whipping fat snowflakes over the central area as well as the worshippers. The whirling blanket of whiteness made it hard to see, and naked skin burned at the snowflakes' touch like acid.

The stone snake struck, flashing forward, fire wreathing its exposed fangs.

"Look out!" Palat yelled, knocking Rhambal from the snake's path.

The demon hunters cleared the area, but not all of the guards got free. Three of the guards were smashed to bloody pulp by the impact. Despite the stone that shattered across the cathedral floor and the chunks that skittered through the pews, the snake wasn't harmed at all.

Gathering his courage, overcoming the doubts that assailed him, Darrick ran toward the snake. Curling in on itself, bloody pieces of the three guards still caught in its fangs, the snake pursued Darrick. Conscious of the unnatural beast closing on him, Darrick cut to the right and hit the ground rolling, sliding up under the snake's own body.

Reaching up, Darrick caught hold of the carved scales with his free hand. The snake head pummeled the cathedral floor, tearing flagstones loose and shattering others. Darrick pushed himself up, clinging to the carved scales along the stone serpent's underside, pulling himself to his feet. He leapt, landing on the snake's snout. Hissing, gurgling flames, the snake opened its mouth, and a forked tongue made of flames stabbed out at him.

The flames singed Darrick's hair as he ran up the snake's snout. Aided by the unnatural beast opening its mouth, Darrick hurled himself into the air toward the platform where Buyard Cholik stood.

Suddenly understanding Darrick's desperate move, Cholik lifted his hands to work his magic. But it was too late. Before the spell was complete, Darrick grabbed the man's robe. Cholik's only saving grace was that Darrick hadn't managed to land on the platform with him.

Knowing that he'd missed the platform in his desperate lunge, Darrick flailed with his free hand and caught Cholik's robe skirts. When his weight hit the end of his arm, Darrick pulled Cholik from his feet, slamming the man against the iron railing and breaking his concentration. Holding on to the robe with one hand, swaying wildly, knowing the snake was curling again, trying to dislodge him and cause him to fall so it could get at him,

Darrick flexed his arm, bending his elbow and pulling himself closer to Cholik.

The blizzard swirled around them with blinding intensity. Cold burning his face and exposed skin, buffeted by the storm winds that Taramis had raised with his magic, Darrick drew back his sword, flipped his hand on the hilt, and threw it like a spear.

Hauklin's enchanted blade sailed true even in the terrible wind. It pierced Buyard Cholik's heart, causing the man to stumble backward, tripping over the robe that Darrick held so tightly to.

"No," Cholik said, clutching the sword that had transfixed him. His hands burst into blue flame as they gripped the sword, but he seemed powerless to let go just as he was powerless to pull the blade from his chest.

Taking advantage of Cholik's inability to fight against him, Darrick caught the edge of the platform in his other hand, then pulled himself up. Cholik stepped backward, freed from Darrick's grip, and fell over the platform's edge.

The sword! Mat yelled in Darrick's head. *Kabraxis is still ahead of ye!*

Clinging to the platform mounted behind the snake's bobbing head, watching the movement around him with his peripheral vision, Darrick held fast to the platform with his left hand and stretched his right out for the sword. He willed it to come back to him just as he had that day at Ellig Barrows's house.

Even as Cholik's corpse fell toward the cracked stone floor below, Darrick felt the power binding him to the sword. He watched as the enchanted blade pulled free of the dead man. Hauklin's sword was in the air, streaking toward Darrick as the snake suddenly popped its head up, flinging him high into the air and knocking the sword away.

Whirling, almost colliding with the cathedral ceiling because he was thrown so high, Darrick flailed and tried to get control of his body. Horrified, he watched as the snake lowered its head below him and opened its massive jaws.

Flames roiled in the snake's throat, promising a fiery death if it caught him.

Get the sword! Mat yelled. *If ye don't have the sword, ye ain't got nothin'!*

Darrick focused on the sword, but he couldn't clear his mind of the snake below as he reached the apex of his flight and started back down. Even if the snake somehow missed him, he felt certain that he wouldn't survive the fall.

The sword! Mat cried. *The sword will protect ye if ye have it. An' I can help ye through the sword's magic.*

Darrick pushed thoughts of death from him. If he died, it would only put an end to the pain he'd lived in for the last year, and from all the pain he'd borne in those years before that.

He concentrated on Hauklin's sword, strengthening the bond he felt between the weapon and himself. Cholik's corpse plummeted toward the waiting stone floor beside the yawning snake's mouth. But the enchanted blade pulled free of the dead man and flew toward Darrick's waiting hand.

Hold to the sword, Mat said. *Hold to the sword that I may help ye.*

Unable to change directions in the air, Darrick fell, dropping like a stone into the waiting snake's mouth. Flames wrapped him, and for an instant he thought he was going to be incinerated. Unbelievable heat surrounded him and stole his senses away.

Stand easy, Mat warned. His voice, even though Darrick was certain it came from within his head, also sounded distant and small. *This is going to be the worst of it, Darrick, an' there ain't no way around it.*

Darrick couldn't believe he wasn't dead. The fall alone against the stone mouth of the snake should have killed him, but the addition of the flames had taken away all chance of his survival.

Yet—

He lived. He knew it from the way he felt, from the ragged and tortured breath he took and the way he hurt all over.

Ye can't lie there, Mat said, and his voice was thin and distant. *This here's the Black Road. The Twisted Path of Shadows. Kabraxis rules supreme here. At least, he believes he does. He'll kill ye if ye lie there. Get up—*

"Get up," a harsh voice grated. "Get up, you worthless bastard."

Darrick recognized the voice as his father's. His eyes snapped open, and he saw the familiar stable area behind his father's butcher shop. He found himself lying on the sour hay that lined the hayloft.

"You didn't think I'd catch you back up here sleeping, did you?" his father demanded.

Instinctively, Darrick curled into a ball, trying to protect himself. His body hurt from the beating he'd remembered getting the day before. Or maybe it was the same day, only earlier. Sometimes after a beating Darrick had lost track of time. He suffered blackout periods as well as lost time.

"Get up, damn you." His father kicked him, driving the wind from his lungs and perhaps breaking yet another rib.

Fearfully, Darrick got to his feet before his father. Something dangled from Darrick's hand, but when he looked he could see nothing. Perhaps he had another broken arm, but this one felt different from the last.

He thought he heard Mat Hu-Ring's voice, but he knew Mat would never come around when his father was in one of his moods. Even Mat's father wouldn't come around during those times.

"Get up, I said," his father roared. He was a big man with a broad belly and shoulders as wide as an ax handle. His hands were big and tough from hard work and long hours and countless tavern fights. A curly mop of brown hair matched the curly beard he wore to mid-chest.

"I can't be here," Darrick said, dazed. "I was a sailor. There was a church."

"Stupid, worthless bastard," his father roared, grabbing him by the arm and shaking him. "Who'd make a sailor out of the likes of you?" His father laughed derisively.

"You've been having another one of those dreams you cling to so much when you hide out up here."

Face burning in shame, Darrick looked down at himself. He was a boy, no more than eight or nine. No threat at all to his father. Yet his father treated him like the fiercest opponent he'd ever encountered.

His father slapped him, causing his head to ring with pain.

"Don't you look away from me when I'm talking, boy," his father commanded. "Maybe I haven't taught you anything else, but you'll know to respect your betters."

Tears ran down Darrick's cheeks. He felt them hot on his cheeks, and he tasted their salt when they reached his quivering lips.

"Look at you, you sniveling coward," his father roared, and raised his hand again. "You don't have sense enough to come out of the rain."

Darrick took the blow on the back of his head, watched the world spin around him for a moment, and remembered how only last week he'd watched his father beat three caravan guards in a fight in the muddy street outside the Lame Goose Tavern. As a butcher, his father was passable, but as a fighter, there were few who could compare.

"Have you fed the livestock like I told you to, boy?" his father demanded.

Peering over the edge of the hayloft, afraid he knew what the answer was, Darrick saw that all the feed bins and water troughs were empty. "No," he said.

"That's right," his father agreed. "You haven't. I ask so little of you because I know that's all I have the right to expect from an idiot like you. But you'd think you'd have enough sense to feed and water livestock."

Darrick cringed inside. He knew there was no winning when his father was in one of his moods. If he had fed the livestock, his father would have found fault with it, would have insisted it was too much or too little. Darrick's stomach lurched as if he were on a storm-tossed sea.

But how could he know what that felt like? Other than

one of the stories he sometimes overheard outside the taverns his father frequented in the evening. His father always tried to leave Darrick at home, but his mother was seldom there in the evenings, and Darrick had been too afraid to sit at home alone.

So Darrick had secretly followed his father from tavern to tavern, having an easy time not being seen because his father had been deep in his cups. As mean as his father could be, he was also the most permanent point of Darrick's life because his mother was never around.

. . . not there . . .

Darrick breathed shallowly, certain he'd heard Mat Hu-Ring's voice. But that couldn't be, could it? Mat was dead. He'd died . . . died . . .

Died where?

Darrick couldn't remember. In fact, he didn't want to remember. Mat had died somewhere far from his family, and it was Darrick's fault.

Ye're on the Black Road, Mat said. *These are demon's tricks. Don't give in . . .*

Mat's voice faded away again.

The weight hung at the end of Darrick's arm.

"What is this, boy?" His father yanked Darrick around, displaying the rope and the knotted noose at the end of it. "Is this something you were playing with?"

Darrick didn't speak. He couldn't. Only a few days ago, using the tricks he'd learned from Mat, who had learned them from his uncle the sailor, Darrick had made the rope from scraps of rope left by farmers who brought their animals to his father's shop to be butchered.

For days Darrick had thought about hanging himself and putting an end to everything.

"You couldn't do it, could you, boy?" his father demanded. He coiled the rope up, shaking the noose out.

Darrick cried and shook. His nose clogged up, and he knew he sounded horrible. If he tried to speak, his father would only make fun of him and slap him to make him speak better, not stopping till Darrick was unconscious or nearly so. He knew he'd taste blood for days from the split lips and the torn places inside his cheeks.

Only this time, his father had something different in mind. His father threw the rope over the rafter support on the other side of the hayloft, then caught the noose when it came back down.

"I wondered how long it might be before you got the gumption to try something like this," his father said. He peered over the side of the hayloft and lowered the noose a little. "Do you want to just hang yourself, boy, or do you want to snap your neck when you fall?"

Darrick couldn't answer.

It didn't happen like that, Mat said. *I found the rope. Not yer da. I took the rope away from ye that day, an' I made ye promise that ye'd never do somethin' like that.*

Darrick thought he almost remembered, then the memory slipped away from him.

His father fitted the noose over his neck and grinned. His breath stank of sour wine. "I think snapping your neck is a coward's way out. I'm not going to let no bastard son of mine be afraid of dying. You're going to meet it like a man."

It's the demon! Mat yelled, but his voice tore apart as if he were shouting through a strong wind. *'Ware, Darrick! Yer life can still be forfeit in there, an' if the demon takes it on the Black Road, it's his to keep forever!*

Darrick knew he should be afraid, but he wasn't. Dying would be easy. Living was the hard part, stumbling through all the fears and mistakes and pain. Death—slow or quick—would be welcome relief.

His father cinched the hangman's knot tight under the corner of his jaw. "Time to go," his father growled. "At least when this story goes through the town, they'll say my son went out with the courage of his da."

Darrick stood at the edge of the hayloft. When his father put his big hand against his chest, there was nothing he could do to prevent the fall.

His father pushed.

Arms flailing—*Hang on to the sword,* some part of his mind yelled—he fell. But his neck didn't snap when he hit the end of the rope. His father hadn't let it down enough for that.

Darrick dangled at the end of the rope, the life choking out of him as the hemp bit into his neck. His right arm remained at his side while he gripped the rope with his left and tried to keep his breath.

"Just let go," his father taunted. "You can die easily. It's only minutes away."

He's lying, Mat said. *Damn ye, Darrick, look at the truth! This never happened! We'd have never gone to sea if this had happened!*

Darrick stared up at his father. The man had knelt down on the side of the hayloft, his face split in a wide grin, his eyes on fire with anticipation.

Look past him! Mat cried. *Look at the shadow on the wall behind him!*

Through dying vision growing black around the edges, Darrick saw his father's shadow on the wall behind him. Only it wasn't his father's. Whatever cast the shadow on the wall there wasn't human. Then Darrick remembered the cathedral in Bramwell, the stone serpent with the flaming maw.

Without warning, Darrick suddenly realized he was full-grown, dangling from the strangling rope thrown over the rafter.

"You're too late," the demon said. His form changed, shifting from that of Darrick's father to his own true nature. "You're going to die here, and I'm going to have your soul. Perhaps you've killed Buyard Cholik, but I'll use you to anchor me to this world."

Anger flamed through Darrick. He fanned it and hung on to it, letting it give him strength. He swept the sword up, slashing through the rope that held him, and dropped to the straw-covered ground below.

Only it wasn't the straw-covered ground of the stable behind the butcher's shop anymore. Now it was a thin black ribbon that hung out over nothingness.

Kabraxis dropped to the Black Road in front of Darrick. Without a word, the demon rushed at Darrick, claws flaring, fangs bared.

With the noose still around his neck, restricting his airways and causing spots before his eyes, Darrick fought. The sword was a live thing in his hands, moving inhumanly quick, but it was only enough to keep his inhuman opponent from killing him.

Kabraxis flicked his tail at Darrick, but Darrick swept the sword out, intercepting the appendage and cutting it off. The demon roared with rage and swung both his arms in a scissoring move. "You can't beat me, you worthless human."

Ducking beneath the blows, Darrick threw himself forward, sliding between the tall demon's legs, slipping on the blood from the amputated tail. Then he was up again, racing toward the demon's back. Darrick leapt, putting aside all thoughts of failing or being afraid of the unending drops on either side of the Black Road, and hurled himself at the demon's back.

Kabraxis tried to brush Darrick from his back but froze when Darrick wrapped one hand around the demon's head and slid Hauklin's blade under the demon's neck against his throat.

"Wait," Kabraxis said. "If you kill me, you're going to pay a price. You're not pure the way Hauklin was. You carry fears inside you that will forever taint you. You'll carry something of me that will haunt you. There is a price."

Darrick froze for only a moment. "I'll . . . pay . . . it . . ." he whispered hoarsely. And he pulled the enchanted blade across the demon's throat, metal grating on bone as lightning filled the darkness around them.

A frantic burst of light filled Darrick's vision, blinding him.

When he opened his eyes again, he stood in the center of the cathedral. Snow covered the floor around him. He had Kabraxis's head in his hand, gripping it by one of the horns.

The stone serpent was still animated, hovering above Buyard Cholik's corpse.

Taramis and the other demon hunters faced an onslaught of church guards, and four of the warriors were down, dead, or severely wounded.

The stone serpent coiled, then struck at Darrick.

"No," Darrick said, feeling the unnatural power that filled him. He struck Hauklin's blade down into the stones of the snow-covered floor.

Cold blue lightning bolts crashed through the cathedral roof and smashed into the stone snake, tearing it into a twisted serpentine pile of bricks and mortar. The flames in its mouth and eyes flickered and died.

Everyone in the cathedral froze as Darrick turned on them.

Lifting the demon's head, Darrick yelled, "It's over! The demon is dead! The false prophet is dead!"

The church guards put down their weapons and backed away. Taramis and his warriors, bloody but unbent, turned guardedly to look at Darrick.

"Go home," Darrick told the worshippers. "It's over."

He told them that, but he knew it wasn't true. There was still the price to be paid, and he was only now beginning to understand what it was.

EPILOGUE

Cold, distant morning sun split the eastern sky, threading the white clouds with violent reds and purples like a fertilized egg that had been cracked too close to term and held blood in the yolk. Despite the cold blowing down out of the mountains, the sun's rays chased the night's shadows away from Bramwell and out into the sea.

Darrick Lang stood atop the garden-covered roof of the Church of the Prophet of the Light as he had all through the long night. He wore his heavy cloak, but the wind cut through it and left him near frozen; still, he wouldn't walk away. His father's voice had rung in his head for hours and had only started to dim a short time ago. Darrick didn't hear Mat's voice at all and didn't know if Mat had continued on through the ghost roads or if he had died yet again during the final confrontation. It was hard not knowing.

Some of Buyard Cholik's mercenaries had threatened to put up a fight, but since their employer had been killed, not many of them had the heart for it. Palat had spat blood and told them they were all mad because they'd lost easy jobs, and if they wanted to lose more than that, all they had to do was step up. None of the mercenaries had. During the confusion, Raithen had disappeared.

Taramis had kept his group together, fearing retaliation on the part of the stunned crowd. At first, it had looked as if the audience would turn on the demon slayers despite the fact that Darrick had held Kabraxis's head and showed them the lie they had been told. They had been there to witness and receive miracles and had seen all that torn away instead. Some of them had sat in the pews for hours,

in faint hope that the Prophet of the Light and the
Wayfinder would return for those who truly believed.

Footsteps scraped the rooftop.

Darrick turned, Hauklin's mystic sword still bared in his
fist. Although he had worked with Taramis and the other
demon hunters and had slain both Buyard Cholik and
Kabraxis, Darrick knew they still didn't trust him. His path
was not theirs; he wouldn't ride off into the new dawn or
find a ship out in the harbor to make war against another
demon.

Another demon. A bitter laugh rose to Darrick's lips, but
he let it die. He wasn't over the last demon yet. Nor was he
over the demons his father had instilled within him.

Taramis Volken walked through the gardens. The sage
still carried the signs of battle—blood, some of it his and
some belonging to others, and soot—on his orange robes.
Shadows clung to his face despite the dawn, and he looked
older somehow in the clean light.

"I wondered if you would still be up here," the sage
said.

"No, you didn't," Darrick said. "You've had Rhambal
watching the passageway from the rooftop."

Taramis hesitated only a moment. "You're right, of
course."

Darrick said nothing.

Walking over to the roof's edge, the sage looked down.
The breeze ruffled his orange robes. "Many of the worshippers aren't leaving."

Reluctantly, Darrick joined the older man at the roof's
edge and peered down as well. The streets in front of the
church were choked with people despite the city guard's
best efforts to move them along. Smoke billowed from a
half-dozen burning buildings.

"They haven't stopped believing," Taramis said.

"Because Cholik and Kabraxis gave them what they
wanted," Darrick said.

"Some of them," Taramis corrected. "And the price was
high. But it was enough to keep the others here, hoping that

they would be picked out next for fortune's favor." He looked up at Darrick. "What the demon did was a terrible thing."

Darrick remained silent. The north wind wasn't any colder than the sage's words.

"The city guard is fighting with roving bands of worshippers in the city," Taramis said. "Many of them are protesting the night's events. They say that Cholik and the Prophet Dien-Ap-Sten were slain by Lord Darkulan out of jealousy and that there never was a demon."

"The demon is gone," Darrick said. "Not believing Kabraxis wasn't a demon isn't going to bring him back."

"No, but they want revenge against the city for the guilt and confusion and anger they feel. If Bramwell is lucky, only a few buildings and a few lives will be lost before the guard gets the situation under control."

Darrick reflected on his own dark anger. The emotion was residue from what his father had done to him. He knew that now, but he also knew that residue was indelible and would be with him forever.

"They say," Taramis said, "that when a man faces a demon, that man comes to know himself in ways he was never shown before. You faced Kabraxis, Darrick, more closely than any man I've ever known before."

"You've fought and killed demons," Darrick countered.

Taramis leaned against the roof ledge and crossed his hands over his chest. "I've never followed them into the Burning Hells to do it as you did."

"Would you have?"

"If I'd had to, yes." No trace of hesitation sounded in the sage's voice. "But I have to ask myself why you did."

"I didn't choose that path," Darrick pointed out. "The snake swallowed me."

"The snake swallowed you because Kabraxis thought he could beat you on the Black Road. And he thought he could beat Stormfury. My question to you is, why did the demon think that?"

For a long while, Darrick held the silence between them,

but he realized that the sage wasn't going to go anywhere. "Because of the guilt I carry," he finally said.

"Over your friend Mat?"

"And more," Darrick admitted. Then, before he could stop himself, he told the sage the story of his father and of the beatings he'd received in the butcher's shop in Hillsfar. "It took me a long time to figure out that my mother had been unfaithful to my father and that I didn't know who my true father was. I still don't."

"Have you ever wanted to know?"

"Sometimes," Darrick admitted. "But the Light only knows what trouble that would bring if I did find out. I've had trouble enough."

"Kabraxis thought he could weaken you by confronting you with your father's anger."

"He would have done it," Darrick said, "were it not for Mat. Always during those times after the beatings, Mat stood by me. And he stood by me again on the Black Road."

"By helping you through Kabraxis's subterfuge."

"Aye." Darrick gazed at the sage. "But the winning wasn't all mine, you see."

Taramis looked at him.

"I defeated Kabraxis in the Burning Hells," Darrick said, "but I brought a part of it back with me." With a quick move, he thrust Stormfury into one of the nearby garden beds. Such treatment to a weapon was unthinkable because the moisture would make it rust. But he knew the mystical sword would suffer no damage. He left the sword quivering there and held out his hand. "The damned demon tainted me somehow."

Darrick's hand shimmered, then began to change, losing its humanness and twisting into a demonic appendage.

"By the Light," Taramis whispered.

"I destroyed Buyard Cholik and Kabraxis's way into our world," Darrick said, "but I became that way." Long talons jutted from his fingers now covered in hairy, green and black skin.

"When did this happen?"

"While I was on the Black Road," Darrick said. "I'll tell you another thing, too. Kabraxis isn't dead. I don't know if he'll ever have another body that will survive in our world, but he's still alive in the Burning Hells. Every now and again, I can hear him whispering to me, mocking me. He's waiting, you see, for me to give up and die or to lose control of myself by getting drunk or not caring if I live or die." He reached for Hauklin's sword, closed his hand around it, and watched as the hand became human again.

"Hauklin's sword grounds you," Taramis said.

"Aye," Darrick said. "And it keeps me human."

"Kabraxis cursed you."

Darrick sheathed the sword at his side. "Kabraxis's gateway from the Burning Hells no longer lies under the ruins of the city on the Dyre River. His gateway is now me."

"And if you should be killed by another?"

Darrick shook his head. "I don't know. If my body were completely destroyed, maybe Kabraxis wouldn't be able to make his way into this world again." He smiled, but it was cold and devoid of humor, holding only bitterness. "By revealing this to you, I feel as though I've put my life at risk."

Taramis didn't say anything for a time. "There are some who would be tempted to put you to death rather than risk the demon's return."

"And you?"

"Doing such a thing would make me no better than the monsters I hunt," the sage replied. "No, you have nothing to fear from me. But should Kabraxis gain the upper hand within you, I'll hunt you down and kill you."

"Fair enough," Darrick agreed. He knew he could expect no less.

"You will need to keep Hauklin's sword with you," Taramis said. "I'll explain the matter to Ellig Barrows, but chances are that he and his family will be glad to be shut of it."

Darrick nodded.

"What will you do?" Taramis asked. "Where will you go?"

"I don't know."

"You could ride with us."

"We both know my place isn't with you," Darrick replied. "Although it would probably prove easier for you to keep your eye on me."

A wry grin fitted Taramis's face. "True."

"There is something more I received from the demon's death," Darrick said. He strode close to the sage. "You're wounded. Show it to me."

Hesitantly, Taramis pulled his robe away and revealed the deep wound in his side. Someone had clumsily bandaged it, but the blood still seeped through.

Darrick clapped a hand over the sage's side, causing him to wince. Power flowed through Darrick, and for the time it took to work, he heard Kabraxis's whispers more loudly in the back of his mind. He took his hand away. "Check the wound."

In disbelief, Taramis pulled the bandage away and inspected his side. "It's healed."

"Aye," Darrick said. "As are the wounds that I suffered last night. But such healing comes with a price. While I do it, Kabraxis has greater access to me. Only Hauklin's sword keeps me sane and human."

"You've healed me more quickly and better than any healer or potion I've ever used," Taramis said. "You could be a great asset."

"But to whom?" Darrick asked. "And at what cost? Perhaps Kabraxis has given me this power so that I will continue to use it and grow closer and closer to him."

"Then what will you do?"

"I don't know," Darrick answered. "I know I need to get away from here. I need the sea again for a time, Taramis. Something to clear my head. I need to find good, honest work again, a sailor's life, so I won't have so much time to think."

"Believe in the Light," Taramis said. "The Light always shows you the way even in the darkest times."

*   *   *

Hours later, with the sun now in the west out over the ocean and a ship's passage secured, Darrick stood on the Bramwell docks. Taramis and the other demon hunters joined him, agreeing to take at least this much of the voyage together.

The docks were congested, people milling around like cattle being herded onto cargo ships. The waves pressed the ships up against the dock pilings, causing sonorous booms to echo over the dockyards.

Without warning, a woman's shrill scream punctuated the noise.

Halfway up the gangplank leading onto the ship he'd booked passage on, Darrick turned and looked back.

Men hauled a young girl from the water, her body torn and shattered in her long dress.

An older woman, probably her mother, knelt beside the little girl as the sailors stretched her out on the docks. "Please," the woman begged. "Can someone help my little girl? Is there a healer here?"

"A healer wouldn't do that one any good," a gruff sailor beside Darrick said. "That little girl had the ill luck to fall between the ship an' the pilin's as she was boardin'. Smashed her up inside. Ain't nobody gonna be able to do anything about that. She's dead, just waitin' for it to come callin'."

Darrick looked at the frail girl, her body busted up from the impact, drenched and in horrible pain.

"Darrick," Taramis said.

For a frozen moment, Darrick remained on the boardwalk. What if the little girl's accident was no accident? What if it was a temptation arranged by Kabraxis to use the healing power again? What if someone in the crowd, a traveling Vizjerei or another wizard, recognized that Darrick's power wasn't given by the Light but from a demon spawn from the Burning Hells?

Then Darrick was moving, vaulting from the gangplank and back to the shore. He shoved people from his path, feeling the old anger and intemperance surging within him. A moment more, and he was at the little girl's side.

Her mother looked up at him, her face stained with frightened and helpless tears. "Can you help her? Please, can you help her?"

The little girl was no more than six or seven, hardly older than one of Mat's sisters the last time Darrick had seen her.

"Ain't no good," a man nearby whispered. "Seen people all squashed up like this before. That little girl's as good as dead, she is."

Without a word, Darrick placed his hands on the girl's body, feeling the broken bones shifting within her. *Please,* he thought, ignoring Kabraxis's harsh whispers fouling the back of his mind. He wouldn't let the demon's words come forward, wouldn't allow himself to understand them.

Power flowed through Darrick's hands, pouring into the little girl. A long moment passed, then her body arched suddenly, and she stopped breathing. During that still moment, Darrick felt certain that Kabraxis had somehow betrayed him, had somehow made him cause the girl's death instead of preventing it.

Then the girl opened her eyes, the clearest blue eyes Darrick thought he'd ever seen. She called for her mother and reached for her. The woman took up her child and hugged her to her breast fiercely.

"A healer," someone whispered.

"That's not just a healer," someone else said. "He brought her back from the dead, he did. That little girl weren't nothin' more than a corpse, an' he done brung her back like it was nothin'."

Darrick pushed himself to his feet, suddenly ringed in by people who were curious and suspicious of him. He put his hand on his sword, barely resisting the impulse to draw the weapon and clear the path from him. In the back of his mind, he heard the demon laugh.

Taramis was suddenly at Darrick's side, as were Rhambal and Palat. "Come on," the sage urged.

"It's the Prophet of the Light," someone else said. "He's returned."

"No," another said. "Those are the people who killed the Wayfinder and destroyed the Way of Dreams. Hang them!"

"We've got to go," Taramis said.

Was this what Kabraxis wanted? Darrick wondered. Would his death at the hands of a lynch mob allow the demon to step back into the world of men? Darrick didn't know.

The mother rose to his defense, holding her child to her. "Don't you men dare touch him. He brought my little Jenna back to me. If he is the one who killed the Wayfinder, then he had to have done it for good cause, says I. This man is a miracle worker, a chosen one of the Light."

"The Wayfinder was leading you to demons," Taramis said. "If he had not killed the servant of the false Prophet of the Light, all of you would have been doomed to the Burning Hells."

Darrick felt sickened. He was no hero, and he was no saint. He forced himself to release his tight hold on Stormfury.

Grudgingly, the lynch mob mentality gave way, surrendering to the people who were looking for something to make sense out of all they had been through with the Church of the Prophet of the Light.

In amazement, Darrick watched as people came forward with wounded friends and family, beseeching him to heal them. He turned to Taramis. "What do I do?"

The sage gazed at him. "The choice is yours. You can board that ship and tend to your own needs as best you can, or you can stay here in this moment and tend the needs of others."

Darrick looked out over the huge crowd. "But there are so many."

Already two dozen litters with men and women lying near death were spread across the docks. People called out to him, begging him to aid their fallen family and comrades.

"But the power I have," Darrick said, "it isn't from the Light."

"No," Taramis agreed. "Listen to me, though. How do you know that in this moment the Light hasn't had a design in placing you exactly in the position you find yourself in now?"

"I'm tainted with the demon."

"You also possess a demon's great power, and you can do a lot of good with it if you choose."

"And what if in using that power I also lose myself?" Darrick asked.

"Life is about balance," Taramis said. "Balance between the Light and the Dark. I would not be able to champion the will of the Light so strongly, so willingly, had I not been exposed to the Darkness that waits to devour us in the Burning Hells. Just as steel must be tempered, Darrick, so must a man. You've come a long way. Your present is balanced between your past and the dreams you might have. You stand between the Light and the Dark as Kabraxis's gateway, but it is your choice to remain open or closed. Your choice to hide the power or to use it. You can fear it or embrace it. Either way, it has already changed your life forever."

Quietly, thoughts racing inside his head, the demon whispering somewhere at the back, Darrick looked at the crowd that waited so expectantly. Then, taking a deep breath, he went forward to meet his future, his head high, no one's unloved bastard child anymore but a man of compassion and conviction. He went to the wounded and the dying, and he healed them, listening to the demon scream at the back of his mind.